WINDS OF CHANGE

Dear Bernice –
Thanks so much for
your support & lunch!
Fasten your seatbelt for
this book. ☺☺

Becky

ALSO BY THE AUTHOR

FICTION BY REBECCA CAREY LYLES

Kate Neilson Series

Winds of Wyoming (Book One)

Winds of Freedom (Book Two)

Winds of Change (Book Three)

———————

Short Stories

Passageways: A Short Story Collection

———————

NONFICTION BY BECKY LYLES

It's a God Thing! Inspiring Stories of Life-Changing Friendships

On a Wing and a Prayer: Stories from Freedom Fellowship, a Prison Ministry

———————

Kate Neilson Series – Book Three

WINDS OF CHANGE

REBECCA CAREY LYLES

PERPEDIT ✓ PUBLISHING, INK

WINDS OF CHANGE
Copyright © 2016 by Rebecca Carey Lyles

Perpedit Publishing, Ink
PO Box 190246
Boise, Idaho 83719
http://www.perpedit.com

First eBook Edition: 2016
ISBN-10: 0-9894624-5-5
ISBN-13: 978-0-9894624-5-7

First Paperback Edition: 2016
ISBN-10: 0-9894624-4-7
ISBN-13: 978-0-9894624-4-0

This book is a work of fiction. All of the characters, organizations and events portrayed in this novel are either products of the author's imagination or are used fictitiously. Any similarity to a real person, living or dead, organization or event is coincidental and not intended by the author.

Cover design by Blue Azalea Designs

Photo credits:
pink badger (bridge)
srnnicholl (kids)
ratkom (adult runner)
Kris Wiktor (mountain)

Published in the United States of America
Perpedit Publishing, Ink

DEDICATION

This book is dedicated to all the caring individuals who give of their time, energy, finances and hearts to help victims of human trafficking escape their chains, recover their self-worth, heal from their wounds, regain trust, and find joy and purpose in life.

PSALM 69:33 (NIV)

The Lord hears the needy and does not despise his captive people.

Chapter One

"We'll only be gone a few hours, Mike." Kate Neilson Duncan eyed her husband's reflection in the bathroom mirror. "Eight or nine, at the most." She opened a drawer beneath the countertop, pulled out her hairbrush and sat on the edge of the bathtub, her bare feet planted on the cool wood floor.

He lifted an eyebrow. "Kate…"

She turned from her husband's "what are you thinking?" stare. Bending over her knees, she began to brush her long, dark hair. Stroke after stroke, she brushed from the nape of her neck downward toward the floor, something she did almost every night.

Her mother had told her years ago a hundred strokes a day would distribute the natural oils in her hair and make it shine. So that's what she did before bed. She didn't always remember to count, but most evenings, she remembered to brush.

Sometimes she thought about her sweet mama while she brushed, determined not to let what memories she had fade. Other times, she thought about her father and her brother, who'd also been killed in the car accident that took her mother's life when Kate was eight. Occasionally, she thought of the years she'd wandered Pittsburgh streets without a dime—or a hairbrush—to her name. And once in a great while, she thought of her prison days, when brushing her hair during a quiet moment was a rare luxury.

Most nights, she talked with Mike. Tonight, they were discussing an outing with the kids from Freedom House, the children's home she and Mike's mom, Laura, had established on their Wyoming ranch several months ago. Kate wanted to treat the children to a fun day in Cheyenne, and she needed another adult to help her keep track of them.

Chin on her knee, she said, "I'm not asking for the whole weekend." She'd originally hoped to add a couple camping days to the outing. But when no adults were available to accompany her and the kids, she'd scaled her plans down to one day.

Mike, who was brushing his teeth, didn't respond until he'd rinsed his mouth. "Kate…" She heard him run water over the toothbrush and tap it on the sink to knock out the excess.

"Kate," he repeated, "you know the only time I can even *think* of getting away is in the middle of the week. Did you forget this is a guest ranch and that Saturday is our busiest day? Guests will be coming and going, like usual. We have trail rides, bison tours, fishing trips and classes scheduled all day long."

She made a face she knew he couldn't see and kept brushing. No matter what she asked him to do, the ranch came first. "That's why you have employees."

"This is the beginning of summer, the beginning of the guest season, and we have a slew of first-time workers. I need to be here to make sure everything runs smoothly." He blew a frustrated breath between his lips. "One of the new hires from town wore tennis shoes today instead of boots and, of course, stepped in a gopher hole. Did a number on his ankle. He'll be out of commission a couple weeks, at best."

"You could put Clint in charge."

"You know he oversees the working side of the WP and doesn't have much to do with the guest side."

Kate loved the Whispering Pines. Their guest ranch was beautiful and welcoming. And she loved that Mike loved his work. But his hands-on management style controlled their lives. She didn't have enough fingers to count the plans that had been ruined by sick cows, runaway horses and natural disasters, like last week's self-combusting haystack, not to mention guests and their emergencies. And then there was his pride and joy, his bison herd...

She pushed the curtain of hair aside. "Just a piece of your day, a handful of hours. That's all I'm asking. Surely you could find someone to cover such a short time."

Mike pulled his t-shirt over his head, threw it in the hamper and left the room. Hands clasped behind his head, he stretched as he walked from the bathroom to the bedroom. Like a magnet, a familiar tug pulled at Kate's heart, drawing her to him.

She sat up. Combing her hair back with her fingers, she watched him balance on the end of the bed and pull off his socks, one at a time. Her husband was as good-looking as the day they met...and just as stubborn.

Finished with her hair, she dropped the brush into a drawer, turned off the bathroom light and walked into the dark bedroom. Mike was already in bed, but before she joined him, she opened the window all the way. She loved to snuggle with him beneath warm quilts while crisp mountain breezes swirled over them.

Like every night, he was waiting for her to slide into his arms, her back against his chest. He kissed her neck. "I love you, Mrs. Duncan."

Kate squirmed around to kiss him on the lips. "I love you, too, sweetheart." She touched his jaw. "Will you at least think about Saturday?"

He grunted, and she could feel his muscles tense. "Don't you ever think about anything or anybody but those kids?"

Kate frowned. "What's that supposed to mean?"

He untangled himself from her and rolled over. "It's late. We can talk about it tomorrow."

~:~:~

Kate leaned on the top rail and watched Clint Barrett, their ranch foreman, usher a small child into the center of the pen. He and the little Asian tyke wore matching red western shirts and navy bandanas with their boots and jeans. Clint's black Stetson was a perfect fit, but the five-year-old's oversized cowboy hat covered his eyebrows and threatened to block his vision.

Someone yelled, "Go, Tieno," and the spectators who had gathered at the Freedom House corral began to clap and cheer.

Laura Duncan, who stood next to Kate, nudged her. "Is our little guy cute or what?"

Kate smiled at her petite, blonde mother-in-law. "Tieno is adorable, even if his hat's too big." She laughed. "Next time Clint goes shopping for the Freedom House kids, he needs to take a woman with him."

The rancher standing on the other side of Laura lifted his chin. "Hey, he'll grow into it."

"Sure…" Kate gave him a dubious look. "In about eight years."

Clint lifted a coiled rope off the dummy calf he'd made for the event by tacking a sun-bleached steer skull to one end of a wooden sawhorse. A frayed piece of twine attached to the other end served as a tail. He raised the rope in the air and the crowd quieted.

"Ladies and gentlemen," he announced, "I'm proud to present our one and only contestant in the calf-roping event this afternoon, Billy the Kid."

The onlookers applauded, but Tieno pushed back his hat and frowned up at Clint. "N-n-not my n-name, M-mister Clint." His features contorted with the effort to speak.

"Oh, I see." Clint turned to those standing outside the rails. "Excuse me, ladies and gentlemen. Wrong cowboy." He placed the coil onto his shoulder, spread both arms wide and shouted, "The Whispering Pines rodeo welcomes Wild Bill Hickok to our arena today."

Again, hoots and hollers.

This time, Tieno placed his hands on his hips and jutted his jaw. "N-no. N-not that g-g-guy."

"Oops…" Clint held out his palms. "What can I say? Will you give me another chance to get it right?"

Squinting against the sunshine, the little boy studied the stocky cowboy. Finally, he offered a solemn nod.

Clint surveyed the audience from one side of the horse pen to the other and then called out, "What a privilege to have such a famous cowboy take time from a busy touring schedule to make a guest appearance at our Wyoming competition. Everyone, please welcome Calamity Jane with a hearty round of applause."

The crowd burst into laughter.

Tieno's eyebrows puckered. He glanced from Clint to the onlookers and back at Clint. Before he could say anything, Amy Iverson, Clint's girlfriend and Kate's best friend since prison days, called from the far side of the corral, "Hey, Clint, I didn't grow up in the West, but even I know Calamity Jane was a girl."

Again, laughter.

Laura murmured, "I'm not sure how much more Tieno can take."

Kate nodded. She had the same concern. Like the other young Freedom House residents, Tieno had been rescued from a Texas brothel called Executive Pride. And like the others, he could easily be overwhelmed by Clint's teasing.

The foreman knelt beside the miniature cowboy and put his arm on the boy's narrow shoulders. "Enough goofing around, bucko?"

Tieno looked down.

Clint squeezed his shoulder. From his position on the ground, he said, "Ladies and gentlemen, you are looking at a calf-roping champion in the making. This young man, Mister Tieno, from right here in Wyoming, will amaze you."

He stood. "But first, we need to warm up our ropin' arms. While we're doing that, Miss Gianna, who's also from Wyoming, will astound you with her bareback riding skills." He handed the rope to Tieno, picked up the dummy calf and carried it to the far side of the corral. The boy followed.

Manuel Ortega, a college student and a longtime friend of the Duncans, opened the gate and led Kate's horse, Estrella Blanca, into the enclosure. Although Manuel wasn't a contestant and most everyone knew he'd done some juvenile-detention time, the crowd greeted him with hoots and whistles.

Kate smiled. This was the life. Spring sunshine warmed her back and a loving community warmed her spirit. Not only was she encircled by friends and family, beauty surrounded her on every side.

Beyond the corral, between stands of evergreen trees and aspen groves laced with new growth, the Sierra Madre Mountains poked their white-topped peaks into a bright blue sky. Freshly sprouted grass and hillsides of wildflowers colored and scented the land. Deer, elk and moose abounded. She even enjoyed sighting an occasional bear or wolf, from a distance.

Since she first set foot onto Whispering Pines property, she'd thanked God every day, sometimes several times a day, for dropping her into the middle of paradise. He'd guided her to the prettiest spot in Wyoming—and led her to the perfect occupation.

Helping children who'd been exploited by human traffickers was an unexpected career change for her. She enjoyed her marketing work for the ranch, but what she was doing at the children's home not only fit her temperament but brought context to her painful past, filling her with a passion to do everything she could to nurture the kids. She'd never known such contentment.

Yet, she rarely mentioned the specific purpose of the children's home. Many of their neighbors, and even some of the ranch guests, knew Freedom House was a place for orphaned and abandoned children, but that's all they knew. They weren't told the young residents had once been forced to prostitute their small, frail bodies.

Kate turned to check the graveled parking area. What was keeping Mike? She considered calling him on the two-way radio in her SUV, but she'd mentioned the rodeo and cookout before they parted ways after breakfast and had left him a note. If he'd wanted to come, he'd be here by now.

Her husband had been such a grouch lately. Any mention of Freedom House set him off, despite the fact he'd been in on the plans from the beginning. She twisted her wedding rings around her finger. He changed the subject, left the room or made crabby comments whenever she talked about Freedom House and the children, even though he knew she intended to work with the kids once the home was constructed.

A gust of wind stirred manure-scented dust and blew hair across her eyes. She anchored the loose strand behind her ear. In the midst of dealing with her great-aunt's dementia and the kids' multiple issues, she needed cooperation and support from Mike, not conflict.

Hearing someone call, "Go, Manuel," she looked back in time to see him walk her horse into the arena. Named for the white star on her forehead, Estrella Blanca was a beautiful dark-gray horse with white "stockings" on her black legs. She was gentle and good with kids.

Manuel led the filly to where an olive-skinned girl wearing a helmet, jeans and a t-shirt sat on the railing. He kept Estrella steady while nine-year-old Gianna grabbed her charcoal mane and slid from the fence to her sturdy back.

"Ah…" Laura placed her forearms on the railing and rested her chin on her hands, her gaze on the young rider.

Kate knew what she was thinking. Gianna had come a long way. When the Albanian child arrived at Freedom House seven months earlier, she was a fearful little mouse of a girl. But she'd taken to Estrella as if the horse was the best friend she'd searched for all her life.

She loved the good-natured filly, and Estrella loved her. Even so, Gianna had sat sidesaddle for weeks before she found the courage to swing her leg over the horse's back. Sexually victimized children had difficulty opening their legs. Other children might do splits or cartwheels without a second thought, but not the Freedom House kids.

Unlike Tieno, whose parentage was a mystery, Gianna knew who her mother was and where her family lived. But when a U.S. emissary visited the woman to discuss reunification, she told the interpreter if they shipped Gianna home, she'd throw her out and bar the door.

Her daughter, the mother insisted, was tarnished and unmarriageable. Plus, she hadn't fulfilled her promise to work hard in America and send money home to help feed and clothe her five siblings.

The emissary, who was also a woman, countered with, "Gianna was told she'd serve as a maid to a wealthy American family, not as a sex worker."

In response, the woman's eyes had blazed and she'd rattled off a string of angry words before shoving them both out the door. As it slammed behind them, the emissary stared at the translator. "What was that about?"

"The girl failed her family," he said. "She's an embarrassment to them. Refusal to allow her back into their home is a matter of honor."

The social worker who informed Gianna she wouldn't be returning to Albania expected tears and was surprised by her response. "Told you they don't want me."

Kate grieved for Gianna's loss, but the girl had moved on, never once mentioning her family. Gianna wrapped her legs around the filly, and pride in her tenacity replaced Kate's sorrow for her past.

Manuel clicked his tongue, and with the lead rope draped loosely over his shoulder, escorted the pair along the railing.

"Good job, Gianna," Laura called amidst other shouts of encouragement.

Kate sneezed when they passed, like she did every time she got close to her horse. Estrella loved to roll in the dirt. No matter how often they brushed her, she was a perpetual dust cloud.

The pair circled the arena once and stopped. "Now, for the best part." Manuel aimed a thumb at the girl. "Miss Gianna here is going to ride with one hand in the air."

"Bravo," shouted Jean, one of the children's therapists who'd come up for the afternoon. All the kids loved Jean, a sweet Chinese-American lady who was able to coax even the most reticent child out of his or her shell during therapy sessions. She also made the best shrimp fried rice on the planet.

Robin, the children's other therapist, yelled, "Show us how it's done, Gianna." While Jean was petite and wore her dark hair short, Robin was tall, with long red hair. Her specialty was play therapy. She helped the children act out their anxieties and trauma with dolls, action figures, plastic animals and other toys in the well-equipped playroom, which included a playhouse. They also spent a lot of time role-playing and reenacting memories and incidents in the free-standing therapy sandbox.

Manuel turned to Gianna. "Ready?"

She hunched her shoulders.

"You did it this morning." He smiled up at her. "You can do it again."

Without responding, she dug her fingers deeper into Estrella's mane.

Manuel walked to her side and touched her knee.

The girl recoiled.

"Oh, dear," Laura whispered. "He forgot she doesn't like to be touched."

"Uh..." Manuel shoved his hand into his pocket. "You want to try it for, like, maybe three seconds?"

Gianna looked away.

Kate felt sorry for Manuel, who appeared to have no idea what to do next.

"Sweetie…" The tremulous voice came from the far side of the corral.

Chapter Two

K ate turned to see Dymple Forbes, an elderly friend from church, wriggle to the edge of the lawn chair she was sitting in, put her hands on the chair arms and push herself to her feet. Even though Dymple was full of vim, vigor and vinegar, as she liked to say, arthritis slowed her down. But it didn't stop her. She hobbled to the railing. "Bring Gianna over here, Manuel."

The youth's face brightened and he hurried the horse to where Dymple stood on the other side of the pole fence. She stretched between the rails to touch the filly's side. Estrella's skin twitched.

"Gianna, dear..." Dymple patted the horse, not the girl. "Remember what we talked about?"

Gianna stared down at her.

"Imagine you're reaching up to take God's hand." Dymple hoisted her own bony hand. "He'll keep you safe and give you all the courage you need."

The girl looked at the horse's head and then back at Dymple, who said, "Try it while the horse is standing still. Reach up to God, honey."

The spectators quieted. Their expectant expressions told Kate they were rooting for Gianna as fervently as she was. *Please, God,* she prayed, *give her the courage she needs.*

"Go, girl," Laura said, "You can do it."

Gianna slowly uncurled the fingers of one hand from Estrella's mane, hesitated, and then let her palm hover just above the horse's back.

Kate smiled and whispered, "Atta girl."

"Very good." Dymple's voice was subdued. "Now, a little higher."

Even from across the corral, Kate could tell Gianna was shaking. Poor baby. She'd experienced so much suffering in her few short years of life.

Estrella nickered and looked back at the girl. Manuel rubbed the filly's neck.

Manuel was a good kid. He'd had his share of challenges, but he'd risen above them to become an honor student and a campus leader at the university. All the Freedom House children adored him, even little Lupita, who rarely spoke but giggled when he pushed her high on the swing.

Gianna wrinkled her nose, screwed her eyes closed and forced her fist upward.

For a short moment, the only sound came from a crow cawing at the top of a tall ponderosa pine. Then applause exploded, accented by whistles and shouts. Kate blinked away tears and hugged Laura, who had tears of her own.

A half-smile tugged at the corner of Gianna's mouth. She opened her eyes.

Manuel grinned. "Ready to ride?"

She unclenched her hand, spread her fingers and offered the briefest of nods.

Manuel led the horse and the girl around the enclosure to the beat of onlookers chanting, "Gianna, Gianna, Gianna…"

They passed Laura and Kate, who sneezed again.

Gianna's hand never wavered. She raised it higher and higher, until it was above her head. After one circuit, Manuel stopped the horse, and she jumped off.

Clint called, "Gianna and Manuel, take a bow."

The duo ducked their heads. More raucous cheers followed them as they led the horse out of corral. Gianna ran to Dymple, who held out her hands but then lowered them to her lap and said something that brought a smile to the girl's somber face.

"Wow," Clint exclaimed as he dragged the dummy calf to the center of the pen. "How are we going to top that, partner?"

Tieno shifted the rope coil to the other arm and shrugged.

"Hey…" Clint tapped the boy's shoulder with his knuckles. "I thought you were a go-getter."

Another shrug. Tieno started to swing the loop end of the rope.

"Ah, I know what's goin' on." Clint motioned to the crowd. "Our man Tieno here is just playing it cool. Doesn't want the dame to look bad."

Tieno dropped the loop and frowned up at him. "D-d-dame?"

Chuckles peppered the air.

Clint grinned. "A dame is a girl, but don't worry about Miss Gianna. She's tough. She can handle the competition."

Tieno didn't look convinced.

Kate shook her head. She had a feeling half of what Clint said floated right over the boy's head.

Clint positioned Tieno several feet from the tail end of the dummy calf. "Go for it, bucko."

Tieno took off his hat and gave it to Clint. Then he straightened, took the loop in his right hand and held the coiled rope in his left. One foot in front of the other and his arm in the air, he circled the loop above his head. His entire body moved with the whir of the rotating rope. On the fifth swing, he flipped his wrist forward and released the loop. It snaked through the air, hit the sawhorse and bounced to the ground.

A collective moan was quickly followed by, "Try again, son." "You can do it." "Twist that wrist."

When the noise quieted, Clint squatted beside his student. Kate could barely hear his words of encouragement. "That was close, champ, mighty close. A few more inches and you'll rope the sucker. Now, remember..." He held out his hand, palm down. "When you release the loop, you gotta flip your hand downward, open it and point your fingers at the calf."

Tieno gave Clint a sideways glance before he concentrated on the dummy again. Kate wondered what he was thinking. He hadn't said much about the mini rodeo, but after Clint gave him the western outfit last week, he'd worn it every day. To get him to change into pajamas at night, the staff had to tell him if he slept in the getup, it would be too crumpled to wear to the rodeo.

One swing, two, three...faster and faster. Five, six, seven—and Tieno released the loop. This time, it caught on one of the horns.

The spectators groaned.

Tieno's shoulders drooped.

Clint whispered something in his ear and he began to coil the rope again.

"Whoo-hoo!," Laura yelled. "You're almost there, baby."

"This is it," Kate called. "Throw a wide loop and you've got him."

Tieno said something to Clint, who nodded and stepped away.

Kate was proud of the determination she saw in the little boy's eyes. She prayed his resolve would transfer to the trials he faced as he walked the long road to recovery.

Tieno began swinging the loop and twisting his wrist, swinging and twisting, swinging and twisting. Three swings, a thrust, a hiss through the air—and the rope dropped around the horns. The calf was his. Like a true roper, Tieno gave the loop a quick yank to tighten and secure the hold.

Cheers and whistles filled the arena.

Clint clamped Tieno's hat on his head, grasped him by the waist, and held him high. "Ladies and gentlemen, the Whispering Pines calf-roping champion!"

Kate clapped until her hands stung. She was as proud of Clint as she was of Tieno. He'd been approved by the Wyoming Department of Family Services to work with the children, but he wasn't a paid staff member. He taught the kids to ride and rope in his spare time.

Rodeo activities were not only fun for their charges, they were therapeutic. Being in control of a rope helped them deal with their fear of bondage. And the ability to unlatch the corral gate or crawl between the rails was also freeing for them.

Clint had patiently persevered through their apprehension and tears and made headway with a couple of them. Slowly but surely, he was learning each child's teasing limit. Sometimes, they even teased back.

In addition to being the ranch manager, Clint was Mike's best friend and had been for years. Tall, blonde, serious Mike and dark-haired, broad-shouldered, fun-loving Clint were as different as the sun and moon, yet they made a great team. With help from a handful of ranch hands, they oversaw the working side of the ranch and kept tabs on the horse, cattle and bison herds. Mike, along with Laura and Kate, monitored guest reservations and activities. Clint helped with related events, like trail rides and bison viewing.

Kate scanned the spectators. Still no Mike. One of the ranch hands was videotaping the event. But a movie wouldn't include rubbing shoulders with their friends and neighbors and thanking them for their support.

Tieno and Clint exited the ring.

Laura turned to Kate. "Is Mike here?"

Kate eyed the parking lot. "I haven't seen him or his truck."

"I hate for him to miss this," Laura said. "The kids' progress is like a reward, a validation for what we're doing." A fierce expression flashed across her face. "We did *not* make a mistake when we opened the children's home."

Kate hugged her mother-in-law. "I feel the same way."

"I don't know what's gotten into my son lately." Laura's eyebrows pinched. "He should be here."

A hawk settled at the peak of a pine tree, head cocked in what looked like an attempt to fathom the noisy creatures below.

"Mike is busy," Kate said, "especially now that you and I spend more time over here than in the office." She hated making excuses for him. Like Laura, she was frustrated with his attitude and beginning to suspect he didn't want anything to do with Freedom House, which was crazy. He'd been enthused about the idea when his mom first suggested it and had participated in the planning, paperwork, training and construction they'd undergone to prepare for the children's arrival.

"That's why we need to hire people for the office," Laura said. "I'll talk to him again."

Hearing applause, both women turned toward the corral, where Clint was again center-stage. "Rodeo fans…" He waved his hat. "We've got a special treat for you this afternoon that'll knock your boots right off your stinky socks."

Children giggled and a male voice yelled, "Speak for yourself, Barrett."

Again, laughter.

"Here they come now," Clint announced. "The Whispering Pines Mutton Busters." Several helmeted children, including those of ranch guests and neighbors, filed into the pen. Manuel and a teenage girl named

Bethany accompanied them.

"For you bronc-ridin' fans, this is where the training begins." Clint motioned to Manuel, who stood by the gate. "Bring on the broncs."

Manuel spoke into a two-way radio and moments later, a truckload of bleating sheep circled the crowd. The ranch hand driving the truck backed it to the corral. Manuel opened the gate and helped him unload five wooly ewes into the pen. The sheep ran first to one side of the corral and then to the other, all the while voicing their distress, but they were soon cornered.

Laura whispered, "Maybe it's best Mike isn't here."

Kate nodded. Her husband was a typical cattleman. He didn't want sheep anywhere near his property. According to him, they ate grass down to the dirt, leaving the land barren for years. After cattle grazed a pasture, the grass grew back fairly fast. Even so, she thought sheep were cute, especially the lambs.

Clint pulled a list from his back pocket. "First up, we have Alison, all the way from Odenville, Alabama." A little girl with curly red hair sprouting from the edges of her helmet burst into tears.

Kate recognized Alison as a Whispering Pines guest. Her family had been with them almost a week.

Bethany knelt beside the child. "What's the matter, Alison?"

"I want my mama."

"I'm right here, honey," a woman called, "waiting to see you ride a sheep."

"Okay." The girl's cheeks dimpled into a smile.

Manuel clamped down on a ewe and Bethany lifted the girl onto her back.

"Look, Mama. Look, Daddy," the girl called in her high-pitched voice. "I'm sitting on a lamb. He's soft."

"Good job, Ali. Hold still while Daddy takes a picture."

After the picture, Manuel said, "Lay your cheek on her back and take hold of her wool with both hands."

The sheep let out a loud bleat.

Bethany steadied the girl. "Squeeze your knees hard."

"Okay."

"Ready?"

Alison lifted her head.

"Put your head down," Manuel said. "One, two, three…go."

They released the animal and stepped back.

As if a coyote was nipping at her hooves, the ewe bolted for the other side of the pen. One bounce and Ali landed face-first in the dirt.

"Ali!" Her mother slipped between the rails and ran to her. "Are you all right?"

The little girl jumped to her feet. Dirt obliterated her freckles. "That was fun, Mama." She swiped at her nose with the back of her hand and shook her head. Dust flew off her helmet. "Can I do it again?"

"That's the spirit," Clint said. "Give Miss Alison a hand."

When the applause subsided and the mother-daughter duo had stepped out of the arena, he consulted his list again. "Next up is Frankie from right here in Wyoming." He didn't mention that Frankie lived at Freedom House.

The sheep trotted to the other end of the corral. Manuel dove after one and caught it by a back leg. Bethany grasped the other back leg.

Shannon, an eleven-year-old blonde girl from Detroit and their oldest resident, made her way to the gate. She had Freedom House's youngest child in tow, a four-year-old boy wearing a helmet. His chocolate skin contrasted with her light complexion.

Frankie was another of their wards whose parents had not been located. Judging by his accent, his speech therapist guessed his roots might be Nigerian. Shannon's parents were known, but they'd been convicted of selling her to a sex-trafficking gang in exchange for drugs— and subsequently imprisoned.

Though the girl refused to participate in the rodeo and had been surly all morning, she'd come alive when she saw car after car drive onto the property. She loved crowds. Kate suspected she would have preferred to see sequined dresses, stiletto heels and glitzy jewelry on the women rather than denim and boots. But at least her mood had lightened.

The instant the gate opened for them, Frankie began to wail.

"I'll go," Laura said. Along with the other staff, they took turns helping Frankie work through his crying jags. She walked to the other side of the corral, took the little boy in her arms, looked at Clint and shook her head.

After a "whatever" shrug, Shannon walked away.

Kate was sad Frankie wouldn't ride today. But he was young and severely traumatized. Just the thought of the cruelty he'd endured broke her heart, over and over.

She smelled meat cooking and glanced toward the patio. Cyrus Moore, their ranch cook, was at the grill. He was starting early, which was wise. They had a lot of people to feed.

Marita, Manuel's mom, was at the other end of the patio, arranging the salads, chips and condiments. Kate left the mutton busters to help the pair set up the barbecue. Anything to get her mind off Mike. He'd not only snubbed her, Laura, the Freedom House kids and staff with his absence, he'd slighted their friends and neighbors as well.

She nudged a pinecone off the path with the toe of her boot. He still hadn't given her a final answer about tomorrow. But she had a feeling his absence this afternoon meant he had no intention of accompanying her and the kids on the trip to Cheyenne.

Chapter Three

Mail in hand, Mike Duncan trudged up the deck steps and stopped at the back door to drop first one muddy boot and then the other on the wooden planks. He opened the screen door, and his big collie, Tramp, bounded into the dining room. Mike followed. After sifting through the mail he'd pulled from the mailbox, he deposited the stack on the table and called, "Anybody home?"

The only response was a tail wag from his dog.

"Figures."

Tramp at his heels, Mike walked through the dining room, past the living room and down the hall. The office and lobby at the end of the long hallway were both empty. He returned to the living quarters to check the kitchen and the bedrooms. Sometimes Kate had a friend stay with Mary until he was done with his work for the day. But no one was home—not Mom, not Kate, not Aunt Mary, which meant he wouldn't have to cook for her tonight.

"It's not that I mind Aunt Mary," he explained to Tramp as he pulled the rubber lid off the dog food bin in the pantry. A smell somewhere between dry cereal and meat-processing plant filled the small room. He shoved a scoop into the reddish-brown chunks. "But I have a hard time following her thoughts when her mind begins to wander. I might as well be eating alone. Know what I mean?"

Tramp whined, more from hunger than conversation, Mike knew.

He also knew Aunt Mary wasn't the real reason he was irritated. Nowadays, he saw his wife and mother at breakfast just before they left for the children's home. And that was it for the day. They also took turns spending nights at Freedom House, which meant he not only ate supper by himself, he often slept alone.

Returning to the patio, Mike dumped the food into one of the dog bowls and picked up the other to fill with water in the kitchen. Tramp dug in with his usual enthusiasm. While filling the water bowl, Mike read the note taped to the window above the sink.

Hi Sweetheart—Just wanted to remind you about the kids' rodeo and barbecue

this afternoon at Freedom House. Rodeo starts at 4:30, barbecue at 6:00. See you then.

All my love, Kate

"Hot dogs?" Mike tugged the paper from the window and dropped it on the counter. She'd reminded him about the rodeo and barbecue at breakfast but apparently felt he needed an additional reminder. "Why would I eat wieners when I have a freezer full of steaks?"

He delivered the water to his dog then retraced his steps to the kitchen. Opening the refrigerator door, he pulled out one of the bison steaks he'd moved from the freezer to the fridge that morning, just in case. He was about to close the door, when he said, "Why not?" and lifted a second butcher-paper-wrapped steak from the meat drawer. Tramp was the only dinner company he had. His dog might as well eat Aunt Mary's share.

Leaving the meat on the counter, he stepped outside to fire up the grill. "Interested in a bison steak, Tramp?"

But all he heard was the collie slurping water like he hadn't just taken a big drink from the creek a half-hour earlier. He turned on the propane and lit the flame. Talking to himself and to his dog was a bit weird, he had to admit. But who else was he going to talk to these days?

Back in the kitchen, where he unwrapped the big steaks, flipped them onto a platter and threw the butcher paper and Kate's note in the pantry wastebasket. Playing bachelor and managing the WP without his wife's help was not his idea of marriage. The guest ranch was moving into its busy season. He needed both Kate and Mom in the office to keep things running smoothly.

He pulled a meat fork from a drawer and walked out onto the deck. The screen door slammed behind him. Lifting the grill lid, he placed one steak in the middle of the grate and closed the lid.

Tramp yipped and perked his ears.

"Hang on, boy." He stabbed the raw steak with the fork and dropped it in the now-empty bowl. "This one's yours."

Tramp wolfed it down, which pleased Mike. His collie might be getting up in years, but he had a good appetite and he was still able to hop in and out of the pickup and chase barn cats and jackrabbits—not that he ever caught one.

He went into the house one more time to rinse the platter, pour himself a glass of tea from the fridge and grab the new *Bison Journal* that had come in the mail. Back on the patio, he fell into a deck chair and opened the magazine. But he couldn't concentrate. Between the smell of the sizzling steak juices, which made his stomach growl, and his growing guilt for missing the barbecue, he found it impossible to focus on the words.

He stared at a cloud that floated overhead, momentarily blocking the sunshine. After more craziness than he cared to recall, life at the Whispering Pines was finally on an even keel. Reporters were no longer calling or banging on their door. Kate's past was behind her and behind the ranch. Thanks to Dymple, almost five-thousand people had signed a petition asking Wyoming's governor to seek a pardon for Kate from the governor of Pennsylvania, where she'd been incarcerated years ago.

The governor had taken his time, but he'd signed the pardon the day he announced he would not run for another term. Evidently, he was no longer concerned about the political ramifications of pardoning a woman who was no longer a resident.

Tramp drank some more and then plopped on his side in an aspen-shaded corner of the deck.

Prior to Kate's pardon, Amy had been rescued from Executive Pride along with the Freedom House kids. And neighbors who'd been conned into giving up their grandparents' homesteads had returned to their ranches. They'd also had a brucellosis scare. But no sign of the disease was found in his or his neighbor's bison herds, and no more bison had been shot, thanks to Todd Hughes's house arrest.

Mike scratched his five o'clock shadow. He should be grateful for all the good things that had happened, but the pardon paved the way for Kate to share responsibilities with his mom at the children's home. And now she was there every day, all day…and sometimes all night.

Between the aspen and evergreen stands that graced their headquarters, he could see glimpses of their barn, dining hall and other ranch buildings his parents had constructed. They'd built the guest ranch from the ground up with the help of neighbors. But Dad was gone. At times like this, he missed him more than ever. If he'd been here, they might have been spared some of the upheaval of these past few years.

Along with Kate and Mom and Clint, Mike did his best to manage the WP with the same expertise and integrity his father had embodied. They'd been a good team, the four of them. But now Mom and Kate were all wrapped up in the children's home. And Clint spent plenty of time there, too.

He got to his feet to turn the steak, wondering what he was going to eat with it. Maybe some of the applesauce Mom and Kate canned last fall. The fridge was nearly empty. No one had driven to town to buy groceries lately. Yeah, he could eat at the dining hall, but people would ask about Kate and he wasn't sure his answer would be civil. He closed the lid and sat down.

The good news was that his nemesis neighbor, Todd Hughes, was now fairly harmless, thanks to his injuries. The bad news was that he'd just gotten off house arrest. Mike had heard the man blamed the Duncans for supposedly ruining his life. Who knew what the crazy rancher might do next.

Todd had been forced to reimburse them for the loss of a bison cow, trauma and damages, plus their attorney fees, which must have fried him to no end. They'd used the money to replace the cow, upgrade equipment in the dining hall kitchen and make some repairs here and there. But without Kate to do the marketing and Mom to take reservations and keep the office running, they could lose the ranch.

Mike snorted. *Might as well let Hughes kill off the whole herd.*

Kate settled next to Amy, who sat across from Clint at one of the new picnic tables scattered about the lawn beside the children's home. "Nice tables, Clint."

"Thanks. I got a lot of help from the guys." He stood. "Think I'll go get another burger and more of Marita's potato salad. Good stuff."

Before he stepped away, Kate added, "Great job with the rodeo. I appreciate all the work you put into the event for the kids."

"Yeah, that was fun." Amy gave Clint a thumbs-up.

"My pleasure." He touched the brim of his hat. "Have to admit I'm mighty proud of Tieno."

"We're all proud of him." Kate smiled at the memory of the earnest little guy beneath his big black hat.

Amy smirked. "I liked your matching outfits."

Clint shrugged and headed for the grill.

Amy watched him go. "I think I embarrassed him."

"He'll get over it." Kate sipped her drink and surveyed the crowd. Nearly all the tables were filled. Their guests' congenial chatter and laughter intermingled with that of birdsong and the shouts of children playing on the Freedom House jungle gym.

"Where's Mike?" Amy asked. "I haven't seen him yet."

"I've been wondering the same thing all afternoon."

"It's not like him to miss a get-together." Amy cocked her head and her auburn hair swung to the side. "Aren't you worried about him?"

"What do you mean?"

"Could be something happened to him. Maybe his truck broke down, or he got stuck. Or, I hate to say it, but what if he's hurt?"

"I should have thought of that." Kate winced. "Instead, I've been annoyed by his absence. Some wife I am."

Amy raised an eyebrow.

Kate shrugged. "He's been grumpy about Freedom House lately, so I assumed he purposely stayed away."

"That doesn't sound like the Mike I know. I hope he's okay."

"I'll call him on the radio if he doesn't show up soon."

Amy pushed her food aside and leaned on the table, hands on her elbows. "Didn't he partner with you and Laura to start this place?"

"He did, but he never comes over. He doesn't want to talk about the home or the children and he complains about how much time I spend here. He won't even let me bring Tramp to play with the kids." Kate swished the ice cubes in her drink. "We all knew the first year would be difficult, but I didn't expect him to turn against what Laura and I are trying to do. He wants us in the office fulltime, like before."

She rubbed at the condensation on the paper cup. "We're not doing a very good job of keeping up at the office. I realize that. But now that we've established Freedom House, we can't walk away from it. These are traumatized kids, as you well know. They need us, every day, all day."

"Like I told you before, I'll be glad to help you out."

"I know." Kate hugged her friend. "We've been trying to get Mike to hire office help. Coach Rob is willing to go fulltime this summer and take over some of Laura's responsibilities. We'd like you to cover the front desk plus assume some of my duties."

Movement beneath a nearby tree caught Kate's attention. She nudged Amy. Lupita, the six-year-old Freedom House resident who was mostly silent and who rarely showed emotion, was watching them, hands clasped to her chest. She and Amy had bonded at the Texas brothel.

Amy jumped up and ran over to give her a hug. "I love you, sweet Lupi."

And then the girl was gone, back to her chair between Kate's Great-Aunt Mary and Dymple.

Amy returned to the picnic table.

"All these strangers make her even more skittish than usual," Kate said. "But I love how she never forgets you and steps out of her comfort zone to make sure you don't forget her, either."

"How could I? She's such a darling." Amy's expression grew serious. "You can't imagine how good it felt to hold her little hand, even for a few short minutes, when we were going through that awful time in Texas—or how thrilled I was to see you again."

Kate watched a chipmunk with a potato chip in its mouth run up the tree Lupita had been standing under. "I thought my heart would explode when we found you, yet we couldn't get near you."

Regret darkened Amy's somber demeanor.

Before the conversation could plunge to depths they'd already mined again and again, Kate said, "So, back to the ranch office. What do you think?"

Amy's smile returned. "I'd love to work in the office, 'cause I like to interact with your guests. But if Mike doesn't want me, then—"

"He doesn't know what he wants. Change is harder for him than I realized when we were first married. But he'll come around. He has to have help to keep WP in business."

"I hate to leave the Raeburns in a lurch at the café," Amy said. "Maybe I could waitress for them two or three days a week and come up here the other days."

"That might work."

"I'd need a place to stay, but I know your cabins are always full in the summertime." Her brow furrowed. "I s'pose I could sleep in a tent, if I could get a shower now and then."

Kate laughed. "We'll find a place for you. You might have to share a bed with Aunt Mary or crash on our couch. One way or another, we'll make room."

"Thanks for your confidence in me. You know how much I love this place." With a wave of her hand, Amy indicated their surroundings. "I'll do my best for you and the ranch, although I doubt I could ever replace you or Laura, especially Laura. She's managed the office for years."

"You'll do great." Kate shooed a determined fly away from her food. "I just thought of something...actually, two things."

Amy gave Kate a sidelong glance. "What?"

"What about your dogs and your cat—and your birds?"

"As long as I can check in on them every couple of days, they'll be okay. If I needed to be away any longer than that, I would call my neighbor. She has a key and has kept an eye on them for me in the past."

"That sounds good," Kate said.

"What's your other question?"

Kate rested her chin on her hand. "What about Clint?"

"What about him?"

"I thought your therapist said you two need to keep some distance between you for a while, 'cause you're not ready to date. If you work at the ranch, you'll see a lot of him."

"She says I've made good progress and I can start dating again, if I want. However, I have to keep it light. Besides, seeing Clint working at the ranch isn't the same as being alone with him."

"Keep it light?"

"You know, have fun together but not get serious or physical. No kissing or hand-holding. I shouldn't make plans for the future or spend a lot of alone time with a guy."

"What if you dated others, not just Clint?"

"She would probably approve of that idea. But Clint knows my background. He knows about Texas." She ducked her head. "And I like him. A lot."

"I can tell he likes you, too…a lot." Kate studied her friend. "But I'm pretty sure intimacy of any sort is going to be a challenge for you." She ran her fingers along the sanded edge of the table. "It's something I've struggled with."

"Yeah…" Amy nodded. "I know what you mean. Some days I don't want to be touched by anyone, not even Clint. Other days I long for a hug. It's crazy."

"You'll get better with time. I did, although I occasionally have ambivalent moments. You'll have to tune into your feelings and figure out your triggers as well as your reactions to those triggers."

"That's what my counselor said. It's not easy."

"No, it isn't. But it's worth the effort." Kate paused. "Just as important is the need for you to be on the same page spiritually with the guys you date."

Clint, who'd been visiting with Manuel and his parents, sauntered toward them, a full plate of food in one hand and a beer in the other—and his gaze on Amy.

"Has he ever mentioned having a relationship with Jesus? Or that he reads the Bible?" Kate asked. "Anything like that?"

"No." Amy, who was grinning at Clint, shook her head. "He's so darn cute, but you're right. I should know where he stands with God before we grow any closer."

Kate put her napkin over her food and stood. "We'll talk more about that *darn cute* guy later. Right now, I'd better give Mike a quick call and then visit with our guests."

Chapter Four

Kate helped Marita and Laura clear the patio and put the barbecue leftovers in the Freedom House fridge. Then she and Cyrus loaded bagged trash into the back of his pickup. He would stop by the ranch headquarters on his way home to drop the garbage in the dumpster.

Before she left, she read the children a bedtime story and hugged them goodnight. Then she said goodnight to the others, saddled Estrella Blanca and rode slowly toward the log home she shared with Mike, Laura and Aunt Mary. At the end of a long day, she was glad their house was only a couple miles away and that Manuel and Bethany had offered to drive her SUV over for her.

As she rode, she thought about the mini-rodeo and barbecue. If laughter and smiles were any indication, everyone had had a good time. The kiddos, as she liked to call the Freedom House residents, had seemed reasonably comfortable with the influx of neighbors and ranch guests.

Lupi and Frankie were jittery, as usual, and neither child ventured far from Dymple and Aunt Mary, but the others did okay. Kate rubbed her neck. Any other time, Frankie would have shadowed Laura, but she'd been on the move, welcoming one guest after another.

The sun dropped behind a mountain, shooting bright rays into clouds backdropped by a darkening sky. Birds called warnings as the horse approached. Several yards ahead, a doe stepped from an aspen grove and stopped to stare at her and Estrella, its long ears high and alert. Behind the animal, lime-green leaves fluttered in the waning light. The deer leaped across the path into the trees on the other side.

Refreshed yet soothed by the forest's fresh scents, Kate wound the reins about the saddlehorn and settled in the saddle. Estrella knew her way home. The horse would trot straight to the barn, anxious for her supper.

Kate placed her hands on her thighs. The day had been beautiful and fun, and now she was blessed with a tranquil evening. She'd learned to relish such opportunities for solitude. Working with children took a lot of time and energy.

A breeze lifted her hair and cooled her neck. She and Laura had been forewarned by those who worked with trafficked individuals that no one could guarantee every Freedom House child would recover. Some might even return to *the life*—or *the game,* as Shannon called it. The thought turned Kate's stomach.

Even so, she'd given herself to the kids, determined to love and guide them to a better future. Just yesterday, using crayons, she'd drawn two faces, one with a frown and one with a smile. And then she'd told them how God's love had turned her own life from sadness to gladness, from hopelessness to hope.

Kate was filling Estrella's feed bin when Mike walked through the barn's wide-open doorway. Tramp followed.

She smiled. "Hi, sweetheart."

He gave her a quick kiss on the cheek.

She patted Tramp's head. "Missed you at the kids' rodeo."

"I was busy."

"That's what I told everyone who asked about you." Kate fumbled beneath the filly's belly for the cinch. "We had a great crowd. And a good time."

Mike opened the gate to the adjoining stall.

She lifted the saddle off the horse and dropped it onto the rail between the stalls. "You could have come over to eat with us. I tried to get you on the radio."

"I don't do hot dogs." He stepped inside the stall.

Kate ignored the comment—she'd seen him eat plenty of hot dogs—and shook out the dusty saddle blanket before hanging it over the rail. "What's wrong, Mike?" She sneezed and rubbed her nose with the back of her hand. "It's not like you to avoid our neighbors."

"Maybe I should have gone." He picked up a rake. "Might have had a chance to talk with my wife."

She lifted her chin. "And what exactly does that mean?"

"I'm lucky to see you a couple times a week." Like a bulldozer scraping topsoil, he jabbed the floor of the stall with the rake and jerked it back, again and again. The violent action stirred up straw particles along with pungent whiffs of urine and manure.

Kate rubbed her nose again. "We have breakfast together every morning, whether I spend the night at the children's home or not."

"And then you take off."

"I went straight to the office this morning and worked for a couple hours." She put her hands on her waist. "But you didn't know that, did you? No, 'cause *you* took off to go check your precious bison herd."

"Oh, so now it's about the bison."

Kate groaned. "We have this time together, Mike, and we're fighting. That's not how it used to be. I miss the old us."

"The old *us* went by the wayside when you opened your blasted children's home."

"Michael Duncan." Kate stabbed her forefinger at him. "You were totally onboard with the home. You prayed with your mom and me about it, did some of the research, worked with the authorities. You helped design the layout and you helped build the house. And now it's *my* blasted children's home?"

"I didn't know it would ruin my life."

"Ruin your life? Are you kidding me?"

A group of guests walking past the barn peered inside, curious expressions on their faces.

She lowered her voice. "We all knew it would take months, maybe even years to get the home running smoothly, to get just the right staff and programs in place for the kids."

"Yeah, well, I'm left running a guest ranch all by myself in the middle of the tourist season."

Estrella snorted and gave them a backward look as if she didn't appreciate them disturbing her dinner.

"We've talked about this before." Kate folded her arms. "You've got to hire help."

"Like I have time to train anyone." He plunged the rake into a corner and dragged the soiled straw to the pile in the middle of the stall.

"You knew months ago you needed to bring on more office staff." Kate smiled at his back and tried to sound cheery. "But lucky you, you don't have to look far. Coach told your mom he'd like to get in extra hours this summer to build his boys' college fund and possibly work some during the school year, too. He understands our operation. You won't have to interview him."

"Yeah, well…"

"He could do more than just bookkeeping. He could answer phones, check people in and out. And the Curtis twins would be happy to help. Every summer, they offer to clean cabins and work in the kitchen in exchange for extra time on the ranch. Whatever you need, they'll do."

He frowned at her over his shoulder. "They're ancient."

"Mamie and Minnie have more energy than most thirty-year-olds. Take them up on their offer, Mike. If your mom or I don't have time to train them, Marita will."

"We need someone to cover the front desk and make reservations. Coach can't be there all the time."

"I've told you before, but I'll say it one more time. Amy is perfect for the position. She's great with people. They love her down at the café."

He stopped raking and turned to her. "Why am I supposed to do the hiring? You can bring on more people to work at the kids' home, which would free you and Mom to work in the office."

"You know how hard it is to find qualified professionals willing to travel all the way up the mountain to work."

"Should have thought of that earlier."

"You're impossible." She shook her head. "Even when someone lives close enough to work at Freedom House, they have to go through a background check, be approved by the state and trained for our unique type of children's work." She paused. "But the WP office needs more employees *now*. What about Amy? Like I said, she'd be great."

He frowned. "I don't think so…"

"Why not?"

He knocked a chunk from one of the tines with his boot. "She'd have to learn our way of doing things and the computer programs we use, which would be crazy when you and Mom already know the ropes."

Kate clenched her fists to keep from grabbing his shoulders and shaking him until his teeth rattled. "You're talking in circles. We're right back where we started."

"We haven't had sex in two weeks."

"Oh…" Kate planted her hands on her hips. "So that's what this is all about." She glanced about to make sure no one else was in the barn.

"Yeah. We don't have sex 'cause you're always at Freedom House or too tired from being over there all day. Those kids are more important to you than our marriage."

"I can't believe what I'm hearing." Kate pivoted and strode toward the exit before she said something she'd regret forever. She charged through the big opening, dodged a ranch hand who was leading a pair of horses into the barn, and ran down the path where she'd first met Mike.

Sometimes the path reminded her of the night sparks of another kind first flew between the two of them and she'd stop for a moment to relive the memory. But not tonight. No, tonight, she wanted to get as far away from her husband as possible.

Seated in one of the rocking chairs clustered on the far end of the dining hall veranda, Kate watched the moon rise above a nearby hill. The daytime's warm breeze danced with the evening coolness. The first cricket chirped.

Voices from within the building suggested some of their guests were playing cards and others were visiting. Judging by the aroma that sifted through the screen door, they'd had lasagna for supper. It smelled good.

She hadn't had a chance to eat much at the barbecue. Under different circumstances, she might have heated a plate of leftovers and joined those inside the dining hall. Tonight, she remained in the shadows.

The sound of boots clomping up the steps at the other end of the porch made her sigh. By the rhythm of the gait, she knew the wearer of the boots was Mike, but she didn't look his way. She didn't want to see him, didn't want to continue the argument, didn't want to kiss and make up—even if he wanted to, which was unlikely.

He stopped and the chair beside hers creaked when he sat. After a moment, he said, "I'm sorry, Kate. Don't know what got into me."

"That's what your mother said."

"You two been talking about me?"

She didn't respond.

"To be honest," he said, "I'm lonely. I miss coming home to you at night. I miss eating dinner with you and Mom. I miss, well, everything…"

Or maybe you just miss sex. Kate closed her eyes. She was tired and she wanted to go to sleep. But Mike was stuck in the past. As a result, their marriage was at a standstill. She reached for his hand. "I miss you, too, and our alone times."

She'd been too busy and exhausted to notice the lack of intimacy, but she wasn't about to tell him that. "Still, I can't abandon the kids, or your mom."

"You can abandon me, not them?"

She pulled away. "Isn't that a bit childish?"

He took her hand again. "We were partners, Kate. You and Mom and I ran this ranch together."

"We haven't left." Kate looked at him for the first time since he sat down. "We cut back our duties, duties someone else can do equally as well, to help children who need a safe place to live and grow."

"That's all you talk about."

"What?"

"The kids."

"Freedom House is a calling, Mike. *My* calling. My past prepared me to work there." She paused. How could she explain her feelings to him, feelings she thought he understood when they decided to open the home. She identified with the children's challenges in a way few professionals could. Using her pain and on-going healing to help salve the kids' wounds was more than rewarding. When she opened her scarred soul and shared from deep within, she sensed purpose in her suffering.

An owl hooted in a nearby tree. In the distance, another responded.

"I love this ranch." She squeezed his hand. "And I like to help out wherever and however I can. But my passion is to nurture the Freedom House children. I want to do everything possible to ease their pain and aid their recovery. Your passion is the ranch, has been almost since you were born, which is great."

"But a ranch wife—"

"Oh, so I'm not fulfilling my wifely duties?"

"Well, my mom—"

"Your mom loves every second she spends with the kids. Yes, she started the WP with your dad and it's grown into a profitable cattle-and-bison operation as well as a beautiful vacation destination. Now she wants to share the ranch with damaged children who desperately need her love, my love, *our* love…and most of all, God's love."

"She and Dad built this place from nothing," Mike said. "They did the bulk of the work themselves. I don't get how she can just up and leave it to other people to manage."

"Why? Because the Whispering Pines—*and* the bison—are your entire life?"

From the pond below the dining hall came the sound of frogs prepping their throats for an evening concert.

"They're not my *entire* life. I lead the worship team at church."

For a moment, Kate was silent. But then she murmured, half under her breath, "Sometimes I wonder which you worship more, God, this ranch or your bison."

Mike jumped to his feet. "That was low, Kate."

She looked up at him. Moonlight outlined his profile with silver. She tried not to think how handsome he was, even when angry. "I don't mean that as an insult. It's just something I wonder about sometimes."

He huffed. "Well, sometimes I wonder if the real reason you hang around those kids so much is because you can't have children. You had that surgery and then the adoption fell through…"

The air chilled another degree. Kate shivered and rubbed her arms. "Speaking of low blows…"

They'd offered to adopt the unborn child of one of the women they helped rescue from Executive Pride. The woman had vacillated between abortion and adoption for weeks and eventually chose to let the pregnancy run its course. But when she delivered the baby, a blond-haired, blue-eyed little boy with dimples like Mike's, she decided to keep him. Kate was heartbroken.

Mike mimicked her. "Of course, I didn't mean that as an insult. Just something I think about now and then." He paused. "What do you have to say about that?"

Brutalized by his words, she couldn't respond to his sarcasm or even look at him.

He kicked a chair. It slammed against the log wall and pitched forward. "If that's the way you feel, you can go your way and I'll go mine." Though his voice was low, it held a razor-sharp edge. "Live your life the way you want. I'll live mine the way I want…with my *precious* bison on my *precious* ranch."

Before he could stomp off, Kate said, "You haven't said whether or not you're going to Cheyenne with me tomorrow." If anyone else had been available, she wouldn't have asked him. "Obviously, this ranch is more important to you than I am." She folded her arms. "Forget about it. We'll do just fine without you."

He scrunched his brow, his disbelief obvious, even in the limited light. "I'm managing a busy, working, sold-out guest ranch by myself. Tomorrow is Saturday, when extra people come up for the weekend. And I've got calves to brand and castrate and a fence to fix. That's Cyrus's job, but half the time he's over at Freedom House."

"You have other employees."

"I told you it's easier for me to get away in the middle of the week."

"But I promised the kids we'd go tomorrow. I don't want to be one more person who betrays them."

The longer they talked, the more certain she was that she needed to get away for more than a day. She'd go without him and she'd take the tent and sleeping bags she'd purchased for the children. The two times they'd slept outside in the play area beside the house, the kids had loved sleeping in the tent.

Mike stared down at her, as if trying to comprehend what she'd just said. Then without another word, he adjusted his hat, leaped over the railing and disappeared into the night.

Chapter Five

Kate twisted to check her backseat passengers. "Seatbelts fastened, kiddos?"

Tieno raised his hands. "M-me f-f-fast."

"Mine is fastened," she corrected him as she made sure the seatbelt was properly attached to his booster seat.

"M-m-me, too." His happy grin was contagious.

Kate laughed. Tieno was excited to go to a park to play and swim. She looked at Lupita, who sat in the other booster seat. "Lupi, what about you?"

No response.

Though Lupita was older than Tieno, she was slow to answer, if she answered at all, as if formulating a response drained her limited resources, as if she'd left her soul in the brothel. But she was making progress. Just yesterday, a look of pleasure had flitted across her normally stoic face when Marita served the children homemade tamales for lunch.

"Mi mama...tamales," Lupita had said, the most she'd spoken since her arrival five months ago. Eyes closed, she'd bent over her plate and inhaled the chili-pepper scent of home.

Kate shifted to check the girl's hands. Just as she suspected, they were fisted against her collarbone. Lupi tended to hold her arms close to her body, even when eating or dressing. Kate understood the urge to protect herself. She also knew how ineffective a small girl was against a man or a group of men or boys.

Another time, she might have urged Lupi to hook her seatbelt by herself. But not today. She wanted the outing to be a fun getaway and an unspoken reward for successfully weathering a series of transitions. After their removal from the Dallas brothel, they'd been placed in the Texas foster care system for several months. From there, they were shipped to the WP, which must have seemed like a different planet to them.

More than anything, Kate hoped a happy day in Cheyenne would instill one more good memory to help counter all their bad memories. The kids had begun treatment for mental and emotional damage as well as for physical ailments in Texas. The healing initiated there made their work less daunting, but some therapies, like trauma and abuse counseling, play therapy and speech therapy, were ongoing.

They'd added other therapeutic activities, including music and art and lots of outdoor playtime. After their confinement in the brothel, the children flourished in the fresh mountain air as well as in the love and safety the staff provided.

Animals were also important at Freedom House. A housecat named Mayo and a duck named Jo-Jo lived on the premises. In addition, Clint brought Estrella Blanca and other horses over regularly. Maybe someday Mike would let Tramp visit, too. The big collie loved children.

Kate swung out of the front seat, opened Lupita's door and knelt beside the car. "We can do it together." With slow, gentle movements, she helped the girl lower her arms.

"Good job." She kept her voice low. "Now, let's click your belt, so we can drive to Cheyenne. We'll eat tacos for lunch before we go to the park. I know how you love tacos."

Lupita blinked, a good sign of connectedness. Kate took her hands in hers, loosening their ferocious clench, finger by finger. "Work with me, Lupita. We need to get going."

No response.

Kate kissed the girl's hair and looked into her eyes. "Pretty please..."

Lupita dipped her head.

Kate felt Lupi's fingers relax. She guided her hands to the seatbelt's metal ends and pushed them together until she heard a solid *clink.* "You did it, Lupi."

Lupita's eyes crinkled in an almost-smile.

Kate closed the door and settled into the driver's seat beside Shannon, whose shaggy hair was so blond it was almost white. She was the only American child of the five they'd acquired from the Texas brothel. After her parents sold her to the trafficking gang when she was eight, she'd been delivered to a pimp in Seattle, who, according to Shannon, said she didn't bring in enough cash and traded her for a younger child.

She'd ended up in the Dallas brothel, where she was held captive for almost two years, if the girl's estimate of time was correct. Like Amy had told Kate, the passing of days, weeks and months was hard to determine when trapped inside a closed environment day and night.

Unlike some of the others, Shannon was able to speak of her past and her abusive, addicted parents. She didn't seem to miss them, yet she talked about the Texas pimp with way too much longing in her voice. The man had evidently become a father figure to her.

Shannon pulled the seatbelt strap over her shoulder. "I knew Lupi would take a long time, so I waited. I hate seatbelts."

Kate gave her an understanding smile. "I know, honey." Bondage at Executive Pride, according to Amy, had been a regular occurrence, whether for punishment or for a client's entertainment.

With everyone buckled, Kate backed the car out of the garage. She didn't like leaving the other two children behind. However, Gianna was sick and Frankie was only four-years old. Separation from Mike's mom at this stage of his recovery upset him.

Laura had planned to accompany Kate and the kids to Cheyenne, but then a team meeting was scheduled for today with all the kids' therapists. They'd offered to drive up to the ranch so she wouldn't have to leave Freedom House. Coordinating the calendars of busy professionals was a challenge, so Laura had opted out of the trip to participate in the meeting.

Kate stopped the car at the end of the driveway and pushed the button to close the garage door, thinking of little Frankie. The mistreatment each Freedom House child had suffered in the past saddened her. But Frankie's history troubled her the most. The melancholy little boy had withstood more abuse and pain in his short life than most people endured in a lifetime.

Shannon leaned close. "Miss Kate, why are you crying?"

Kate swiped at the tear that trickled down the side of her nose. "I just thought of something sad." She smiled. "But today is a happy day. We're going to have fun in Cheyenne. Right, Tieno?"

He clapped. "R-r-righto, b-bucko."

Kate laughed. No doubt Clint had taught him that phrase.

"Gianna come?"

"What did you say?" Kate glanced in the mirror. Had she really heard Lupita speak?

"Gianna?"

Kate met Lupita's questioning gaze. The two girls didn't say much to each other, yet they sat together at meals and sometimes played side-by-side in the outdoor sandbox. "Gianna is sick, sweetie. Miss Laura said she threw up in the night and again after breakfast. I'm sorry she can't be with us."

Gianna was obsessed with food. The staff had to lock the cupboards and the refrigerator because she'd get up in the night and eat everything in sight. Last night, they'd left chips and cookies from the barbecue on the counter and Gianna had evidently overindulged again.

Lupita blinked but made no comment. Kate knew that allowing themselves to make attachments was hard for these kids, and when they did, small disappointments were often magnified way out of proportion by their injured psyches. She prayed Gianna's absence wouldn't trigger an anxiety attack for Lupita.

Laura and Aunt Mary waved from the front door. The children waved back. Kate rolled her window down. "Bye. I love you. See you tomorrow night."

Tieno and Lupita began pushing buttons. The back windows rolled down and up, down and up, down and up. Kate brought the SUV to a standstill in the middle of the dirt road and angled the mirror so she could see them both. "While we're driving on the ranch, let's leave the windows down, okay? That way you can smell the pine trees and watch for deer and porcupines. Remember the porcupine we saw the other day?"

Tieno nodded and the windows slid down.

Kate tapped the controls on her door panel to lock the windows. "When we get on the highway, you can close them." She had just started down the road again when she felt movement. In the mirror, she could see Lupita rocking and staring straight ahead, hands to her chest, something she did frequently at Freedom House. Readjusting the mirror, she decided the rhythmic motion helped the girl deal with Gianna's absence.

The only wild animal they saw on the way to the ranch headquarters was a chipmunk, which thrilled Tieno, who clapped and clapped. "Ch-chip-chip."

Driving between ranch buildings, Kate slowed the car when she saw a dented, faded-blue Dodge pickup parked in front of the barn. Mike had inherited the truck when his dad passed away. It still ran great and he drove it almost every day.

Kate was glad to see thick leather gloves on her husband's hands. He was wrestling a heavy roll of barbed wire into the back of the pickup. The wire screeched and scraped when he shoved it across the truck bed. The sound was horrendous, but Kate knew the barbs couldn't hurt Old Blue, Mike's dad's nickname for the tough old truck.

Shannon covered her ears.

In the corral beside the barn, wranglers were saddling horses for the morning trail ride. Expectant guests propped their arms on the top rails, watching their every move. A horse whinnied and a child called, "I want one with spots."

Kate stopped the car beside the pickup. The smell of horse manure wafted through the window. "Wave goodbye to Mister Mike."

Shannon wiggled her fingers and Tieno, who was closest to Mike, thrust his little arm out the open window. "B-bye, M-m-mister Mike."

Mike raised a forefinger in acknowledgement, but he didn't smile or make eye contact with Kate, who sighed and looked away. He was still mad at her. She'd had a feeling the hasty post-breakfast kiss was a show for his mom's sake. She also suspected the only reason he'd slept in their bed was because he didn't want Laura to find him on the couch.

Weaving between ranch buildings, Kate drove past the combination home and office she shared with Mike, Laura and Aunt Mary. Someday, she and Mike would build their own place. But right now, living with Mike's mom and working down the hall enabled them to all keep an eye on Aunt Mary. Despite the multiple sclerosis that forced her to use a walker, and thanks to the Alzheimer's disease that sometimes disoriented her, she had a knack for disappearing in a flash.

Now that Kate and Laura were at Freedom House most of the time, they took Mary with them almost every day. The kids loved her, even when she didn't make sense, and she loved being with them. With only two children to monitor today, Kate was confident Laura and Marita could keep track of them and Aunt Mary, too. They'd give her the supplements and coconut oil that kept her Alzheimer's in check when they gave Gianna and Frankie their meds.

She lowered the sun visor and turned onto the dirt road that led to the highway. So much on her mind. All Mike had to think about was the ranch. He didn't worry about the kids and Aunt Mary like she did.

Frowning, she slowed the car. He'd said he needed to stay close to keep things running smoothly. Yet, he was loading fencing materials into his pickup, which meant he'd be leaving the ranch headquarters. Had he put someone else in charge? And if he'd done that, he could have driven to Cheyenne with her and the kids.

Ticked by his rude behavior, she stopped in the middle of the road to punch out a text. "You could have at least said goodbye." Cell reception on the ranch was spotty. He might not receive the message for a week, but she didn't care. Tapping the "send" button made her feel better.

Shannon asked, "What's wrong?"

"Just needed to send a text."

Shannon eyed her briefly and then switched on the CD player. One of Mike's favorite country-western artists was singing about his first car. Shannon rolled her eyes but she didn't change the music.

Kate dropped the phone into the cup holder and picked up speed again. The argument still ate at her and, apparently, at Mike, too. She knew he was afraid to be near the Freedom House children, worried they might feel threatened by him or think he expected sexual favors from them.

He'd said he was concerned the prematurely sexualized children might come on to him when they wanted something, like dessert or a ride on his horse. True, Shannon acted a little flirty around men, but she was easily diverted. Mike even worried he might go to jail for accidently touching one of them in the wrong place. What if he picked up a child to put him or her on a horse and his hand slipped? Would they scream? Cuddle inappropriately? Report him?

"Clint does okay with children," she'd told him. "He doesn't get hung up by what *might* happen."

"Clint is comfortable with kids. I'm not."

Kate shook her head. Talking in circles again. Maybe he'd lived with her aunt too long.

Thinking of Aunt Mary made her smile. What a precious gift God had given her in her great-aunt. Earlier that morning, she'd asked, "What's the matter, dear? You're not yourself today." Even with dementia, Aunt Mary was tuned to her emotions.

Though Mary's eyes had been clear and she'd appeared to be lucid right then, Kate had hesitated to explain her disagreement with Mike—until she remembered how much she'd relied on her prayers throughout her life. Back when she'd felt too messed up to ask God for help, knowing Aunt Mary prayed for her comforted her and gave her hope for a better future. Kate decided she couldn't miss an opportunity to talk with her while she was coherent.

Leaving Marita and Laura to get breakfast for the kids, she steeped two cups of green tea three-and-one-half minutes, just the way Aunt Mary like it. Then she added a teaspoon of honey to each cup, along with the "splash" of cream her aunt requested.

She grabbed two of the blueberry scones Dymple had made for the household and took a seat beside her aunt on the patio. Between nibbles, she gave her a brief overview of her conflict with Mike, all the while trying not to badmouth him. She concluded by asking, "Did you and Uncle Dean ever fight?"

In response, Aunt Mary had lowered her cup to the table and laid her wrinkled hand on Kate's arm. Chipmunks chittered and birds sang in the treetops, but Mary said nothing. Kate hid her disappointment and tried to be grateful for fleeting instances of clarity.

Before they walked out the door to drive to Cheyenne, her aunt had let go of her walker, wrapped her slender arms about Kate's waist and looked up at her. "Your wedding day was one of the best days of my life."

Her breath smelled of the pink wintergreen mints she kept in her pocket. But unlike the mints Kate remembered from earlier years, these were sugar-free. She and Laura had eliminated sugar from her diet to help slow the Alzheimer's progression.

"I was so happy for you, my sweet Katy," Mary said. "After all your wandering, you'd finally found a wonderful home. Mike is a good man. His love for you is strong. Don't let a little spat steal your joy." The corners of her wrinkled mouth turned up and her green eyes twinkled. "Remember, the best part about an argument is making up after the heat dies down."

Kate nodded. Aunt Mary was right. Her marriage to Mike had been the happiest day of her life. And they'd found so much happiness together since. Somehow, they'd work through the Freedom House issue and become partners again, instead of adversaries. She glanced at her phone. *Shouldn't have sent that text.*

Chapter Six

In the distance, Kate could see the log portal that straddled the entrance to their guest ranch and distinguished their road from the other dirt roads that branched off the mountain highway. A cast-iron *Whispering Pines* sign dangled from the top log and a metal cattle guard spanned the dirt beneath the portal.

She glanced in the rearview mirror at Tieno and Lupita. She hadn't spoken to the kids since they stopped at the barn. It was time to change her focus. This was about them, not her and her problems. She'd call Mike later to apologize and tell him how much she loved him.

Smiling, she glanced at the children. "Everyone ready for a fun day?"

Tieno clapped, but the girls didn't respond.

The car rumbled over the cattle guard.

"Tieno and I are going to have a great time," Kate said. "And I think you girls will have fun, too." She unlocked the windows. "Lupi and Tieno, you can roll up your windows now."

The two younger children fell asleep almost as soon as the SUV bumped from the dirt road onto the highway and the wheels began to roll a hypnotic rhythm over the asphalt. The pair had an amazing ability to nod off in almost any situation. Kate checked them in the mirror. Was sleep a subconscious self-defense mechanism they'd developed at the brothel?

The musician switched to a slow, melancholy song about his aging dog. Kate turned down the volume on the CD player. "What's new with you, Shannon? You look like you're deep in thought."

The girl turned from gazing out the window. "I was just wondering about something."

Kate waited, but when Shannon offered no further explanation, she gave her a questioning look. "What's that?"

"Something about you."

"Okay…" *This should be interesting.*

"Did you…um…?"

Kate swerved to avoid running over a dead skunk but caught a potent whiff as they passed. She grimaced. If the scent adhered to the tires, her car would stink for weeks.

Shannon plugged her nose. "That's disgusting."

Her nasal whine made Kate laugh. She touched the controls to roll both front windows down several inches. The air cleared and she raised the windows again. "You're safe now, Shannon. You can breathe."

The girl released her hold on her nose. "So, did you?"

"Did I *what*?"

"You know, stuff like…" Shannon flipped the visor down to peek at herself in the mirror. "Like, um, turn tricks, hook up with johns."

"Why do you want to know?"

"You say you've done stuff like us, but you never say what." As if readying for a fight, she pooched her bottom lip and jutted her chin. Her white-blonde hair fell in random layers down to her shoulders. "Maybe you're making it all up."

Kate searched her mind for a good response to the challenge. She didn't like to talk about her past, especially that aspect of it. However, Shannon was a bit of a loose cannon. If her own experiences would help the girl move forward into a better life, then she'd share them. Although still a child, Shannon was far from innocent. Brutal honesty might be what she needed right now.

"Depends on your definition of a trick."

Shannon's eyebrows puckered. "Like, what do you mean?"

"I first hooked up with johns in foster homes."

"In their *houses*?" Her blue eyes widened.

"They were my so-called foster fathers. The state placed me in their homes. But I didn't go after those men. They came after me, uninvited."

Shannon returned the visor to its original position but said nothing.

Kate clenched the steering wheel. "They *raped me,* Shannon. Not only was I underage, what they did was *totally* against my will. I fought and yelled, but they waited until everyone else left the house and no one was there to hear me.

"I don't know how many times that happened." She took a ragged breath. "Way too many. Every time I was assaulted, I ran away. But the cops always found me and took me back." Breathing hard, she paused to stifle memories that in a weak moment could overwhelm her.

"That must have sucked." Shannon gave her a sidelong glance, as if seeing her in a new light. "My foster dad in Texas didn't do anything like that to me. In fact, he pretty much ignored me."

"Not all the men raped me." One finger at a time, Kate loosened her grip on the steering wheel. "Some of them were okay. But there was one guy who beat me." She clenched again.

"He and his wife made me their slave. I scrubbed their toilets, washed their clothes, shoveled their walks, changed their toddler's diapers. Everything. Once in a while, the wife would give me money to go to a movie with my friends." She lifted a shoulder. "That was my pay, which I guess was better than nothing."

Shannon was quiet for a long time. "Actually," she said, "I was asking about walking the track, like what I did in Seattle. I worked my way up to bottom girl."

"Do you realize how absurd that is…working your way *up* to *bottom*?"

Shannon shrugged.

Kate signaled and moved to the passing lane to go around a semi-truck lumbering toward the summit of a long hill. "Yes, like you, I worked the track. But the streetwalking came later, when I was a couple years older than you and on my own."

Shannon twisted to stare at her, eyebrows raised.

Kate bit her lip to keep from smiling. *Thought that would get your attention.* "Eventually, I'd run away so many times and was so close to aging out of the system that Family Services and the Pittsburgh police quit chasing me down."

"That was good."

"No, it was bad."

"Why? The cops didn't bug you anymore. Right?"

Kate passed the truck and returned to the right lane. "I about starved to death. I was too young to get food stamps, so I dug through dumpsters for food, most of it rotten." She cringed at the memory. "I slept behind those same stinking garbage bins at night. Things got so bad I almost turned myself in to Family Services. But that all changed the day I decided I didn't need foster parents *or* food stamps."

"So you…"

Kate blew out a long breath and let her mind venture down a dark alley she normally avoided. "Just as the sun went down, I hid between a couple of those filthy dumpsters and removed my bra. Wearing a tank top and the shortest shorts in my backpack, I headed for the busiest street corner in the Hill District. Somehow, I managed to be the first girl there that night.

"I stood against the light pole and, uh, made my presence known. It wasn't long before I got my first customer. All night long they came. I earned enough money before dawn to buy a breakfast tamale from a street vendor and rent a cheap motel room.

"First thing I did was take a hot shower, a long one. I felt filthy, inside and out. And I hurt everywhere." Kate squeezed her eyes closed but blinked open, surprised at the intensity of the pain and humiliation that still lingered. "After that, I fell asleep and slept hard all day, even though the motel was in a noisy neighborhood."

Kate rolled her window down partway. She needed air. Cool wind blustered noisily through the opening, but she preferred the ebb and flow of fresh air to air-conditioning. She'd spent too many years trapped inside institutional-green concrete walls.

"That's what I did," Shannon said. "Worked at night and slept during the day. Wasn't so bad."

Oh, baby, how quickly you forget. "One night, I was gang-raped." Kate shuddered. "That was bad. Very bad. And one of the reasons I'm not able to have children." She pointed at a herd of antelope grazing alongside the fence that bordered the highway. The animals were a welcome diversion.

Nibbling on a fingernail, Shannon turned her head to look out the window.

Tieno shifted in his car seat but didn't awaken.

"I try not to think about all that happened that night." Kate drank from her water bottle. "The short version is the attack was a turning point for me. I decided it was time to let a pimp handle the business end of things. Thought he'd keep me safe and make sure I got paid."

She shook her head. "What a fool I was. I didn't realize he'd own my soul and control *every* aspect of my life, keep *all* the money and beat me or burn me when I didn't meet my quota. He didn't care how the johns treated me, if I was sick or having a period or so tired I passed out.

All he cared about was the money. Life went from terrible to unbearable."

She gave Shannon a hard look. "Sound familiar?"

The girl ducked her head. After a while, she said, "Still, I miss some things about the game."

Kate winced. What would it take to get through to her? "Like what?"

"Like makeup. You guys won't buy me makeup. When I look in the mirror, I see a zombie. Men used to tell me I was the prettiest girl they'd ever seen. Now I'm a zombie."

Oh, please...

"And jewelry and perfume and high heels." She pulled the mirror down again. Staring at her reflection, she flicked her hair away from her neck. "And highlights and lowlights in my hair and having my nails done every week."

"Ordinary eleven-year-old girls, girls who aren't forced to work in brothels, don't wear makeup or high heels."

"Just sayin'… I miss real food, too. And lights. It's so dark in the mountains at night."

"Real food?"

"Yeah, like we're gonna get today at Taco Bell."

Kate didn't bother to respond. Between Juanita, Laura and Cyrus, the children ate three excellent meals each day. They'd all gained needed weight since their arrival at Freedom House.

"And I'm sick of looking at trees." Shannon stuck her finger in her mouth and made gagging sounds. "Sick. To. Death."

"You seemed pretty interested in that moose that wandered out of the forest a couple days ago." Kate waved a hand at the rolling grass-covered prairie outside the window. "And this is a change of scenery."

"It's a whole lot of nothin', if you ask me."

Kate tapped the steering wheel and prayed for patience. Robin and Jean had taught her to ask questions and acknowledge emotions rather than react defensively to Shannon's querulous comments. Times like this, her coping skills tended to fly out the window.

Seeing a sign for the first Laramie exit, she considered pulling into a truck stop for gas. But the two in the backseat were asleep and she had enough fuel to get to Cheyenne. Her biggest concern was Shannon. The girl was so enamored with city life that Kate feared she might regress into hooker mode and convince a trucker to help her escape the boring mountains.

Shannon must have seen the same billboard because she sat taller. "Are we stopping? I need to go to the bathroom."

"There's a nice rest area between Cheyenne and Laramie. Much more pleasant than a gas station. Great view, clean bathrooms…and a surprise. Something you've never seen before."

Shannon snorted. "Yeah, sure."

They drove the highway, which curved along the city's outskirts, in silence. Shannon slouched in her seat. Kate concentrated on the road. She thought about Mike and the sense of unease growing in her spirit. Was it apprehension about their unresolved conflict or concern about spending a weekend alone with the kids? Or was it the white van in her rearview mirror that triggered her anxiety? Mile after mile, the vehicle had stayed a good eight-to-ten car-lengths behind hers and seemed to travel at the same rate of speed.

Kate gave herself a mental slap. Once upon a time, she'd been hypervigilant, her street antenna constantly tuned to her ever-changing, often-threatening environment. But that was Pittsburgh and what she had to do to stay alive. This was Wyoming. The interstate highway that spanned the sparsely-populated state was a far cry from Pittsburgh's crowded Hill District, and the white van was just another vehicle driving east on I-80.

At the top of a long, steep incline, she took the turnoff for the rest area. Nearing the rock-sided building, which hosted a visitor center as well as bathrooms, she wondered how she'd keep her eye on three children yet use the restroom herself. She pulled into a parking spot in front of the building and turned off the engine. If Mike had come with them, she wouldn't have this dilemma.

Tieno and Lupita began to stir.

"Did you see it?" Kate asked Shannon.

"See what?"

"The surprise."

Shannon looked from side to side. "Don't see nothin' special here."

"Over there." Kate pointed to a giant bust of Lincoln balanced atop a huge stone pedestal. He appeared to be keeping a watchful eye on the I-80 traffic that swished back and forth in the valley below.

"Oh, that? Yeah, I saw it. Ugly dude."

"Know who it is?"

The girl shrugged.

"Ever heard of President Lincoln?"

Shannon's forehead creased. "Should have known it'd be some government guy."

Kate pressed her lips together and got out to help Lupita with her seatbelt.

"S-s-swim?" Tieno asked.

"No, but we're almost there. This is a bathroom stop."

Shannon was out of the car and standing on the sidewalk before Lupi was unbuckled. Through the car window, Kate followed the eleven-year-old's gaze to the lower parking area, where a handful of trucks idled. *Oh, great.* She pictured Shannon fluttering her long curly eyelashes at some overly attentive trucker. Not that all truckers were bad, but…

She pushed her hair behind her ears. *God, help me watch over the kids in the restroom…and all day long.* Maybe this outing wasn't such a good idea after all.

They'd barely stepped inside the visitor center when someone said, "Kate Duncan. Fancy seeing you here."

Because her vision hadn't yet adjusted from the bright light outside, Kate didn't immediately recognize their neighbor, Betsy Williams, walking across the vestibule. With her wide-brimmed hat, tall boots and fringed leather jacket and skirt, she looked like a cowgirl straight out of the early 1900s.

Kate hugged her friend. "Love your outfit, Betsy."

Betsy grinned. "This is my docent-for-a-day getup."

"Docent-for-a-day?"

Betsy embraced each of the children and kissed their cheeks. She occasionally volunteered at Freedom House, so they'd learned to tolerate, maybe even appreciate, her unrestrained affection. She straightened. "Arnie and I come over here a couple times a month to greet travelers. We answer questions and help visitors learn about our beautiful state."

She motioned toward her husband. Beneath his Stetson and his handlebar mustache, Arnie wore a plaid shirt under a dark leather vest trimmed with antique-silver conchos. Levis and black boots completed his attire. Gesturing lavishly, he was telling an elderly couple how the Lincoln sculpture arrived at its present location.

Kate chuckled. "Arnie is in his element."

Just beyond Betsy, Kate could see Shannon perusing the room, one hand on her hip. With her other hand, she twisted hair around her finger. Could have been her imagination, but the girl seemed especially interested in the men who entered the building.

Lowering her voice, Betsy said, "We love Wyoming and after what we've been through, well…we like to give back, if you know what I mean."

Kate nodded. Betsy had told her the loss of their ranch and the resulting move to a relative's Nebraska farm, followed by a sudden return to Wyoming had been a painful, unpredictable roller-coaster ride. That chapter of their lives had stretched their finances and their emotions as well as their faith.

Arnie finished talking with the tourists and ambled over. He shook Kate's hand before he crouched in front of Tieno and reached for his ear. When he retracted his hand, he held a nickel between his thumb and forefinger. "Well, lookee here what I found in your ear, Mr. Tieno."

All three children stared at him, obviously awestruck.

Kate took Betsy's elbow and pulled her aside. "Could you watch the kids, so I can use the restroom?"

Betsy nodded toward her husband, who'd given Tieno the nickel and was eyeing Lupi's ear. "Looks like Arnie has their attention. Why don't you run in now? When he's done teasing them, he can take Tieno into the men's room and I'll take the girls. Sound like a plan?"

"Oh, yes. Thank you. You're an answer to my prayers."

Inside the stall, Kate speed-dialed Mike's cell phone. This might be the only chance she'd have all day to try to make amends. Several other stalls were occupied. The women would hear her, but she needed to at least attempt to clear the bad air between her husband and herself. With any luck, he'd carry his phone with him while he was fixing fence and drive to a high spot to check it, something he tended to do when she was out of town.

He didn't answer, so she left a message. "Hi, Mike. Just wanted to say I don't like what happened last night. I'm..." The bathroom door squeaked open, followed by Betsy's voice. Kate pushed the send button. She'd intended to apologize for the cranky text she sent earlier. Oh, well. She'd try again later.

Chapter Seven

By the time they got to Cheyenne, stomachs were growling. Kate drove straight to Taco Bell.

"Yum." Shannon rubbed her stomach. "I love the Bell. We used to eat there in Seattle, when I was on the streets...not like, you know, Executive—"

Before the past could shroud them all, Kate turned to those in the backseat. "Unbuckle your... What's wrong Tieno?"

A tear trickled down his cheek. "S-s-swim?"

Kate stretched between the seats to pat his knee. "You'll get to swim soon. We're eating lunch now, so you'll have lots of energy to play at the park and swim in the lake. Okay?"

"K-kay. S-s-swim p-pants?"

"Yes, you'll wear your new swim trunks."

His happy smile threatened to melt her to tears. He was such a sweet, grateful little boy.

She slid out of the car and opened Lupita's door. The girl was staring at the restaurant, arms folded against her chest. Kate decided not to pressure her to unbuckle her seatbelt and, instead, released it for her. They needed to stay on schedule. She and the kids had a lot to accomplish in the few short hours they had in Cheyenne. And she couldn't forget to shop for camping food before they left town.

Placing their order took longer than Kate had hoped. But, eventually, everyone decided what they wanted to eat. She led them to a booth, where she spread hot sauce packets in the middle of the table—mild, verde and fire.

Lupi's eyes brightened. "Caliente, bueno." She plucked three of the hottest from the pile. The hint of a smile on her sweet face was as moving to Kate as Tieno's gratitude.

If only Mike could see the changes she saw in the kids, no matter how small and seemingly insignificant. But even if he didn't want to hear updates on their progress, she knew Laura would be interested. She'd ask all kinds of questions about their adventures when they returned home.

As soon as they were done with lunch, Kate hurried the children to the car.

"S-swim?" Tieno asked.

"First, you get to play in the park." Kate rubbed his head. "You'll have fun." After helping Lupi with her seatbelt, Kate drove the short distance to the Children's Village, a learning center nestled in a corner of Lion's Park. Copperville friends had shared such glowing reports about the village that she could hardly wait for her trio to experience it.

"Oh, look, a rainbow." Shannon pointed at the multicolored archway over the entrance. The girl had become a little less sullen since they got to town. Maybe she'd allow herself to be a child for the afternoon.

Inside the village, Tieno beelined for a pond off to the right. "S-s-swim."

"That's not the lake, Tieno." Kate ran to catch up with him. "We'll go to the lake later to swim. But you can wade in this water."

"W-w-wade?" His features scrunched. Speaking was hard work for Tieno.

"That means you can walk in it, 'cause it's not very deep. Remember when we waded in the creek at the ranch?"

He ran ahead and was about to step into the pond when she called, "Don't forget to take off your sandals."

Tieno plopped down on a rock to remove his shoes. Shannon joined him and was the first one in. She giggled. "This is like walking in the gutters at home after the rain."

Frustrated with Shannon's constant references to city life, Kate was reminded that, like herself, cities were all the girl had known before the Whispering Pines. In time, she'd grow to love the stars that shimmered overhead more than neon nightlife with its glitter and glamour...if she stuck long enough.

Tieno slid one foot across the pebble-lined bottom and squealed. "F-f-funny."

Kate knelt beside Lupita, who'd crossed her arms and was clutching her shoulders with her small hands. "Want to take off your shoes so you can play in the water with Shannon and Tieno?"

The girl shook her head.

"Okay. We can sit over there."

They settled onto a bench flanked by flowering bushes, Kate's bag on one side of her and Lupi on the other. A hint of a smile tugged at the little girl's lips as she watched her friends splash in the water. Soon, she lowered her hands to her lap.

Kate laid her arm across the back of the bench, breathing in the flowers' fragrant scent. Butterflies flitted from one bright blossom to the next and sunshine caressed her shoulders. A breeze lifted her hair, momentarily cooling her neck. Children's eager voices accompanied the burble of the tiny creek that trickled into the pond.

Yet, no matter how tranquil and gorgeous the day, her world was upside down. She was anxious to return to the ranch to make things right with Mike. But that wasn't all. Kate scratched at a mosquito bite on her arm. Once her street senses had activated, they hadn't stopped tapping at the back of her brain.

She surveyed their surroundings. Parents and grandparents watched little ones pull themselves across the pond on a small platform and discover how augers, waterwheels, windmills and pumps worked. Others relaxed on benches while their children played in the water or helped volunteers plant seedlings.

Peaceful. It was a peaceful scene with cheerful background chatter to boot. Why did she feel so uneasy? The children's village appeared to be the safest, happiest place in Wyoming. Still, something felt off-kilter.

Kate hugged Lupita and kissed the top of her head. The little girl smelled sweet and her skin was soft and warm. Tieno and Shannon were laughing and having fun. All was good in her world. She was just nervous because this was the first time she'd taken the children on an outing by herself. She should save her apprehension for camping.

Her thoughts switched to the campsite she'd reserved in the Vedauwoo Recreation Area. Situated between Cheyenne and Laramie, not far from the Lincoln Monument, the campground had seemed like the ideal spot to spend the night on their way home to the ranch. But she couldn't help but wonder if bears or wolves frequented Vedauwoo. How about coyotes?

She'd heard hungry coyotes sometimes became aggressive. Three little kids with only a nylon tent between them and the elements would be tempting. She should have brought bear spray or a handgun. Chewing at her lip, she had to admit she'd gone forward with the camping idea partly to spite Mike, who loved to camp. She should have waited until he could accompany them.

"G-go, go," Tieno said. He and Shannon splashed over to the rocks, put on their sandals and raced to the puppet theater. Kate and Lupita followed. Lupita sat directly in front of the mini-theater, her hands folded in her lap, watching the other two perform silly puppet shows.

Every time the puppets elicited a smile from the broken little girl, Kate had to blink away tears. She couldn't wait to tell Laura. Mike wouldn't understand, but her mother-in-law would cherish the priceless memory.

She wished she could take pictures of the children to record all the fun they were having. Not only would Laura enjoy the photos, they would serve as good reminders of happy times for the kids. However, after being photographed and filmed for pornographic purposes, they cowered whenever a camera appeared.

From the puppet theater, they walked over to check out the tall windmill. Shannon said, "We have one of those at the ranch."

Kate grinned. Shannon had just expressed ownership in the ranch. That comment added to Lupi's smile was like seeing a double rainbow. *Thank you, Jesus.* Maybe today wasn't such a bad idea after all.

The four of them crawled inside teepees, snuck into the secret garden and toured the greenhouse. By the time they'd investigated the entire village and made tissue-paper flowers in the craft room with the help of a volunteer, the kids were ready for a snack. And Kate was ready for a break.

They found an empty table shaded by a vine-covered shelter. Kate pulled the protein bars Marita had made for them from her bag. "I'm glad God gave us such a beautiful day."

"S-s-s-swim," Tieno said.

"That's right." Kate smiled. "You can change into your new swimsuits when we're done with the snack."

Walking from the children's village to the beach that ran along the south side of Sloan's Lake, they passed paddleboats tied to a dock. Lupita pointed at the boats and looked up at Kate.

"I'm sorry, Lupi." Kate squeezed her hand. "We don't have enough grownups today. They require an adult in each boat and we'd need two boats. We'll have to come again and bring Miss Laura with us."

She pressed her lips together. If Mike had joined them, she wouldn't have to refuse a rare request from the sweet little girl. But, she reminded herself, she couldn't hold it against him. She had to move on.

"I did that once at a zoo," Shannon said.

"You rode in a paddleboat?"

"Yeah."

"Did you like it?"

"I guess, but it made my legs tired."

Farther along the beach, in the midst of sunbathers and watchful parents, a young lifeguard sat in a short tower. He glanced at them and returned to scanning the swim area. Kate was glad to know someone with lifesaving skills was there to help her if one of the kids had trouble in the water.

The children changed into their swimsuits in the restroom and then Kate found an open spot amidst the families and teens scattered across the sand. She dropped her satchel on the sand and pulled out a swim tube still in the package. Handing it to Shannon, she said, "Blow this up and slip it under your arms while I tighten the straps on Tieno's and Lupita's life jackets." When everyone was ready, Kate walked her little brood to the edge of the lake.

"S-s-see p-pants?" Tieno pointed at the colorful superhero printed across the backside of his trunks.

"You're looking sharp, buddy." Kate loved the light that had appeared in his eyes not that many weeks ago. She prayed today's outing would be one more dab of healing ointment God could use to salve his frail, wounded spirit.

She knelt beside the girls. "And you two look very nice in your new swimsuits."

Lupita, as usual, said nothing.

Shannon peered down at her one-piece suit. "I had sexier work outfits in Texas." She wrinkled her nose.

The attitude was back.

"That's not what this is about," Kate said. "This is about having fun in the lake."

"Whatever."

Kate sighed. Maybe Shannon wasn't ready for city outings, even to a town as small as Cheyenne. She forced a smile. "Who's going to jump in first?"

"M-m-me." Tieno ran into the water, gasped and ran back. "C-c-cold." Arms clasped across his chest, he hopped up and down.

June was a bit early for swimming in some parts of Wyoming, but a dozen other children and at least two adults were in the lake and seemed to be having a good time. "Jump all the way in," Kate said. "You'll get used to it faster that way."

He looked at her, looked at the water and dashed into the lake, where he fell forward with a big splash and came up gasping and giggling.

She gave him a thumbs-up and turned to Shannon." Your turn."

The girl hesitated.

Tieno called, "C-c-can't c-catch me." He was halfway to the floating dock that sat thirty-feet out.

Kate raised her eyebrows. She didn't know he could swim.

Never one to let a younger child best her, Shannon plunged in. She squealed, but she stayed in the water and dog-paddled all the way to the dock.

Kate laughed. The girl was still a kid after all. She knelt beside Lupita. "Ready, Lupi?"

Lupita dug a hole in the sand with her toe.

"Tieno and Shannon are having fun in the water."

No response.

"Okay. You can sit with me. First, let's take off this flotation vest so you don't overheat. We can put it on later if you change your mind." After they removed the vest, Lupi helped her spread out a beach towel and ready other towels for Tieno and Shannon.

Kate lifted her phone from a side pouch on the bag. "I need to call Mr. Mike while I have service." The tension between them felt like rotten food had permanently lodged in her stomach.

Seated on the edge of the towel, Lupita began to sway, rocking forward and back, forward and back. But then she slowed, opened a fist and grabbed a handful of sand, which she trickled through her small fingers. She brushed her palms together and stuck her hand into the sand again. Pulling up another fistful, she let the grains filter between her fingers.

Kate rubbed her palm across the warm pebbles. According to Robin, the tactile stimulation and free-play in sand aided the kids' healing. Opening her bag, she found a plastic cup and gave it to Lupita. "Want to use this? You could make something with the sand."

Lupita eyed the cup.

"You don't have to play with it." Kate set the cup on the towel. "I'll leave it here, just in case you'd like to try it out."

Lupita picked up the cup, slid it into the sand and filled it to the brim.

Once again, Kate speed-dialed Mike. And once again, she got his voice mail. Ending the call, she began to type. *I hate what's happened to us. I love you and I love the kids.*

She looked across the lake. Tieno and Shannon were talking with other children on the dock. That's what she liked to see—kids being kids, hanging out, having fun.

Someone opened a lawn chair beside her. The metal legs scraped against the sand. Kate frowned. All kinds of space on the beach and someone had to park right next to her, someone wearing way too much aftershave.

She angled away from the chair and returned to the text, which was an inadequate way to express her feelings, but that was all she had right now. She tapped—*I want to do what's best for all of us*—and hit "send" just as Shannon jumped into the water.

Tieno, who was seated on the edge of the float, kicked water at her. Shannon splashed him back. Soon all the children were slapping the lake and shooting streams of water at each other.

Kate rubbed her nose. The guy's aftershave was invading her sinuses. They'd just gotten settled, but if she started to get a headache, she and Lupi would have to move. She dropped her phone into the satchel pocket and leaned back on her elbows. Maybe she could finally relax for a few minutes. Tilting her chin upward, she closed her eyes and let the sun warm her cheeks and throat.

"Hello, Kate."

She blinked, turned her head and saw a clean-shaven man wearing sunglasses and a floppy hat. "How do you know my name?" Hand on Lupita's back, she checked the two in the water. Maybe she had an overactive imagination, but something about the man felt sinister—and familiar.

"I don't just know your name..." He propped his elbow on the chair arm and slanted his body toward her. "I know *you*."

Kate recoiled. *Jerry Ramsey.* The correctional officer who'd followed her to Wyoming and ended up behind prison bars had found her again. She swallowed an oath. No wonder alarm bells had been banging in her head all day.

"They let you out." She squinted, trying to see through his dark glasses. How did he know she was in Cheyenne today?

He must have seen the question on her face. "You know you can't hide from me, baby." He sneered. "GPS works every time."

Why hadn't she connected him with the aftershave? Just when she'd stopped having nightmares about him and his greasy, slicked-back hair, and just when the smell of Brut no longer turned her stomach, he'd weaseled into her life again.

Chapter Eight

"Leave. Me. Alone." Kate kept her voice low. She didn't want to scare Lupita, who was dumping sand onto a growing pile. "I'm married."

"So?"

Lupita gave Ramsey a wary glance.

"You're a free man now, Jerry." Kate shifted away from him. "Enjoy your freedom. Find a job. Start over." She looked out across the water. Shannon was hanging onto the edge of the floating dock and Tieno was standing on it, laughing.

"I don't want a job," he muttered. "I want *you*."

"No!"

Lupita dropped the cup and stared up at Kate with wide, frightened eyes.

Tieno, who'd been poised to jump off the dock, froze.

Kate waved. She hadn't meant to yell. "It's okay, Tieno. Go ahead." She squeezed Lupita's knee. "We're moving to a different spot, sweetie. Bring your cup with you."

She jumped to her feet, snatched up the bag and towels and grabbed Lupi's hand. Weaving between the other beachgoers, she headed for an open area on the far side of the sandy stretch. When she'd distanced herself and Lupi from Ramsey yet could still see Tieno and Shannon, she unfurled the towel with a snap and spread it across the sand. This was just one more reason Mike should have been with them today. Jerry Ramsey wouldn't have dared to come near her.

Lupi stood at her side, her face pinched and her gaze darting from Kate to those nearest them and back again.

Kate knelt to hug her. "This is a good place for us. You can play in the sand some more."

A doubtful expression crossed the girl's face.

Kate sat Lupita on the towel with the cup, positioning her so that her back was to Ramsey. Praying the little girl could relax, she rummaged through her bag for the biography she'd brought. She had to get both of their minds off Ramsey.

She found the book and rolled onto her stomach to read. But all she could see on the page was Jerry Ramsey's leer. She glared at the book. *If Mike had come...* She massaged her temple, warning herself not to focus her irritation on the wrong man. Mike was a saint compared to Ramsey. If it wasn't for the kids, she'd pack up right now and go home to him.

"Look, Miss Kate," Shannon called.

Kate glanced up in time to see her flip off the float into the water. She clapped. "Good job, Shannon. Nice dive."

Lupita, who'd been dragging her fingers through the sand, began to fill her cup again.

Between watching the children, thinking about Mike and checking Ramsey's whereabouts, Kate couldn't concentrate on the book. Only when she saw her nemesis fold his chair and leave the beach did she relax. With any luck, she'd never see him again. Otherwise, she'd have to report him as a stalker.

Tieno and Shannon had been playing for over an hour when she waved them to shore and bought all three children snow cones at the snack shack. Lips colored by the blueberry syrup, Tieno held his cone high. "B-b-blue ice. Y-yum."

With prompting, Lupita asked for a banana-flavored snow cone. Shannon ordered cherry syrup and walked away with the cone. When Kate turned from paying the attendant and didn't see Shannon with the others, her heart skipped a beat. She searched the crowd and saw the girl strutting in front of the lifeguard, one hand on her hip and a wide smile on her cherry-tinged lips. But the lifeguard appeared to be ignoring her. A teenage boy walked by and she turned her attention to him.

Kate dashed over to her. "Shannon, what are you doing?"

She shrugged. "Just being friendly."

The boy kept walking.

"Looked to me like you were flaunting your body. Do you know what that word means?"

Shannon shook her head and stared out over the water.

"It means showing off, trying to get attention by using your body." Kneeling beside her, Kate added, "But you don't have to use your body to get people to notice you or like you. Beauty comes from the inside. If people see the real you, they'll love you for who you are, not how you look."

Shannon lowered her head. "I'm ugly on the inside."

"That's not how Jesus sees you. Remember when you asked him to come into your life and make you white as snow on the inside?" Not long ago, a long conversation between Dymple and Shannon had concluded with prayer.

"Uh-huh…"

"When you learn to love yourself like he loves you, you'll see the beauty of your sweet spirit. I see that beauty when I observe how kind you are to Dymple and Aunt Mary and to the other children at Freedom House."

Shannon's only response was a shrug.

They rejoined the others and the four of them returned to their towels. Seated in a circle, the children slurped their treats, happy grins lighting their faces. Kate reapplied sunscreen to their backs and shoulders while Shannon and Tieno chattered about their new friends and the water games they'd played.

During a lull in their conversation, Lupita said, "Bad man gone," as if she felt they should know Ramsey had left.

The other two looked at Kate, questions in their eyes.

"Yes." She nodded. "The man who sat beside us is a bad man, but I saw him leave a few minutes ago."

"How do you know he's bad?" Shannon asked.

"I knew him when I lived in Pennsylvania. Somehow, he found me today. I told him I don't want to be his friend and he left." Kate inspected the beach again, just to be sure he hadn't returned.

Snow cones consumed, Shannon and Tieno scurried back to the lake and their friends. They invited Lupita, who shook her head and continued building her sand mountain. Kate lay on her stomach again to read. The warm beach beneath her and the sun on her back soothed her spirit and lulled her senses, but she wasn't about to fall asleep on the job. Every time she turned a page, she looked up to check the two in the water and to survey their surroundings. Still no Ramsey, thank God.

Kate let the children play all afternoon. Lupi's happy murmurs and Shannon and Tieno's laughter told her the outing was a success, one she wasn't about to ruin. They'd have to come back another time with Frankie and Gianna and Laura.

By the time the lifeguard called the swimmers in at six o'clock, very few people remained on the beach. Shannon and Tieno waved goodbye to their friends, sad smiles on their sun-burnished faces. The lifeguard said something to the teenage girl who was closing the snack-shack window and walked toward the parking lot.

"Can we swim some more?" Shannon asked.

"S-s-swim l-like f-f-fish." Tieno rotated his arms.

"You are a little fish," Kate said, "but we need to leave, like everyone else." She dropped a towel onto his shoulders. "I'm glad you had fun today."

After another round of Marita's protein bars, Kate had the children change into the shorts, t-shirts and flip-flops they'd worn earlier. She wrapped the wet swimsuits and towels in plastic bags and placed them at the bottom of her satchel, beneath the paper flowers the kids had made earlier.

Just as they were about to exit the bathroom, Tieno wound his thin arms about Kate's leg and gazed up at her, his little face contorted with concentration. "L-l-love you, M-miss K-kate."

"I love you, too, Tieno." She combed his wet hair with her fingers. "You liked swimming in the lake?"

He nodded, his eyes big. "A-a-gain?"

"Yes, we'll come again."

Despite his enthusiasm, Tieno looked exhausted. Kate handed the bag to Shannon. "Would you please take Lupi's hand and carry this to the car?" She lifted Tieno and settled him on her hip. "Let's give those swimmer legs of yours a break."

Shannon did as she was asked without grumbling. Kate smiled. This Shannon was much more pleasant than the earlier version.

Due to the lateness of the hour and the kids' exhaustion, Kate decided to eat in town rather than wait until they purchased food, drove to the campsite, put up the tent and prepared a meal. "Anyone here ready for supper?"

Lupi clapped her hands. "Bell?"

"You mean Taco Bell?" Shannon asked.

The girl nodded, a broad smile on her face.

"We'll have to see what Shannon and Tieno think about returning to the same place where we ate lunch," Kate said. "This town has lots of restaurants."

Shannon hoisted the bag to her shoulder. "I love the Bell."

Tieno hugged Kate's neck. "M-me l-like t-t-tacos."

Kate laughed. "That settles it. Back to the Bell we go." Whatever made them happy made her happy. They'd stop by a grocery store to pick up camping supplies after they ate and then buy groceries for the house on their way through Laramie tomorrow night. She had a feeling their empty cupboards weren't helping Mike's disposition.

She made a mental note to add tiramisu ingredients to the grocery list. Mike had tried the dessert for the first time in Texas and loved it. Since then, she'd fixed it for special occasions. Surely making up after a fight was as worthy of tiramisu as a birthday.

When they neared the parking lot, Kate put Tieno down. "You're getting heavy, mister."

Apparently revived, he ran across the grass to the car, which was parked beside a white cargo van. Only three vehicles remained in the parking lot. The third one sat alone beneath a tree in the far corner.

She heard a short cry and gave Shannon a quizzical look. "Was that Tieno?"

"I think so. Maybe he fell."

Kate hurried to find out what was wrong with the little boy but stopped when she saw Ramsey standing between the vehicles in the van's shadow, his shoulders hunched. She frowned. What was the jerk doing now?

Shannon and Lupita ran up beside her. Shannon breathed, "Tieno."

Kate gasped, now understanding what she was seeing. With one Latex-gloved hand, Ramsey clutched Tieno's shoulder. With the other, he held a knife just below the child's trembling chin.

Tieno's eyes bulged and his mouth stretched in a silent scream.

"Stop!" Kate shrieked. "Don't hurt him."

"I won't..." Ramsey pointed the knife at her. "If you do what I say."

She glanced toward the lake and then across a grassy expanse to the street. No help in sight. But if she got close enough, she could shove Tieno away and take care of Ramsey with his own weapon, if that's what it came to. Her street skills might be rusty but she hadn't forgotten how to handle an attacker.

She was about to rush him when Shannon cried out. Kate spun and saw a flash of skin and strawberry-blond hair—and then Lupi was jerked off her feet. Kate's first reaction was to yank her out of the attacker's grasp, but then she saw that the woman, like Ramsey, held a knife to the child's throat.

Tara Hughes? Kate stared at her. *When did she get out of prison?* "You can't do this to little kids."

"Oh, yes, we can." Tara smirked. She was dressed in her usual summer attire—halter top and short shorts. Like Ramsey, she wore Latex gloves and... *A gun belt?*

Kate held out her hands to the frightened little girl, who reached for her, her eyes wide and pleading. "Give her to me, Tara. Do it now and I won't press charges."

"Get over here, Hughes." Ramsey snarled. "Where no one can see you."

Tara shot him a dirty look. "Don't tell me what to do."

Kate scanned the park again. This was a public place. Surely someone had already seen them. *What happened to all the people? The swimmers were gone, but what about bikers and joggers and picnickers?*

She inched closer to Tara.

Tara spat, "How stupid do you think I am?" Dropping Lupi to the ground, she grabbed a handful of her dark hair and hauled her across the lawn.

"Don't..." Kate charged after her.

Tara stopped in front of Ramsey and Tieno and turned. Still holding Lupi by the hair, she leveled the knife just above the girl's collarbone.

Ramsey said, "Get in the van, Neilson, and we won't hurt the brats."

Tears rolled down Lupi's cheeks, but like Tieno, she was mute.

"Release them and I'll do whatever you want." Kate pointed at Shannon. "She can take care of the little ones." Once the children were out of danger, she'd deal with Tara and Ramsey.

Tara shook her head. "You're *all* coming with us."

Kate whispered, "Run, Shannon. Run fast."

The girl dropped the bag and took off.

Ramsey bellowed, "You run, I shoot."

Shannon faltered mid-stride.

Kate pivoted. "No!"

Ramsey leered at them over Tara's shoulder. He had swapped the knife for a gun and was aiming it at Shannon. "I'll blow your kneecap off *and* make your little friends squirm." He rapped Tieno's head with the gun barrel.

Shannon sucked in a breath. Kate back-stepped to stand beside her. She pulled the girl close. "What do you two want from me?"

"Get in the van," Tara ordered.

"Jerry..." Kate looked past Tara to the man she'd hoped to never see again. "You said you wanted me, not the kids. Let them go."

"Oh, we want the kids, all right." Tara jutted her chin. "You're just, shall we say…frosting on the brownies. Right, Jerry?"

He waved the gun. "Cut the chitchat and load up. Nielson, get over here."

Tieno and Lupi gaped at Kate, silently begging her to save them. She had a sick feeling she knew Ramsey's plans for the kids. If she got in the van with them, her presence would lessen the terror, but how could she help them if she was a captive, too?

Ramsey holstered his gun, jerked Tieno's arm out to where Kate could see it and slid his knife across the boy's tiny bicep. A line of red popped up in the blade's path. Tears poured down Tieno's face and he sobbed out loud.

Kate cried, "Stop it!"

Ramsey thrust the knife at her. "You comin' or not?"

She picked up the bag Shannon had dropped. "Yes, I'll come." If she could pull her keys from the cell phone pocket, she—

"Don't even think it, Neilson." Ramsey sheathed the knife, told Tara to cut the girl's throat if Kate tried anything and dragged Tieno close enough to wrench the satchel from her hand. "You're not going anywhere."

Tara laughed. "Except with us." With a flip of her head, she tossed her hair behind her bare shoulders.

"Where?" Kate glanced across the empty, open lawn to the quiet street in the distance.

"You'll find out soon enough." Ramsey tucked the bag under his arm and pulled his gun. "March."

Kate and the children walked single file alongside the van, their abductors with them every step.

Ramsey stopped at the back. "Cover me, Hughes."

Kate followed his gaze as he looked over the parking lot and the park that surrounded it. No one. *God help us.*

He opened the van's two back doors. Heat poured out like steam from a radiator. "Nielson..." He lowered his voice. "You can join me in this gig. I'll dump Hughes and we'll—"

"Never."

His jaw twitched. "I won't ask again."

Kate stared into his sunglasses. "Release the children and then we can negotiate."

"Get in." The disgusting way he curled his lip was all too familiar.

A folded metal-frame lawn chair lay just inside the opening. Two bench seats and a gallon of water were the only other items in the windowless cargo area. A wire screen separated the front of the van from the back. Every cell in her body urged her to run. But how could she desert the children?

She started to pick up Lupi.

Ramsey stopped her. "You first."

"What does it—?"

He swore, threw her bag on the grass and yanked the girl from her arms. "Cooperate, Neilson or the brats will pay." He pinched Lupita.

The girl yelped.

Kate had never heard such a loud sound from her. "Jerry, don't. Please."

The vein that ran up the middle of his forehead pulsed. "Get. In. The van."

Kate squinted at him. If prison had changed Jerry Ramsey, it was for the worse. She crawled inside and felt Lupita fall onto her legs. Then Tara shoved Shannon in, knocking her against the metal wall.

"Ouch, you hurt me." Shannon clasped her sore arm.

Ramsey flung Tieno next to Shannon.

"Leave the kids," Kate pleaded. "They're orphans, like you and me. They've had a rough life. You know what that's like. Take me, but let them go."

By now all three children were crying.

"Rough life? Ha. They're alive, aren't they? You didn't give *my* kid a chance to live." He slammed one of the doors and then stuck his head in the open side. "I hear any more bellyaching back here, I'll tape your mouths shut." He glowered at Kate before he shut the other door with a loud, jarring thump followed by the sound of a steel lock sliding into place.

Chapter Nine

Balanced on her knees, Kate ran her fingers over the warm doors, searching for an inside handle, but she found nothing. She turned to the sniffling children and pulled Tieno, who was crying the hardest, to her chest to muffle his cries. With her free arm, she hugged the other two.

She was wiping Tieno's nose with his t-shirt when she heard Ramsey's voice from the other side of the van wall. "Hughes, find the keys and throw the bag inside. Then follow me—after I pull the GPS from the wheel well. That thing cost me a fortune."

A car door opened—and closed. A moment later, Kate heard her car start.

She groaned. She'd just lost her cell phone and her connection with Mike and the ranch. Like a vine, panic climbed her chest and wrapped her throat, threatening to strangle her. Would anyone understand why she abandoned her car and everything in it?

Mike would put two and two together. He could figure out what happened to them, but… She groaned again. He didn't expect her home until tomorrow night.

The driver-side front door opened. Kate peered through the metal screen. Ramsey dropped onto the seat and closed the door with a clunk that shook the vehicle. He peeled off the gloves. "These things are hotter 'n blazes." He tossed the gloves aside and started the engine.

Shannon swiped at her tears with the back of her hand. "Where are they taking us?"

"I don't know," Kate whispered, "but we have each other and God is watching over us."

Their prison-on-wheels backed out of the parking space, turned and jerked forward. Kate grabbed onto a seat to steady herself. "We'd better sit down and fasten seatbelts."

Shannon and Lupita sat on one bench and Tieno climbed onto the other beside Kate. Once their belts were secured, she put her arm across his shoulders. Shannon did the same with Lupita.

The van wound through the park, past a municipal swimming pool with a full parking lot, to a light at Central Avenue, the street they'd taken into town. Kate squeezed Tieno's shoulder and shifted her position to face forward. Sitting tall, she could see cars whizzing back and forth in the intersection. Such a busy area. Why hadn't some of those drivers been in the park just now?

She dug her fingernails into her knees. She couldn't dwell on what-ifs. For all she knew, someone saw them climb into the van and had already called the cops. But they were on the edge of town, near the interstate, which was very likely Ramsey's destination.

Would the police stop them before they got on the highway? She couldn't tell what lane they were in, but she knew a right turn led into the city center. The other direction accessed the highway.

The light changed and the vehicle swung right. Good. They were headed back into town. She held onto the edge of the seat and tried to collect her thoughts and calm her pounding pulse. Sweat trickled down her temples.

Ramsey did not take the road into the heart of Cheyenne. Instead, he turned left, drove past the airfield and took a right again. Kate recognized the road as one of the busiest streets in town, one with businesses on each side, including a large mall. If the cops had been alerted, surely this road would be one they'd check first.

At the light in front of the mall, Ramsey turned left and drove into the parking lot. He slowed the van then yelled out the open window, "Park it over there in the middle of all those cars, where no one will notice it. Then lock it and keep the keys."

Kate frowned. Ramsey had a plan. This was no spur-of-the-moment abduction.

He followed Kate's car as it wove through the parking lot and stopped amidst dozens of other vehicles, many of them SUVs like hers. Soon Tara was climbing into the van, jingling Kate's keys. "Good idea, Jer. I've seen cars parked here late at night. No one will think twice about one more."

"If they do, we'll be long gone."

"Whoo-hoo, we did it!" Tara lifted her arms and danced in her seat.

"Shut the door. That woman over there heard you."

The instant she slammed it shut, Ramsey hit the gas and charged through the parking lot toward the exit.

Tara grabbed the dashboard. "I didn't give anything away."

"Just keep your mouth shut and don't attract attention." He turned right at the exit, driving back the way they'd come.

Panic clutched Kate's throat, tightening it so that she could barely squeak out, "Jerry…"

He didn't hear her, so she tried again. "Jerry, let us out now and—"

"Shut your trap, Neilson."

"You can't—"

He glared at her in the rearview mirror. The screen failed to filter his ruthless stare. "I can do anything I want," he said. "Keep harping at me, and the brats will suffer the consequences." He snorted. "You know me,

I always keep my promises."

Kate broke away from his haughty gaze.

After retracing most of their route from the park to the mall, Ramsey turned onto the road leading to the highway. Kate's heart sank.

Tieno touched her arm. "M-m-me h-hot."

"Me, too," Shannon whispered. "What are you going to do, Miss Kate?"

The children fixed their gazes on her, hope obvious in their teary eyes.

"I don't know." With a sad shake of her head, she added, "But I'll try to think of something."

Their narrow shoulders sagged.

Kate clenched her fists. She was their only hope. But what could she do? Her heart hammered her ribs. She should have run to the nearest phone and called the police. Leaning forward, she read highway signs as they came into her limited range of vision. A right turn would lead north, deeper into Wyoming. A left turn would lead south to Denver.

Ramsey chose the route to Denver.

Denver. What was waiting for them in Colorado? Kate sat back, trying to make sense of their circumstances. Neither of their abductors could be considered a good citizen, by any stretch of the imagination. But kidnapping? This was stooping low, even for them.

Had Ramsey and Tara followed them all the way from the ranch? She hadn't noticed... *Oh.* She stiffened. The van behind them on the highway.

Why had she ignored her instincts? She buried her face in her hands. Why did she put the kids in danger? She should have turned around the first time she felt uncomfortable, gone home and waited until another adult could accompany them.

Tieno patted her back.

She sat up. She had to get a grip on herself. Truth was, she hadn't been looking for trouble. She'd merely been driving children to Cheyenne for a fun outing. She had no reason to be on the alert. But now, she couldn't let her guard down, even for a second.

"M-miss K-Kate?" Tieno tapped her leg.

"What, Tieno?"

He folded his hands. "W-we p-pray."

Before she could bow her head, he said more clearly than she'd ever heard him speak, "J-Jesus loves me." He paused. "M-men."

"Amen." Kate rubbed the sober little boy's hair, amazed a child who'd just been sliced with a knife could calm her frantic thoughts. She peeked at his arm. The bleeding had stopped.

Shannon wrinkled her nose. "How's that going to help?"

"Tieno's right," Kate said. "As scary as this is, that's all we need to know—Jesus loves us. He's with us right here, right now."

Shannon turned her head, but Lupita studied Tieno, her expression thoughtful, maybe curious. Hands gripping her shoulders, she began to rock against the seatback.

"Remember the song Aunt Mary taught you?" Kate asked. "'Jesus Loves Me'? Let's sing it real soft. Jesus loves me, this I know…" Tieno, who could sing easier than he could talk, joined her. The girls watched them but didn't join in. "For the Bible tells me so. Little ones to him belong. They are weak but he is strong."

Oh, Lord, I am so weak. But you are strong.

"Yes, Jesus loves me." Lupita's rocking slowed to match the tempo. "Yes, Jesus loves me. Yes, Jesus loves me. The Bible tells me so."

When they finished the song, Kate heard Ramsey and Tara talking. She strained forward in an attempt to hear over the van's vibrations and the road noise.

"I'm calling..." Tara lifted a cell phone.

"Do you have...every blasted thing...?"

"I promised...as soon as...let him know."

Ramsey gave her the finger.

Tara tapped the phone and put it to her ear. "Daddy? Daddy, it's me." Her voice grew louder. "Can you hear me?" She paused. "We're in the van, leaving Cheyenne."

Another pause. "That's right. We got three of them plus Neilson. They're all in the back and we're on our way. Easy as pie, just like you said."

Kate sucked in a sharp breath. *Daddy? Three of them? Easy as pie?*

So Todd Hughes was in on this too. Not just in on it. He was likely the mastermind. The other two weren't smart enough to pull off much on their own. But with Todd at the helm... She winced. *Please, God, protect your children.*

"Yes, three. Neilson, too." Tara was quiet for a bit and then she shouted, "Three. I swear nearly freezing to death last year ruined your hearing." She glared through the divider. "Thanks to the Duncans."

Kate squinted at her. Was she really that deluded? Todd Hughes was solely responsible for his near-demise. Determined not to waste energy butting heads with Tara, she surveyed the van's scuffed interior. It looked like it had hauled many a load. And smelled like...she wasn't sure what. Old tires? Rusty metal?

"Daddy. Daddy, are you there?" Tara lowered the phone. "Must have lost him."

The van swayed and turned. Kate read all the signs she could see. They weren't going to Denver after all. They were driving west onto I-80, toward Laramie...toward home. Maybe they were going to the Hughes ranch, which bordered the Whispering Pines. She'd find a way to escape. They'd walk home or hitch a ride on the highway.

Thoughts of home reminded her of Mike. If only he were with them right now. Of course, if he'd been with them, they wouldn't have been abducted. She was sure of that. Yet, she couldn't blame their kidnappers' criminal behavior on her husband.

And she had to forgive Mike. If she'd learned nothing else during all the counseling she'd received over the years, she'd learned the importance of forgiveness. Dymple said it best. *To refuse to forgive someone is like wallowing in manure, thinking the other person is the one who stinks, when in reality, it's you.*

Kate clutched her wedding rings, wishing she could call Mike or send him another text, one that ended with *I'll love you forever.*

One by one the children fell asleep, sedated by the heat and the sound of tires turning beneath them. The girls were propped against one another. Tieno's sweaty head was on Kate's lap. He stirred and she loosened his seatbelt so he could sleep more comfortably.

Both of their abductors lit cigarettes, which made the draining heat all the more intolerable and inflamed her sinuses. Kate fought to stay awake. She had to be aware of their location at all times in case they had an opportunity to escape.

They looped past Laramie without stopping. Miles later, they passed the Saratoga exit, which led to the Hughes and Duncan ranches. Slumped against the vinyl seat, which was now slick with her sweat, Kate circled her rings around her damp finger. On the other side of Rawlins, another exit accessed the ranches. Maybe they were going to sneak in the back way.

Rawlins and the second ranch exit came and went. She choked back a sob and tried to catch the few bits of conversation that floated between Tara and Ramsey. But she couldn't hear enough to make sense of their words or find out where they were going. Oh, how she longed for the

Whispering Pines and her husband—and a bathroom. She prayed they'd stop soon.

Several miles back, Ramsey had pulled off the interstate and said they could get out if they had to pee, but all she saw through the window was prairie, asphalt and highway traffic. The fresh air would have felt good, even if the breeze was hot, but no way could she squat beside the van with the whole world *and* Jerry Ramsey watching her. No one, not even Tara, took him up on his offer.

When he returned to the driver's seat, Tara had laid into him. "I'm a woman," she'd ranted. "I can't pee outside like you can. I need a bathroom, a real bathroom."

"Yeah, yeah." He flicked his hand at her. "You can use the john when we stop for gas."

"No I can't. Those things are filthy. Besides, I need one *now*." She motioned toward the back of the van. "So do they. It'll stink in here if the brats wet their pants. We have to stop at the next rest area."

"Too dangerous." He shook his head. "Nielson might cause problems."

Kate clenched her fists. *You bet I'll cause problems. First chance I get.*

"You worry too much. Remember, we're the ones with the weapons." She leaned close and massaged his neck. "I'll make it worth your while, Jer."

He pulled the van onto the highway.

Kate wasn't sure how long ago that was, but if her bladder was any indication, it had been way too long. Just when she was about to beg them to stop, the vehicle slowed. Were they coming to a town? She squinted through the window into the twilight and saw a sign for a roadside restroom. Tara had evidently won this round. For the first time since she met Tara Hughes, Kate was grateful for the woman's obstinate nature.

She nudged Shannon with the toe of her sandal and shifted Tieno to an upright position. "Wake up, kiddos. Bathroom stop." She hoped this wasn't a false alarm.

One at a time, the children sat up, their confusion obvious, even in the hazy light.

The vehicle stopped moving.

"We're still in the van…with the bad people." Kate kept her voice low. "This is a rest area. We'll use the bathroom and stretch our legs. Try not to cry or do anything to make them angry, okay? And be sure to drink water." They'd long ago finished the solitary gallon of warm water.

The children nodded and reached for their seatbelt buckles. The resigned expressions on their young faces made Kate sad. They knew the drill when it came to vicious captors. Tieno hadn't once complained about the cut on his arm and she hadn't mentioned it, for fear of reminding him of that awful moment.

Ramsey's door opened, then Tara's.

Please, Lord…

The lock turned at the back of the van and the doors swung open. Purple-and-orange clouds colored cliffs to the west of them, silhouetting Ramsey's body in the dusky gloom. He grunted. "Outhouse stop."

They started to get up, but he raised a hand. "Not so fast. We got rules."

Tara appeared at his side. "Yeah, we got rules." By the sound of her voice, she apparently enjoyed tormenting little children.

Ramsey pointed at her. "She'll walk the girls inside. The boy'll go with me."

"I can take care of him," Kate said. God only knew what Ramsey would do to frighten Tieno further.

He lifted his chin. "All right, but no monkey business." Stabbing his finger at each of the children, he said, "Don't forget. I have a gun." He touched the pistol at his side. "And she has a gun." Tara pulled her handgun and pointed it upward.

"Hughes," Ramsey hissed, "put that thing away before someone calls the cops."

She pouted but returned the gun to the holster that dangled on her bare leg.

Kate stared at the pair. Felons weren't allowed to have guns, yet they wore theirs in plain sight.

"And knives." He touched the case on the opposite side of his belt. "We both have knives."

Tara slipped hers from the case, reflecting the parking lot lights in the blade, first one side then the other. She put her hand on her waist and cocked her hip. "I should be on one of those shopping channels."

Ramsey scowled. "You're supposed to be the lookout."

She spun around, her bare back to them.

Again, he pointed at the children. "If even one of you tries to run away, I will…" He slashed his hand across his throat. "You won't get far—and *everyone* will pay." He snorted. "A little nick here, a little blood there..."

Kate could feel Tieno begin to shake again. "You don't have to be so graphic, Jerry."

"Don't tell me what to do." He glared at her. "Just get in there and make it fast."

Chapter Ten

K ate jumped out to help the children from the van. The less physical contact Ramsey had with them, the better. The man was pure evil. Maybe the threatening words were meant for her, but he could have told her in private. She took Tieno's hand, Shannon took Lupi's, and the four of them hurried toward the bathroom.

The only other vehicle at the rest area backed out of a parking space and sped away. Dots of artificial light reflected off its back window. Kate mourned the loss of a potential rescuer.

Just outside the narrow cement wall that shielded the women's entrance, Ramsey grabbed Shannon's arm. "Stay here, blondie. Hughes, you're in charge of the Spicaninny. Wait 'til Neilson is done."

Kate whirled. "Don't call her that."

"Shut up and get in there with the kid." He motioned with his knife. "Do something stupid and these two'll suffer the consequences."

She hated to leave the girls, but Tieno's bladder was at its limit, not to mention her own. She pushed the door open and the bathroom's overhead lights flashed on. Once she got Tieno settled in a stall, she held the door for him while she inspected the room.

The empty bathroom had only one door and the windows were high, without any means of accessing them. They were open but blocked on the inside by a heavy metal screen. Escaping the building through the windows didn't appear to be an option. Air-freshener spray spit from a nearby dispenser, filling the room with its cloying aroma.

Kate sneezed.

Ramsey pounded the door. "What's going on in there?"

She considered ignoring him but didn't want him to charge into the room, which she was sure he'd do if she didn't respond. "I sneezed."

"Cut the noise and get out here, pronto."

She and Tieno switched places. Later, after they'd washed their hands, she lifted him so he could drink from the faucet. The door opened. Kate pulled Tieno away, ready to plead for help.

But it was Tara, a knife in one hand. With the other, she clutched Lupita's shoulder. The frightened little girl reminded Kate of a big-eyed puppet in the hands of a sadistic puppeteer. She longed to hold and comfort her. Instead, she pushed the dryer button and held Tieno close enough to dry his hands.

Tara gave Kate an arrogant smirk as she clomped past on her high-heel sandals.

Kate considered suggesting Tara not act so superior. She was an ex-felon, just like Kate. However, that's as far as the similarities went. Tara's shorts were as tight and short as ever and her top revealed as much cleavage and as many butterfly tattoos as before. The gun belt hanging low on her hips was a new addition to her summer attire, but her overkill makeup and egotism hadn't changed. Evidently her morals hadn't improved either.

Stealing from the Whispering Pines cash drawer was one thing, but stealing children was another. Prison should have convinced her to never take even a paperclip that didn't belong to her. Yet, Kate knew from experience that prison could serve as a training camp for further criminal behavior for inmates who didn't focus on redirecting their lives while incarcerated.

Turning back to the sink, she encouraged Tieno to drink some more.

Prison had to be where Tara and Ramsey learned about the market for young flesh. They hadn't said they were planning to sell the kids, but she had a feeling the intent was to deliver them to a pimp or to a gang that had expanded its illegal activities to include human trafficking.

Drugs could only be sold once, but bodies could be sold again and again and again. Plus, the chance of arrest was slight for pimps, as were the penalties in most states. The sex workers, who were actually victims, were more likely to be arrested than pimps.

She hoped that wasn't Ramsey and Tara's purpose, but she couldn't think of any other reason why two people who didn't like children would abduct three of them. And why Ramsey kept her after she refused his offer to hook up with her and dump Tara. Could be he thought they could sell her as a sex worker, along with the kids.

But she doubted that would happen because traffickers paid more for young bodies than they did for adults. She lowered Tieno to the floor and turned off the water. Even if they considered her too old for a brothel, she wasn't too old for factory work. Certain factory owners, even some in the US, used slaves as laborers. Was that her destiny?

Taking Tieno's hand, she walked over to Tara, who stood outside Lupita's stall, holding the door closed. "Tara," she whispered, "what are you doing with a creep like Jerry Ramsey? You deserve better."

Tara's snort was so loud it echoed between the walls of the concrete room. "Oh, yeah?" She thrust her knife at Kate's chin. "Like my boyfriend you stole?"

Kate pulled back. "Mike?"

"Well, duh…" Her eyes blazed. "Who else?"

"How did you ever get the idea he was your boyfriend?" Kate knew she was stepping into dangerous territory, but she couldn't help but ask. "He never saw it that way."

Tara's face reddened. "You don't know beans about me and Michael. We have something special." Brandishing the knife, she spewed a string of swear words. "But *you* wouldn't understand. You married him for his money, so you wouldn't have to go back to streetwalking."

Kate clamped her teeth together. Arguing with a crazy woman would get her nowhere.

"Oh, don't act so innocent." Tara pointed the knife at Kate. "I know all about you and your—"

"Please, Tara. Don't do this to the kids. Think about the consequences of kidnapping three children. You'll go to prison for a long, long—"

"I'm *never* going back." Her voice grew louder. "It was your fault I was sent away." Tara raised a manicured eyebrow. "But sweet revenge is just around—"

Ramsey hammered the door. "Get out here, all of you, or I'm coming in."

With a shake of her head, Kate turned toward the exit. "Let's go, Tieno." Tara's delusions were as deep as they were varied.

A toilet flushed and a moment later, Kate heard Lupita whisper, "Done." She stopped to wait for the girl.

Tara yelled, "Be there in a minute, Jer," and entered the stall.

After Lupi had quenched her thirst and dried her hands, Kate opened the door. Sheathed in the jaundiced glow of a solitary light, Ramsey was leaning against the wall, a cigarette dangling from his lips and his arm draped across Shannon's shoulders. Her arms circled his waist.

Kate opened her mouth, but before she could react, Ramsey whacked Shannon on the head. "Get in there, blondie. And make it quick, or your precious *Miss Kate* gets a slug in the ribs." He aimed his gun at Kate.

Shannon stumbled, caught her balance and blinked up at him with wide, surprised eyes.

He pushed her toward the door.

Waiting outside the bathroom with Ramsey, Kate focused on the parking lot with its pools of light, praying for other cars to join them. But no other vehicles appeared before they were herded into the van and Ramsey drove onto the highway.

Kate read the mileage signs. Salt Lake City, Utah, was almost three hours away, but Rock Springs, Wyoming, was coming up soon. And Green River was only eighteen miles past that town.

She touched Shannon's knee, a white spot in the dark.

"What?"

Kate released her seatbelt and knelt in front of the girl. She spoke just above a whisper. "Back there, you were all over him." She aimed her chin at Ramsey. "Smiling up at him like you'd gladly do anything he asked. What was that about?"

"Nothing."

"It was something." She remembered Robin and Jean's instructions to respond with questions rather than an emotional reaction to a behavior, something she should have practiced with Mike. "Why were you cozying up to the guy who kidnapped you?"

"I...I just thought..." Her voice trailed away.

Kate waited.

"I thought I could maybe help him like us better."

Kate could tell she was talking to her lap.

"Did any pimp ever treat you better because you *did* him?"

"Well, maybe..."

"Yeah, maybe for about twenty minutes. Ramsey hit you and shoved you just now. People don't slap people they care about. Violence and affection don't mix, even if some pimp says he loves you after he beats you. That kind of thinking is as warped as working your way up to bottom girl."

Kate hoped she wasn't being too hard on Shannon. It was one thing to remove a child from an abusive, controlled environment, and quite another to wipe a warped mindset from a child's psyche.

"Like we talked about at the beach, your body is a precious gift from God, not a tool you use to convince men to like you. You are beautiful in God's eyes and his love for you is pure and true. Asking him to help us is better, much better, than trying to change an evil man's mind. Right, Tieno?"

"P-p-pray to J-Jesus."

Kate squeezed Shannon's hand and returned to her seat. "Please don't do that again."

Shannon didn't respond, but neither did she argue with her, for which Kate was grateful.

Tieno's stomach growled. Kate rubbed his back. They'd have to stop for gas and food soon, maybe Rock Springs or Green River. That's where she'd beg for help. Or grab the kids and run. Whatever it took, she'd be ready.

Mike dropped the mail on the desk and fell into his chair. After today, he knew what Cyrus meant when he said he was "bone weary." With the help of two young ranch hands, he'd dug countless post holes, planted dozens of fence posts and stretched what felt like miles of barbed wire. He could have hung around the office to keep an eye on things, but after the argument with Kate, he needed to get away. The staff had done fine without him. They'd only radioed him four times with questions.

Tramp plopped down next to the desk. With a long sighing moan, he rolled onto his side, closed his eyes and dropped his head to the floor.

Mike nodded. "I know how you feel, buddy." He'd worked late. Too late. On top of the exhaustion, he was extra dirty, thanks to the dust devil that had spiraled across the pasture while he was checking bison on his way back to the barn.

In spite of the long day, knowing one section of fencing was repaired and posts set for another section felt good. In addition, the conflict between a ranch hand and an irate guest was resolved to everyone's satisfaction. And he and Clint had repaired the tongue on one of the wagons they used to transport guests on the ranch.

He hung his hat on the corner of his monitor, ran his fingers through his hair and began to sort the mail. Bills. Lots of them. He looked at the stack that had already accumulated on his mom's desk. If she didn't catch up soon, they'd lose their longstanding rapport with their suppliers.

Kate's mail consisted mostly of advertisements and catalogs, but two envelopes from the state looked important. He glanced at her desk. Yep, her mail was out of control, too.

Mike sighed. His mom wanted him to hand all her bookkeeping duties over to Coach, who was helping in the office again this summer. Rob Murphy not only coached all the junior high and high school sports teams, he taught bookkeeping at the high school. The man was more than capable, but the idea of their finances being monitored by someone outside the family didn't sit well with him.

One piece at a time, he tossed his own mail on the far side of the computer. Yeah, he had his fair share, too. He'd get to it one of these days. Life on a guest ranch in the summer was beyond busy.

In addition to housing, feeding and entertaining guests, he had to deal with haying, fencing, branding, never-ending repairs, animal issues and a great deal more. The list was endless. He shook his head. And then they had to go and add the children's home to the mix, which consumed way more of Mom and Kate's time and energy than he'd ever imagined.

The final piece of mail, an oversized postcard, captured his attention. He turned it over and saw the cover of a book about bison management, one he'd read years ago when he started the bison herd. "Added chapters," the flyer informed him, "updated information, video links plus a live-action DVD showing hands-on, how-to close-ups."

He rubbed his jaw. Maybe he'd order the new edition. He needed to stay current with the industry.

The phone rang. Mike glanced at the clock before he picked up the handset. His first thought was that Kate was calling. But then he remembered she and the kids were camping and probably didn't have cell service at the campsite. Even if service was available, she wouldn't answer. The first thing she did when the two of them camped was switch off her phone.

He let out a long sigh. One more night without her. "Hello."

"Hi, Mike. This is Calvin Gardner."

"Hey, Cal. How you doing?" Calvin was the deputy assigned to their corner of the county.

"Good. Just wanted to give you a heads-up."

"Not sure I want to hear it." Mike took off his boots and leaned back in the chair. "Last call, you told me Todd Hughes was no longer under house arrest." He put his feet on the desk. "I hope you have better news this time."

"Sorry. No can do. In fact, this may be worse news. I just heard his daughter was released from prison early due to good behavior."

Mike groaned. "Good behavior and Tara Hughes are contradictory terms, in my book."

"You're telling me. My guess is she slept her way out of the slammer."

"When was she released?"

"A couple days ago. Keep your eye out for her and her dad, will you? I think my job just got harder."

"Heard anything about their partner in crime, Darryl Pratt?"

"Didn't anyone tell you they let him go a while back?"

"Nope."

"Sorry about that. I heard he got a scholarship to that auto-body tech school in Laramie. Your tax dollars and mine at work."

"Might be worth it, if he cleans up his act." Mike scratched his gritty forehead. He'd always thought there was hope for Darryl.

"Yeah, you're right. This job makes a guy cynical at times. Hey, I gotta go. I'm on duty and I see a car on the side of the road. Better check it out."

"Thanks for the Tara Hughes update."

"Her old man has been calling the department every hour on the hour to get his ankle monitor removed. Well, it's actually a wrist monitor because, as you know, he has no ankles. I'm on my way over there now. Catch you later."

Mike put the phone down. Todd and Tara Hughes both back in circulation. Not good. Still, what could Todd do without the legs he'd lost after the bison cow fell on him? He'd tried to feel sorry for him, but the man had been asking for trouble for a long time.

Then there was Tara. He pulled a pen from his shirt pocket, put his feet on the floor and started a to-do list on the back of an envelope.

1) Tackle mail on desk.

2) Remind Kate and Mom to deal with their mail.

3) Tell Mom, Kate, Clint and Cyrus about the Hughes duo.

Now that he was married and Tara had done time for stealing from the ranch, surely the nutcase woman would forget her obsession with him and the WP. And Todd would forget his obsession with the bison herd— and Mike's mom. But it wouldn't hurt for everyone to be on the alert.

Tramp rolled to his other side. Mike caught a whiff of dusty dog and something else not quite so pleasant. Only God knew what he'd wriggled in today. If Kate were here, she'd be sneezing. And telling him he ought to bathe his dog.

Chapter Eleven

K ate blinked awake. Jostled from side to side and startled by the sound of a long, loud horn, she didn't know where she was or why it was so dark. But the nightmare returned when Tara shouted, "Jerry, wake up! You're going to get us all killed."

"Stop your hollering."

"Let me drive."

"You'd run us off the road."

"And you didn't almost do just that?"

"Shut your trap."

"God," Kate whispered. "Keep him awake and alert." *Unless, of course, you arrange an accident where none of the kids are hurt and we're rescued from these jerks.*

The lights of an oncoming vehicle silhouetted Tara's head and shoulders as she slanted her body away from Ramsey and lit a cigarette. Kate knew the urge to distance herself from the nasty man, but she wasn't the least bit sad Tara was getting a taste of the real Jerry Ramsey. No doubt he'd eventually turn on her. But he'd keep her on a tight leash until he no longer needed her.

Kate peered at the children. All three were asleep, which was good. They weren't thinking about how hungry and thirsty they were. Ramsey had stopped for gas after the rest area, but he hadn't let them out of the van or offered them any food. She rubbed her nose. The cigarette smoke made it itch.

While he was pumping gas and Tara was in the convenience store, Kate had waved at the man washing windows on the minivan ahead of them. But he didn't see her. The children watched in silence. They'd learned from past horror that keeping quiet was safer and smarter than shrieking out the terror that rocked their insides.

When she heard Ramsey remove the gas nozzle and screw the cap on, she hurried back to her seat. She was fastening her seatbelt when Tara opened the passenger door and climbed inside. And now, here they were, driving down the highway, again.

"Where are we?" Tara asked.

"Outside of Brigham City, Utah," Ramsey said, "headed for Idaho."

He glanced back, as if remembering they had passengers, and lowered his voice.

Staring through the screen, Kate tried to make sense of their travels. Other than the lights of three oncoming vehicles in the distance, inky darkness drenched the night. Was their destination Idaho—or somewhere beyond? Traffickers shuttled victims up and down the coast, so Ramsey could be aiming for Washington or Oregon…or even Canada.

Her stomach gurgled and Tieno, who lay across her lap, stirred. She laid her hand on his narrow back. One of the girls whimpered, but that was all. Unlike other children, they didn't bawl for their mommies— probably because they either had no mommies or their mothers didn't want them.

From what little she could see in the headlights, they were driving through mountains, mountains that reminded her of the Whispering Pines…and Mike. What was he doing now? Was he still mad at her? Did he miss her?

They'd said such angry words to each other. If only she could take hers back. Her husband was a man of character and integrity, the polar opposite of Jerry Ramsey. Mike was good. He was kind. He was faithful. He loved God and he loved her. *Oh, Mike...*

But what was said was said. Kate slid her rings, her only physical attachment to her husband, over her knuckle and held them in her palm. If she ever got a chance to talk with him again, the first thing she'd tell him was how much she loved him. And then she'd let him know how sorry she was for her unkind words.

She replaced the rings, thinking of the times he'd saddled her horse for her or gassed her car at the ranch pump before she went to town. He grilled bison steaks for her, brought her wildflowers and rubbed her feet. She pictured her husband and her mother-in-law pacing the floor, waiting for word of their whereabouts.

Just as quickly as the vision came, it shattered. Mike and Laura thought she was camping. Kate sighed and rubbed her forehead.

Did she and the kids leave any evidence behind, other than what was in the car? Had the Cheyenne police noticed her SUV in the mall parking lot yet? Probably not, if she hadn't been reported missing and no one was searching for her and the kids.

The obnoxious smell of Brut tinged with cigarette smoke snaked into the back of the van, carried by the cool air that whooshed through Ramsey's open window. Too bad the cops couldn't follow his aftershave trail. Maybe he'd left fingerprints on her car. Then again, maybe not. He'd worn the gloves until he got into the van.

Tara's phone call to her father could be traced. But why would anyone have reason to suspect either person? Unless, of course, they found *her* fingerprints on the car...but Tara had also worn gloves.

Kate crumpled against the seat. She despised the horror the kids were experiencing and the upheaval and heartache their disappearance would cause at the ranch. She'd promised they'd return home tomorrow night— and maybe they would. But here they were, driving farther and farther into the night, farther and farther away from the ranch. And it was her fault.

Trust me.

"What?" Kate looked from side to side.

Trust me.

I want to trust you, God. She buried her face in her hands. *Really, I do. But I don't understand why these traumatized little ones have to go through this awful ordeal.*

She waited but no response came. Kate lifted her head to look at the ceiling. Knowing God was with them, close enough to speak, was enough. They weren't alone or forgotten.

The words of a worship song Mike wrote based on Isaiah forty-one sifted into her mind.

> *Do not fear, for I am with you*
> *Do not fear, I am your God*
> *I will give you strength and help you*
> *Hold you with my strong right hand*

Yes, Lord," Kate whispered. "You are my God. I will trust your strong right hand."

Later—she didn't know how much later, only that the sky was still dark, Ramsey pulled off the highway into a brightly lit gas station. He turned to Tara. "I'll top the tank while you get me coffee, so I can stay awake."

"I have a better idea. You sleep while I drive."

"I'm not taking any chances with our cargo."

"Thanks for the vote of confidence." She opened her door. "Buy your own coffee."

He grabbed her arm. "You'll do as I say or find yourself hitchhiking home with no dough in your pocket."

"I've got money." Yanking from his hold, she twisted to the door.

"You *had* money. Two-hundred and seventy-six dollars, to be exact."

Tara hesitated. "How do you…?"

"It's right here." He patted his shirt pocket.

"You can't—"

"I already did." He jutted his chin. "Want to do something about it?"

For a long moment, they stared at each other. Then Ramsey pulled a solitary bill from the pocket. "Coffee and candy bars—that's it."

She cursed him loud and long before snatching the money from his fingers. "I'm not using the john here. You better stop at the next rest area, like you promised."

By now, all three children were wide awake.

"I'm hungry," Shannon whispered.

"P-potty?" Tieno looked hopeful.

Ramsey got out of the van.

"Jerry," Kate called, "the kids need a bathroom break."

He stuck his head back inside. "Not now."

"What if—?"

He slammed the door shut. A moment later, Kate heard him fiddling with the gas cap. She took a breath to stifle her rising anger and released it through her nose. "I'm sorry, Tieno. You'll have to wait a little longer."

He didn't respond. Just laid his head against her arm.

The children's docile demeanors disturbed Kate. Yet, their compliant behavior, learned through abuse, kept them from triggering Ramsey's temper, which could get ugly fast. She kissed Tieno's head, unbuckled her seatbelt and stood.

Head and shoulders hunched, she checked the front window. No cars or people in sight. She motioned to the others. "Move your muscles, kiddos, while you can." She stretched her arms out and circled them in the air.

They got to their feet and mirrored her actions.

She brought her hands to her chest, straightened her arms and did it again. Light from the gas station's canopy filtered through the screen into the rear of the van. Her charges looked wan and tired, but they seemed to be holding up okay. She had them do squats and then they all touched their toes.

Jesus, Kate prayed, *help them understand what I'm about to say. And help Tieno to not wet his pants.* The little boy's bladder control had improved since he'd been with them, but this trauma could set him back.

She knelt before them and looked into their eyes. "Next rest stop, I'm going to find someone to help us. I'll have to be real sneaky, maybe hide behind the bathrooms, but I'll get us help. I promise."

Shannon's forehead creased. "Are you going to leave us?"

"Oh, honey…" Kate stroked her hair, running her fingers through the tangles. "I'll ask someone to call the authorities for us and then hurry right back to you."

"But what if we drive away without you?"

"I'll tell the police what you look like and what the van looks like. I memorized the license plate, so the highway patrol can watch for the van and stop it."

Lupita flung her arms about Kate's neck, clinging like a kitten on a tree branch.

"N-no go," Tieno whispered.

"I've got to do whatever it takes to get help for all of us." Kate laid her cheek on Lupi's head. "No matter what happens, the Bible says God is with us, wherever we go."

Shannon, who'd been twisting her hair, yanked at the strand.

Kate touched her arm. "Please don't do that, Shannon. Your hair is growing so good." She smoothed the girl's hair again. "The bald places are almost filled in."

"W-w-we p-pray," Tieno rasped. Kate wondered if he was dehydrated.

"You want to pray for us?"

He nodded, folded his little hands and bowed his head. "D-d-dear J-Jesus." A long pause. "M-men." Raising his head, he tapped his chest. "P-pray…h-h-here."

"Thank you, sweetie." She looked at the others. "We can all pray silently, inside our spirits."

First one front door then the other opened.

"Remember," Kate whispered, "you can talk to God anytime, without those two hearing you."

The younger ones climbed onto the seats. While Shannon helped Lupi and she helped Tieno latch their seatbelts, Kate strained to hear the conversation in the front.

"Here's the coffee I bought with *my* money," Tara said. "And a candy bar."

"I see you got something for yourself."

"Of course. It's my money."

"Keep the change."

Kate turned in time to see him tear open a candy wrapper and toss it out the window. *Jerk.* She felt for the kids, who watched with longing on their sad faces and whose hunger pangs had to be as great as hers or worse.

They drove out of the gas station and onto a dark highway. Loosening her seatbelt, she twisted to watch the road through the window, all the while praying other travelers would stop at the rest area when they did. If no one was there, she'd find a place to hide and wait until a car came along. She hated to leave the children and upset them further, but if that was the only way to get help, she'd do it.

The thought of Ramsey injuring the kids because of her actions turned her stomach, even though she was fairly certain he wouldn't do serious damage to their bodies. The better they looked, the higher the price he'd get for them. She shivered, despite the lingering warmth of the van. *Oh, Lord, don't let these babies suffer.*

When a road sign indicated an upcoming junction that led to either Pocatello or Boise, she knew they were in or near Idaho. Shortly after that the van slowed and she saw the lights of a rest area. At this time of night—or morning—few people would be using the facility, which was the way Ramsey wanted things, no doubt.

Kate sat Tieno upright and unbuckled his seatbelt, then hers. "Shannon, Lupi," she called softly. "Wake up. Bathroom stop." They blinked awake and released their seatbelt buckles, which could barely be seen in the dim light. Ready to make her escape, she gave each child an extra hug and reminded them to drink water while they were in the bathroom.

When the back doors opened, Kate sucked in the cool, fresh air and jumped from the van to help the children out before Ramsey could touch them. First Tieno, then Shannon and Lupita hopped down to the asphalt.

"Same drill," Ramsey said. "Get in, get out. No monkey business." He pointed at Tara. "She'll be inside. I'll be by the door. We're both armed."

Kate reached for the plastic jug to fill it in the restroom, but Tara grabbed it first. "I'll toss this."

"Please fill it for us. The children are parched."

Tara arched her eyebrows, sauntered to the nearest trashcan and dropped the jug inside. "No liquid in, no liquid out. You wouldn't want them to make a mess and stink up the van, would you?"

Kate clenched her fists to keep from knocking Tara to the cement. She itched to pound the coldblooded woman's face into pulp. But instead of giving in to her instincts, which could backfire and cause more trouble, she swiveled to scan the parking lot. A solitary car was parked in front of the bathroom. On the far side of the wide lawn that separated cars from trucks, five semis were lined up nose to tail.

Their lights were off, but she could hear the sound of idling motors, which meant the sleeping drivers were running their air-conditioners. The doors on the driver's side of the trucks faced the restroom. If she knocked on the passenger doors, she wouldn't be seen by Ramsey or Tara, even if they were outside the restroom. The drivers might resent being awakened, but she'd talk fast and explain their situation.

Tara on their heels, Kate ushered the kids into the bathroom in time to hear a gray-haired woman say, "We won't get any prettier staring at ourselves in the mirror." The teenager beside her laughed and they walked out a door on the far side of the sinks.

Another exit. Kate bit back a grin. Perfect.

"You take the boy into that one." Tara pointed to a stall, one of three. "The girls can go in the far one. I'll be in the middle. Coffee ran right through me." She rushed Shannon and Lupita to the end stall and darted into her chosen spot.

Kate opened the stall door for Tieno and pointed at the toilet. Putting her finger to her mouth to signal silence, she backed out, quietly pushing the door shut. With any luck, it wouldn't swing open and he wouldn't cry. No matter what happened, she had only seconds to put her plan into action.

Trusting that Ramsey would be in the men's room, she darted out the far door without checking to see if he was nearby. She ran to the nearest truck, swerved around the front and rapped the passenger door with her knuckles.

No answer.

She knocked again, this time harder.

Still no answer.

Hurrying to the next semi, she pounded on the door with both hands. She was about to knock again, when the window rolled down.

"Leave me alone."

"I need help." She couldn't see his face, but she kept talking. "I have children. We've been—"

"Get a new line. I've heard that one before."

"But—"

"Try another guy. I'm too tired to screw tonight."

Kate gasped. "No, that's not—"

"Beat it, *lot lizard*."

The window slid upward and Kate ran for the next truck, right into Jerry Ramsey, who slammed her against the trailer. "Stupid broad." He slapped his hand over her mouth. "Who d'ya think you're messin' with?"

Chapter Twelve

Kate bit Ramsey's hand and kicked his shin. He swore, jerked his hand away and slapped her cheek, but he didn't release his grip on her arm.

She screamed with all the pent-up fury inside her and drove an elbow into his ribs. Ripping the other arm free, she took off. But two strides from the truck, he grabbed her shoulder.

Kate stopped and he thudded into her. She yanked his arm across her chest with one hand, grasped the back of his neck with the other and flipped him over her shoulder onto the ground.

He landed on his back. A growl sputtered from his lungs, but he was on his feet again, his fingers extended like claws.

Her own hands and feet spread wide, Kate squinted at his dark form, trying to anticipate his next move.

"What's going on here?" demanded a deep voice behind her.

Kate flinched but didn't take her eyes off Ramsey. "He abducted me."

"Hey, dude, that's her pimp." She recognized the voice of the trucker who told her to go away. "She's just trying to get out of work."

"Yeah," Ramsey interjected, breathing heavy. "She slacked off. Time to move on."

"That's a lie," Kate cried. "He kidnapped me and three little kids—"

"Kids?" the first man said. "I don't see no kids."

"They're in the bathroom."

Ramsey inched closer.

Kate backed away. "You can see for your—"

"Take it somewhere else."

Kate turned to the men. "Please help me."

Ramsey clamped her arm, his fingers like steel. "Too many drugs. She needs to sleep it off."

She held out a hand to the men as he dragged her away, but they turned their backs and disappeared behind their trucks. Digging in her heels, she twisted her arm and tried to wrench free.

Ramsey slammed his gun barrel into her ribs. "Slut," he hissed. "Did you forget I promised to hammer down on those brats every time you mess up? A slice here, a nick there." He snickered. "Maybe I'll blow off a toe or two."

She whirled. "Do whatever you want to me, but don't hurt them."

"You were warned. And you know me…I keep my promises." He shoved the gun deeper, forcing her toward the van, where Tara hovered above the children. The parking lot lights reflected the tears that streamed down their sad faces.

Kate groaned. Instead of helping them, she'd worsened the situation.

All three children ran to her. Kate dropped to her knees and pulled them close, but Ramsey yanked Shannon from her grasp. "This one pays for your stupidity." He slapped the girl so hard she sank to the asphalt.

Kate pulled Shannon close, all the while staring at their abductors. "How can you be so cruel?"

Tara shrugged. "You do something else dumb and it's my turn to come up with a, let's say, reward." She rubbed her hands together, as if anticipating the likelihood. "For every action, there's an equal and opposite reaction. That's how things work with us." Her dangling earrings and the spangles on the tight t-shirt she'd pulled over the halter-top glittered under the streetlight.

Ramsey pushed them aside. "Outa the way."

The kids toppled, dragging Kate onto the asphalt.

He opened the van door. "Get in."

She got to her feet and started lifting the kids into the van. A motorcycle rumbled by, followed by a car. Kate spun around, Tieno in her arms.

Ramsey gripped Tieno's neck. "Don't even think it, Neilson."

Teeth gritted, she waited until he'd released Tieno before she turned to place the boy in the van. After the doors slammed behind them, she gave each child a hug, with an extra squeeze and an apology for Shannon. Kneeling between them, she took their hands and bowed her head.

"Jesus, only you can save us." She swallowed the frustration lumped in her throat. "Show us what to do and how to act. Show others how to help us. Those truck drivers didn't understand."

By God's power, she would forgive them. Dymple had told her, "When you forgive, you don't change the past, you change the future." That's all that mattered right now—the future.

"Thank you for loving us," she continued, "and being here with us. Please help Shannon's cheek to be okay. In Jesus' strong name, amen."

Tieno whispered, "M-men, J-Jesus." And then he began to sing so softly she could barely hear him. But she joined in. "…loves me this I know, for the Bible…"

Kate returned to her seat as Ramsey backed the vehicle out of the parking space. Not until darkness overtook them again did she let the tears flow. She'd been so close yet so far from help. What could she have done differently? What words would have convinced the truckers to get involved?

On the other hand, if the sleepy truckers had tried to assist her, Ramsey would have shot and possibly killed both of them. She was grateful that hadn't happened.

Wiping her face, Kate hugged her ribs to stop the shaking, which was as much due to hunger and dehydration as adrenalin letdown. She'd taken a chance and failed. But that wouldn't stop her. Every opportunity she had from now on, she'd fight for the kids, if it took her last breath and every fiber of her being.

"I say we get rid of Neilson." Tara's voice was loud.

Kate assumed her volume was intentional.

"She's a liability."

Ramsey grunted. "She's worth some cash."

"Not as much as the kids," Tara said. "If she runs again, we could lose the brats, too."

"If we're gonna divvy the dough three ways…not that your old man has done anything worth getting an equal—"

"Yes he has. He made all the arrangements for—"

"The more ways we split the cash, the more we need up front."

The next time Kate awoke, her shoulders were sliding across the vinyl seatback. Sensing the van had slowed, she turned her head to look through the grid. The night sky had faded to a graphite gray and they were on a curve that felt like an off-ramp. A moment later, the horizon brightened, tinged with a hint of gold. They must be facing east now.

When the curve ended, Ramsey merged onto what appeared to be the main road into a town, if the number of lights in the distance was any clue. Were they still in Idaho?

Only one other car was on the highway. She yawned and stretched. Seemed like they'd been driving for days, yet she knew better. This was Sunday morning, wasn't it?

The van was cooler now, almost chilly. But it would heat up soon enough. The way her armpits reeked, she hated to think how bad she'd smell after another day inside the hot, airless tin can. She swallowed, surprised she had enough saliva to coat her dry throat.

A highway sign flashed past with a jagged boot-shaped outline and *Idaho* in big letters at the bottom. Yes, they were still in Idaho.

Tara held out her phone and said something to Ramsey.

Was that a map on Tara's phone? They wouldn't need a map to get gas at an exit. Maybe this was where they were delivering her and the kids.

The headlights caught a sign that read "Binford," and below the name, "Pop. 9,341." *Binford, Idaho*? She'd never heard of it, but that didn't mean much. With such a small population, the town obviously wasn't a major Idaho city. At least she knew where they were in case she had a chance to call Mike.

Street lights began to appear along the road. They passed two gas stations, one on the left and one on the right. Apparently gas wasn't Ramsey's objective. A MacDonald's sat adjacent one of the stations. Next was a bridge. A sign on the railing read *Snake River*.

Copperville and the Whispering Pines were near the Little Snake River, but it didn't flow off an Idaho river. Or did it? Mike would know. He knew all the rivers in the West. She twisted her rings around her finger. *I miss you, sweetheart.*

They crossed the bridge, which was fairly long, and drove into the town. Bright signs and parking lot lights flickered through the partition. An Arby's and a grocery store were followed by a strip mall and another gas station. Tara continued to hold the phone at eye level and whisper to Ramsey. And he continued to drive straight ahead.

Kate unbuckled her seatbelt, slid away from Tieno and dropped to the floor of the van to crawl closer to the grid. Off to the left, the beginning of a sunrise outlined a large building…actually, several decrepit-looking buildings crammed together. The dark place had no lights and appeared abandoned. A faded sign beneath a streetlight read *Binford Flour Mill. Trucks enter here.*

"Turn on that street." Tara jabbed the phone to the left.

Ramsey slowed the van.

"Hurry," Tara said, "before the sun gets high."

He swore and stomped the gas. "What d'ya think I'm doing?" The van jolted over a series of railroad tracks.

Kate spread her hands and knees to keep from falling over and peered through the dim light at the children behind her.

Shannon sat up.

Kate crept back to her seat.

The girl shivered and hugged herself. "Where are we?"

"Idaho," Kate whispered. "Binford."

The vehicle slowed, turned left again and stopped. Headlights illuminated a ramshackle guardhouse with broken windows and peeling paint. The outhouse-size building tilted against a chain-link fence. Its sagging double gate was secured by a thick, rusted chain and an equally corroded padlock.

Kate leaned forward. Why were they stopping here? She couldn't see much of the old mill, but it had to be dangerous. No place for kids. She sat back. *Not that they're in a safe place now.*

"Jerry," Tara snapped, no longer whispering, "I didn't tell you to turn yet. He says it's a tan metal building in the middle of trees." She waved the phone at him. "Which, according to the directions, is down the road two more miles."

Kate knew Todd Hughes owned property all over the West. Maybe their destination was one of his ranches.

Ramsey slapped the phone away. "This place looks fine to me."

"It also looks locked. What're you going to do about that?"

"I'm gonna crash that gate." He revved the engine.

"Shannon," Kate whispered, "Hang on." As nasty as the mill looked, it would have dozens of hiding places where she and the kids could disappear. They'd find their way out, eventually.

"Jer…" Tara's voice took on a pleading tone. "Just do what they want, so we'll get our money."

They? Jerked to attention by Tara's words, Kate gaped at the pair up front. Her hunch was right. All these miles, she'd hoped and prayed she was wrong. *Oh, God, no. Don't let the kids be sold again.*

Ramsey swore, rammed the gearshift into reverse and backed onto the road. Grinding the gears, he jerked the van forward again.

Kate clung to her seat. Were traffickers waiting at the metal building in the trees? She had to keep them from taking the kids. But how? *Help me, God.*

By now, all three children were awake.

Tieno said, "H-h-hungry."

"And thirsty," Shannon added.

The road surface changed from asphalt to dirt. The van bucked and rattled.

In the growing light, Kate saw tears roll down Lupi's cheeks. "Shannon, would you please release Lupi's seatbelt?"

Shannon unclasped the belt and Kate motioned to the younger girl. "Come sit with me."

Lupita climbed off the seat, struggling to keep her balance.

Kate lifted her onto her lap. The little girl's hair no longer smelled sweet. "I know this is hard, for all of you." She pulled Tieno to her side and smiled at Shannon, who was becoming more visible in the growing light. "But I think we might stop soon."

"Will they give us food?" Shannon asked.

"I hope so." If she'd been able to promise food and water and safety, she would have done so. But all she had to offer was hope. There had to be a way to put feet to the hope. She pursed her lips. *Put feet to hope...* Yes, that's what she would do.

"Turn left by that haystack," Tara said.

The van slowed and they jolted onto an even rougher road.

Kate tightened her grip on Lupi to keep her from bouncing off her lap. She only had a few more minutes, at best, to finalize her strategy. Closing her eyes, she thought through the sequence.

When Ramsey unlocked the first door, she'd shove it at him, knock him over and race as fast as her legs could run to town. She'd alert the police, and they'd rescue the children before the traffickers got away with the kids.

She chewed at her lip. The kids would be terrified. She knew that. But if they thought about it, they'd realize she was running for help, not running away from them.

A dark clump of trees came into view, backed by a mountain range edged with a golden-pink glow. Under different circumstances, Kate might have enjoyed the sunrise, but freeing the children and memorizing the return route to Binford was her priority. Two turns so far.

Were any businesses open this early on a Sunday in a small town? The gas stations and fast-food places had appeared to be open, but they were too far away. She needed to get help *fast*. If businesses weren't an option, she'd knock on residential doors and plead for help. Surely someone would be more understanding than the truckers had been.

The van bumped and clattered closer to the trees. Beyond the grove, flat farmland rolled toward the mountains. "Turn in there." Tara aimed the phone at the trees.

Another turn. *This one's a right turn.* She had to remember to reverse direction when she sprinted back to town.

The turnoff led directly into the stand of cottonwoods. A quarter of a mile later, the trees parted and a solitary metal structure came into view. No other vehicles were in sight. With a large overhead door and a smaller normal-size door beside it, the tan building looked like a mechanic's shop. Maybe it was. And maybe the traffickers' car was inside.

Ramsey rolled the van onto the graveled driveway and Tara hopped out.

Kate unbuckled her seatbelt, set Lupi beside Tieno and slid to the edge of the seat. She watched Tara stride to the smaller door, study her phone and then punch a keypad next to the doorframe. She opened the door and motioned toward the van.

Ramsey shut off the motor. "We're going in."

Still holding Lupi, Kate unlatched Tieno's seatbelt. "Don't forget," she whispered to the children, "Jesus is with us."

Their only response was silent, unblinking stares.

When Ramsey got out, Kate made her way to the back door and knelt on one knee. She raised her palms, ready to slam him with the door.

She heard him insert the key. But he didn't turn it. "Neilson," he yelled, "I've got my knife ready. If you care about the brats, you'll mind your p's and q's."

"Miss Kate," Shannon whispered. "Don't leave us."

Kate turned to the children, who were watching her with big worried eyes—and saw her nine-year-old self staring up at a big, burly policeman. She'd never forgotten the grim-faced officer who'd interrupted her childhood and dumped her at Family Services without explanation.

The shock, the terror and the loss of everything familiar, compounded by abandonment came back to her. She lowered her hands to her thighs. She couldn't leave them. Like her, they were orphans in a strange and violent land. There had to be another way. "I love you guys," she whispered. "We'll do this together."

Chapter Thirteen

The van door opened and crisp air smelling of alfalfa fields rushed in. Goose bumps prickled Kate's skin. When she hopped onto the gravel driveway, she swayed, dizzy from dehydration and hunger.

Ramsey grabbed her arm. "Don't play games with me."

Games? She squinted at him, willing her vision to clear. He was selling children into the hands of perverted people who would use and abuse them until their little bodies gave out. The first chance she had, she'd do a lot more than *play games* with him and Tara.

She helped the children from the van, avoiding eye contact with Ramsey. As soon as the children were out, he flipped her around and jabbed a gun barrel into her back. "Move it."

Kate stumbled with the kids through the weeds.

Ramsey goaded her. "Get in there."

Kate tripped into the lighted building, took two steps to catch her balance and stopped. Another older-model panel van, this one brown and grimy, was parked at the far end of the building, nose toward the big door. She scanned the room for other people but saw no one. Even Tara had disappeared.

Ramsey shut the outer door behind them with a solid thunk, elbowed Kate aside and plowed into the room. "Outa the way." Gun in hand, he walked straight to the van, opened a door and retrieved keys from the side pocket. Apparently, no one was inside.

Kate murmured a prayer of gratitude.

With its high ceiling and oil-smudged cement floor, the place looked like an auto repair shop—and smelled of oil and gas. Bunk beds lined two of the walls. The other wall hosted a microwave oven, a small refrigerator, two cupboards and a countertop. She counted four windows, all barred. The bars she could understand, but why did an apparently unused country garage have beds and appliances?

A narrow wall with a closed door was angled across the corner by the kitchen area. She hoped that was a bathroom.

Ramsey pointed at the beds. "Sit."

The sound of a flushed toilet and running water filled the room. Then the door to the corner room opened and Tara walked out.

"The children need to use the restroom," Kate said.

Ramsey gave her a dismissive nod. "After me." Jutting his chin at Tara, he said, "Keep 'em in line." He lowered his gun and tramped across the cement floor to the bathroom.

Gun extended, Tara sauntered over to Kate. "Like our new digs?" She sniffed. "You stink."

"Your criminal behavior is what stinks."

Tara slapped her. "Don't judge me, you jailbird."

Though she'd instinctively recoiled, Kate stood her ground. "Doesn't matter what I think. The only opinion that matters is what God thinks of what you and Jerry are doing to these kids."

"Shut up." Tara waved the gun toward the beds. "And get over there."

Kate turned to the frightened children staring up at them. She hoped they saw Tara for what she was—a ruthless predator. She also hoped they understood God was bigger than both Tara and Ramsey and that the pair would have to answer to him.

Each bed was topped with a thin mattress and a green-brown Army surplus blanket. She sat on the edge and watched Tara high-heel strut to the cupboards. One by one, she opened and shut the doors, doing the same with the refrigerator and the microwave oven.

The odors that emanated from the dusty wool blanket and the stained mattress became too much for Kate. She sneezed.

Ramsey, who was exiting the bathroom, gave her a dirty look. "Keep it down."

Tara pounced on him. "There's nothing to eat here, Jer. I checked. Not even a can of tuna."

He grunted. "Come outside."

They stopped by the door at a keypad Kate hadn't noticed. *What kind of garage has keypads on both sides of the door?* Tara pushed buttons again and the pair walked out, closing the door firmly behind them.

One at a time, the children used the toilet and drank from the sink faucet. Kate studied the exits, the high ceiling and the barred windows covered with a dark film. "Jesus," she whispered, "you know a way out of here. Please show us what it is."

She was the last one to use the windowless bathroom, which smelled only slightly better than an outhouse. But it was a bathroom and she was grateful. A quick survey of the small room told her it held no options for escape or anything to use as a weapon—not even a plunger or a toilet scrubber. The bathroom was also without a mirror. Was that because glass could be broken into sharp shards?

She splashed water on her face before she pulled up her shirt and slapped handfuls onto her armpits. A shower, a change of clothes and a thorough tooth-brushing would be nice. But her personal comfort was the least of her concerns. Right now, her primary purpose, her *only* purpose, was to get the kids away from Ramsey and Tara and whoever else was involved with the abduction.

Her shoulders against the wall, Kate tried to orient herself. Thinking back to the Saturday afternoon kidnapping and the hours of driving through the evening and all night across Wyoming to Idaho, she decided her earlier calculation was right. This was Sunday morning. Was Mike getting ready for church, strumming his guitar and humming in preparation to lead the worship team?

Any other Sunday, she'd soon be seated in a Highway Haven House of God pew surrounded by smiling friends and family members. The log church's ancient oak benches would groan beneath squirming children and parishioners singing along with the worship band. She pictured the raised hands and peaceful expressions that would emanate from the sincere hearts of fellow worshippers.

Kate wiped her damp hands on her shirt. If they had an idea she and the kids had been abducted, today would be different. The atmosphere would be solemn and the singing cut short by voices crying out to God to bring their missing loved ones home. She smiled, encouraged by the thought.

The sound of the outer door opening returned her to reality. Kate flushed the toilet and took another drink from the faucet. She had to get back to the kids and find out what Ramsey and Tara—and their cohorts—were planning.

Kate exited the bathroom, took a quick peek at the kids and then focused on Tara and Ramsey who both stood by the door.

"…find another buyer," Ramsey was saying. He cursed. "Sitting in this hole for two days is a waste of time."

"But, Jer," Tara pleaded, "Daddy says a chicken in the frying pan is better than two in the henhouse."

Kate lifted an eyebrow. She'd never heard the "bird in the hand" idiom put like that before.

"I don't care what the nitwit says." Ramsey slammed the door shut.

"Sounds to me like the California crew is backing out."

"No, no, no." Tara shook her head back and forth, hair flying. "This says they're anxious to meet with us and look over our merchandise. This is just a delay. They have the money and will notify us when we can get on the road again and make the exchange."

She squealed and jumped up and down. "Isn't this exciting?"

Ramsey checked the door and stepped around her to jab a finger at the children, who huddled together on one bunk. "Separate beds. Now."

Shannon and Tieno scrambled to nearby bunks.

"Wait. They want more pictures." Tara read from her phone. "He says they liked the swimsuit shots I took earlier, but they want front and back close-ups."

Kate winced, sickened by the knowledge the children had been stalked and photographed for evil purposes.

"Line up against that van," Ramsey demanded.

They slowly crawled off the beds and shuffled over to the brown vehicle, heads down.

"Face me…" Tara raised her cell phone. "And move closer to each other."

Kate wanted to rip the phone out of her hands and throw it against the wall.

The children obeyed but continued to stare at the floor.

"Look at me."

They lifted their chins.

Tara snapped several shots, the flash lighting the room each time. "Now turn around. They want to see your butts up close." She snickered.

Kate crossed the room, hand raised to slap the evil woman but halted when Ramsey snarled, "Keep your distance, Neilson." He wagged his gun at Tara. "You finished?"

"I need to see if they turned out okay." She scrolled through the pictures. "Yeah, these should make them happy."

Ramsey flicked his hand at the kids. "Back to the beds."

They scuttled to the bunks.

He sniggered, apparently enjoying their fear, and then pointed both forefingers at Kate. "We're taking off, but don't you even *think* about trying to get out of this place." Cocking his chin, he added, "It's foolproof, designed especially for fools like you."

Kate glared at him, arms folded.

"Don't you worry, hon." Tara placed her hands on her hips. "We'll be back before you have time to miss us."

The instant she heard the van drive away, Kate dashed to the keypad. Tara had punched five buttons each time, hadn't she? She tried combination after combination without success before she gave up and sprinted to the far side of the bigger door, which had an identical keypad. Again, she tried different sequences, and again, the door did not budge.

Darting to the nearest window, she discovered that not only was it coated with a dark film, it didn't open. She rushed to the next window, and the next. All were sealed tight and had exterior bars spaced so close even Lupi couldn't slip through them.

From the center of the cavernous room, Kate scrutinized every corner of the building. Knowing the children watched her every move, she tried not to let her shoulders drop in defeat. Someone had designed or modified the building for this very purpose—to imprison people. What kind of sick mind...? She narrowed her eyes. A mind like Ramsey's, or worse.

"Miss Kate...?" Shannon's voice quavered. "Are you trying to get out?"

"Uh-huh." Kate tapped her chin. She'd broken into plenty of buildings in her criminal career, but she'd never before tried to break out of one, not even prison. Most structures had weak areas. This one was a basic four walls and a roof. She couldn't ask for more simple construction. *God,* she prayed, *show me, fast.*

"Are you going to leave us?"

Kate looked over her shoulder and saw tears running down all three children's faces. She hurried to Shannon, who turned her head, eyes downcast. Motioning the others over, Kate pulled them close. "If I can—"

Lupi clung to Kate's waist. Tieno hugged her neck with his thin arms. "D-d-don't l-leave." They all smelled like they could use a bath. And their breath wasn't any better.

"I don't want to leave you." Kate fought back tears. "But if I can slip through a weak spot, I can run to town to get help."

"You said we'd do this together," Shannon whispered. "Please take us with you."

Kate kissed her forehead, fully understanding her apprehension. "I'll do my best." She didn't want to distress them any further. But she had to do whatever it took to notify authorities.

She disentangled herself from the children. "I'll look for a way out of here, for all of us, while you guys ask God to show me where it is. Okay?"

Tieno took Shannon's and Lupita's hands and bowed his head. "D-d-dear J-Jesus…"

Once again, Kate turned her attention to the larger door, which was wide as well as tall, big enough for a motor home—and windowless, like the smaller door. She stared at the garage-door opener attached to the ceiling. If she triggered it, the door would rise and they'd all run to freedom.

Or…drive. She ran to the van. She hadn't hotwired a vehicle in a long time, yet it was worth a try. The van was old enough she ought to be able to figure it out. Then they'd race to the police station, provided she managed to open the door.

Kate climbed onto the bumper and then the hood, got a foothold on the windshield wipers and clambered to the roof. Once she stood to her feet, she balanced on her tiptoes and reached for the door motor that hung above the vehicle. But as high as she was, she was at least two, maybe three feet short.

She looked about the room. What could she stack on top of the van? The only loose items in the room were thin mattresses and even thinner blankets. The microwave oven would be perfect, however, it was attached to the wall. She'd already checked.

Dropping to her belly, Kate slid off the roof and yanked a mattress from a nearby bed. A quick toss landed it on top of the van, but it slipped over the side. She grabbed another. Three mattresses deep, she stopped. More mattresses would be required to gain the height she needed and the likelihood of sliding off the slick roof increased with each addition. They'd have to crash the van through the garage door to get out.

She ran to the driver's-side door and jerked it open. God only knew how much time she had left. She crouched beside the steering wheel. Oh, for a screwdriver. Sitting back on her heels, she thought for a moment. Maybe she could tear a metal piece off a bed. Then she remembered the toilet tank. She'd rip the flush lever out and use it to remove the steering column cover.

Kate was almost to the bathroom when she heard a vehicle rumbling up the road. *No...* Disappointment knotted in her throat like a wad of bubblegum. She pivoted and motioned to the children. "Someone's coming. Back to separate beds." She wanted to tell them to hide, but there were no hiding places.

Hurrying to the van, she slammed the door shut, shoved the mattresses off the top and grabbed a blanket to wipe her footprints from the dusty hood. After she'd replaced the mattresses and blankets on the bunks and smoothed the wrinkles, she turned to the kids. "Lie down."

Tires crunched over the gravel toward the building, stopped and started again. The sound of the motor receded then came close again.

Who was it? Their abductors or the traffickers? What if Tara and Ramsey had been paid and sent on their way? Known enemies, as nasty as they were, were better than unknown.

Kate dashed across the floor to the bathroom. Instead of running around like a headless chicken, she should have dismantled the toilet mechanism and made a weapon. She turned the light on but left the door open—and reminded herself the time wasn't a total loss. If nothing else, she'd figured out a way to escape in the event they were left alone again.

She lifted the tank lid, set it on the seat and peered inside the stained reservoir with its metallic-smelling water. Good. The guts, as Mike called toilet mechanisms, were simple and easy to tear apart. She turned the shutoff valve at the toilet base and separated the rubber float from the rusted lever. She was attempting to detach the lever to use as a weapon, when she heard a car door open and close.

Kate whirled, switched off the light and pulled the door almost shut. Footsteps crunched over the gravel but the motor continued to run. She crouched, ready to fly at anyone who went near the children.

Through the crack, she saw Tara's form outlined by sunshine. She released the breath she'd been holding. Never in her life would she have expected to be relieved to see Tara Hughes walk into a room.

As silently as she could, Kate closed the bathroom door, careful to not let the latch snap into place. She turned the light on, picked up the float and stood over the tank to reattach it.

"Neilson, you in the bathroom again?"

"What do you want?" Kate replaced the float, set the lid on top of the tank and cranked the shutoff valve on.

"Stay in there 'til I tell you to come out. Same with you three. Don't move."

Kate frowned. What was that about? A loud clatter and the squeal of metal against metal shook the building. For a split second, she couldn't place the sound. Then she realized the big door had been activated. She jumped to her feet and opened the bathroom door.

Tara, who was standing between her and the growing gap in the wall, swiveled, the gun in her hands leveled at Kate's chest.

Chapter Fourteen

Kate ignored Tara and watched Ramsey walk through the opening. He climbed into the brown van and started it, blowing exhaust in the kids' faces. With a series of maneuvers, he re-parked the vehicle so that it faced the bathroom side of the building, not the front. By then, the fumes had everyone coughing, even Tara.

He killed the engine, got out and tromped toward the opening. "Watch 'em." He pointed at Tara. "I'm gonna back the other one in."

A malevolent smile spread across Tara's freshly made-up face. She positioned her arms on the hood of the van, pointed her gun at Kate and said, "Don't move."

Kate ducked and raced toward the opening.

"Neilson!" Tara screeched. "Get back here."

Ramsey jumped from the white van, leaving the door open behind him.

Kate charged at him with enough momentum to bowl him over and dive into the van, which was still running. She'd be halfway to town before he had the other van out of the garage.

"Miss Kate," Shannon screamed, "don't leave."

Kate faltered.

Ramsey whipped out his gun and pointed it at the children. "Go ahead, Neilson. Your choice."

She jerked to a stop. He knew her Achilles heel. She was certain he wouldn't kill the children. But she also knew he wouldn't hesitate to injure them. If she kept running, he'd shoot her and she could no longer protect the kids from him.

"I've got her." Tara jabbed her gun into Kate's spine.

Ramsey backed the vehicle into the garage, accompanied by more exhaust fumes. Kate pulled the neck of her t-shirt over her nose and motioned for the kids to do the same.

When he got out, he gestured with his gun. "Get over there. I'll deal with you later."

Shoulders back, head high, Kate walked to the bunks nearest the children, sat on the bottom bed and pulled her trembling knees to her chest. She'd blown it again. If only she hadn't hesitated. Why couldn't the kids believe she'd return for them?

Tara pushed buttons on the keypad beside the garage door. The big door noisily rolled down the wall and hit the cement floor with a resounding thud that was as loud and forceful as any prison gate Kate had ever heard clang shut behind her. She winced.

"Miss Kate," Shannon whispered. "Look."

She lifted her head in time to see Tara haul two jugs of apple juice from the van to the counter then go back for a grocery sack. Her mouth watered and she swallowed, appalled that the mere sight of food caused her to drool. She hated her frailty.

Ramsey dropped a magazine and a six-pack of beer on the counter and tore open a package of sweet rolls. He ate two, guzzled the juice and poured a second glass, which he downed in loud chugs.

From her position behind the children, Kate could tell they ogled his every move. She pictured hopeful yet resigned expressions on their sad little faces. Shannon twisted and tugged at a strand of hair. Lupita swayed back and forth. Tieno, who sat in front of her, clutched his growling stomach. Surely their captors would feed the kids.

Ramsey plopped the paper cup on the counter, belched and swiped the back of his hand over his mouth. "I'm gonna go catch some sleep. You know the drill."

Tara, who was eating a roll, nodded.

He picked up the magazine and the six-pack and stomped across the garage floor to the white van, which was only a few feet from where Kate sat. She could see the magazine was a pornographic one and shook her head in disgust.

He glowered at her. "What?"

She didn't respond.

"Keep the brats quiet." He climbed into the van and dropped onto one of the bench seats. "You try another foolhardy stunt like that, Nielson, you and the brats'll all get a taste of my temper."

Kate rolled her eyes. Forever the macho man. She glanced at Tara, who crammed the remains of the roll into her mouth and crooked her finger. Kate got up off the bed and walked over to her.

"Feed these to the brats," Tara said. "And these." She pulled bananas out of the bag. "They can eat as much as they want. I've had enough. And this," she said, producing a loaf of white bread, a package of bologna and a bag of potato chips, "is lunch. We'll be sleeping, so save some for us, or Jerry'll…" Her eyebrow twitched. "Well, you know what to expect from him."

"Tara," Kate whispered, "Let the children go. I'll give you whatever you ask."

Tara snickered. "As if you're in any position to bargain with me."

"Mike and Laura will make sure you're well paid. Just don't do this to the kids."

"Don't even mention her name to me. I can't stand that woman."

Ramsey belched. "Hughes, come here."

"Don't tell me what to do." Tara dropped her and Ramsey's cups inside the empty sack and placed it on the counter. "Trash goes in here. We have to leave this place spotless." With that, she flipped her hair behind her shoulder and hurried into the bathroom.

Kate stared at the bathroom door. *Leave this place.* Would they leave together or separately? Where were they going? When? She pushed away her questions and motioned to the children, who scurried to her side.

"First, you need to drink," she said. "Then save your cups so you can get water in the bathroom." She poured juice for each of them. Tieno drank greedily. The golden-brown liquid dribbled down his chin.

"Slow down," she whispered. "There's plenty." She handed Shannon a banana and broke another one in half for the younger children.

Tieno's grin twisted with his effort to speak. "Y-y-yum."

Tara exited the bathroom. "I'm going to get in the van with Jerry." Her voice was low. "And lock the doors. You can't disturb us in there and you can't get out of here. Don't bother trying. This place has alarms."

Swallowing her pride, Kate said, "Thank you for feeding the children. Please think about what I said."

Tara smirked. "You can thank yourself, Neilson."

Of course. She should have known they'd taken her cash. With any luck, they'd also stolen her credit cards and had left a charge-card trail across the West. She squinted at Tara. "Name's Duncan. Kate *Duncan.*"

Tara slapped her. "You may have stolen my last name…" Her voice grew louder. "But you won't keep it. When we're done with you, Mike will be mine again."

"Shut your mouth, Hughes," Ramsey ordered, "and get in here. You owe me for those rest stops."

With a haughty lift of her stenciled eyebrows, Tara swiveled and marched away, hips swinging.

Kate gripped the counter edge, breathing hard. Her instinct was to fight back—not because her cheek smarted or because Tara was foolish enough to think Mike would have anything to do with her, but because she was a callous, mercenary woman. She and Ramsey had evil plans for her, just like they had evil plans for the kids.

She stared at the metal ceiling high above. Today's johns lusted after teen and pre-teen bodies. The traffickers wouldn't pay much for her and they'd sell her cheap to a factory or to a farm for slave labor. Whether she ended up in this country or another, it didn't matter. She'd eventually be worked to death or...

Biting her bottom lip, Kate wished she didn't know so much about human trafficking. Her body would be used until she could no longer meet the demands of whoever owned her at the time and then they'd auction off her organs on the black market, one by one.

Shannon touched her hand. "What was she talking about?"

"I don't know." Kate sighed. "She's a crazy lady."

"Mean lady." Lupi leaned against Kate, who squeezed her shoulder and nodded.

"D-d-dear J-Jesus," Tieno whispered.

"Yes, dear Jesus..." Kate bowed her head. "Thank you for the food and the water and the juice. And for a bathroom. Amen."

She tore the sticky rolls apart, handing them to the children one by one. For their sake, she would pray. But she was beginning to wonder how much good it did.

The Bible said the Lord was with her, that he was her refuge and strength. But where was he now? He said he'd never leave or forsake his followers...just like she'd promised the kids. But she hadn't kept her promise. Had he reneged on his too?

Kate dozed off and on throughout the hours that Tara and Ramsey slept in the white van. The kids were good. Too good. They didn't play, didn't horse around, and they only awakened her to ask permission to use the bathroom or to tell her they were hungry. Once, she thought she heard Tieno singing *Jesus Loves Me.* Maybe she just dreamed it.

Mike sighed and leaned his chair back. Another long day under his belt. He looked at his watch. Kate should be home by now. He checked the phone for messages. Nothing. Normally, she would have called or left a message informing him when she expected to return. But after the argument, she might not care to talk to him.

He was about to close his eyes for a few minutes when he remembered he needed to call the vet. He sighed, pushed upright again and dialed the number.

Doc Hall answered immediately. "Hey, Mike. What's up?"

"Hey, Doc. Nothing much. Sorry to call so late."

"No problem. I just hung up from talking with my brother in Wichita. What can I do for you?"

"I'd like you to take a look at one of my bison cows when you have a chance. Eyes look funny. I was thinking possibly pinkeye, yet they're more whitish than red, as far as I can tell."

"Any other symptoms?"

"Nose is dripping as well as the eyes and she's coughing, which I know could also indicate pinkeye. Weight may be down."

"Diarrhea?"

"Not that I noticed. Why do you ask?"

"Could be something else. I'll take a look. You going to be there Tuesday morning? I have a meeting in Laramie tomorrow."

"I'll be here all day Tuesday. I don't stray far from the ranch this time of the year."

"I'll aim for morning." Doc chuckled.

Mike raised an eyebrow. "Care to share the joke?"

Tramp yipped and his feet began to flap like he was chasing a rabbit across a field.

"Can't say it's a joke. Not even funny, really," Doc said. "I was just thinking about the days when every time I turned around, you were calling 'cause one of your bison had been shot. Thank God those days are over."

"Don't drink on it. I just learned Todd Hughes is off house arrest. Plus, his daughter got out of prison early."

"Well, don't that beat all."

Mike could picture the vet's bemused expression beneath his salt-and-pepper crewcut.

"I doubt either one of them is up to raising havoc," Doc added, "especially Todd, without legs."

"I'd like to think so, but…"

"Yeah, his old man was a scoundrel and he and his daughter followed suit." He paused. "On a brighter note, how's that children's home of yours doing?"

"Good, I guess. I never see my wife or my mom. They're over there with the kids day and night."

"Starting a new venture takes time, Mike. Tell Kate and Laura I'm proud of what they're doing for those little ones. They have my full admiration and respect."

Mike tilted his head to stare at the ceiling. Everyone who knew about the kids' place said the same thing. But they weren't the ones trying to keep a busy guest ranch in operation. "I'll do that. See you tomorrow."

He put the handset down, pushed away from the desk and slowly got to his feet. He ached all over. A hot shower was beginning to appeal to him even more than sleep.

His stomach growled. Oh, yeah. He still needed to eat. And feed Tramp.

As if on cue, his dog lifted his head and whined.

The phone rang again. Mike picked it up and glanced at the readout. Freedom House. He pushed the on-button. "Hey."

"Are Kate and the kids over there?"

Mike frowned. It was his mom's voice, not Kate's. "Uh, no. I thought she might be with you."

"I tried her cell phone, but she didn't answer. Has she called?"

"Not yet." He didn't tell her Kate didn't want to talk to him. Could be she was dawdling on purpose, avoiding another awkward evening with him.

"That's not like her. She usually keeps us informed when she goes to town. Do you think we should call the sheriff?"

Mike clamped his jaw. The bad publicity from previous years was finally dying down. He didn't want to stir the pot again. "They could have stayed late at the campsite and then stopped in Laramie for supper. Add in ice cream cones at the Big Dipper, bathroom and gas stops, grocery shopping..." He hoped she hadn't forgotten the groceries. "That adds up to a long day."

"Maybe." Laura sounded doubtful. "But it's getting late. What if she had car trouble or got in a wreck?"

"The highway patrol would have let us know by now." Though he was trying to calm his mom, his heart hammered his ribs. Truth was, they should have heard from Kate by now. He glanced at the clock. Eight thirty-nine. "How about we give her twenty more minutes? If she hasn't shown up over there by nine, let me know."

"This is out of character for Kate," Laura insisted. "I hate to wait."

"Maybe she lost her phone. Or the battery died. I don't want to get the authorities searching for her when she might be just down the hill. You know how reception is here." He rubbed his wedding band with his thumb.

"Well, okay…"

"If neither of us has heard from her by nine, I'll call Cal Gardner. He's on duty right now."

~:~:~

Mike, who hadn't slept all night, paced from the living room to the office and back again, the wood floors creaking with each step. Tramp monitored his progress from the bearskin rug in front of the fireplace. Early on, the aging dog had tried to keep up with his master, but it didn't take him long to find a comfortable spot where he could keep track of Mike yet stay out of his path.

The first rays of sunrise were just beginning to shoot between the mountains when Laura walked in from the kitchen, coffee pot in hand. "Care for another round?" Mascara streaks highlighted the puffiness beneath her eyelids. As soon as Mike had reported Kate and the kids missing, she'd left Gianna, Frankie and Aunt Mary in Marita's care and joined him at the ranch house.

Mike yawned and held out his cup. "Smells good." With any luck, his stomach would endure one more cup.

The living room phone rang. He handed Laura the cup and grabbed the phone. "This is Mike."

"Detective Bledsoe from the Cheyenne PD." The officer's voice was so loud that Mike had to hold the phone away from his ear.

"Did you find them?"

Laura stood like a statue before him, coffee pot in one hand and the cup in the other, her eyes wide and expectant.

"Have an update for you."

Mike frowned. Not what he wanted to hear.

Laura's shoulders drooped.

"Your wife and three children visited the Children's Village Saturday afternoon, like you said," Bledsoe continued. "We showed pictures to the employees and volunteers who were there on Saturday. They remembered a dark-haired woman with three children who matched the ethnicities you mentioned. Estimates as to how long they stayed ranged from two to three hours."

He paused. "We're not sure about the lake. The lifeguard had no recollection of them but the snack-shack girl thought she might have seen them. A lot of people were at the beach that day."

"Did they act like everything was okay? You know, no stress or odd behavior." Mike wanted to kick himself. Odd was not the best word to use. The kids were damaged and easily triggered, according to Kate, which sometimes elicited unpredictable reactions.

"The witnesses said the children appeared healthy and happy, like they were having a good time."

Laura tensed. "Mike…"

"Hang on, please, Detective." He lowered the phone. "What is it, Mom?"

"Have they checked the lake?" Her eyebrows crumpled. "I hate to suggest they might have drowned, but…"

Before Mike had a chance to repeat her question, the detective said, "I heard that. We considered the possibility. Although it's highly unlikely, fire department personnel are searching Sloan's Lake from one end to the other, even as we speak."

Mike could tell his mom was only partially relieved.

"You are aware," Bledsoe continued, "that we found your wife's vehicle in the Frontier Mall parking lot. Correct?"

Chapter Fifteen

"Yes, you told me about her SUV." Mike didn't remember Kate saying she planned to take the kids to the mall, but maybe she needed to pick up something there.

"We just finished running prints. Hers, with her, uh, history, are on file. We also have your fingerprints and your mother's. Evidently those were taken after you had a theft a couple years ago. The car has other prints, including smaller ones, probably those of the children. If needed, we'll have the sheriff's department up there do some fingerprinting for us."

"Did you find anything in the car?"

"A large bag."

"Grocery sack? She was planning to get groceries."

"No, something like a big purse. One of our female officers called it a satchel. Had a wallet and a cell phone in it. Apparently both belong to your wife. Someone in the department is checking phone messages right now. The wallet contains a driver's license, a library card, credit cards and such, but no cash." He paused. "Do you have any idea whether or not your wife carried cash?"

"Knowing Kate, she had cash with her, but I don't know how much."

"We've had a couple cash-only thefts in that part of town. Could be a connection." The detective cleared his throat. "The bag also had some snack items, what looks like a kids' craft project, and wet children's swimsuits and beach towels. From what we can tell, two of the children swam, but your wife and one child, a small girl, did not swim, judging by the dry swimsuits."

Laura said, "I had a feeling Lupi wouldn't be comfortable in a strange place. She's the youngest girl. And Kate told me she thought she'd do a better job watching the kids from the shore than swimming with them."

Mike rubbed his jaw. "What's next?"

"Like I said," Bledsoe responded, "we have someone checking out the cell phone. If we get a lead, we'll follow it."

"But if you don't…"

"Can't track a cold trail."

"But this isn't cold. It just happened."

"What do you think happened, Mr. Duncan?"

Oh, so he was still a suspect. They'd already grilled him like he was Jack the Ripper. "All I know is my wife and three kids went on an outing yesterday and didn't come home." He struggled to control his voice. "Have you checked the Vedauwoo campgrounds?"

"Sheriff deputies are out there right now. But…"

"But what?"

According to the campground host, no woman with three kids camped there Saturday or Sunday. And although your wife made a reservation, the site sat vacant all weekend."

Mike frowned. That didn't make sense. "Anything I can do from here? Or should I drive to Cheyenne?"

"Hang tight. We'll keep you informed. Stay close to home and call immediately if you hear anything or they show up."

Mike shook his head. Kate was gone. The kids were gone. He had to do something. "Please let me know if there's anything I can do to help find them."

"Will do." The detective ended the call.

Mike replaced the phone. "Could you hear all that?"

"Uh-huh." Laura poured coffee into his cup and handed it to him. "Couldn't miss it."

Tramp stretched and then ambled to the patio door.

Mike walked over to let him out. "I hate sitting here doing nothing."

She opened a drawer in the hutch, pulled out a trivet and placed it on the hutch. Setting the coffee carafe on top, she said, "I feel the same way, but we'll be busy, at least for a day or two, lining up help to keep things running smoothly."

"You make it sound like Kate's not coming back."

"Mike..." Laura folded her arms. "Whether Kate and the kids are missing for one day or a week or more, you and I will be too distracted to be much use around here. We need to find people to cover for us at the ranch and at Freedom House."

"You're right." He ran his hand across his eyes. "I'll ask Cyrus to help Clint with the work crews. Fletcher can take over for Cyrus in the dining hall."

"This would be a good time to have Coach assume more responsibilities," Laura said. "And to ask Amy to man the front desk."

"I don't like the idea of other people running our business."

"I'm a partner in this business and I trust Coach. Kate's also a partner. She trusts Amy. So do I, for that matter." Laura pushed stray hair away from her tired eyes. "Just because we're busy with Freedom House doesn't mean we aren't equal partners with you."

He swirled the coffee in his cup. Finally, he nodded. "True."

"Time to trust our friends, Mike, and to trust God to help them manage our operation. We now have multiple businesses to run, with the guest ranch, the livestock, the bison products and the children's home. We're no longer a mom-and-pop...well, mom-and-son operation. You're spread too thin. I'm spread too thin. We can afford to hire more help, so let's do it."

He jutted his chin. "You're talking like it's just you and me, like Kate won't be back for a long time."

"I'd *like* to think she'll walk in the door before we breathe our next breath. However, from the looks of things, she didn't just disappear."

Mike raised an eyebrow.

"I'm convinced someone abducted her and the children." Her eyes misted. "I hope I'm wrong, and I pray, pray, pray no harm comes to any of them, but I have a feeling we're in for a long haul."

"Kidnapped?" He stared at her. "Why in the world would someone kidnap them? We're not wealthy people. We haven't received a ransom note."

A tear spilled down her cheek. "Traffickers don't ransom their victims. They sell them." She stepped past him. "I need to get something from the office."

Traffickers. Mike groaned. After all they'd learned about trafficking before they opened Freedom House, he should have thought of that. *Oh, God, please, no...* He set his cup on the dining room table, pulled out a chair and fell into it.

Laura came back with a notepad and pen and sat across from him. She swiped at her cheeks, which were now both wet. "I'll make a list of everyone we should call, starting with Dymple. She can activate the church's prayer chain for us." She wrote something on her pad and then pointed the pen at him. "You're going to talk with Clint, Cyrus and Fletcher, right?"

He nodded through the gray haze that blurred his vision. He felt numb all over, like he'd been shot with a massive dose of Novocain. *Trafficked.* If his mom was right, Kate and the kids could be sold to a brothel like the one in Texas. Or to a porn studio. Or a street gang. God only knew where they'd end up. Another state? Another country? Might already be there.

Mike ran his thumb along the underside of his wedding ring and thought about the fight he'd had with Kate and the times she'd taken lunch out to him when he worked far from the house. And how she massaged his back when he'd had a hard day and left him sweet notes when she knew she'd be spending the night at Freedom House.

"I'll call Coach and Amy." Laura tapped her chin with the pen. "I know Amy rents that little house down in Copperville, but I'd like her to stay up here until this situation is resolved. She can sleep in Mary's bedroom and Mary can stay over at Freedom House, where she won't be disturbed by a lot of commotion and tension."

She scribbled again. "And the Curtis twins. If they're free, I'm sure they'd be thrilled to come up early to clean cabins and wash sheets for us."

"So it's a done deal, huh?"

"What?"

"Coach and Amy."

"Yes, Mike. It's a done deal."

He tapped his fingers on the tabletop. "The Raeburns won't appreciate us stealing Amy from the café."

"I've already talked with Joyce about the possibility of Amy working for us. Their daughter is home from college for the summer and a niece is staying with them. Both girls are anxious to get in more hours to save money for school."

"What do we tell Aunt Mary? Kate's absence could throw her for a loop."

"Good question." Laura looked thoughtful. "I'll talk with Marita about what to say to her. But with her memory problem, it may not matter. When Kate's not with us and Mary asks about her, we tell her she'll be over later. Later might be the next day, yet she never seems to get upset. Time is no longer an issue with her." She paused. "I'll also talk to the kids' counselors regarding what to tell the two children still with us."

She wrote another note. "I'm glad Kate put the coconut oil and supplement doses the naturopath prescribed for Mary on the chart with the kids' medications. And Marita knows about her special diet, so that's good." She paused. "I hope the other three children don't have to go too long without their vitamins and meds."

Mike pushed back his chair. "So we call everyone and tell them what they can do to help us out." He stood. "Then what? I can't hang out here all day twiddling my thumbs."

Laura got up, took his arm and led him to the couch. "Sit."

He lowered onto a cushion with a groan, tempted to stretch out and give his body the rest it craved. But he knew he couldn't sleep, even if he tried.

"We do the most powerful thing any human can do." She settled across from him in a chair. "We talk to the Creator of the universe, who knows exactly where Kate and the kids are and what's happening to them at this very instant."

Mike bent forward, elbows on his knees, and rested his forehead on his clasped hands. He prayed first and Laura finished. When he lifted his head, he said, "I'm going to call Cal to find out what he knows about the investigation. And then I'll go looking for Kate."

"Good idea," Laura said. "But you'd better eat something before you leave."

Mike nodded. "My head's in a fog and my stomach's burning from all the coffee. Maybe food'll help." He got to his feet. "I think I'll fix eggs and toast. Want some?"

"I'm not hungry, but I s'pose I should eat."

He opened the refrigerator and pulled out a carton with two eggs inside. Good thing neither of them had much of an appetite. Maybe they should go back to raising chickens. They'd torn down their chicken coop years ago, following a losing battle with a fox. He found a partial loaf of wholegrain bread, deposited two slices in the toaster and pressed the lever.

Laura walked into the kitchen with the coffee pot in her hand.

"How about one egg, over easy?" Mike opened the fridge again to get the butter.

"Perfect." She poured the remainder of the coffee into a cup. "Looks like I'd better brew another pot."

"I thought you were a tea drinker, Mom."

"I was. Now I need something stronger."

"How about whiskey?"

"Don't tempt me."

When the eggs were done and the toast buttered, they took their plates to the dining room table, where they picked at the food and sipped at their coffee without speaking. The sun was barely over the mountain when the phone rang. Mike pushed his chair back and hurried into the living room.

He grabbed the phone. But before he answered it, he checked the readout. Amy, not Kate. He punched the button. "Hey, Amy. What's up?"

"Hi, Mike. Sorry to call so early."

"No problem. Mom and I are awake."

"I was just listening to the news. They're already talking about Kate and the kids. Did you hear it?"

"Haven't turned on the radio or TV this morning."

"I'd like to strangle that reporter."

"Oh, yeah?" Mike glanced across the room at his mother.

"He talked about Kate doing time at Patterson and then hinted she might have run off with the kids. They're even trying to get a statement from the governor who pardoned her. But so far, he's not taking their calls."

Mike groaned. "Guess I should have expected it."

"This has to be a nightmare for you and Laura."

"Yeah."

"I try to imagine what they're experiencing. And then try not to, if you know what I mean." She paused. "Hang on a minute. My oatmeal is boiling over."

Mike heard the clank of metal against metal and then Amy came right back. "Have you heard anything more about Kate and the kids?"

"Just that the Cheyenne police have proof they were at the children's village in the park but that they didn't show up at the campsite Kate reserved in Vedauwoo."

"That's strange. So something happened between..." Amy interrupted herself. "I need to get to work. We'll talk more later."

"If you can spare half a minute, Mom needs to speak with you." He handed the phone to Laura, who arranged for Amy to start training for the front desk that afternoon.

He'd just taken a bite of cold egg when the phone rang again. Jumping to his feet, he strode across the floor to the living room and picked up the phone. Though he didn't recognize the number, it had a Wyoming area code. Was it Kate?

"Hello."

"Good morning," boomed a cheery male voice. "Is this Michael

Duncan?"

Mike frowned. Definitely not Kate. "Yes, this is Mike."

"Nathaniel Strauss here with the *Laramie Boomerang*. I'd like to ask you a couple questions about your wife and the three missing children."

Media. He should have known they'd come calling. "Isn't it a bit early to be bothering us?"

"I, uh, well… Sorry." Nathaniel chuckled. "I tend to forget others may not get going as early as I do. But you're a rancher and ranchers are early risers, or so I've been told…"

"I won't waste your time or mine, Nathaniel. We're not doing interviews at this time. Goodbye."

Hearing the crunch of tires in their graveled parking area, Mike walked over to the window and pulled a curtain aside. A minivan with KGWN plastered across the doors was pulling up in front of their office.

Laura came to the window. "Oh, great, the Cheyenne television station."

Right behind it was a vehicle from the Casper station, K2TV. Mike frowned. Photogenic Whispering Pines would be all over the news before lunch.

He dropped the curtain. "I'll talk with them."

"What are you going to say?"

I'll tell them Whispering Pines is private property open to registered guests only." He squared his shoulders and steeled himself to face the intruders. "We have nothing to hide, but I don't want nosy reporters disturbing our guests' vacations. They pay good money for peace and quiet."

"However…" He snorted. "I'm beginning to think tranquility is an illusion found only in our brochures."

Chapter Sixteen

The second morning in the garage, as Kate lay staring at the bottom of the bunk above her and praying for wisdom, Tara had exited the van waving her phone. "Neilson, you made the news." Her eyes sparked with excitement. "Not just Copperville news or Wyoming news but *national* news. They're all talking about the Wyoming woman who disappeared with three little orphan kids."

Kate gawked at her. Why was Tara so happy? The more people aware of their disappearance, the more likely they'd be found and Tara and Ramsey arrested.

Ramsey crawled out after her, his usual scowl twisted across his face.

"And guess what…" Tara giggled, near hysterics. "They think *you* kidnapped the kids, 'cause you're an ex-con." She laughed and elbowed Ramsey, who gave her a dirty look. "They didn't use those exact words, but I know that's what they meant.

"I can't wait to tell Daddy, if he hasn't already heard. We never once thought about how your record would make it look like *you* stole the brats." She raised the phone above her head and danced a jig. "We'll make out like bandits."

Ramsey flapped a hand at her, as if swatting away a fly. "Yeah, and now the fuzz'll be looking for us."

Tara pointed the phone at Kate. "You said it matters what God thinks of me." She smirked. "Appears he's on *my* side, not yours."

Determined not to react, Kate bit the insides of her cheeks and willed her facial muscles to go slack. Her heart, however, beat a frantic rhythm. She'd done her time, paid her dues. She'd tried hard to be a good citizen. She'd been pardoned. Yet the media had immediately jumped to conclusions and assumed she'd done something horrific.

She clenched her fists. Those who rubbed shoulders with her day in and day out might have faith in her character, but she'd tarnished the WP's reputation, again. Freedom House and what she and Laura and others were trying to do for the children would be questioned.

How could she ever forgive herself? She'd wanted to help the kids recover from the brothel trauma, but instead, she'd caused them more harm. And now, Mike, Laura, two governors and the Wyoming and Texas agencies involved with the children's home would all be called on the carpet for trusting her.

On top of that, she could return to prison for something she didn't do…if she survived the trafficking ordeal.

Mike dropped onto the couch. "Well, that was a waste of time. I didn't find anything at the campground or the park."

Laura sighed. "How could they disappear without leaving a trace?"

The moment the media drove away, Mike had called his dog, hopped into his mom's SUV, and driven the two hours to the Vedauwoo campground. All the campsites were empty but two. He'd talked with the occupants as well as the camp host, who insisted Kate had never been there.

Just to be sure, he checked the vacant sites but found nothing and drove another half hour to Cheyenne, where he searched the children's village and walked the path all the way around Sloan's Lake. But everywhere he went, he struck out.

"If I had a clue where to look for Kate, I'd take off this minute." He sat up, hands on his knees. "I hate not knowing what to do. Maybe I'll go move cattle with Clint."

"Good idea," Laura said, "before you start pacing again and wear a hole in the floor. I can monitor things from here."

She shooed Mike and Tramp out the door, promising to radio him if she heard any news. He made sure his radio was on his belt and trudged to the barn to saddle Lightning. His horse needed the exercise and he needed the fresh air—and to do something useful for a couple hours.

When he joined Clint at the corral to help him and the other ranch hands drive cattle from one pasture to another, his foreman gave him a funny look. "What're you doing here, Mike?" He mounted his horse. "I've got a crew to cover this."

Mike shrugged. "I can't handle staying at the house, waiting for the phone to ring."

"Yeah, but…wow, I mean, Kate being gone and all…"

"I gotta do something besides sit."

Clint motioned to the others. "Head on down to the pasture."

Two men, a teenage boy and two teen girls climbed onto their horses and filed out of the corral. Either they were being polite or they hadn't heard about Kate and the kids yet. They nodded and greeted him, but none of them asked questions.

Mike followed on Lightning, Tramp close behind.

Clint, who'd stopped to latch the gate, caught up with Mike. "What's the latest?"

"The Cheyenne detective called this morning. He said people saw Kate and the kids at the park but she never showed at the campground." He loosened the reins. Lightning would follow the herd. "Just to be sure, I drove to Vedauwoo and to the Cheyenne park. I walked all over the place, but I didn't find any sign of them."

"The police will come up with more leads today."

"I hope so."

"Wish I knew how to help." Clint adjusted his hat. "It's not much…" He paused. "But I'm praying for Kate and the kids—and you and Laura."

Mike arched an eyebrow. "Didn't know you were a praying man."

"I wasn't. Until a couple weeks ago." Clint guided his horse past a gopher hole. "When I read that book you gave me."

"What book? I don't remember giving you one."

"It was a while back…on that winter hayride where you gave everyone copies of your favorite bison book."

"Oh, yeah. *Thundering Herd* by Zane Grey."

"Yep, that's the one. Good book. The night I finished reading it, I went outside to look at the stars. Tried to imagine what it was like for those buffalo hunters camped out on the prairie month after month. Skinning smelly hides, cutting out the horns, eating nothin' but bison steaks day after day."

"Ah, now that's high living."

Clint laughed.

Something rustled a clump of sagebrush alongside the trail. Lightning snorted and Mike turned to see a jackrabbit pop out and bound across the hillside. Tramp tore after the rabbit. Lightning shied and pranced in a circle, but Clint's horse took the commotion in stride.

"Whoa, boy." Mike pulled the reins tight. "Whoa." He patted his horse's neck. Lightning settled and was soon walking alongside Clint's horse as if nothing had happened. Tramp rejoined them, his tongue hanging out the corner of his mouth.

Mike turned to his foreman. "You were saying?"

"Yeah, well, I hadn't been outside ten minutes, when I saw a meteor shower. Big one."

"Nice."

"And I got to thinking only a supreme being, someone bigger than I can begin to imagine, would have the power to create those millions of stars in the universe, actually *universes*." He swept his arm across the landscape. "And all this, from boulders and hills down to bugs and lichen and bacteria."

Mike glanced at their surroundings. "Yeah, it's mindboggling." He'd gotten so caught up in worrying about Kate that he'd forgotten to appreciate the beautiful afternoon. He inhaled the sagebrush-spiced air.

"And then I remembered this church school I went to in Colorado when I was a kid."

"I didn't know you went to parochial school."

"No, not regular school. It was summer. The teachers told us stories and we played games and made stuff. I always looked forward to snack time."

Mike chuckled. "They call that vacation Bible school."

"So I went to this Bible school with a kid named Tommy. First time I'd ever been inside a church. We went every day for a week, maybe two—seemed like a long time back then. On the final day, the teacher said anyone who didn't have Jesus in his heart could pray to ask him to come in." He shrugged. "So that's what I did, but not out loud."

"Hey, that's great news."

Clint grinned. "I went with Tommy to Sunday school several times. Then we moved away. My parents didn't attend church and I never thought to ask to go by myself. Guess I just put God on a shelf for a while, along with Grandpa's Bible."

He brushed away a horsefly. "But while I was watching that meteor show, I heard this voice…or maybe a thought came out of nowhere into my head." He screwed up his face, as if he was thinking hard. "Not sure which."

"You think God was talking to you?"

"Yeah. It was like he said, 'You may have forgotten me, but I haven't forgotten you.' I can't explain it, but I felt loved, not condemned." Clint fidgeted with the reins. "Sounds strange, I know."

Mike shook his head. "I don't think it's strange."

"Hearing those words out of nowhere hit me hard, like a punch in the gut. I waited a while, but I didn't hear the voice again. After a while, I went inside to get my grandpa's Bible. I keep it in my closet, kind of like a good luck charm." He gave Mike a wry smile. "I know, not the smartest thing to do."

"God's Word is powerful. Inviting his presence into your home can't be a bad thing. What did you do after you found the Bible?"

"I opened it and saw this underlined part that said something like, 'God stretched out the heavens by his understanding.' Bam. I was clobbered again. I'd been thinking about exactly that. I looked at the other, uh…you call them verses, right?"

"Yep."

"Somewhere before that verse, it says we shouldn't boast about strength or wealth but boast that we know God." Right then, I realized the God who made the heavens might know me, but I didn't know him." He shook his head. "Crazy."

Cattle lowed in the distance. The lead cows were nearing the pasture.

"I was thinking…that is, if you don't mind," Clint said, "maybe you'd help me understand the Bible. I read some other parts last night that didn't make much sense to me."

"Some of the Old Testament is tough going. Most people are better off reading the New Testament first. That's near the back of the Bible." Mike raised his eyebrows. "I like your idea to study together. Maybe read a short section and talk about it. Get out my Bible dictionary—and call Pastor Chuck when we get stuck."

"I'd like that."

"So would I. But I don't think I'll be worth much until Kate and the kids come home."

"Gotcha." Clint gave him a sympathetic smile. "In the meantime, I'll keep praying." He flicked his reins and took off to catch up with the crew.

Mike slumped in the saddle. He was a fraud. One minute he acted like a jerk to his wife and the next, he pretended to be Mr. Spiritual with Clint. He heaved a long sigh and vowed to apologize to Kate first thing when she came home. If she came home.

Mike and Clint followed the others up the road to the ranch headquarters.

"That went good," Mike said.

"Other than the calf that tumbled into the ravine."

"Yeah, but it wasn't hurt, thank God." And it gave him a reason to stop thinking about Kate for a few minutes.

The horses snuffled and sidestepped, spooked by a rattlesnake winding across the road. The men reined to a stop, but Tramp tiptoed toward the reptile, sniffing. Mike called him back. Although his dog knew not to mess with rattlers, he was too close. This one was long and meaty. If it decided to coil, its strike distance could reach up to two-thirds of its body length.

Clint leaned on the saddlehorn. "Any word about Kate while we were working the cattle?"

"Nope." His radio had been silent the entire time.

"Sorry, man. Something has to break soon."

"Yeah, I'm counting on it." Mike rubbed his jaw and changed the subject. "Did you tell Amy what happened to you the other night? About the meteors?"

"Not yet."

The snake slithered into a pile of rocks and they urged the horses forward again.

"I think she'd like to know. So would Mom and Kate."

"I'll get to it." Clint adjusted his hat brim, shading his eyes. "But I have to admit this thing with Kate has me rethinking my relationship with Amy."

"Oh, yeah?" Mike cocked his head. "How's that?"

"I, uh, well… I don't mean this bad, but—"

"Spit it out." Mike was too tired to be patient.

"Seems like ever since Kate came to the WP, one crazy thing after another has happened." Clint shrugged. "I mean, it's not like she causes drama. Todd Hughes is the one who shot the bison, not Kate. But that scene with Tara Hughes at the parade. And then there was that Ramsey guy who followed her here."

He lifted a palm. "Now this. Like I said, those situations weren't her fault, but..." He shrugged. "Amy's past is just as sketchy, especially considering what happened in Texas…"

"What are you getting at?"

"I'm just wondering. Is it worth it? I know you love Kate and all that, but being married to an ex-felon can't be easy."

Mike blew out a long breath. No, life with Kate hadn't been easy, but he'd often said marrying her was the best thing he'd ever done. "Marriage has been great, Clint." *Other than that stupid fight Friday night.* "Yeah, it's been wild at times, but it hasn't been boring. And you usually get to be part of the excitement."

"Glad to help." Clint chuckled. "But looking from the outside in is a lot easier than what you're going through right now. Single life has its advantages."

"I haven't forgotten those days, but I never want to go back. Marriage is far better." The more they talked about Kate, the more he missed her. Mike lifted his hat and ran his fingers through his hair. "Give it time, Clint. Ask God to guide you. Amy is like Kate. She's a great gal who got off to a rough start."

"I understand, but she worked in that Executive Pride place for months. And now she's doing all that counseling. I'm not even supposed to touch her right now. Will she ever be ready to marry anyone, whether it's me or some other guy?"

"Only God knows the answer," Mike said. "That's why we pray and read his Word—to get guidance. I'm glad you suggested a Bible study. I need to spend more time reading my Bible. It helps ground a person for times like this."

Back at the barn, Mike and Clint removed the horses' saddles, wiped their backs and led them into the corral. Both horses trotted straight for the water trough. The men walked over to the office.

When they stepped into the lobby, Amy was standing behind the counter at one of the computers. "Hi, Amy," Mike said. "I see you're already hard at work."

Clint, who'd followed Mike in, gaped at her. "What are you doing here? I mean…"

I'm working." She laughed and shook her auburn hair. "Can you believe it?"

Laura walked through the office doorway. "Mike didn't tell you?"

Clint looked at Mike. "Uh, no."

"Sorry." Mike yawned. "I meant to tell you while we were moving cattle."

"Our foreman ought to know who's on staff." Laura put her arm on

Amy's shoulders. "We've talked for some time about bringing Amy up to help cover the front desk two or three days a week." She sighed and tilted her head. "But now that we're dealing with this crisis, I asked her to start immediately and work fulltime. She graciously agreed. Coach has also agreed to work fulltime this summer, so you'll see more of him, too."

"I, uh, wow," Clint stuttered. "Guess I should say 'welcome aboard.'" Instead of offering his usual contagious grin, he shoved his hands into his pockets.

Amy's smile faded.

"Is this temporary, until Kate…?"

Laura leaned on the countertop. "We'll take it one day at a time."

"The most important thing right now is to find Kate and the kids." Amy stood tall. "You two helped Kate rescue me. Now it's my turn to give back."

The screen door creaked open. Mike looked over his shoulder and saw Doc Hall step inside. "Doc, you're a day early."

"I was driving by on my way home from the meeting and thought I'd check your bison cow now, so I don't have to bother you tomorrow. I hear all hell broke loose around here after we talked."

Chapter Seventeen

Mike drove the veterinarian down to the bison pasture in Old Blue. Doc had insisted he could drive himself and report in later, saying he didn't want to bother the Duncans during such a difficult time. But Mike was grateful for the distraction. Besides, he wanted to be with the vet when he examined the cow, not only to see what he saw, but to make sure he was safe.

He'd brought a tranquilizer dart gun in case they had trouble getting close enough for a diagnosis. His bison were intelligent, playful creatures with lots of personality, but they were also wild and unpredictable. Unlike cattle, bison could not be tamed or domesticated and could revert to instinctual behavior without warning.

He cringed every time he saw an Internet picture of someone with a "pet" buffalo. A twelve-hundred-pound cow that could broad-jump eight feet from a standing start or a two-thousand-pound bull that could easily clear a four-foot fence and run thirty miles per hour was not an animal to attach to a leash.

Clint followed them in his pickup. Mike appreciated his foreman's desire to learn about bison caretaking. Not everyone shared his enthusiasm for the primeval beasts.

Once they were inside the pasture and Clint had shut the gate behind them, Mike slowly motored through the herd. He'd never lost his awe of the animals' massive proportions. Their huge shaggy heads with their big eyes, curved horns and long beards were supported by enormous shoulder humps.

"I read somewhere that dried buffalo chips make good fires," Doc said. "Is that true?"

"Yep." Mike nodded. "They ignite easily and burn down to hot coals with low flames. Our crews use them to warm their hands on cold days." He chuckled. "But even though the chips burn clean and are odorless, I have yet to convince my mom to burn them in the fireplace."

Doc laughed. "I have a feeling my wife would have the same reaction."

Bumping over hillocks, Mike circled boulders and searched for the cow with the eye problem. He'd marked her with fluorescent-green livestock spray paint so he could find her again. They worked their way diagonally from one fence corner to another and then did the same with the opposite corners, creating an X of tire tracks across the prairie grass. But he saw no sign of the cow.

Mike started around the perimeter, following the fence line. "Sorry to tie up your time like this, Doc. Maybe she wallowed in the mud and covered the paint. Still, you'd think her eye issue would be obvious."

"No problem. I enjoy seeing your place." He laughed, pointing at two rust-colored calves running circles, chasing each other.

Clint honked his horn and Mike stopped the truck. But they didn't get out. A cluster of curious but cautious bison thirty-feet away eyed them, tails extended from narrow hindquarters that looked out of proportion with their bulky front quarters. A rigid tail was a warning sign Mike heeded every time.

The two-way radio on his belt sputtered to life. Clint's voice rasped through the airwaves. "I think I see her."

Mike scanned the prairie from one side of the pickup to the other. He lifted the radio and pushed the button. "Where?"

"In those trees on our right. Could be a downed cow on her side, or it could be a mossy log. What caught my attention was a flash of bright green."

Mike depressed the speaker button again. "Let's park our trucks so they block the view of that bunch on the left. Then we can get out to look her over. But be careful. If that's a cow, she might just be resting." He returned the radio to its holder. "What was that you were saying, Doc, about no more dead bison these days?"

"I trust that's not the case here."

Mike circled a rock pile to angle his truck nose to nose with Clint's. He peered between the trees. Yes, that was definitely a bison on the ground, not a log with fluorescent-green moss.

Doc cleared his throat. "She's not moving."

Mike opened his door, checked the area for bison and walked slowly into the trees. With the tranquilizer gun aimed at the inert cow, he cautiously stepped around sagebrush and over pungent manure piles.

The other men followed, Doc with his medical bag in hand.

Mike knelt by the lifeless form. "Don't need to tranquilize this one. Should make your job easier than expected, Doc."

The vet pulled exam gloves from his bag. "Doesn't look like she's been dead long."

Mike touched the carcass, which stunk but was still warm and not yet stiff. How he hated to lose another cow.

The vet bent over the big head and waved away the flies crawling on the eyelids. He separated one set of eyelids, then the other. Both eyes were cloudy with evidence of discharge drying on the lower lids as well as from the nose. He moved to the back end of the animal and lifted the tail, which was caked with feces and what looked like dried blood. "Dysentery, just as I suspected."

"What do you think caused her death?" Clint asked.

"Can't say for sure without testing, but I suspect malignant catarrhal fever. Not a nice way to die."

"Cattle can get that disease, too, right?"

"That's right." Doc got to his feet. "MCF is a herpes virus carried by sheep and goats, which are not affected by the virus. But it can be deadly for cattle and bison as well as deer, elk and moose. Bison are especially vulnerable, far more so than cattle."

Mike frowned and stood. "I've read a bit about MCF, but I don't see how the virus could get into our herd. The closest sheep operation is fifty miles away."

"MCF can lie dormant in an animal for quite some time. Or, an animal can test positive but never show symptoms." Doc pulled a small camera from his pocket and started snapping shots of the cow. "Ever had sheep on this ranch?"

"Not for as long as I remember. Dad didn't allow them on the property and neither do I. They'll graze a pasture down to the roots."

"All a matter of land management," the vet said.

Mike didn't respond. He and Doc had had this discussion before. Neither man was ready to change his opinion.

"Uh…" Clint kicked a stubby cactus aside. "We had sheep here last week."

Mike pivoted. "You're joking, right?"

Clint's eyebrows puckered but he looked Mike in the eye. "Wish I was. I leased some sheep from a small farm near Laramie for the kids' rodeo on Friday. Brought 'em in a week early so they could get used to the place and not be too frightened when we put them in the arena. I didn't want them to injure a kid."

Mike narrowed his eyes. "What arena?"

"I meant the corral. We had a mutton-busting competition as part of the kids' rodeo. You know, where little kids ride sheep."

"I know what mutton busting is. Why didn't you ask me?"

Clint's brow furrowed. "Never occurred to me that pasturing a handful of sheep for a few days on the other side of the ranch would be a concern."

"Where were they?" Doc asked.

"At Freedom House, the kids' place Mike and Kate and Laura started. We brought in five sheep for the event."

"How far is Freedom House from here?"

Clint looked at Mike. "Four or five miles, as the crow flies."

Mike stuffed his hands in his pockets so he wouldn't slug his foreman. Good thing he'd skipped the barbecue. He'd have blown his top when he saw the sheep.

"Your cattle herd is even farther away, right?"

"Right," was Clint's only response.

"Any lambs?" Doc returned the camera to his pocket.

"One of the ewes had triplets. The kids got a kick out of the lambs."

"Eight," Mike muttered, his jaw tight. "You brought *eight* sheep onto the WP?"

Clint sighed. "I had no idea that would be a problem. They were only here a week." He turned to the vet. "Why did you ask about lambs?"

"MCF is most commonly spread by nasal secretions from lambs five to nine months of age. He pointed to Clint's boots. "You wear the same boots every day?"

Clint nodded.

"Drive the same pickup around the ranch?"

"Only one I got."

Clint was looking more miserable by the minute, but Mike didn't care.

"Some people," Doc said, "theorize that the virus can travel on the air or on equipment. But," he added, "we don't know that this cow had MCF or that it came from those sheep—or that your clothing or vehicle transmitted the virus. I was just speculating out loud."

He continued. "The good news is that bison can't transmit the disease to other bison. Same with cattle. So we shouldn't have to quarantine your herds. However, that doesn't guarantee you won't have an outbreak in either herd."

He indicated the cow that lay prostrate on the grass. "I could take some samples, but it'd be better if you'd let me haul the body to the university's veterinary pathologist. He has a crack team of researchers who'd love a fresh carcass to necropsy."

Mike frowned. "Who's going to pay for all this?" He'd wanted a diversion, but this was too much, a nightmare on top of a nightmare.

"I think the university will work with us on that." Doc turned to Clint. "I'll need contact info for the farm where you got the sheep. I have a hunch the pathologist will want to test the entire flock."

Like a nightmare on replay, day two in the garage had been much like day one, except that their kidnappers never left the building. Kate had slept, eaten the same food as the day before, tried to wash in the bathroom, prayed for escape or rescue, and searched for a way out.

Ramsey and Tara had spent most of the day inside the white van, which was fine with her. The less she interacted with the obnoxious pair, the better—and the more freedom she'd had to investigate their surroundings. But though she'd circled the building dozens of times, she hadn't found any weakness in the structure.

To pass the hours, she and the kids had done dozens of stretches, jumping jacks, lunges and squats, and they'd run in place. They'd also thumb-wrestled and played hand games. Kate was glad when the games elicited an occasional smile.

Their free-time ended shortly before sundown, when Ramsey and Tara crawled out of the back of the van, grabbed the leftover food and trash and herded them all into the brown van. After that, Ramsey shuffled vehicles again, moving first the white one then the brown one outside.

Finally, he returned the white vehicle to the garage and shut the door. At least that's what Kate assumed from the confines of their latest prison, where they breathed exhaust fumes and listened to Tara sing off-key with the radio.

Shoulders hunched, Kate moved to the grate that separated her from the front. "Quick, Tara. Jump in the other seat and drive us out of here. You can be a hero, not Jerry's accomplice."

Tara whipped around. "Keep hassling me and I'll remove your tongue." She stabbed her knife into the grate.

Kate jerked back.

Tara snickered, upped the radio volume and continued to sing along with the nasal country-western vocalist.

Ramsey opened the door and Kate hurried to her seat. He put the van in gear, stomped the gas and took off across the bumpy road.

"This is it, Jerry." Tara squeezed his shoulder. "The final leg of our journey. Just think—we're about to get rich. Gloriously rich."

He pushed her hand away.

She gave him the finger and sang along with the next song, this one about a two-timing spouse.

Ramsey switched off the radio.

Tara slouched against the door. But once they were on the highway again, she straightened and read the latest news reports out loud. According to the media, Kate was the prime suspect in a *possible* kidnapping case. Authorities were scouring the West for them. Lowering the phone, she peered through the divider into the dark rear of the van. "What do you think about that, Neilson?"

Kate didn't answer. She wanted to kick out the back doors and scream her innocence to the world, but she couldn't let her focus waver. Far more crucial than defending herself was thwarting the meeting with the traffickers.

Ramsey growled, "Quiet."

Tara snickered and leaned on the door again.

They stopped for gas once but bypassed rest areas. "Jerry," Kate called above the van's rattles, "The kids need a bathroom."

"They can hold it."

"You want them and the van to smell like an outhouse?" Tara asked. "That'll lower the price we get."

His only response was a shoulder shrug. But it wasn't long before he pulled off the interstate onto a dark, wooded side road. Outside the van, Kate could see no signs of life, other than the vehicle lights flashing past. Their only hope was to run to the highway.

Ramsey grabbed Tieno. The blade he held against the boy's throat gleamed red in the taillight. "Make it quick, Neilson."

She glared at him and touched Lupi's shoulder. "You go first, behind that bush. I know it's dark, but I'll be close by."

Chapter Eighteen

The sun had settled behind one mountain and the moon was rising above another by the time Mike walked into the house. Trusting that exhaustion would replace frustration, he'd worked on one project or another until it was too dark to see. He was mad at himself for the cruel things he'd said to Kate, mad at her for leaving, mad at God for letting her disappear, and mad at Clint for bringing sheep onto their property.

He hadn't been home two minutes when Laura offered to warm some of the casserole a friend had dropped by earlier. And he hadn't been there three minutes when the telephone rang.

One hand on the microwave door, she turned to Mike, her tired eyes bright. "Maybe that's Kate."

He grunted. "Or another reporter." He tried not to get his hopes up. The roller coaster of emotions that charged through him like a stampeding buffalo every time the phone rang was wearing him down.

He stepped into the living room and picked up the phone. "This is Mike."

"Evening. Detective Bledsoe from the Cheyenne PD." He didn't waste time with niceties. "Have an update for you."

Mike swallowed. Another update. That was all. But at least they had something to report. "Shoot."

"It's not a bona fide clue…" The detective hesitated. "Just a possible sighting."

"Okay…"

"A woman who contacted the Idaho Highway Department today said she drove from Oregon to Colorado over the weekend. She saw several children, she wasn't sure how many, with two women plus a man at an Idaho rest stop late Saturday night.

"But she couldn't remember which one. One woman had light-colored hair and the other woman's hair was darker. Both were of medium build, as was the man. She said the children were young, maybe ages four to nine or ten."

"How could she tell all that in the dark?"

"Most rest areas are well lit."

"Okay, I'll give you that. But why would anyone assume Kate was one of them?"

Laura came into the room and stood next to him. He pushed the speaker button on the phone.

"This may be a false lead not worth a pot of beans," the detective said. For a moment, he was quiet, and then he asked, "Did your wife mention visiting friends in Cheyenne or elsewhere in Wyoming?"

"No."

"How about Utah or Idaho?"

"We don't know anyone in either state."

"Maybe your wife knows people there you don't know."

"That's possible but not likely. She's from Pennsylvania. Did the woman get a license number?"

"She said she didn't think of it until she exited the bathroom. Unfortunately, the van was gone by then."

"She gave you a description of the van. Right?"

"Yeah." He paused, as if looking at notes. "Apparently, it was a white utility van. No idea of make or model. We've alerted highway patrol in multiple western states."

Mike rubbed his eyes. Time to go looking for Kate. This was taking way too long. He would check every rest area between Cheyenne and... He frowned. That couldn't have been Kate with those people. So where in the world was she? He pulled out a dining room chair and sat.

Laura sat across from him, hands clasped.

"I'm about to go off this case," Bledsoe said. "The chief is sending Detectives Moore and Schroeder up to your ranch tomorrow to ask a few questions."

"Isn't that what you've been doing?"

"They'll be knocking on your door bright and early. Be sure to be there when they arrive. Good evening, Mr. Duncan."

Mike dropped the phone on the table and put his head in his hands. "That couldn't have been her at the rest stop."

"How do you know?" Laura asked.

Mike sat up. "She wouldn't take off with other people without telling us. You know that."

"But if she and the kids were kidnapped, those *other people* might be the ones who abducted them. Have you forgotten that we talked about the trafficking possibility?"

He rubbed his brow. "I wish I could forget." They'd spent months researching modern-day slavery before opening the children's home. Human beings exploiting other human beings was far more pervasive than he would have ever guessed. The evil practice entailed a wide range of atrocities in addition to sex trafficking.

Individuals were bought and sold and shipped back and forth across the globe to work in hotels and restaurants as well as in brothels. They toiled long hard hours in private homes, fields, factories, mines, mills, ships, construction projects and anywhere else owners were too selfish and greedy to pay their workers. In some countries, they were forced to serve as soldiers. Those deemed unfit for labor were sold for parts.

Mike got to his feet. He had to find Kate before she disappeared forever. "I'm going to check maps in the office and then take off. Time to follow the trail before it gets any colder."

Laura stood. "I'd tell you to leave the investigation to the authorities, but I remember what you and Clint and Kate accomplished in Texas when the authorities were stymied."

True, their foreman had helped them find Amy... Mike's jaw twitched. But he'd also brought sheep onto the WP. His mom hadn't told him about the mutton busting, even though she knew he didn't want sheep anywhere near their ranch.

If he told her the cow's death was possibly caused by Clint's actions, she'd say it was an honest mistake, even if it would make Dad roll over in his grave. Maybe it was a mistake. However, it could cost him his entire herd.

And Kate hadn't said a word about the mutton busting at the kids' rodeo. Of course, that's what their argument had been about—the rodeo.

"I'd like you to wait until tomorrow afternoon to leave."

"What?" Mike gave her an incredulous look. "It's been almost twenty-four hours since we reported them missing."

"I know." Laura sighed. "Feels like an eternity. But I'd like you here with me to answer the detectives' questions tomorrow. I don't want to have to explain your absence, which they might find suspicious."

"Searching for my missing wife isn't a crime, Mom. Any number of people can sit with you during the questioning. Cyrus, Coach—"

"Leaving the ranch right after you learned they were coming up here might be considered suspect. But my primary reason for you to stay..." She pushed in her chair. "We could learn something from them, something more specific than a possible rest-area sighting. That's not much information to go on."

Mike jammed his hands into his pockets. "If I stay, Kate and the kids will be another ten or twelve hours down the road."

"If you stay, you might learn which road."

Lulled by road noise and the van's vibrations, which were worse than in the other van, Kate fought to stay awake. They were in Oregon and still driving on I-84. She knew that much from the signs. The kids were asleep again, momentarily unaware they were being driven to their doom.

God, you may not care about me, but surely you care about the kids. Please send help or provide an escape. A patrolman could stop Ramsey or he could have an accident or... She sighed. God didn't need her suggestions. He could come up with his own ideas. But time was running out. He had to do whatever he was going to do soon.

She reached for one of the juice jugs she'd filled with water and took a sip to still the grumbling in her gut. She tried not to drink too much because she didn't want to deprive the others. Might be hours or days before they were offered more. Tara had objected to the jugs, but Ramsey overruled her, saying dehydration could affect the appearance of the merchandise. Kate had ignored the degrading comment and placed the water in the back of the van.

She twisted her rings, missing Mike more by the mile. By now he was probably wondering where she was. Would he come looking for her or leave the search up to the authorities?

The two of them had planned to travel through Oregon and along the coast someday. She wanted to see the ocean, the waterfalls, the giant trees and mountains, especially Mount Hood. She loved the picture of Mount Hood on their kitchen calendar. Backlit by a stunning sunrise, the beautiful snowcapped mountain stood alone, strong and majestic. Every day it reminded her of God's power and glory.

All she saw now was darkness, which mirrored their situation. She'd escaped the murky shadows of her past and so had the kids. But here they were, once again prisoners of evil.

A psalm she'd prayed often in prison came to her. *Hear my cry, O God, listen to my prayer. From the ends of the earth I call to you, I call as my heart grows faint. Lead me to the rock that is higher than I. For you have been my refuge, a strong tower against the foe.*

The Lord had been her rock and her refuge, her strong tower against her enemies in prison. He wouldn't desert her now. One phrase replayed again and again in her head. *Lead me to the rock that is higher than I.*

"I'm in a deep valley, God," Kate murmured, "the deepest of my life, and at the end of my wits. I'm weak, but I need to be strong for my kiddos...your kiddos." She rubbed Tieno's back. *Lead me to the rock that is higher than I. Plant my feet. Strengthen my spirit and my body.*

Closing her eyes, she waited for him to speak, to reassure her. But she was tired. Oh, so tired. And sore and angry and lonely—and scared. She dropped her chin to her chest.

No matter how much bravado she displayed before Ramsey and Tara, she was petrified they'd hurt the children. The traffickers they were meeting had to be even more callous, if that was possible. Her pulse pounded in her ears. She couldn't let their plans come to fruition. Whatever it took, she'd fight with all she had for the kids.

But... She sagged. She was only one person.

Stand on the rock.

She bowed her head. *Yes, Lord. You're the Rock, a Rock higher than I, much higher. I'll plant my feet on you.*

Kate opened her eyes in time to see a mileage sign that said Troutdale was eleven miles away and Portland twenty-seven. *Portland?* They'd driven clear across Oregon. If they drove much farther, they'd end up in the ocean.

Just before Troutdale, she saw a sign for the Mount Hood National Scenic Byway. Someday... Lord willing, *someday* she and Mike would drive the byway and hike the mountain.

Near Portland, traffic picked up. Scattered taillights stretched as far as she could see. Oncoming traffic created a long line of sporadic headlights. Were people on their way to work already? Seemed early, yet life began early on the ranch too.

Oregon and Wyoming were in different time zones. If it was five o'clock here, it would be six o'clock at the ranch, and Mike and Laura would be awake. Had they slept? She ran her finger over her ring, wishing she could send Mike a mental message to tell him where they were and that they were okay but to come quickly.

Aunt Mary, who was an early riser, would also be awake. Had Laura or Marita remembered to give her the supplements and coconut oil that eased her confusion? She was lost without her vitamins and herbs. Kate wondered if her great-aunt had been told about her and the kids' disappearance.

Even if no one told her, she must have noticed their absence. She'd always sensed Kate's needs, whether she was in foster homes, on the streets or behind bars. Yes, Aunt Mary knew. She always knew.

Kate thought of Frankie and Gianna, the Freedom House kids still at home. They would notice their friends' were no longer there. Laura must have her hands full caring for them and dealing with the fallout resulting from the disappearance of the others. *Give her strength, Lord. Plant her and Mike's feet on the Rock.*

No doubt Dymple and other friends were already praying. Kate closed her eyes. *Thank you, Jesus.* Just knowing people were supporting them, pleading for the miracles they desperately needed, gave her courage.

Signs for an upcoming juncture appeared. She was surprised when Ramsey took the 205 south rather than staying on west I-84 into Portland's City Center. Maybe the city wasn't their destination, after all, which might be good. She'd heard it was a hub for juvenile sex trafficking.

Tara lifted her phone to her ear. At first Kate couldn't hear her, but then she yelled, "Daddy, we're getting close."

Close? Close to what?

Shannon sat up, stared from one end of the van to the other, and then focused on Kate. "Where are we?"

Kate whispered, "Portland, Oregon."

"Where's that?"

"Near the ocean, next to Washington. Didn't you say you lived in Seattle for a while?"

"Yeah, but I didn't go to the ocean." She yawned. "I'm hungry."

"Me, too. When we get out of this mess, we'll pick up some fried chicken and coleslaw and have a picnic on the coast before we go home to the ranch." Shannon loved fried chicken.

The girl slumped against the seat.

Kate wished she hadn't mentioned fried chicken. Just the thought made her mouth water. She checked the dim figures of the other two children, who were both fast asleep. She was glad for them. They weren't feeling hunger pangs gnaw at their little stomachs.

"Miss Kate…" Shannon's whisper was barely discernible.

Kate hunched closer.

"What did he mean when he said you didn't give his kid a chance?"

"Wha…?" What was the girl talking about? And then she remembered. "Oh, you mean him?" She indicated Ramsey.

Shannon nodded.

"I'm afraid that's another sordid chapter of my history." Kate pushed hair away from her face. "I was a prisoner in a Pennsylvania prison. He was a correctional officer." She lowered her voice. "If I needed something from the commissary—shampoo, deodorant, snacks, he was an easy mark. All I had to do was mention our little hideaway."

She stretched across the space between them to take Shannon's hand. "That's what I was talking about earlier. I didn't offer my body in love, which is what marriage is all about. I used it to get something I wanted. As a result, I got something I didn't want. Pregnant."

"You did? But you don't—"

"Prison officials pressured me to abort the baby. I didn't want an abortion. Something about it seemed wrong to me. But I hated the idea of having Ramsey's baby." Kate shuddered. "Even worse was the thought of sharing custody with him or that he might be the one to raise the child while I was in prison." Kate bent closer. "As you may have noticed, he's not exactly fond of children."

Shannon nodded, her eyes wide.

"I also didn't want the child to end up in the foster-care system, where I spent much of my childhood. In my mind, that was an unthinkable option. Eventually, I agreed to the abortion, a decision I regret every day of my life. I let them kill the only baby I'll ever have."

Kate paused, fighting tears. "Ramsey never cared about that child. When I called off the relationship, he beat me within an inch of my life, which also endangered the baby's life. The warden fired him, and he's been fuming ever since. He says he wants me, but what he really wants is to control me and punish me for supposedly causing him to lose his job."

"Wow…" Shannon glanced toward the front. "He's wacko."

"Just as wacko and wicked as Tara. Funny how evil attracts evil." Kate undid her seatbelt. "I'd better go see where we are." She got down on her knees and crawled to the front to read signs. The more location hints she had, the better.

They passed exit sign after exit sign, but it wasn't until the "Oregon City/West Linn" sign that Ramsey slowed the van and turned off the freeway.

Chapter Nineteen

K ate swallowed. Was this the end of the journey? What was waiting for them in Oregon City or West Linn—or beyond?

They drove past a gas station onto a dark two-lane highway. Trees lined both sides of the road, reminding her of Pennsylvania. They were going even slower now, slow enough she could hear their kidnappers talking.

"Should be somewhere along here," Tara said. She tapped the window. "I hate all these trees. They make me feel claustrophobic."

Was this another layover location or was this where they'd hand her and the kids over to the traffickers? Kate's brain balked at the possibility. But she had to face it, accept it and be ready to fight for the kids.

"This is it," Tara declared in a triumphant voice.

A rustic sign beside the road read *West Bridge Park.* The van passed the sign and jolted onto a dirt road. Tieno bounced awake with a small cry. Lupita moaned and stirred.

Kate returned to her seat.

"I should tell Daddy we made it here okay." Tara sounded excited.

"You just called him."

"He wants to share our triumphs."

"Why don't you text the man?"

"He says texting is for sissies."

Ramsey shook his head. "And we're letting the idiot run this operation."

"Don't you call my Daddy an idiot. You don't even own a phone. You have no idea how to text."

"I'll call him anything I want."

Their voices were loud. Kate was sorry the children had been startled out of dreamland by fighting. She and Mike had fought, but at least it wasn't in front of the kids. Thinking about her husband hurt. She longed to tell him how much she loved him. How much she missed him…

"Daddy, we're here," Tara shouted.

"Quiet." Ramsey yanked the phone from her hand. "You'll wreck everything."

"We're out in the boondocks. Nobody can hear me."

"Did you see all the traffic? And the houses we just passed? This isn't Wyoming." He cursed. "I should have brought someone with brains."

"Give me my phone. I need to talk to Daddy."

"No you don't."

"Yes I—"

"Where's the next turn?"

"The directions are on my phone."

He handed it to her. "Hang up."

Tara snatched the cell phone from his hand. Without comment, she lifted the phone, tapped it and began to read. "After a quarter mile, take the dirt road on the right and drive into the trees."

Less than a minute later, Ramsey swung the van to the right. The van rattled over a bumpy road and jerked to a bone-jarring stop. He grunted. "End of the road. Give me the flashlight from the glove box."

Tara complied. Kate was amazed the obstinate, self-absorbed woman did whatever he asked, even when he treated her like trash. Evidently she thought he was her path to riches.

Ramsey got out of the van.

Kate moved to the front and tried to watch him but saw only circles of light flicker off tree trunks and over the ground. "Tara…" She grasped the grid. "There's still time. You can drive us out of here and save yourself another trip to prison. But you need to hurry."

"I told you to leave me alone." Tara stared at the window. "You're just trying to save your ugly hide."

"Take the kids to a safe place and then you can do whatever you want with me."

"I want you dead." Tara swung around, her flying hair colored by the dash lights. "That's what I want. If I had my way, we would have dumped your body beside the road miles ago."

Kate recoiled, surprised by the depth of her animosity. "Please, Tara, the kids—"

"You stole Michael from me, you stole the Whispering Pines from me and you, you…set me up for prison. You're the one who got me arrested."

Kate lifted her chin. Tara had sealed her own doom.

"Every day in prison—every single day, I thought about how much I hate you and how I was going to get revenge." She pounded the metal screen between them. "This is it. No way am I going to let it slip through my fingers. It's a win-win in every way for me—and for Michael."

"Michael?" Kate tilted her head.

"He's—"

The driver-side door creaked open.

Kate crept back to her seat. She'd gotten nowhere with Tara, except deeper into her delusions.

Ramsey put the van in gear, lurched between trees and over roots and rocks into an even darker thicket. The engine had barely died, when he growled, "Neilson."

Fingering her wedding rings, she waited to respond. For all he knew, she was asleep.

"Neilson, answer me."

"What?"

"Wake the brats."

She turned to the children. "Sounds like we're getting out. Hold hands and stay together."

Lupita yawned. "Where?"

"I don't know, sweetie, but Jesus will go with us." She stretched to pat the girl's leg. "Release your seatbelt."

The back door screeched open and a moist, fecund smell crowded into the van. Were they near a lake or a river? Or was this the way coastal Oregon smelled? She heard a steady rumble in the distance. What was that?

Ramsey directed the flashlight at them. "Out."

Kate lowered her head to avoid the glare and saw a gun in his other hand. She jumped from the van to help Tieno, then Shannon and Lupita drop to the soft ground. When she straightened, Ramsey slammed the side of her head with the gun.

Kate staggered and fell against the van.

Shannon cried, "Don't hurt Miss Kate."

He swung toward the girl. "Shut it."

The light flashed Kate's direction. "Payback, like I promised. Now stand up and do what I say."

Using the side of the van for support, she pushed upright, her head reeling.

"Hughes, you take the girls. Stick your gun in the back of the big one, grab the Spicaninny's hand, and walk ahead of me. I'll take Nielson and the kid."

"I need light," Tara said. "So I don't trip."

"Shouldn't have worn such stupid shoes. Move it."

Kate took a breath to try to clear her throbbing head and grabbed Tieno's hand. Together they stumbled forward, propelled by the gun in her ribs. Though Ramsey's light flickered between the feet of those in front of them, Tara tripped again and again, dragging Lupita with her. Kate prayed Tara's finger wasn't on the trigger. If so, Shannon was in great danger.

A terrible heaviness settled on her shoulders. She touched her sore, swollen temple, longing for sleep, and pictured herself curled against her husband in their warm, safe bed. But even as the image shot through her brain, she knew it was an impossible dream. *Revive my senses, God, and give me strength for whatever is ahead.*

They filed onto what she assumed was a path because it had fewer obstructions. The noise got louder. She looked up. Not too far away, traffic flowed over an elevated freeway, most likely the one they'd just exited.

Tara stopped. "Here's the river." She rubbed her bare arms. "It's chilly."

Ramsey skimmed his light across the water and then over a small boat.

Kate glanced at the river. Pinpoints of light from the opposite shore rippled on the current, reflections of businesses and homes. They were near civilization, thank God. The more people, the better her chances of finding someone to help them.

The river was wide but not as wide as some she'd seen. She could swim it, if needed. Beyond the lights and the cloud that dimmed the moon's light, a meteor zipped through the midnight-blue sky into a hazy indigo horizon.

Ramsey pulled Tieno from her grasp, dumped him in the rowboat and handed him the flashlight. "Hold this." He waved his gun at Kate. "Nielson, help me."

Kate took hold of the other side of the boat and they slid it into the river. In less than ten steps, she was wet to her knees. The water, which was cool but not unbearably cold, felt good and smelled fresh. She considered diving in for a quick bath, but Ramsey was already ushering the others to the boat.

He positioned himself at the front, facing backward, and told her to sit in the middle and man the oars. Tieno and Lupita were crammed between her and Ramsey. Shannon and Tara sat behind her.

Tara read from her phone. "Row under the bridge on the right and across the river."

"Get moving, Neilson." Ramsey's voice was a low growl.

Kate tugged at the oars. Flexing her arms and shoulder muscles felt good after being confined for so long. But she was rowing against the current. How long could she keep at it? A line from Mike's song came to her. *I will give you strength and help you.*

She repeated the phrase in her head as she rowed. *I will give you strength and help you. I will give you strength and help you.* And then she hummed the entire song under her breath.

Do not fear, for I am with you
Do not fear, I am your God
I will give you strength and help you
Hold you with my strong right hand

"Faster," Ramsey ordered.

Kate was tempted to capsize the boat and make a scene. But what if no one came to their rescue and the kids drowned? They didn't have life jackets and she didn't see any other boats on the water, except a handful of empty ones moored along the shore.

Something crawled from the paddle onto her hand. She shook it off into the river, glad she couldn't see whatever it was.

A different kind of roar came from the well-lit buildings they were approaching on the right. A factory maybe. Or a power plant. White clouds illuminated by the lights rose above the edifices, bright against the night sky. By now the sound was really loud. If she called for help, she'd never be heard, even if someone were on the shore.

Kate rested her arms. *Do not fear, for I am with you, do not fear, I am your God* played in her head. Ramsey was staring at the buildings. Thanks to the noise, he couldn't hear if she was paddling or not. She hoped the thunderous sound wasn't scaring the kids.

Tara poked Kate in the back. "Aim for the single yellow light."

She shook out her arms and began to row diagonally across the current, which was becoming more and more turbulent. Choppy waves rocked the boat. She strained, breathing hard. Humidity clung to her skin like plastic wrap. *I will give you strength and help you, hold you with my strong right hand...*

At least now she knew their destination. The rowing would end soon. Trouble awaited them on the other shore, but defending the children on dry land would be easier than on the water.

The factory noise receded, replaced by the sound of rushing water. Soon, they were so close to a waterfall she could barely hear the boat paddles splash in and out of the river. Thanks to the lights across the river, she could tell the water plummeted over a wide cliff but that's all she could make out.

The buildings they approached were also vaguely illuminated by the lights from the other side of the river. Some were large, others smaller or round. The profiles suggested warehouses or a factory, maybe a flour mill like the one in Idaho.

When they neared the shore, Tara called, "He says to tie the boat beneath the wharf, Jer, and climb the ladder."

Ramsey aimed his flashlight beam below the yellow light. "Over there." Evidently neither abductor was concerned someone might hear them. The waterfall noise was loud, but not so loud they couldn't be heard. Was the complex deserted? It wasn't brightly lit like the buildings on the other side of the river.

Stained concrete stanchions rose up before them in the gloom. Kate slowed her rowing. This would be a good time to turn the boat around. But any kind of confrontation on the flimsy vessel would cause them all to topple into the river.

They drifted beneath the pier to a moss-covered rock foundation. Kate caught a whiff of mold and sneezed, jerking the oars. The boat rammed the wall.

Tara cried, "Watch out."

Ramsey swore. "Clumsy broad." He ran the light back and forth on the rock wall until it landed on a corroded metal ladder. "Over there." Rung by rung, his beam highlighted the ladder's rusty condition. Kate paddled closer. She'd never seen such a tall ladder.

Balanced on his knees, Ramsey tied the boat to the bottom rung. "Come here, brat." He motioned to Tieno. "You're going up top with me."

"M-m-miss K-kate…" Through the dusky light, Kate saw the little boy reach for her.

Before she could respond, Ramsey wrapped one arm across Tieno's chest and latched onto a rung with the other. Shoving off from the boat, he shifted their weight to the ladder.

The rowboat rocked and banged against the wall. Tara shrieked.

Shannon gasped but Lupita made no sound. Kate struggled to stabilize the boat with the oars, all the while praying the ladder would support the pair. And that the boat wouldn't tip and drown the others.

Ramsey disappeared over the top but his light soon reappeared. "Nielson, bring up the Spicaninny."

Kate clamped her teeth. She hated it when he called Lupi names. Touching the girl's back, she said, "Crawl to the front of the boat, Lupi."

Lupi hesitated.

Ramsey swore and waggled the light. "Now."

"Let's get on our hands and knees," Kate said. "I'll be right behind you." They crawled to the front, rocking the boat as they went. With each wobble, Lupita let out a frightened squeak. Behind them, Shannon's moans offset Tara's curses. Kate stood, grasped a rung to steady her stance and lifted Lupi, who clutched her shoulders with painful desperation.

"Good girl," Kate said. "Now let's scooch you to my back. I'll hang onto your arm while you change positions."

Lupi began to shake.

"Move it, Neilson." The light twitched.

"Please, Lupi." Kate angled her head away from the light. "I'll hold you."

The boat swayed as they made the switch. "I need both hands to pull us up the ladder." Kate spoke over her shoulder. "Don't let go of me."

No response.

"Promise me you'll hang on all the way to the top." The decay stench irritated her sinuses, but she stifled the sneeze that threatened. No way would she chance knocking Lupi off her back.

The little girl's trembles vibrated Kate's ribs. "Say it, Lupi."

Lupi whispered in her ear, "I hold tight."

Chapter Twenty

M ike gave up on sleep and crawled out of bed just as dawn broke over the ranch. He wandered into the kitchen to find Laura already there, making coffee. The radio was on but the volume was so low he hadn't heard it in the bedroom.

"Morning, Mom. Any news I should know about?"

"Same stuff as yesterday, except they added descriptions of Kate and the kids and used all our names." She switched off the radio. "Former inmate *Kate Neilson Duncan* disappeared with three children from Freedom House, the children's home she started with her mother-in-law, *Laura Duncan*, co-owner with *Michael Duncan* of the Whispering Pines Guest Ranch near Copperville, Wyoming. Her abandoned car was discovered in the parking lot of the Cheyenne Frontier Mall, but no trace of Duncan or the children has been found."

She offered a wry smile. "Everyone in the country will know our names by the time this is said and done."

Mike scowled. "Why'd they have to name the ranch?" Bad publicity year after year could hurt business.

"Mike…" Laura's forehead creased. "Worse than that, Freedom House was named. We've made it a point to fly under the radar to keep the curious as well as the nefarious away from the children. Most of our guests come from far away and know very little about the WP's history, other than what they read on our website or in a brochure or other marketing material. The ranch will survive negative publicity as it has in the past, but the children's home, that's a horse of a different color."

"I hadn't thought about Freedom House." Mike rubbed his jaw. After all his bellyaching, the idea of losing the children's home should have made him happy. Yet, the kids needed Freedom House as much as he needed his wife. And Freedom House needed to be a safe place for the children and the staff.

"There's more." Laura leaned back against the counter. "The reporter interviewed the director of a children's home on the other side of the state, a woman, who said the case brings up important questions. Why does an isolated ranch have a children's home? What are we hiding? Why was a previously incarcerated person not only given free access to the children but allowed to travel alone with them? And why did the Pennsylvania governor pardon a woman who's no longer a resident?"

She folded her arms. "And then she said, 'Thanks to the governor of another state, the citizens of Wyoming are suffering the consequences of an unwarranted pardon. A criminal who apparently hasn't been fully rehabilitated has slipped out of sight and taken children with her.'"

"That's pure conjecture." Mike scowled. "She knows nothing about Kate."

"Right. On top of that, they aired her words without a rebuttal. We know our sweet Kate hasn't done anything wrong." She paused. "But most people don't know her like we do. They just see her record."

He looked at the floor. He thought he knew his wife. But the argument they had before she left was the worst one ever. Had he pushed her over the edge? Mike swiped his hand across his eyes. "I need coffee."

Laura took a hot pad from a drawer, opened the oven and pulled out a pan of muffins. "I know neither of us feels much like eating, but we've got to preserve our strength for whatever is ahead." She placed the pan on a trivet.

"So that's what smells so good."

"I had to substitute a couple ingredients. Used some of the applesauce Kate and I canned last fall in place of bananas and replaced the eggs and oil with mayonnaise. But I think they'll be edible."

"You could borrow food from the dining hall."

"I know, but I hate to cut into Cyrus's inventory." She closed the oven and opened the refrigerator. "I'll warm the breakfast casserole Betsy brought over yesterday. You have any idea when the detectives are coming?"

"Bledsoe said 'bright and early,' whatever that means."

"I have a feeling they'll be here before long."

"Hope so. I need to get on the road." Mike plucked a muffin from the pan.

"Are you taking Clint with you? You two make a good team."

He tossed the muffin from palm to palm to cool it. True, they worked well together, most of the time. And he could use Clint's help. Two heads were always better than one.

The bell on the lobby counter rang. Mike frowned. He must have forgotten to lock the front door. "That's them right now." He started toward the lobby. The detectives were certainly early enough. The sun was just now silhouetting the mountain.

"Ask if they'd like breakfast. We've got plenty."

He walked past the office door and into the lobby, where he halted. "Cal…what are you doing here so early? Stop by for a cup of coffee?"

"Sounds good. I'm dead on my feet. But the real reason is to give you a heads-up about the next step in the investigation before I go off-duty for the day."

"Come on back." Mike led him into their living quarters. "Coffee is perked and breakfast should be ready soon. You're welcome to join us."

"If it's not too much trouble. I hate to barge in on you."

"As long as you're not a reporter, you're welcome at our table."

"Gotta be tough for you and your mom." Cal shook his head. "News reports are getting dicey, from what I hear."

They stopped in the kitchen long enough for Mike to pour the deputy a cup of coffee. "You take it black, right?"

"Right. Thanks."

Mike refreshed his own coffee and the two sat at the dining room table, the scent of their coffee mingling with that of muffins, sausage, eggs, onions and peppers.

"I appreciate your hospitality," Cal said, "but this isn't a social call."

"What was that about the next step?" Mike asked.

"Hi, Cal." Laura came around the corner. "I thought I heard your voice."

Cal nodded. "Good morning, Laura."

Mike lifted his cup. "I invited Cal to breakfast, Mom."

"Great. It's almost ready." She sat down. "Thanks to friends, we've got more than enough for the two of us. I'm glad we can share with you, so it won't go to waste."

"Like I told Mike, I appreciate your hospitality, but this isn't a social call." Cal glanced from Laura to Mike. "The Cheyenne PD is sending detectives up here today. You knew that, right?"

"We were told they'd show up first thing this morning," Mike said.

"Then I'd better talk fast." The deputy set his cup down. "Just so you know, they may ask to search your computers, your paper files, your phone records, your home, your cars, the barn, the children's home…anywhere Kate and or the kids spent time. Plus, they'll try to figure out why an ex-con was allowed to establish a treatment home for children."

"That's easy," Mike said. "The governor of Pennsylvania pardoned her. Besides, Freedom House is in Mom's name, not Kate's." He might not be able to set the record straight with the media, but he could tell the police the truth.

"They'll dig deeper than the obvious. Ask plenty of questions—like, what do you know about your wife's past? Why was she pardoned? Was the governor bribed? Why was a license granted for a children's home so far away from civilization? Were votes or money or power involved?"

"They can find answers to those questions through their government sources," Laura said.

"They'll ask you, just the same." He took a sip of coffee. "They may ask why you don't have children of your own, Mike. And why an ex-con was allowed to be alone with the kids. How did Kate act when she was them? What was her role at the children's home? Why did she have only three of the five children with her? Were they her favorites?"

The room brightened with the sun's rising but not so much that they switched off the ceiling lights.

"Did her behavior change before this happened?" Cal continued. "Was she upset about anything? How did she interact with your staff?"

Motioning to Laura, Cal said, "They'll ask personal questions. Did Kate get along with you, her mother-in-law? What about all the WP's legal wranglings in recent years? How is the ranch doing financially? Does Kate have access to ranch records, to bank accounts? Has she withdrawn any large sums lately? How does she handle personal money and family finances? Who are her relatives?"

The kitchen timer dinged. "Excuse me," Laura said. "I'll be right back."

Cal turned to Mike, whose head was beginning to spin. "They'll ask about your marriage. Might even ask about your sex life and what activities or interests the two of you share."

Mike rubbed his finger along the table edge. How would he avoid talking about the argument?

"Yeah, I know," Cal said. "Invasive. But they have to dig up all the weeds, turn over every boulder and find the worms. We'd do the same thing." He winked. "Although I like to think we'd be kinder and gentler and all that warm fuzzy stuff."

The deputy turned serious again. "They'll question your ranch hands, your cleaning staff, your cooks. Maybe even your guests."

Mike sighed and shook his head.

Laura slid placemats onto the table and returned with plates filled with muffins and egg casserole.

"Thanks, Laura. Smells great. Can't think of a better way to come off a graveyard shift." Cal picked up his fork and cut into the casserole. "Back to the detectives. Be careful not to get your hackles up. Their goal is to help you, even when they're abrasive and accusatory. The more open and cooperative you are, the better they'll treat you."

Mike pulled the salt and pepper close. "I'll try to remember that."

"If I were you," Cal said, "I'd back up your computer files on a cloud server and whatever other means you have and plan on leasing other computers for the duration."

"You think they'd really take our computers?" Laura poured him a glass of orange juice.

"Strong possibility."

She groaned. "Bad time of year to switch out computers." She picked up her plate. "Thanks for the heads-up, Cal. I'll go start a backup now. I ran one a couple days ago, so it shouldn't take long."

The deputy watched her walk away before he turned to Mike. "Seems like every time I talk to you, I give you more bad news."

"I s'pose that comes with the territory." Mike leaned across the table. "Can I count on you to pass along any news you hear about Kate? I have a feeling the detectives may not be generous with their findings."

"I'll do what I can."

~:~:~

"Here goes." Kate released Lupita's arm and grabbed the highest rung she could reach. Grasping the ladder with both hands, she hopped onto the bottom rung. But one foot slipped off the slick surface into the water.

Trying not to panic, she held tight and felt for a foothold in the rock wall. Finding an indentation, she shoved the toe of her sandal into it, regained her balance and lifted her foot to the rung.

"Get up here." Ramsey's flashlight glared in her eyes.

"You just blinded me."

"You don't need to see. Keep moving."

Kate closed her eyes against the glare and felt for the next crusted rung. Lupita's stranglehold made breathing difficult. And she was growing heavier by the second. *I need your strong right hand, God.* Seizing the rung, she forced one foot upward, found traction, and then lifted the other.

One hand, one foot at a time, she fought to make it to the top, muscles burning. She grasped the final slimy rung with one hand. But before she could take hold with her other hand, she lost her grip.

Lupi squealed and squeezed even harder, her heels digging into Kate's abdomen.

Kate caught the next lower rung in time to avert a plunge into the dark river below.

Ramsey held out a hand but she wasn't about to touch him. Mustering all her strength, she pushed upward to the top rung and pulled the two of them over the crumbling cement edge.

They'd barely gotten to their feet when Ramsey thrust them out of the way and yelled down to the boat, "Send the girl up, Hughes, and then you come."

Tara called, "But who's gonna steady the boat for me?"

"Nobody," he hollered back.

"I can't—"

"Stay in the boat then. Fine by me. I can handle this operation on my own. But if you come up, cut the boat loose after you're on the ladder."

Despite Tara's yelps and curses, both she and Shannon made it to the top. Kate drew the children into an embrace. Only God knew how they would escape this nightmare. For now, she was grateful they were together and none of them had dropped into the river.

Mike picked up his and Cal's plates and took them to the kitchen. He was rinsing them when the lobby bell rang. Tramp followed him into the lobby, where two men waited. Both were of medium height, but that's where the similarity stopped. The huskier man was steely-eyed and balding. The other man had a lanky build and dishwater-blonde hair.

"Good morning." Mike nodded. "How can I help you?"

Tramp wagged his tail.

Mike could tell the slender guy was fighting the temptation to pet his dog.

The somber man held out his ID. "I'm Detective Moore with the Cheyenne Police Department." He aimed his chin at the other man. "And this is Detective Schroeder."

After they shook hands, Moore said, "Was that the sheriff or a deputy who just drove away?"

"Deputy."

"What was he doing here? Something going on?"

"Deputy Gardner patrols this neck of the woods. He's the one I called when Kate and the kids didn't come home from Cheyenne." Just to be sure they understood that Cal's concern for his neighbors went beyond the time clock, Mike added, "He worked the night shift last night and stopped by on his way home to check on us."

Moore motioned to Schroeder. "Make a note to speak with Deputy Gardner." To Mike, he said, "Mr. Duncan, as I'm sure Detective Bledsoe told you, we're here to investigate the disappearance of your wife and three children. We'll begin by talking with key players at the ranch and at the children's home this morning. Our afternoon and evening interviews will depend on what we learn this morning."

Schroeder lifted a clipboard, wrote something and said, "We need a private place to conduct our interviews. Do you have a vacant office we can use?"

"Good morning, gentlemen." Laura walked from the office to stand behind the counter.

The detectives turned to her.

She smiled. "We only have one office shared by several people. But you're welcome to use our private quarters."

"This is my mom," Mike said. "Laura Duncan."

After the men shook her hand, Schroeder handed her and Mike business cards.

"Thank you for your offer." Moore gave each of them a card. "May we take a look?"

"I've got work to do here," Laura said, "but Mike can show you around."

Chapter Twenty-One

"Follow me." Mike led the detectives to his family's living quarters at the back of the building. The detectives bypassed the couch and chairs clustered in front of the fireplace and walked directly to the dining room table on the far side of the open room.

"Perfect." Moore glanced at the door that led to the patio. "Unless this is a high-traffic area."

"Shouldn't be." Not with Kate and Aunt Mary gone and Mom busy up front. She'd man the phones, which would start ringing again soon. More and more friends were calling for updates. And then there were the reporters...

"You want to talk with me first?" He'd already been grilled by Bledsoe. This wouldn't be much different. The sooner they were done with him, the sooner he could go looking for Kate.

"We'll begin with you. When we're finished, we'll speak with Mrs. Duncan and then those in your employ who work directly with your wife. After that, we'll talk with individuals at the children's home."

"Have a seat." Mike indicated the chairs and pulled out one for himself. "Bathroom is around the corner. Coffee in the kitchen. I can pour you a cup, if you'd like."

Moore eyed him. "Maybe later."

Mike lifted an eyebrow. Did the man think he was going to drop rat poison in their coffee?

Schroeder pulled a small device from his shirt pocket and pushed a button. "This is a recorder. Michael Duncan, are you aware this discussion is being recorded?"

"Guess I am now."

The questions were standard, ones he'd answered previously or Cal had warned him about. He was just beginning to relax, when Moore asked, "Do you own a cell phone?"

"Yes."

"Is it on your person?"

"I don't carry it with me."

"Why not?"

"You may have already noticed that cell service doesn't extend to this ranch. No use carrying a phone I can't use." Mike touched the radio on his belt. "We use two-ways."

"Where is your cell phone?"

"In my bedroom."

"I'd like to take a look at it."

Mike got up and walked to the bedroom he shared with Kate. Why the detective asked to see a phone he didn't use was senseless. But he'd cooperate so they didn't think he was trying to hide something.

When he returned, phone in hand, he said, "Don't know if it's has power. I haven't charged it in a while."

"Flip phone, huh. Didn't know they still made those." Moore pushed the "on" button and waited for the phone to power up.

Mike dug his fingers into his thighs to slow his jiggling knees. The detectives might interpret the action as nervousness, when impatience was what spiked his blood pressure right now. He needed to get on the road to find his wife. And they needed to get off their duffs and look for his wife. Yet, here they all sat. Doing nothing.

Moore showed Schroeder the readout.

Schroeder nodded. "No service."

Mike refrained from commenting. Did they think he'd lie to them?

Moore put the phone down and pulled a folded piece of paper from his shirt pocket. He laid it on the table, smoothing the creases. "Apparently your wife sent you text messages and tried to call you on your cell phone."

"What?" Mike jerked upright. "When? Why didn't she call the house? She knows I don't use that phone on the ranch."

The detective raised his palm. "From what we can tell, these messages were left before she disappeared."

Mike bent closer. "What kind of messages?"

"Here's the first one, sent Saturday morning." Moore read from the paper. "You could have at least said goodbye." He studied Mike. "Any idea what that means?"

Mike rubbed his palms against his Levis. If he were a swearing man, he'd be coloring the air with a few choice words right now. "Yeah, well...it's like this. We had an argument the night before she left. I was still fuming the next morning." He shook his head. "As you might guess, I now regret how I acted."

"Give us the specifics of the disagreement."

"I can't give you a verbatim account." Mike crossed his arms. "But the short of it is I thought she was spending too much time over at Freedom House, the children's home we opened a few months ago, and not enough time with me."

Talking about his behavior made him realize how selfish he was. He rubbed his neck. "She wanted me to go with her and the kids to Cheyenne. But I said I was too busy. Now, of course, I wish I'd gone."

Moore's deadpan visage did not alter. "A couple hours later, someone at her number left this voice message." He pulled a recorder just like Schroeder's from his pocket and pushed a button. "*Hi, Mike. Just wanted to say I don't like what happened last night and I'm...*"

Mike clenched the sides of the chair to keep from ripping the recorder from the detective's hands. It was her. Kate. The sound of her voice deepened the lonely ache in his gut. First chance he had, he'd drive up on top the nearest rise just to hear her voice on his phone again.

"Is that your wife's voice?"

He nodded, unable to speak.

"Please speak up for the recording."

He cleared his throat. "Yes."

"Can you explain the message?"

Mike shrugged. What more could he add?

"She sounds angry," Schroeder said.

"Terse, maybe, or rushed. But not angry. Remember, she had three young children with her. That's why she wanted me to go with her. My guess is she was interrupted." He clamped his jaw. Other men, total strangers, had access to personal messages from his wife before he did. But they expected him to interpret those messages. His world had flipped upside-down.

"Next was a hang-up," Moore said, "followed by this text. He read from the paper. "*I hate what's happened to us. I love you and I love the kids. I want to do what's best for all of us.*"

Schroeder rested his forearms on the table. "She loves those kids."

"And she loves me. You just heard it."

"How bad was the fight?" Moore asked. "Did it get physical?"

"It wasn't a *fight*. It was a disagreement." Mike gripped the table edge. "And it wasn't physical. I didn't touch Kate. She didn't touch me."

He wiped his sweaty palms on his jeans. "We rarely have conflicts. We would have worked it out."

The detectives studied him, doubt written across their faces. Moore asked, "How often do you argue?"

"Hardly ever. And, like I said, when we have a disagreement, we eventually work it out."

Schroeder tapped his pen on the notepad. "Medical records show your wife is incapable of conception. Could it be disappearing is her way to escape your disapproval and be with the children she loves somewhere far away from you?"

"Are you serious?" Mike stared at him. "After all we went through to set up the children's home? All the training, all the government red tape? You should understand that."

No response.

He flattened his palms on the tabletop and straightened his elbows. "Kate wouldn't take those kids away from Freedom House. They're traumatized children who need the help that's provided there."

Moore lifted his hands. "Women and hormones…" He raised his eyebrows. "Let's just say they sometimes act irrationally."

Mike gaped at the man. "You gotta be kidding me."

"Was your wife on hormone therapy?"

"Not that I know of. But you should know. You have access to her medical records."

Out of the corner of his eye, Mike caught sight of Tramp standing at the backdoor. He got up to let the dog out, glad to have an excuse to move. "Check our medicine cabinet. We have nothing to hide."

"We'll speak with her doctors."

What happened to doctor-patient confidentiality? Mike clenched his jaw. When she was hospitalized, Kate's doctor wouldn't discuss her health with him without written authorization from her.

"We'll also do a room-by-room examination of this building." Schroeder lifted an official-looking piece of paper from his clipboard. "Search warrant."

Moore stood. "I'll use your restroom now and pour myself a cup of coffee, if you don't mind."

Mike was about to tell the men where to find the cups but decided they could search the cupboards themselves. They were going to do that anyway.

"We don't want to disturb ranch activities," Schroeder said. "But please ask your staff to stay this afternoon in case we need to ask—"

"Excuse me, gentlemen." Dymple Forbes hobbled into the room, canvas bags hanging from each arm. "I'm sorry to interrupt, but I'll just be a minute."

Ramsey on her heels, Kate followed behind the children as they trudged single-file in and out of ramshackle buildings and over mossy paths. Inside the buildings, their footsteps echoed and water dripped. Outside, the roar of the paper mill across the river melded with the waterfall's thunder and rolled between the structures.

Tara led the way, using her phone for directions as well as for a light inside the dark structures. She squealed every time her high heels slid on the slick, pitted catwalks that spanned pools of stagnant water. Ramsey's flashlight beam bounced off the green water below them, revealing massive concrete supports.

"Be careful, kiddos," Kate called. "Watch out for holes in the floor." Red plastic warning strips hung from wires along each side of the narrow walkways, but the solitary lines provided scant protection.

Ramsey growled, "Quiet."

The smell of mildew and the sound of trickling water shadowed them through the dank, suffocating grayness. Kate swallowed the urge to sneeze and fought for balance every time she tripped over debris. She tried to keep the children on their feet, but their abductors, who made no effort to help, cursed them and called them foul names.

Between buildings, the early morning light revealed grayed, pocked sidewalks. Vines drifted across damp walkways, over moss-darkened wood piles and up mineral-streaked walls, interrupted here and there by corroded metal doors. The place was creepy, yet the random structures and the heavy vegetation that had overtaken the place offered plenty of hiding places.

Tara screamed, "Snake," and jumped backward, knocking Tieno down.

He rolled to his feet and ran to Kate, Lupita and Shannon close behind. "I hate snakes," Shannon whispered. Kate had a good idea where her fear originated. She'd seen the rattlesnake pit the Texas brothel used to control their workers and had had horrible dreams for weeks after. How much worse the experience was for the children, she could only imagine.

"Oh, for crying out loud." Ramsey directed his flashlight at the sidewalk. "It's small, just a—"

"I don't care what it is." Tara's voice shook. "A snake is a snake."

Sensing a weak moment, Kate started toward Tara, but Ramsey jabbed her ribs with his gun. "Throw a rock at it, Nielson."

She bit back a retort and crouched on her heels. Barely able to see in the dim light, she ran her fingers over the path and picked up what felt like crumbled cement. She tossed the lump at the reptile but missed. The chunk bounced off the sidewalk and the snake slithered into a tangle of foliage.

Ramsey ordered Kate to stand, rapped the kids on their heads and said, "Back in line."

Tara lifted her foot to step over the spot where the snake had been and then led them into a tall building where wan daylight filtered through dirty windows high above. They passed rusted elevator doors, oxidized machinery and green-coated walls. At the far end of the building, they stopped at the base of a metal staircase.

One by one, they climbed the steep steps to a catwalk. Kate tried not to think about how rickety the structure was or how it swayed. She held the railing with one hand and grasped Lupi's hand with the other, all the while praying for safety. Shannon held Tieno's hand.

A vast expanse of emptiness, barely visible in the faint light, spread below them. *What is this place?* Large, peeling letters stretched across the adjoining wall. She could barely make out the faded words. "Blue Heron Paper Company." Next to the washed-out lettering, a blue-tinted bird with a wide wingspan appeared to be in flight.

They reached the end of the catwalk. Stepping through a short doorway, Kate breathed again and relaxed her hold on Lupi's hand. She didn't know what awaited them here, but at least they were off that wobbly walkway.

They stood in a huge open area with thick wooden support posts, wide overhead beams and big windows. Massive machinery lined both walls. Walking from darkness into the beginnings of daylight gave Kate hope. Now she could see where they were. Now she could plot their escape.

"Stop dawdling, Neilson." Ramsey rammed the gun into her ribs again. Did he aim for the same spot each time? Her back was beginning to hurt worse than her head.

From the open area, they were shunted into a long unlit hallway with doors on each side. Tara stopped in front of one marked "Human Resources" and read from her phone. "Key in hole in red chair cushion." She pointed at a faded red office chair propped against an open door across the hall. "Isn't this fun? It's like a treasure hunt."

Kate rolled her eyes. *And you're a pirate on a slave ship, stealing people to sell them into slavery.* With any luck, Tara would walk the plank, along with Ramsey. She peered down the dark hallway. If she could get Shannon's attention while their captors were looking for the key, the two of them could grab the younger ones and make a run for it.

But before she could nudge Shannon, Ramsey handed Tieno the flashlight. "Hold this." He grabbed the boy's arm and marched him to the chair. Kate could tell from the shivering beam that Tieno was shaking. She ached for the frightened child.

Ramsey growled, "Hold still," and dug the key out of the chair. Then he dragged Tieno across the hall to the HR office, where he ordered the boy to shine the light on the doorknob while he unlocked the door.

Tara bounced on her toes. "We did it, Jer, we did it. We're here."

He opened the door and jerked the flashlight from Tieno's hands. "Get in there, all of you."

Chapter Twenty-Two

M ike stood. "Morning, Dymple. You're out and about early today."

"Good morning, Mike. I'm just here to drop off some goodies."

"You're spoiling me again." He motioned toward the two men. "Dymple Forbes, I'd like you to meet Detectives Moore and Schroeder from the Cheyenne Police Department."

The men stood and spoke in unison. "Nice to meet you."

Mike watched them look the elderly woman over, from her bright blue eyes, wrinkled cheeks, red lipstick and the long white braid that hung down her back, to her canvas bags, denim jumper and hiking boots.

"Nice to meet you, too." Dymple set her bags on the table and shook their hands. "Looks like you three could use a scone break."

"Dymple's scones are the best." Mike raised a thumb.

She stood on tiptoe to kiss his cheek. "My favorite grandson."

Moore raised his eyebrows. "You're his grandmother?"

"Adopted," Dymple said. "Never had chipmunks. But this guy is better than a dozen kids or grandkids."

The detectives shared a questioning glance.

Mike grinned. Dymple's aphasia had struck again.

She lifted a Mason jar filled with purple liquid from one of the bags. "You can put this in your refrigerator, Mike. I know you like it cold. Unless..." She turned to the other men. "Would you gentlemen care to sample my chokecherry wine?" She winked. "Folks in these parts call it Dymple's Delight."

"Uh, thanks for the offer." Moore looked like he was trying to contain a smile. "But we're on the clock."

"Then you're both welcome to stop by my house for a sip when you're off-duty." She pulled a foil-covered plate from the second satchel. "Fresh from the oven walnut-cinnamon scones." She folded back a corner of the foil.

A warm spicy scent filled the room. Schroeder inched closer and breathed deeply. He looked at Moore, who said, "We don't usually..."

Mike saw the longing in their eyes. They'd probably skipped breakfast to get an early start this morning. But that was their problem, not his.

"Do you gentlemen drink coffee?" Dymple asked.

They nodded.

She put her hand on Mike's arm. "If you'll bring out the coffee pot, I'll be glad to pour Mr. Schroeder and Mr. Moore each a cup of coffee."

Mike peered down at her, frowning. He saw no reason to share the scones with men who questioned his and Kate's integrity.

She raised an eyebrow.

"Uh, sure." He hurried to the kitchen, where he placed the wine on a center rack in the nearly empty refrigerator and pulled three mugs from the cupboard. Rather than take the coffee pot to the dining room, he decided to pour the coffee himself. Dymple could serve the scones, *his* scones, to the detectives.

His hands trembled and his vision was so blurry he could barely see to fill the cups. What was Kate trying to say? Did she want to work things out? Or had she taken off with the kids, like the detectives suggested?

From the kitchen, Mike heard Moore say, "Please have a seat, Miss…Forbes was it?"

"Correct. Dymple with a 'Y' Louise Forbes."

For a moment, the only sound was that of chair legs scraping the wood floor.

"Do you live in the area?"

"I live on the other side of Copperville, by the church just off the highway. It's called Highway Haven House of God. I'm sure you saw it when you drove into town." She paused. "Actually, I live next to the cemetery, which is next to the church. I'm the crankshaft."

Mike almost dropped the mug he was filling. *Crankshaft. Good one, Dymple.* He was sorry he couldn't see the detectives' faces.

"I pick up the flowers the wind blows around, trim tree branches, wash headstones in the summertime. A teenager mows the grass."

Tramp barked in the distance. Mike listened. Didn't sound serious. He was probably chasing a barn cat.

"So you're employed by this Highway Haven place?"

"Oh, no. I'm a volunteer, but I do my best to keep it nice. I'll give you a tour when you stop by for that glass of Dymple's Delight. It's a lovely graveyard."

"I'm sure it is."

Mike smirked. Just what he needed. A Dymple intervention.

He replaced the grin with a serious expression and returned to the dining room with napkins, spoons and a mug of coffee, which he placed in front of Dymple. "Dymple is a retired schoolteacher."

"That's right," Dymple said. "I taught third grade in Copperville for thirty years. Many of my students migrated to the far corners of the earth, but many stayed or eventually returned to our beautiful valley to raise their families." She removed the foil from the scones and set it aside. "I'm as proud of their aquariums as if they're my own children."

Mike spun on his heels and headed back to the kitchen.

"Aquariums?" This time it was Schroeder's voice.

"Oh, dear. Is that what I said?"

"I may have misunderstood—"

"I'm sorry." Dymple released an exasperated sigh. "I fell and hit my noggin on a tombstone several years ago. Ever since, I garble my words now and then." She paused. "People around here seem to be able to figure out what I'm trying to say. You're smart men. What do you think I meant?"

"Attitudes?" Moore's voice.

Schroeder added his guess. "Accomplishments?"

"Bingo. You got it, Mr. Schroeder."

Chuckling under his breath, Mike poured the last cup of coffee. He'd gotten so he could usually figure out her intended meaning. Yet her word substitutions never failed to amuse him.

He set the coffee in front of the men and returned to the kitchen for cream and sugar. Back in the dining room, he said, "I'll go tell the others you want to talk with them."

Moore raised a forefinger. "Hold on." He turned to his partner. "Show him the photo."

Schroeder pulled a sheet of paper from his clipboard and handed it to Mike. "Look familiar?"

Mike took one glance, frowned and sat down beside Dymple, holding the sheet with both hands.

Dymple leaned in to study the enlarged photographs. "Oh, yes."

"Ms. Forbes seems to recognize the object. What about you, Mr. Duncan?"

Mike blew out a breath. "It's an earring from a set Mom and I gave Kate when we made her a full partner in the ranch." The W-shaped gold earring in the photo had a small diamond at the peak. "The other one is a P. And the necklace has both a W and a P, for Whispering Pines."

He looked at Schroeder. "Where…?"

"A trucker found it at a rest-area parking lot and gave it to the caretaker. Evidently, sunlight flashing off the diamond caught his attention. That necklace you mentioned—was she wearing it?"

Mike stared at the photograph. He'd barely looked at Kate that morning. He had no idea what she was wearing. "I don't know."

"Do you know where she keeps her jewelry?" Moore asked.

He nodded.

"We'd like to see the necklace, if it's here."

His knees had gone weak when he saw the photo and he wasn't sure he could stand, but he did. Schroeder trailed him into the bedroom and watched him rifle through Kate's necklaces, which along with several scarves, dangled from decorative hooks on the wall. Her perfume lingered on the neck scarves, distracting him.

The WP necklace hung near the front. He lifted it from the hook, handed it to Schroeder and followed him to the dining room, where they slid out their chairs and sat.

Moore took the jewelry, studied it and then told Schroeder to photograph it.

Mike picked up the earring picture. "So you know the exact rest stop where the earring was found?"

Schroeder, who'd just extracted a small camera from his pocket, said, "It's the same Idaho rest area where a dark-haired woman was allegedly soliciting sex early Sunday morning."

"What?" Mike stared at him.

"Just what he said," Moore interjected. "Another trucker had mentioned the solicitation to the caretaker, who thought there might be a connection between the woman and the earring, so he gave it to the next patrolman who stopped there."

He turned to Dymple. "You may want to remove yourself from this conversation."

"No." Mike held up his hand. "I want her to stay."

"I know all about Kate's past, Mr. Moore." Dymple pointed a finger at him. "A past that's exactly that—in the past and under the blood of Jesus."

"Be that as it may, we still need to pursue this line of reasoning." He eyed Mike. "Records show your wife pleaded guilty to prostitution in Pittsburgh, Pennsylvania, more than once."

"Like Dymple said, that's history." Mike clutched the paper. "Who has the earring?"

"It's in good hands."

Yeah, sure. Mike dropped the paper and stood. Time to move on. He looked at Moore. "You done with my phone?"

Moore shook his head. "We'll hang onto it a while longer."

"But what if Kate calls?"

"We'll handle it."

Mike reached across the table to grab a scone and then stepped to the back door. He hated to walk out on Dymple, but he'd had enough and he knew she could hold her own with the detectives. Lifting his hat from the deer-antler coatrack, he opened the door.

"Stay close," Moore said. "We may need to speak with you again."

Mike stepped onto the patio.

Tramp followed him across the deck and around the building to the lobby. Inside the office, Laura looked up from her desk, where both she and Amy sat in front of a computer monitor. "Done with the detectives?"

"Yeah." He swiped crumbs from his mouth with the back of his hand. "You're next, after Dymple. She walked in with scones and they started asking her questions."

Tramp trotted directly to Amy, who kissed his head and rubbed his ears. "Tramp, I'm so glad you came to see me."

He sniffed her leg and she laughed. "I know, I know. You smell my dogs, but they stayed home today."

"Scones?" Coach, who sat at a desk on the other side of the room, looked offended. Despite being wheelchair-bound, he was muscular and athletic-looking. "Police detectives get Dymple's scones but we don't?"

"If you're lucky," Mike said, "there might be a morsel or two left when you talk with them."

"They want to talk to me? I don't know the kids."

"But you know Kate. They plan to speak with those who work the closest with her." He turned to Amy. "Even though you just started working here, they'll probably want to interview you, too."

"Oh, great." Amy's forehead creased. "After prison and Texas, I was hoping to never talk to another detective—or any other law enforcement officer, for that matter."

"Sorry, honey." Laura squeezed Amy's shoulder and then motioned to Mike. "How did the interview go?"

"Uh…" Mike shrugged, not sure what to say regarding the experience. "I'll tell you about it later. Right now, I need to tell Cyrus, Clint and Fletcher the detectives want to interview them this morning. They'll talk with our other employees later, after the Freedom House visit. Everyone is supposed to hang tight until after they've been interviewed."

He gave his mom a wry smile. "That could be either late this afternoon or this evening and could cost us some overtime."

"Then we should make sure they have something to do while they're waiting," Laura said.

Dymple shuffled through the office doorway. "A couple good-looking young men are anxious to talk with you in the living room, Laura."

"I bet they are." Laura looked unconvinced. "Did you straighten them out?"

"I interrupted their questions so I could pray for them. And then I let them know they were barking up the wrong tree when they suggested Kate did something wrong."

"Good for you. They need to erase that idea from their minds." Laura smiled at Amy. "Keep working on this reservation. Just follow the step-by-step guide." She slid an open notebook closer to Amy. "I'll check your work when I return."

Laura stood and walked over to Dymple. "Will I see you over at Freedom House in a bit?" She hugged her friend. "I plan to tag along with the detectives to make sure they're not too hard on Aunt Mary."

"I'm going over now." Dymple patted Laura's arm. "Mary might surprise you. She's a sharp one beneath her confusion. But I'm glad you'll be there. The kids are missing you and Kate and their little friends."

"I'm sure they are. And I miss them." Laura sighed. "This is all so sad, for everyone." She stepped into the hallway. "Better go meet with the detectives before they come looking for me."

Chapter Twenty-Three

K ate knelt to pull the quivering little boy close. The girls hovered at her elbows. She scanned the office they'd just entered. In addition to the hall door behind her, it had a closed door on the left and an opening at the back plus two windows.

The nearest window faced the hallway and the other was on the back wall by the corner. Both were covered by aluminum blinds. Gray light seeped at the edges. If she had the direction right, the far window faced the water. How close was the river? And the distant roar she heard, did it come from the waterfall or the paper mill?

A rusted metal desk, the only piece of furniture, had been shoved against the windowless wall on the right. Somewhere nearby a persistent drip ticked like the secondhand on a clock. No wonder the place smelled moldy. Kate's nose itched.

No evidence of recent occupation was obvious, but she had a feeling the place had been used many times to transfer victims. If Tara and Ramsey had been instructed to leave the garage in Idaho spotless, no doubt that was the norm here, too.

Ramsey, who'd been whispering to Tara in the hall, steered her into the room, shut the door and locked it.

Kate pulled all three children into a quick hug and stood, bracing herself for the next round of abuse. But their abductors remained by the doorway, their heads bent over Tara's phone. The harsh white light accentuated their evil features.

A malicious smile twisted Ramsey's mouth. He muttered something undiscernible and herded them through the office into a smaller room with three walls of empty shelves. Kate assumed it was once a supply closet.

"Outa the way." Ramsey thrust himself between her and the kids. "Hughes, keep a bead on 'em."

Tara giggled. "My pleasure."

Kate took a shaky breath. Tara's giddiness could only mean one thing—the transfer was imminent.

Ramsey's light darted from shelf to shelf. He reached out, tugged at a shelf in the center section and then tugged again. A creaking sound filled the room just before a strip of pallid light cut into the supply closet gloom.

A secret door in an office? Kate drew the children close.

Ramsey turned off the flashlight, widened the opening and ushered them into an even smaller room. A hint of the increasing daylight came through a barred window high above their heads. Kate guessed the room once held an old-fashioned metal safe or possibly personnel files.

"Sit."

Kate backed against a wall and slid down. "We need a bathroom."

"After the watchman makes his rounds." He lifted Lupita by the arm and dropped her in front of Tara. "Keep 'em quiet, Hughes, while I track him. Use the knife on the Spicanniny if Neilson is dumb enough to do something stupid again." He sneered at Kate. "Up to you, Neilson." With that, he stepped out.

The sound of a bolt rasping into place grated deep into her chest. She put her arms across Shannon and Tieno's shoulders.

Tara, who sat with her back to the door, raised her knife. "You heard the man. Keep the noise down."

"Don't worry about us," Kate whispered. "We'll be quiet. Right, kiddos?"

They nodded.

Kate pointed to Tara. "You should worry about you."

Tara's eyebrows pinched. "What's that supposed to mean?"

"You'll go to prison for a long time for being Ramsey's accomplice."

"No I won't. Our plan is failsafe."

"Maybe, maybe not. Either way, you have to live with your conscience, if you have one." She felt more than heard reverberations through the wall. Again, she wondered if the tremors came from the waterfall or the paper mill…or both.

"Don't get religious on me, Neilson."

"That's *Duncan* to you."

"Give it up, woman." Tara leveled the knife at her, dangerously close to Lupi. "When we're done with you, your name won't matter to anyone and Michael won't remember he was ever married to you."

"What does *that* mean?" This was a bizarre conversation, but the more information she could get out of Tara, the better. Kate motioned to Lupi, who crawled onto her lap. Tara didn't seem to notice.

Tieno whispered, "D-don't h-h-hurt Miss K-kate." He wrapped his arms around Kate's waist.

"I'll give Michael children," Tara said. "I'll give him heirs."

Kate flinched. Tara was closer to the truth than she knew. But no matter how upset Mike was with her, he'd never think of marrying Tara.

"And I'll get rid of that stupid children's home. Michael wants *real* children, children of his own, not someone else's rejects."

"Kiddos," Kate said, "Tara's mom died when she was young. Maybe that's why she's so heartless. Her father is a convicted felon and so is she. In fact, she just got out of prison."

Tara slammed the wall with her fist. "You spent time behind bars too."

Good. I'm getting to her. The more noise, the better. "One difference," Kate said. "I let prison and Jesus change my ways. You can do the same. Start by steering clear of people like Jerry Ramsey. He's a loser. He'll ruin your life."

"Don't tell me what to do."

"You can do better, Tara. Jesus will give you a new life. You can begin again."

"Oh, I plan to do just that. Won't be long before I'll be *Mrs. Michael Duncan.* And the Whispering Pines will be mine." Her eyes glittered in the growing light. "Then Daddy and I will combine ranches and create our exotic game ranch." She waved the knife in the air. "Like we were planning to do before you nosed your way into our world."

"If you're in this to get rid of me, why not let the kids go? Kidnapping will put you back in prison, for years longer than the time you just served."

Tara jutted her chin. "We need cash to purchase the exotics—"

The harsh sound of metal scraping against metal bounced between the walls of the small room. Tara moved away from the entrance and the wall opened. Ramsey stuck his head inside. A cigarette hung from the corner of his mouth. "Get up. We're going to the hole."

Kate stumbled after the kids as they were piloted from the room behind the shelves into the supply closet. From there, Ramsey and Tara goaded them through the office and the hallway, across the open area they'd earlier traversed and into a corner crowded with corroded machinery. Rotted rubber hoses, rusted levers, dirty switches and dangling wires and knobs sprouted from the metal behemoths, reminding Kate of the kids when they first climbed out of bed in the morning.

"Keep moving." Ramsey drove them deeper into the dark corner then stepped in front of them and switched on his flashlight. He aimed it at a jagged hole in the floor. "One at a time."

"I don't care what our contact says." Tara crinkled her nose like she'd been asked to scrub a septic tank with her bare hands. "I can't do that. There has to be a real bathroom here somewhere."

"The guard has a port-a-john down below."

Her lips twisted. "You think you're so funny."

Kate took Lupita's hand and started for the hole. She'd help her straddle it, so she wouldn't fall in.

Tara pushed them aside. "Me first. Everyone turn around."

Kate swiveled. The door they'd used to enter the room was directly across from them. She hated to risk their lives on that rickety stairway again, but if—

Ramsey jammed his gun in her side. "Don't get any ideas."

Tara tromped from behind the metal pile. "On the way home, Jer…" She stopped in front of Ramsey. "I *insist* we stay at five-star hotels with king-size beds and Jacuzzi bathtubs. And eat at restaurants that serve steak and lobster and flaming…flaming whatever. I've had my fill of bologna sandwiches and sleeping in cars."

She huffed. "Now this. On top of everything else, a stinkin' hole for a toilet. It's worse than an outhouse. And I'm cold." She rubbed her arms. "I have goosebumps all the time."

"Should a worn more clothes." Ramsey brandished the gun. "Move it, Neilson. Get the brats in and out, pronto."

When they returned to the office, enough light leaked at the blinds' edges that Kate could see the room more clearly than before. As far as she could tell, it didn't have the elaborate touch-pad security the previous place had. Breaking out would be easy.

Ramsey locked the door behind them, told Tara to aim her gun at

Shannon's head and went into the other room. He returned with a loaf of white bread, a package of bologna and a bag of potato chips. He dumped the food on the desk.

"Bologna again." Tara swore. "If I wasn't so hungry…"

"Keep your gun on the brat." Ramsey pivoted and strode into the other room. This time, he carried in a case of bottled water and dropped it beside the chips.

Tara pooched her lower lip. "I prefer flavored water."

Kate was tempted to ask if the Wyoming prison warden had provided her with flavored water but decided to save inflammatory comments for more important issues.

Ramsey stabbed the cover, ran his knife through the plastic and tore it apart. He wrenched a bottle from the middle, twisted the lid and emptied it in a series of loud gulps.

While the others watched, he ripped open the chip bag and stuffed a handful in his mouth, chewing while he made himself a sandwich. After three sandwiches and countless chips, he belched long and loud. "I'm gonna go sleep. Wake me at four so I can check the guards when they change shifts."

"I'll set my phone alarm." Tara handed him her gun. "Keep an eye on 'em for a minute." Within seconds, she said, "Done," and slid the phone into the back pocket of her skin-tight shorts.

Kate sat against a wall, her gaze on the ceiling. When Ramsey left the room, she'd wait until he was snoring. Then she'd kick Tara in the head and sneak away with the kids. They'd be long gone before Tara regained consciousness or Ramsey awakened.

But Ramsey didn't leave. Instead, he motioned with the pistol. "Over there, Neilson."

What now?

"Stand by the pipe." He pulled a set of handcuffs from his pants pocket.

She hesitated.

He motioned to Tara. "Show Neilson your blade. If she doesn't get up, start cuttin' on the girl."

Kate got to her feet, glaring at him. She hated how he threatened to injure the kids to get her to comply.

He stuck the gun in the back of his pants. "You fight me on this, Neilson, you'll be watching the girl lose a finger."

The thought of being chained again felt as if someone had a stranglehold on her throat. She shuffled closer, weighted with dread, barely able to breathe.

Ramsey backhanded her and her head snapped to the side. "That's for whoring after those truckers." He grabbed her wrist, hooked it to the pole and left the room, leaving a trail of Brut and cigarette breath.

Kate blinked, fighting to recover her senses. She sucked in one shuddering breath after another. This couldn't be happening.

Tara slid the knife into its sheath. She pushed Shannon away. "Go sit down."

The girl joined Lupita and Tieno on the floor. The three huddled close to Kate.

Tara slapped a piece of lunchmeat on a bread slice, folded it in half and took a bite. She waved the sandwich at Kate. "Look what happened to the tough ex-con. Not so tough now, are you, honey?"

"Please feed the children."

"They can fix their own food." Tara continued to chew. "When I'm done."

Kate slid down the wall to the floor. Her jaw ached, her wrist hurt and her vision was hazy. The handcuff triggered memories from the days when pimps and johns had shackled her at will as well the times she'd been arrested, jailed and imprisoned.

How can I help the children, God? How can I protect them locked to a pole? She eyed the door. She might be restrained, but the kids weren't. If she could get Shannon's attention, she'd use eye signals to encourage her to leave. The girl was smart. She'd find her way through the labyrinth of buildings.

But the children's focus was on the food.

When Tara finished, she said, "Eat all you want." She snickered. "Gotta fatten you up for the big sale." Walking over to the hallway door, she stood on her tiptoes and slid a bolt across the top. On her way to the other room, she said, "Wouldn't want anyone to slip out and get lost in this big ol' place."

Kate stifled a groan. Thanks to the dim lighting, she hadn't noticed the extra lock, but she should have known the exit would be secured.

The children looked at Kate as if asking permission to eat.

She nodded and they rushed to the desk. Shannon took charge. "First, we make Miss Kate a sandwich." She laid a bologna slice on a piece of bread, folded it and handed it to Lupita. "Take this to her. Tieno, you can give her chips."

Kate smiled, touched by Shannon's thoughtfulness and their teamwork. Before she took the food, she caressed Lupi's and Tieno's dirty cheeks with her free hand. "Thank you. You kiddos are sweethearts." She looked at Shannon. "Thank you for taking care of me."

After they'd eaten and drunk their fill, the children curled against her and fell asleep. She prayed God would bless them with sweet dreams in the midst of the terror.

She knew of ways to escape handcuffs when both hands were cuffed. One should be easy enough. But the children made it hard to move and Tara, who'd returned, was watching her. Seated on the floor, the woman leaned against the door, elbows on her knees, smoking a cigarette and staring at Kate through the smoky, muted light.

Chapter Twenty-Four

Mike was about to leave the office, when Pastor Chuck entered, dressed in his usual summer attire, a white t-shirt, cargo shorts and flip-flops.

He greeted everyone before asking, "Where's your mom, Mike? I was hoping to visit with both of you."

"She's talking with a couple Cheyenne detectives," Mike said. "Shouldn't take too long."

"Oh, yeah? Have they made any progress?"

"Some, but not much." Mike glanced at the clock. "I'd like to run something past you, if you have a minute."

"That's why I'm here, to help however I can."

Mike, with Tramp at his side, led Chuck through the lobby and out onto the porch. He pointed to a picnic table under a nearby evergreen. "Would you like coffee, or maybe a glass of Dymple's Delight? She just brought us a jar."

Chuck laughed. "Thanks, but I've already had my caffeine quota for the day and it's a little early for Dymple's concoction. That stuff has a kick."

Mike sat across from his pastor, fists on the table. For a long while, he stared up into the tree branches.

Chuck rubbed Tramp's ears and scratched his back.

"The night before Kate went to Cheyenne, we had a fight." Mike looked Chuck in the eye. "A big one." She wanted me to go with her and the kids. I refused, said I was too busy and she was spending too much time at Freedom House." He shook his head. "If I'd gone with her, none of this would have happened."

"What was Kate's response?"

"I don't remember her exact words, but the gist of it was that I was being juvenile and selfish, which I was."

Chuck arched an eyebrow but said nothing.

"I didn't intend to tell anyone about the fight."

Tramp settled near his feet.

"But..." Mike folded his arms. "The police found messages from Kate to me on her cell phone, messages that hinted at our argument. I'm afraid the fight will be used against her. The media has already jumped on her ex-felon status. They're suggesting she ran away with the kids. And the detectives are all but saying she took the kids to get away from me and to have a family I apparently don't want."

Chuck rested his forearms on the table, hands clasped.

"What if...?" Mike scratched his forehead. "What if...?" He looked toward the house then lowered his voice. "What if that's true?"

When Chuck's eyebrows puckered, Mike quickly added, "After that emergency surgery in Nebraska, Kate can't get pregnant."

For a long moment, Chuck rubbed his hands together, his gaze on the table. Finally, he looked at Mike. "Speaking from experience, I can say that one fight doesn't ruin a marriage. And blaming a difference of opinion suggests your marriage was so bad that Kate not only walked away, she took others with her. We both know better than that."

"Yeah, well..."

"I don't know much about detectives. My guess is that it's their job to suspect the worst, maybe even suggest the worst. But that's not your job right now."

"What exactly is my job? The only thing I can do here is answer invasive questions over and over and fend off nosy reporters."

A pinecone plopped onto the table. Tramp lifted his head.

"Your job is to trust your wife and ignore the false accusations. Believe in Kate. Tell anyone who'll listen what a wonderful woman and wife she is and how much you love her, how you know without a doubt she's done nothing wrong." Chuck cocked his head. "Are you praying for Kate?"

"Of course."

"What else are you doing for her?"

Mike motioned to his pickup parked in front of the office. "As soon as I can get out of here today, I'm gonna go looking for her."

"I'm glad to hear that. If it were me, I'd have been long gone by now."

"If I'd had any idea which direction to go, I would have taken off yesterday. We got a hint of a possible location last night and the detectives passed along confirmation today."

"What kind of clues?"

"Someone saw a dark-haired woman with kids at an Idaho rest area yesterday. And then someone else found one of her earrings. It was custom-made, so I was able to make a positive identification."

Chuck straightened. "Same rest stop?"

"Yeah." Mike didn't mention the solicitation.

"So..." Chuck's eyes grew wide. "Now you know where to head."

"She could be anywhere by now."

"But you know which direction she went. That's a start. You taking anyone with you?"

Mike shook his head.

"Wanda and I are driving to Denver this afternoon to be with my mom when she has surgery tomorrow. Otherwise, I'd go with you." He looked at his watch. "I need to stop at the bank, so I'd better get a move on. Tell your mom I'll call her later. In the meantime, I'll be praying for all of you." He swung his leg over the bench seat and stood.

"Thanks for your prayers." Mike stood to shake his hand. "We certainly need them."

Tramp scrambled out from under the table. He nudged Chuck's leg with his nose, and Chuck stroked the dog's head. "I hate to see you tackle this thing alone, Mike. I'll pray you find someone to travel with you."

Mike walked into the barn. He'd notified all the employees about possible interviews, but he couldn't leave yet because the detectives' vehicle was still parked in front of his house. This was as good a time as any to try to figure out Kate's messages and to think about what Pastor Chuck said.

At the base of the hayloft ladder, he told Tramp to "stay" before he climbed up the ladder onto the wide platform and sat on a hay bale. Any other day, the sweet aroma of warm hay, the solid rafters above him and the peaceful solitude would calm his spirit. But today…

Why were Kate's messages so brief? Was she angry? Or speaking some kind of code? What was he missing? Whatever the intent, hearing her voice again melted his insides.

Chuck was right. One fight didn't ruin a marriage. He and Kate had a good marriage, a happy marriage. He never should've doubted her.

He stared through the sunlit opening at the end of the hayloft where they lifted in the hay bales. Ever since he was a kid, this had been his favorite place to look out over the ranch. The WP was his life, Kate's life. How many times had she told him how much she loved the ranch—

and how much she loved him? How she thanked God every day for leading her to Wyoming.

A mouse skittered past.

"Hey, Mike...you up there?" Clint's voice.

"Yeah, come on up."

The ladder creaked twice and then Clint's head and shoulders appeared through the gap in the loft floor. "I knew Tramp wasn't sitting down there staring at the ceiling for nothin'."

"He'd try to climb the ladder, if I didn't stop him." Mike motioned to his foreman. "Pull up a bale. Take a load off your feet."

Clint settled on a hay bale directly across from Mike. "Hope I didn't interrupt anything."

"Just trying to get my head screwed on straight. Too much craziness going on."

"You can say that again." Clint leaned his elbows on his thighs and clasped his hands. "Is this a good time to talk?"

"Shoot."

"I would have said something when we talked earlier, but too many people were around." Clint straightened, hands on his knees. "I owe you an apology for bringing sheep onto the WP. Should have checked with you first. I'll pay you for the dead cow, if you don't mind taking it out of my paycheck, over time, that is."

"Thanks for the offer..." Mike shook his head, realizing he hadn't thought about the bison cow for hours. "Insurance should cover it. And like Doc said, those sheep may not be the source of the MCF, if that's what it is."

"I still think I should reimburse you for your loss."

"It was an honest mistake." Now that he'd cooled down, he could see the truth in that statement.

Clint looked doubtful. "Let me know if the insurance doesn't come through or you have a deductible, or whatever."

"First the shootings…" Mike took off his hat and ran his fingers through his hair. "Then the brucellosis scare. Now this." He shrugged. "We'll make it through. I just pray it's true the state won't quarantine the herd."

He put his hat back on. "I have to admit, I honestly don't care what happens to the bison any more. All I want is to have my wife back."

"Sure wish there was something I could do to help." Clint stood and walked to the opening, his back to Mike. "I'm itching to dig in, get my hands dirty, like what we did for Amy."

"Exactly my thoughts."

Clint turned to Mike. "You want to go after Kate and the kids?"

"Yep."

A wind gust wafted in. Hay particles swirled in the wide shaft of sunlight.

"Where would we start? We don't know where Kate is. With Amy, we at least knew she made it to Dallas before she disappeared."

"We have a couple clues. Plus, I just learned a new one."

"Oh, yeah?"

"Some trucker found one of Kate's earrings at an Idaho rest stop. The detective showed me a picture. They didn't say which rest area, but I left a message for Cal. Maybe he can help us out when he goes back on duty."

"How did they know it was Kate's earring?"

"It's a one-of-a-kind piece of jewelry from a set Mom and I had a jeweler make for Kate." Mike lifted his gaze to the rafters. "Mom is convinced human traffickers took Kate and the kids. If that's the case, someone could be transporting them through Idaho to the coast."

Clint groaned. "Not good."

"No, not good." Mike heaved a long sigh. "I've heard traffickers ship people in and out of the country through Oregon and Washington ports. And the California coast is always a possibility—or Canada. But that doesn't mean they'd be sent to another country. There's plenty of buying and selling going on right here in the good ol' US of A."

"And I thought we'd abolished slavery." Clint shook his head. "When do you want to take off?"

"Did you talk with the detectives yet?"

"Yeah, just finished. I didn't have much to say, except that Kate is great with the kids and you two have a good marriage, as far as I can tell. They kept harping on the marriage bit for some reason, but I didn't give them any fuel for their fire."

"Thanks, man." Mike stood. "I'd like to take off the minute Moore and Schroeder head over to Freedom House. If we push it, we can make it to Idaho before nightfall and follow the trail from there."

One corner of Clint's mouth turned up. "I wonder if they'll talk to Kate's aunt."

"Bet she gives them a run for their money, like Dymple did." Mike grinned. "I had a hard time keeping a straight face. I didn't hear it all, but later she said she prayed for them and scolded them for suggesting Kate did something wrong."

"Good for her." Clint started for the ladder. "I better go track down Cyrus to let him know what we have going with the livestock the next couple weeks." He shrugged. "Just a precaution. I'm sure we won't be gone that long."

"Tell him to call your cell phone if he has questions Mom or Coach can't answer. We've got a lot going on."

In addition to the working side of the ranch that Clint oversaw, the WP offered their guests a smorgasbord of opportunities, from trail rides to chuck-wagon dinners, fishing expeditions, bison tours, bird watching and whitewater rafting. They also provided classes and hands-on training in horsemanship, fly fishing, calf roping, archery, firearm safety, target shooting and outdoor survival.

For the first time, Mike realized the wisdom of bringing Amy into the office. She'd be a big help to Mom and Coach and Cyrus. Along with taking reservations and greeting guests, she could remind leaders and instructors of times and locations for their activities and post the information for the guests.

"Which rig are we taking?"

Mike got to his feet. "Long trip for Old Blue. Maybe I'll drive Kate's SUV."

"You forgetting something?"

"What's that?"

"Kate's car is down in Cheyenne."

"Oh, yeah…." Mike yawned. "I'm not thinking straight. Guess we'll use Mom's. If she needs to go somewhere, I'm sure one of the staff would be glad to drive her or loan her a vehicle."

"We could take my pickup."

"You sure?"

"Hasn't been out on the highway for a while. Good opportunity to burn off the cobwebs."

Chapter Twenty-Five

From his hayloft vantage point, Mike could see the ranch office. He waited until the detectives drove away before he descended the ladder and returned to the house to pack. Walking through the living room, Tramp at his heels, he noticed the message light blinking on the phone. Had Kate called and they'd missed her? He pushed the voicemail button.

"This is Cal." The deputy sounded sleepy. "I've been trying to sort out what I saw over at Hughes's place the other night, and I finally figured it out." He paused, like he was trying to collect his thoughts. "My assignment during his house arrest has been to do random, unannounced visits. As you can imagine, he's never been, shall we say, welcoming."

He chuckled. "I make it a practice to park a ways from the house and slip behind a bush to check his computer monitor before I ring the doorbell. The computer sits beside a big window, so I can see what's on his screen before he knows I'm there. When I went to his house to retrieve the wrist monitor, I did my usual—"

The message ended and a second one started. "Sorry about that. I'll talk faster. I did my usual routine and saw a picture of a kid on his screen who looked familiar, but I couldn't place him. I've been thinking about him ever since, and just now, I think it figured it out. He could be one of your Freedom House kids, the little Asian guy who was doing the roping at that kids' rodeo a few days ago. I stopped by for a few minutes but must have missed you."

He was quiet for a moment. "That's it. Might be the same kid, might not be. We can talk later. Right now, I'd better get some shuteye."

Mike left a voice message for Cal. "Got your message about Hughes. Not sure what to think about it, but thanks." He paused. "A heads-up for you. The Cheyenne detectives saw you leave our place this morning and asked why you were here. Expect them to contact you soon, if they haven't already done so."

Still talking, he walked over to the table. "I'm taking off for Idaho in a few minutes and could use some help locating a rest area. I'll give you a buzz when I'm on the road." He made a mental note to make sure Clint took his cell phone.

Ending the call, he laid the house phone on the table and picked up the plate Dymple had left behind. Only two scones and some crumbs remained on it, but that was okay. The pastries would be great for the trip. One for him and one for Clint.

He lifted the foil to wrap the scones and saw his cell phone lying right where Moore had laid it earlier. *Nice work, Dymple.* She'd been a big help today, in more ways than she knew.

He pulled Moore and Schroeder's business cards from his shirt pocket and entered their numbers into his contact list. He might need to call them, and their names would show if they called him, which would enable him to decide whether or not to answer.

In the bedroom, he stopped long enough to read the Bible verse Kate had taped to her mirror. *With God all things are possible. Matthew 19:26.* He'd read the words almost daily. But today the *all things* took on greater significance. Only God could lead him and Clint to Kate and the kids.

He tossed a razor, toothbrush and toothpaste, plus shirts and underwear into a duffle bag. Opening a drawer, he found a cell-phone charger and exchanged the two-way on his belt for a phone case. He would charge the phone in Clint's truck so it would be ready if Kate called.

The police had her phone, but she might call from another number, and he needed to stay in contact with his mom and Cal. Question was, would the Cheyenne police track his calls? Mike shrugged. Didn't matter. He was taking the phone with him.

He found Clint in the office, visiting with Amy and Coach. "You ready?"

"Truck's gassed and waiting by the front door."

Amy eyed Mike's duffle bag. "Where are you two going?"

Mike slung the bag over his shoulder. "After Kate."

"Are you sure?" Coach folded his arms, biceps bulging against his broad chest. "You don't have much information to go on."

"The detectives gave me another clue and Cal left a message saying he saw a picture on Todd Hughes's computer that looked like it could be Tieno. I'm not sure if there's a connection, but I wouldn't be surprised if Hughes is somehow mixed up in this mess. At any rate, more clues will come up as we go along. That's what happened in Texas. Right, Clint?"

"Yep."

Amy jumped to her feet. "I saw that Hughes guy yesterday morning at the café."

"Oh, yeah?" Mike wondered why she was so excited. "Sounds like he's joining society again, for better or worse."

"I didn't know who he was, but he was so rude and grumpy that I asked the other waitress about him. He was in a wheelchair, so I should have put two and two together. Anyway, I was wiping the table behind his booth when his phone rang. He squished way into the corner and started talking real soft. But I heard some of what he said."

The three men leaned toward Amy.

"I don't remember exactly what I heard, but it was something like,

'Don't worry about…he can handle her.' And then I'm pretty sure he said 'three.' Caught my attention because he said it kind of proud like. And then he said, 'Quite a haul. I hear it's usually just one at a time.'"

She sighed. "If I hadn't knocked over a salt shaker right then, I might have heard more. He turned his head, gave me a dirty look and ended the call."

Mike frowned. "Thanks, Amy. I'll pass that information along to Cal."

Coach rolled closer. "What did the detectives tell you?"

"One of Kate's earrings was found at an Idaho rest stop."

"Huh?" Amy scrunched her eyebrows. "How do they know—?"

"It's one Mom and I had custom-made for Kate."

"Oh, her 'WP' earrings." Amy turned to Coach. "You've seen those, haven't you?"

"Uh, sorry…" He lifted his palms. "I don't normally notice jewelry, unless I'm hunting for a birthday present for my wife."

"I know what you mean," Mike said.

"I don't have a wife," Clint said, "but I agree."

Amy tossed her hair to the side. "Okay, guys, I get it. I'm just glad there's finally some concrete evidence. With almost nothing to go on, you flew all the way to Texas to look for me. I'm forever grateful." Her eyes misted. "I'll be praying for you."

"Yeah, uh, I'll be praying for you-all, too." Clint thrust his hands into his pockets. "You're going to be shorthanded 'til we get back."

Amy gave him a funny look.

"What?"

"I didn't know you prayed."

"I'm learning."

Coach shook both men's hands. "We'll hold the fort down. You be careful out there."

"Thanks, man." Mike shifted the bag on his shoulder. "Tell Mom I'll call her."

"Will do."

"And tell her I have my cell phone. If you hear any news about Kate, call us ASAP."

"Better check to see if I have both of your numbers." Coach returned to his desk. "We so rarely use cell phones in these mountains, I may not have it."

"I'll check mine, too." Amy pulled a phone from her purse.

Coach rattled off Clint's number, and Clint said, "You got it."

Then he said, "This is what I have for you, Mike," and read another number.

Mike replied, "That's it."

"Say that again, please." Amy tapped her phone. After she added the number, she stood and hugged Mike. "Take care and give Kate and the kids hugs for me."

She turned to Clint, whose hands were at his side. "No goodbye hug for me?"

"I'm not s'posed to touch you. Remember?"

"This is different." She wrapped her arms around his neck. "This is an 'I care about you and I'll be thinking of you and praying for you' hug." She looked like she was about to cry. "Stay in touch. Okay?"

Clint pulled her close and buried his face in her hair. "Yeah, I'll do that." His voice was husky.

Amy stepped back. "If they were taken by traffickers..." Her voice caught. "You'll be walking into a hornets' nest. Words can never describe how evil pimps and their gangs are." She swiped at her eyes.

"Sorry, Mike. I don't mean to upset you. I try not to think about what Kate and the kids might be going through and pray for them instead. But it's hard to forget the bad and remember God can take care of them, like he took care of me."

Mike swallowed. Yeah. He needed to trust God and not allow his imagination to get the best of him.

"I thought I'd never see any of you again when I was in Texas. Now I have that same fear." Tears spilled down Amy's cheeks. "Will I ever see you again? Will I ever see Kate and Tieno and Lupi and Shannon again?" She fell into Clint's arms. "Oh, God, please. Please bring them home."

Mike nodded at Coach and walked out the door. He hadn't expected that reaction from Amy. She was normally such an upbeat person. But she was right. They could be walking into a hornets' nest. She understood better than any of them how vicious human hornets could be.

Seeing Amy in Clint's arms hurt. Like Clint, he longed to hold the woman he loved. His arms were empty without Kate.

Mike made his way down the steps and over to his pickup to get the handgun he kept under the seat. Tramp followed. He closed the door and patted his dog's head. "Stay here, Tramp. I'll be home soon…with Kate." He climbed into Clint's truck in time to see his foreman walk out the door, wiping his face with the bandana he kept in his back pocket, his shirt stained with Amy's tears.

When Clint settled into the driver's seat, Mike said, "Got my gun. You have yours?"

"Under here." Clint pulled a metal box from beneath his seat, unlocked it with a key on his key ring and pulled out a pistol, which he began to take apart. "Who knows where we'll end up or what the gun laws will be. To be safe, I think we need to break our guns down and lock 'em up while we're traveling."

Mike disassembled his handgun, laid the pieces and ammunition in the box and slipped the holster beneath the passenger seat. Clint slid the box under his seat before starting the truck. They drove away from the ranch headquarters toward the highway in silence.

A short time later, they rattled over the cattle guard at the entrance. Mike turned for one last look at the ranch. Between the rifles on Clint's gun rack, he could see the Whispering Pines sign swaying with the breeze. Would they return to the WP? Would Kate?

Clint stopped at the highway and looked both ways. As usual, no vehicles were in sight either direction. "Didn't expect that reaction from Amy. Caught me off-guard."

"Yeah, me too."

Clint pulled onto the blacktop. "She doesn't talk much about Dallas."

"Her words were sobering." Mike scratched the bottom of his nose with his knuckle. "But I needed the reminder about who we'll be dealing with."

"I already miss her."

"Amy getting under your skin?"

Clint grunted. "I thought I had things all figured out."

Kate closed her eyes and slept a dreamless slumber, until something awakened her. She didn't know what. Maybe Ramsey's raucous snores. Whatever it was, it hadn't disturbed the children.

She had no idea how long she'd slept, but the light that sifted from behind the blinds was brighter. Her muscles ached and her fettered arm tingled. She longed to shift her position, yet she remained still so she wouldn't disturb the children.

Tara, who must have been awakened by the same sound, stretched her arms and arched her back. "Some mess you got yourself into, Nielson."

Kate ignored the comment, which wasn't worth the breath it would take to counter it, and whispered, "See how sweet these sleeping children look, Tara? How can you sell them to people who'll sell their little bodies over and over *and over*?"

"Calves look sweet, too. But we eat veal. It's delicious."

"You're a sick woman."

"Besides, selling brats happens all the time, right under your holier-than-thou nose. One of my cellmates in prison was a meth addict. Whenever she needed a hit, she'd take her kid to the mall and sell her for a day. Pick her up at night. Or drop her off at night and pick her up in the morning. All her friends did it. Some of the prostitutes had babies just so their pimps could make money off 'em."

Kate shuddered. "Please, Tara, you—"

"Don't *please* me."

"You can't be that callous."

"Bet me."

"Selling little children just for money?"

"We'll need cash to buy exotic animals for our ranch. Michael is going to love it."

Michael. Hearing his name come from Tara's lips was painful for Kate. But she would play along with the delusion. She circled her rings around her finger. "The WP has plenty of money. You don't need to do this."

"You should give me those rings."

"Why?"

"Because after midnight tonight, you won't have any use for them."

"What happens at midnight?" With any luck, Tara would turn into a pumpkin and Ramsey into a rat.

"Depends on what the buyers are looking for. They may want you for factory work. They may want you for organs." Tara snickered. "Or both. Work you 'til you drop and then farm out your parts. Get their money's worth from that ugly old bod."

"You really are heartless, aren't you?"

"And proud of it." She lifted her chin. "As you well know, a girl can't be weak in prison. Those bitches will eat you alive."

"Just because a person cares doesn't mean they're weak."

"That's not how I see it. Give me the rings."

Ramsey's snores, which had increased in volume, overpowered the children's quiet snuffles.

Kate closed her fist and hooked her thumbnail behind the rings. "What in the world do you want with my wedding rings?"

"Mike'll trade them in for nicer, more expensive ones for me."

"Think I'll keep my rings."

Tara jumped to her feet, knife in hand.

Kate untangled her legs from the children and pushed up the pole, sorry she had to interrupt their dreams.

Tieno cried, "W-w-what?"

Kate braced to fight with one hand—and her feet, if needed.

Ramsey snores were momentarily interrupted by a loud snort.

Tara glanced at the door to the next room. She hesitated. Was she afraid the commotion would awaken Ramsey?

The children sat up.

"Tell you what." Kate stood tall. "I'll give you the rings *and* Mike's cell phone number, if you let me call him."

Tara came closer. Her perfume's potency had lessened, but it had also soured. "You're trying to trick me." Tara spat the words at Kate. Her smoker's breath was as nasty as her perfume. "You just want to tell him where you are."

"I don't know where we are. All I want is to say goodbye." She paused, swallowed her grief and added, "Then you can talk with him."

"Tell me the number. I'll dial it."

"No."

Tara slapped her. "You're in no position to tell me *no*."

Kate stared defiantly into her captor's angry eyes.

The cell phone alarm sounded. Both women jumped. Tara gave Kate the finger, spun around and stomped into the other room.

Ramsey was with her when she returned. He pulled a key from his pocket and released Kate while Tara stood guard. Again, he marched them all into the back room, which had more light than earlier. This time, he took Tara's phone with him, insisting he needed it in case he ran into trouble. He pointed the phone at Kate. "No monkey business."

She looked away.

Tara waited until they heard the bolt slip into place before she demanded, "Tell me the number, Neilson, or I'll cut one of these kids."

Chapter Twenty-Six

"I'm tired of your threats." Kate massaged her sore wrist. "You hurt a child and you'll never—I mean *never* get the number from me. All I ask is that you give me five minutes with Mike. You'll automatically get the number on your cell phone...and I'll give you the rings."

Tieno tugged at Kate's arm. "G-g-got t-to go."

"Me, too," Shannon said.

Lupita moved her head up and down, her eyes wide.

"When he comes back," Kate said, "we'll ask."

"Five minutes is too long." Tara waved the knife. "You could tell him too much."

"Like I said, I have no idea where we are." A cloud floated past the window above them.

"You could tell him about...about this." Tara swept her hand over the children.

"That you kidnapped and are terrorizing three beautiful, precious, sweet children?"

"Lay off the guilt-trip mush."

"Three minutes." Whatever it took to make a solid connection between the phones. Even if she didn't get Mike and had to leave a message, he'd have Tara's number, which could be traced.

"I'll think about it."

"We're running out of time."

"Yeah." Tara's eyes glistened. "Payday is coming in just a few hours. I can't wait."

Kate felt the bologna sandwich roil in her stomach. "My Aunt Mary would say, 'Don't count your chickens before they hatch,' and the Bible says, 'The hopes of the wicked come to nothing.'"

Tara jumped to her feet. "Don't you call me—"

The bolt slid noisily from the lock and the door opened. Ramsey stood in the opening, his thumb aimed over his shoulder. "Out."

"Jerry," Kate said, "we need to use the hole."

He lowered his brow. "Last time."

After the trek to the hole, Ramsey again handcuffed Kate to the pipe. And again, he guzzled water and devoured sandwiches and chips. When he finished, he wiped his mouth with his shirt sleeve and told Tara to watch the kids until they went to sleep. "Then come to our room and make papa happy."

Kate choked. *Papa?* He was a vile, greedy, evil, cruel child-stealer, not a papa.

Tara knelt in front of the exit door, her gun balanced on her knee and a cigarette between her fingers. The children were soon asleep. But their kidnapper remained in the room.

A train roared past. By the sound of it, the train was short—not more than an engine and a couple cars—and fast, on tracks that must run right past the mill. She and the kids could follow the tracks into town or somehow alert the engineer that they needed help.

Ramsey began to snore.

Tara laid her cigarette on the desk and stood. After holstering her gun, she pulled out her knife and sidled over to Kate. She held out her phone. "Keep it short."

Kate reached for the phone.

Tara stuck the knife under her nose. "One false word and I start the organ removal early."

"Back off." Kate stood, careful not to disturb the children, and waved her away. "Give me space. Your perfume is so nasty I can't breathe." She didn't mention the cigarette breath.

"Give me those rings."

"After the call."

Tara bent over Shannon's head. "She won't miss a chunk of ear, but it'll bleed like hell."

Kate blew out a frustrated breath, shoved the phone into her pocket and slid the rings over her knuckle. *God, help me not to cry,* was all she could manage as she surrendered the symbols of her marriage and her love for Mike. She would not cry. She would not cry.

Tara puffed her chest and smiled the proud smile of a victor. She slipped the rings onto her finger and held out her left hand, whispering, "A dream come true. *My* dream come true."

Kate turned her back. She couldn't let Tara's lunacy distract her. Holding the phone with her chained hand, she dialed Mike's number. Like before, he wouldn't answer, but at least she could hear his voice one more time.

Two rings. Three. "Hello."

"Mike." Surprised he answered his cell phone, she stopped. But then she blurted, "It's me. Kate."

"Kate. Sweetheart." Shock laced with happiness and relief colored his voice. "It's so good to hear your voice. I've been worried. Where are you?"

"I don't have much time." She took a breath, determined not to break down and waste the connection. "Remember how we like to watch the blue herons at the river?" Before he could say he had no idea what she was talking about, she added, "And how we wanted to climb that tall mountain—I think it starts with an H—and see really big waterfalls? I'm so sorry we can't do that now." Her voice began to shake. "So much we wanted to do together, but—"

Mike broke in. "Are you in danger?"

She thought fast. How could she answer with more hints about their whereabouts? "Yes, we talked about canoeing by the factory—"

Tara yanked the phone from her hand. "Michael, guess who this is."

Kate slid down the pipe to the floor, her shackled wrist limp above her head. *Goodbye, my love. I'll love you forever.*

Mike looked at the Wyoming prefix again and then put the phone back to his ear. "Who is this?" He'd been talking to Kate, when another female voice broke in. What was going on? He and Clint were on the highway. Was he catching someone else's conversation?

"You silly ninny. You know me. This is Tara."

"Tara Hughes?" His jaw dropped.

Clint, who'd pulled to the shoulder and stopped the truck when Mike said, "Kate," stared at him, eyes wide. He switched off the engine.

"Aren't you s'posed to be in Rawlins, in the pen?"

"I got out early." She sounded proud. "Good behavior."

"Good behavior? You?"

"Michael…" Her voice was low and husky. "You'll understand just *how good* I can be when we're married, darling."

"I'm already married. You know that."

Clint crossed his eyes and circled a loco sign by his ear.

"Not for long." The sultry tone took on a teasing lilt.

Mike frowned. "Let me talk to my wife."

"Hughes," A man's voice called, "quit the yacking and get in here."

She whispered, "Catch ya later, love."

Mike heard a smacking sound and then silence. He waited. "Kate, are you there?" Nothing. He peered at the readout. The call was gone, but he couldn't stop staring at the phone. Had he really just talked with Kate…and then Tara Hughes?

"What was that all about?" Clint undid his seatbelt and faced Mike, his elbow on the steering wheel.

Mike couldn't speak, couldn't think. Nothing computed. Kate and Tara sharing a phone was like a rattler and a kitten eating out of the same food dish. "That was Kate." He rubbed his forehead, staring at the darkening sky beyond the truck window. "I know it was. She said crazy stuff, but it was her."

"How did she sound?"

He pursed his lips. "Sad, like she was about to cry. That's the best I can describe her voice. Then that, that bimbo came on." He ran his fingers through his hair. "I, we, we've got to do something, Clint."

"What did Kate say?" Clint held up a hand. "Wait. Inside the glove box should be a pen and the notepad I use to track gas mileage."

Mike opened the glove box, pulled out the notepad and dug through it until he found the pen.

"I'll take those." Clint rolled the windows down part way. "You tell me everything Kate—and Tara—said and I'll write it down. Has to be something we can offer the detectives in addition to the number Kate called from." He wrote the date and time at the top of the page. "How about you give me the number now? That way if it disappears from your phone for whatever reason, we'll have it on paper."

Despite his shaking hands, Mike found the number and read it to Clint. "Has a 307 prefix, so we know the phone belongs to someone from Wyoming. Or someone who got their phone *in* Wyoming."

Clint copied the number above the date and time. "Okay, shoot."

"None of it made sense."

"It's all we've got to go on."

"Okay. First, Kate's voice came on. She sounded surprised that I answered. Then she said something about how we like to watch blue herons at the river. And how we wanted to climb a mountain that starts with an H and visit waterfalls." He scratched the beard stubble that had erupted on his chin. "I don't remember having that conversation. Maybe she said something in bed when I was falling—"

"You're knocking on the wrong door, boss."

Mike squinted at his foreman. "Huh?"

"What mountain has a name that starts with an H?"

"I don't know. Could be dozens." He shrugged. "There's the Himalayas."

"Yeah, but those are in Nepal. If Kate and Tara are together, seems they'd be in the US, not far from home."

"We could check the map or look up mountains on your phone."

"Or we could go with Mount Hood. I saw a billboard advertising the Mount Hood Scenic Byway several miles back." A motorcycle and two trucks whooshed past, sending tremors and a gust of warm diesel-tinged wind through the pickup.

"Mount Hood, in Oregon?"

"Yeah." Clint rolled his window up.

"Kate likes the picture of Mount Hood on our calendar, a lot."

"Where do blue herons live?"

"Near water, as far as I know."

"She also said something about waterfalls. Those have to be clues."

"Clues?" Mike shook his head to clear the cobwebs. He'd been in such a fog since the argument, and then the kidnapping…and now, hearing Kate's voice again, talking with her. He had to snap out of it. "Yeah, you're right. She was trying to tell me something. She wasn't just babbling."

Clint looked like he was about to jump out of the truck and run up and down the highway. "Unless I'm mistaken, Mount Hood, blue herons and waterfalls all add up to Oregon."

"Yeah…" Mike looked out the window. "Oregon is a big state."

Clint tapped the notepad. "What did she say when you asked if she was in danger?"

Mike turned away from the vehicles flashing past. Think. He had to think. "She said, 'Yes'…" He paused, trying not to dwell on what "yes" might mean. "And then something about canoeing… Yeah, canoeing on a river by a factory."

"Interesting." Clint made a note. "I bet that's crucial info. Anything else?"

"That's all, except at the end, when she said she was sorry we'd never be able to do those things. Something like, 'So much we wanted to do together…' I think that's when Tara butted in." Mike snorted. "That woman has been the bane of my—"

He stopped. "What if Kate meant she doesn't expect to…" His voice trailed off.

Clint's forehead furrowed. "I was wondering the same thing. We have to get on this, fast."

Mike swiped his hand across his eyes. They'd checked every rest area from the Utah border on, including the one Cal told them about, and found nothing to indicate Kate and the kids had ever been there. No earrings, no toys, no shoes or articles of clothing, no caretakers present to answer questions. Nothing. They'd have to call Cal for help with these new clues.

Clint wrote some more and then looked at Mike. "What did Hughes say?"

Mike didn't want to talk about Tara, didn't want to think about the crazy woman. But her involvement in the disappearance confirmed Kate's innocence, at least in his mind. Kate would never partner with Tara Hughes for any reason, good or bad. He took a long breath and blew it out his nose. "She said she got out of prison early due to good behavior, which I already knew."

Clint raised an eyebrow.

"Cal warned me about her release a couple days ago, but I figured she'd leave me alone, now that Kate and I are married." Mike shook his head. "Should a known better."

"What else did she say?"

"Get this." Mike grimaced. "She said I'd understand how good she can be when we get married."

Clint gaped at him. "What a nutcase." He made another notation in the notebook.

"And then some man told her to get off the phone."

Clint did a double-take. "The plot thickens." He slowly nodded. "Adding in a male fits the rest-area story about a man and some women and kids."

"You're right." Mike found Cal's number on his phone and was about to dial when it rang. Was it Kate again? He looked at the screen. No, it was Schroeder. He pushed the send/receive button. "This is Mike."

After a pause, he heard Schroeder's voice. "I see you took your phone."

Mike pointed at the phone and mouthed *Schroeder.*

Clint whispered, "Good timing."

"We stopped by the office," Schroeder said, "but you weren't there. And no one seemed to know where to find you. Where are you?"

"Idaho." He looked at Clint and shrugged. Might as well be honest.

"Good luck finding your wife," Schroeder said. "Hope you get your marriage back together."

"We're dealing with four missing persons and you're talking marital problems?"

Clint sat back, his forehead creased.

"Our investigation today found nothing to indicate anything more than a tiff between you and your wife. And because she has legal custody of the children, we have no reason to pursue a kidnapping angle." He cleared his throat. "The chief says we're off the case. He wants us back in Cheyenne."

"You're not going to look for—?"

"That's right. Goodbye, Mr. Duncan."

Kate held back the tears as long as she could. *God, please help Mike figure out what I was trying to say.* How he could help from so far away, she didn't know. But hearing his voice again gave her hope.

Feeling naked and vulnerable without her rings, she ran her finger across the place at the base of her finger where her rings usually sat. Now the tears began to flow. Another woman had just called her husband "love." Another woman was sending him kisses.

But that wasn't what bothered her. What hurt was knowing she might never see Mike again. Never feel his arms holding her again. *Jesus, help me.*

She prayed he understood and had already given the authorities the phone number. According to the news reports Tara shared with her on a regular basis, authorities were looking all over the West for them. But would they find her and the kids before the traffickers arrived?

"Miss Kate." Shannon's voice.

"Yes, sweetie..."

"I'm sorry."

"Sorry about what?" Kate wiped her cheeks.

"I'm sorry she stole your wedding rings and took the phone away when you were talking to Mr. Mike. She's a stupid lady. I know he would never marry her."

"I know that, too." She sniffed. "But I miss him."

"I want to go back to the ranch. We were safe there."

"Yes, we were safe...and happy."

"What's going to happen to us?"

Chapter Twenty-Seven

Kate was tempted to lie about their future, but Shannon was trusting her to tell her the truth. "I hate to say it…" She put her free arm around the girl. "But it appears they plan to sell us all to traffickers."

What light there was in the room dimmed. Kate wondered if a cloud had covered the sun or if it had lowered behind a building.

"Yeah," Shannon said, "I had a feeling." After a long pause, she added, "I know I said I miss the game. But that's not true. I just thought I did. Know what I mean?" She chewed at a nail.

"Mm-hmm." Kate dried her face with her t-shirt. "I thought maybe you forgot. Could be you had a case of temporary amnesia."

"Like Aunt Mary?"

Kate chuckled. "Yes, a bit like our sweet Aunt Mary." Thinking she might never hold her great-aunt again was painful, especially knowing her absence could worsen her frail condition.

Her aunt's words of advice came to her. "Mike is a good man. Don't let a little spat steal your joy." Tears welled in her eyes again. How she longed to hug Aunt Mary and make up with Mike. Kate closed her eyes. She had to be as honest with herself as she was with Shannon. Unless God intervened, she'd never see her loved ones again.

She touched an earlobe. At least she still had the WP earrings Mike and Laura gave her. Tara hadn't taken those. She fingered the other side—and then felt both ears again. The "W" was missing. When did that happen? She moaned. The loss hurt almost as much having her wedding rings taken from her.

The door between the rooms opened. Kate blinked away her tears. What little daylight remained revealed Tara's scantily clad form. She closed the door quietly, whispering, "He'll be snoring soon and then I can get back with Michael."

Kate shook her head. Tara's obsession was maddening. However, if she played it right, she could use the woman's fantasy to their advantage. "I didn't finish talking with him."

"You had your say. Now *I'm* the one with Michael's number—*and* his rings." Tara pulled out her cell phone. "He's *all mine*." The phone's light revealed the triumphant glow on her face. She dialed and put the phone to her ear.

You are truly off your rocker, woman. Kate sucked in air, filling her lungs to capacity. The instant Mike answered, she'd scream for help. No holding back this time. The traffickers were close. Ramsey wouldn't damage "the goods" now.

Tara lowered the phone. "He didn't answer. Must be busy."

"Leave a message." Kate tried not to sound pushy. "He'll listen soon, I promise."

"I'll call later," Tara said. "Michael prefers to hear my voice." She crossed the room. Standing in front Kate, she held the phone over her left hand, illuminating Kate's wedding rings, which sparkled in the screen's light. "They're a perfect fit," Tara said. "Maybe I'll keep them."

Kate didn't respond.

"Those are Miss Kate's rings," Shannon said. "She's the one married to Mr. Mike, not you."

Tara kicked the girl. "Shut up."

Shannon yelped and Kate shouted, "Stop it, Tara!"

Tara swung back, hand raised. "Don't you tell me what to do."

The door between the rooms flew open, slamming against the wall with a loud bang. "What's going on out here?"

"Nothing," Tara simpered. "Just visiting with our mouthy prisoners."

"Get in here with me, so I can get some sleep."

"I want to wait up for our contacts. Don't you? This is exciting."

"It'll be hours before they show."

"They're s'posed to be here sooner than that."

"Something came up. They're gonna be late. I talked to them earlier."

Tara's phone rang. "Maybe that's them."

The bright screen lit her face.

"No," Ramsey said. "Can't be—"

"Hello." Her voice was loud. "This is Tara. Who's this? Oh…" Her voice softened. "You called back. How sweet."

Kate sucked in her breath. Mike.

"Who is it?" Ramsey demanded.

Tara twisted away from him. The phone's light darted about the room.

Kate wished the kids, who were all now wide awake, weren't sitting in the middle of a war zone.

Ramsey yanked the phone from her hands. "Should a known." He cursed. "A Wyoming number."

Tara screeched. "Give me my phone."

Kate felt little hands grip her legs. She crouched closer to the frightened children. Could Mike hear the commotion? She was about to yell "help" when Ramsey spoke.

"It's your blasted daddy again." His ruthless features bleached by the screen's glare, Ramsey held the cell phone close to his contorted mouth, highlighting his crooked teeth. "Hughes, listen up and listen good. You're outa the game."

"What do you mean, out of the game?" Tara tried to wrench the phone away from him.

"Your idiot daddy is history and so is this phone." Ramsey stomped to the window that faced the river, jerked the blinds up and pounded the cell phone against the glass until it broke. The last dregs of twilight outlined his rigid body. He reared back and with a mighty heave, tossed the phone between the glass shards. River-scented air poured through the opening in sync with the waterfall and factory noises.

"Jerry!" Tara pounded his back. "What's wrong with you? That phone was our connection with our contacts—and Daddy."

And my connection to Mike. From what she remembered, the shore below the mill was littered with boulders. If the phone landed on rocks, it would have shattered. If it landed in water… Did the GPS in cell phones work in broken phones or underwater?

Ramsey lowered the blinds and the darkness deepened. "Your old man is a worthless cripple. I'm the contact now."

"But…"

"Take this key and unlock Nielson. You're all going to the back room. I need to get some sleep."

"I'll be quiet."

"Just do as I said."

"I can't see. It's too dark."

Light pierced the shadows and stabbed at Kate's eyes.

Tara released the handcuff.

"Give me the key," Ramsey said, "and guard Nielson. I'll cover the brats."

Tara's gun barrel against her back, Kate followed the children through the supply closet into the gloomy hideout. Almost as soon as Ramsey locked them in, Tara began to sob. "Michael, oh, Michael," she wailed. "He'll think I hung up on him, and I can't call him back to explain."

"Cut the noise," Ramsey pounded on the wall.

"Nobody can hear me." Tara lifted her middle finger even as she muffled her cries.

Kate settled against the wall to mull their latest circumstances. Tara's phone would do them no good smashed on the rocks or at the bottom of the river. But, thank God, before Ramsey destroyed the phone, she'd been able to talk with Mike. Surely he'd notified the authorities by now.

She thought of a sermon Pastor Chuck preached about storms. He'd said Jesus was Lord of the storms of life. If there ever was a storm, this was it. *You've walked with me through so many storms, Lord. But this is far worse than anything I've ever faced. Worse than losing my family. Worse than the worst foster home. Worse than living on the street. Worse than prison. It kills me to watch Ramsey and Tara mistreat the children.*

The room was darkening, but Kate could still see the sad faces of her three charges. *They've suffered so much already. We're running out of time. Unless you step in, they'll go right back into the hellholes they escaped.*

A scene from one of the westerns Mike loved to watch unfolded before her. Two men, one an old-timer and the other a greenhorn, stood on a mountainside, watching a huge dust storm billow toward them. As it crossed the vast empty desert below, gathering dirt and sand as it traveled, it obliterated the sun and dimmed their world. A coyote ran for cover.

The older man instructed the younger one to tie his shirt around his horse's nose and lead it into the shelter of a shallow cave. They moved the horses as far into the cave as they could and then wrapped bandanas over their own mouths and noses.

"A person can't see a bloomin' thing when these blasted dirt clouds come rollin' in," the old codger said. "And breathin' is nigh unto impossible." The bandana flapped with his words. "We gotta hunker down and wait for the storm to pass and the dust to settle. Could be a matter of hours, could be days." With that, he untied the blanket roll behind his saddle, shook it out, squatted against a rock and covered his head.

Kate stared into the darkness. *So, what does that mean, God?*

The storm will pass.

Is that what I tell the kids? Just wait for the storm to pass?

Tell them I love them. That's enough.

Yes, Lord. She nodded. *More than enough.*

She pulled Lupi, Shannon and Tieno close. "Jesus loves you," she whispered, "and so do I."

Mike was glad he'd activated the phone's speaker before he returned Tara's call. He would have had trouble describing what he heard, but Clint had caught every word of the bizarre conversation and the noises that followed. After they compared notes, he called Cal.

"Glad you called back, Mike," Cal said. "I used cell phone triangulation software to locate the phone with the number you provided and learned it belongs to Tara Hughes." He grunted. "That, of course, is no surprise. I was able to triangulate it to a point between towers near two Oregon towns located on the banks of the Willamette River—West Linn on the west and Oregon City on the east. They're about fifteen miles south of Portland.

"Blue Heron," he said, "could refer to an old paper mill called the Blue Heron Paper Company that's no longer in operation. It's on the Oregon City side next to Willamette Falls, which is touted as America's second largest waterfall. I assume Niagara Falls is the biggest. The Blue Heron is across from an active paper mill on the West Linn side of the river, which may be the factory Kate referred to.

"Mount Hood is due east of there," he added, "as the crow flies."

"Great." Mike smiled. Kate's clues were on target.

Cal paused. "Keep in mind the fact we could be barking up the wrong tree or, if the triangulation does get you close to Kate the kids, they could take off before you get there."

"Right." Mike hated to admit the possibility of failure, but he knew he had to be realistic.

When the call ended, Clint raised his hand for a high-five and the two slapped palms. "I feel like we just won the grand championship," Clint said.

Mike grinned. Everything Kate said now made sense. But she was in grave danger. And so were the kids.

Clint shifted in the driver's seat. "Ready to get back on the road?"

"Ready. But I can drive. You've been at it for hours." He wouldn't be able to sleep, so he might as well drive—and listen to Kate's message on his phone. And pray.

They got out of the truck. Cars flashed past, pummeling them with airwaves. Even so, the night air felt good. Mike stretched, hands clasped behind his head, before he climbed into the driver's seat, turned on the lights and pulled back into I-84 traffic.

Clint found Oregon City on his phone map. "Looks like we can be there in about three hours. We'll head toward Portland, but we can bypass the city." Clint held his phone so Mike could see it. "Interstate all the way."

"Great. The faster we get there, the better."

"Hey…" Clint touched his phone. "We can also get there by circling Mount Hood. Would take twice as long, but it's more proof Kate wasn't just shooting the breeze."

"Maybe we should drive that route, in case she's near the mountain."

"We wouldn't see much in the dark."

"Yeah, you're right." Mike switched to the passing lane. "We'd better take the fastest route."

"Mind if I call Amy?"

"No, not at all." Mike gave Clint a sideways glance. "You don't need to ask."

"You can't talk to Kate. I don't want to rub salt in a sore—"

"Call her, Clint, but—"

Clint cocked his head. "But what?"

"Her cell phone won't work at the ranch."

"She gave me the number for the phone in Kate's aunt's bedroom. Said she's been staying in there."

"Oh, yeah. I forgot we added a private line for Aunt Mary when she first came to live with us. But I haven't heard her make a phone call in months. Kate says numbers confuse her."

Clint tapped the phone and a moment later, said, "Hey, Amy, it's me." Pause. "Yeah…" He leaned his head against the headrest. "It's good to hear your voice, too."

Mike sensed a new tenderness in his foreman. Yep, Clint was smitten, which was okay by him. Amy was a great gal, although rough around the edges. She'd been through a lot, yet she was thoughtful and generous and had been a faithful friend to Kate. Best of all, she was determined to live life differently than she had in the past. And Tramp adored her.

"We're okay," Clint said. "Haven't slept much, but I plan to get some shuteye after we hang up. We have new clues."

"New clues? Whoo-hoo!"

Clint grinned and held the phone away from his ear. "I'm putting this on speaker, Amy, so you can talk with Mike, too."

"Hey, Mike."

"Hey, Amy."

"So, tell me about the clues. You know I'm dying to know."

Clint said, "Mike talked with Kate."

"You did?" Amy gasped. "Oh, Mike. That's wonderful. How is she? Where is she? What—?" She interrupted herself. "Sorry. I should let you talk. I'm just so excited."

"It was short," Clint said. "And she talked in code. I guess that's what you'd call it. And then—get a load of this—Tara Hughes came on."

"No way. I thought she was in prison.'

"Just got out," Mike said. "Her dad seems to be involved with whatever's going on, like you suspected, along with another man. Could be others. Those are the only ones we know about right now."

"Wow, that's mind-boggling."

"You're telling me."

"What did Kate say?"

"She talked about blue herons," Mike said, "and Mount Hood and waterfalls. Cal traced the phone, Tara's phone, that is, to a specific area in Oregon. We're headed there now."

"You mean you know where Kate is?"

Chapter Twenty-Eight

"We *think* we know." Mike wanted to believe they'd find his wife at the mill, but he knew anything could happen to thwart a rescue. "Nothing's for certain at this point."

"Oh, I hope so, Mike. I hope and pray so."

"Thanks."

"Any idea what this is all about?"

"All we know for sure," Clint said, "is that Tara Hughes still has the hots for Mike and she still thinks the WP belongs to her."

Mike grunted. "She's a nutcase. Hey, Amy, do me a favor. Would you pass all this along to my mom?"

"She's over at Freedom House. Do you want me to call her tonight or tell her first thing in the morning?"

"I hate to bother her if she's busy with the kids or resting. Tomorrow morning is soon enough. But please ask her not to give the media details, or anyone else for that matter."

"Okay. We'll be careful with what we say. Can I tell Coach?"

"Yeah. And Cyrus and Dymple and Marita. They'll keep it under their hats." He paused. "How is my mom doing? Is she holding up okay?"

"She's tired, but she says she can't stop to rest. If the media isn't hounding her, someone from the staff is asking her questions about running the ranch. Your neighbors and friends bring food, so she has to take them to the kitchen and visit with them a bit, not that she minds. If they don't stop by, they call to ask for an update. And, of course, the Freedom House children and staff need her."

She sighed. "Laura is being pulled in so many directions. I wish I knew more, so I could be more help to her. I've gone over to the kids' place a couple times to visit with Aunt Mary and play with Frankie and Gianna, just to give the children a diversion and Laura a break."

"I'm sure you're a great help to Mom. More than you know." Mike wanted to kick himself. Amy would have been trained months ago, if he hadn't been so obstinate. "Glad you're there to support her and the others—and us."

"My privilege. I love my WP family. You-all are the best."

Mike was about to respond, when she said, "I hope you don't mind, Mike, but I took Tramp with me. He's so sad and lonely without you. He loves the kids and they love him."

He raised an eyebrow. "Did he behave himself?"

"He and Mayo the Cat and Jo-Jo the Duck had to get acquainted. But once they figured out he just wanted to play, they allowed him into their domain. Gianna and Frankie giggle and giggle when the animals chase around the yard. And they like it when Tramp licks their faces. They pet him and hug him and call him *puppy*."

"Bet he's lovin' all that attention." Once things were back to normal, he'd let Mom and Kate take his dog to Freedom House every day. The question was, would *normal* ever come again?

"I'd better get some sleep," Clint said, "and give Mike my phone so he can use the map. He and his flip phone are still in the Dark Ages."

"Hey," Mike interjected. "I rarely use the thing, so I don't see any reason to spend all that money to upgrade."

"Yeah, yeah." Clint chuckled. "I miss you, Amy. With any luck, I'll call back soon with even better news."

"I miss you, too, Clint. Call anytime. Aunt Mary's phone is right by the bed. Oh, I forgot to tell you, Mike. Your vet, Doctor Hall, called. He wants you to *give him a jingle*—his words, when you get a chance."

Clint winced. "Sorry, man."

Oh, yeah, the bison cow. Mike frowned. He'd forgotten about the dead bison and the possible introduction of MCF into his herd. "I'll call him tomorrow, if I get a chance." Right now, rescuing Kate and the kids was all that mattered.

"Dymple stopped by today to pray with us," Amy said. "She asked me to tell you she's holding you and Clint up before the thistle."

"Thistle?" Mike looked at Clint, who shrugged.

"That's what I asked." Amy giggled. "She meant to say 'throne,' God's throne."

"Oh, I get it." He grinned. "Please thank her for us."

"She also said to remind you that those who hope in the Lord will renew their strength."

"I appreciate the reminder." He had no idea how to rescue Kate and the kids. Strength and wisdom for whatever lay ahead would have to come not from his limited resources but from God, who was their *only* hope.

Mike slowed the pickup and pulled off I-205 at the Oregon City/McLoughlin Boulevard exit. Clint lifted his head from the denim jacket he'd rolled and pressed against the window.

"We're here," Mike said. "Oregon City." He braked and took a left at a light. "The Blue Heron Paper Company is close." He lowered his window. The smell of humidity and vegetation wafted into the cab.

"After a long curve, we turn right and we'll be on Blue Heron's doorstep."

His insides jittered. They were less than a mile from his wife—*if* Cal's findings were correct and *if* she was still there.

Clint yawned and sat upright. "Surprising amount of traffic this time of night—or morning." He picked up the cell phone. "Yeah, morning."

At the curve's end they were stopped by a traffic light.

"Cool mural." Clint pointed to the bar-and-grill on their left. Dimly lit by the corner street light, the painting that stretched across the bricks featured a river and a waterfall and what looked like mills or factories. Native Americans, loggers and other workers provided a glimpse into the area's early history. "Interesting place," Clint said. "I read somewhere that the Oregon Trail ended right here in Oregon City."

Mike eyed the panorama. "We studied the trail in Wyoming History class and visited places like Fort Laramie and Register Cliff. But I don't remember talking about where it ended." God willing, this was where Kate's journey along a similar route would end.

A quaint-looking shop occupied the opposite corner, but cattycorner from the bar, the buildings were more industrial. Mike glanced up the side of the tallest one. "This is it, Clint."

Clint followed his gaze and read aloud, "The Blue Heron Paper Company. What d'ya know." A big blue bird with a wide wingspread "flew" above the company name.

The light changed. Bouncing over the railroad tracks that ran down the middle of the road, they turned south on Main Street and drove half a block. Streetlights illumined the paved road that led into the compound. Ahead of them, a chain-link fence glinted in the headlights. Almost as soon as Mike stopped the pickup, a uniformed man exited the small but well-lit guardhouse on the other side of the fence. Behind the guardhouse, random solitary lights hinted at multi-shaped buildings.

A short train roared past on the left, vibrating the truck. Mike saw only brief flashes of light as the passenger train zipped by, but it was fairly close. The track it followed apparently ran along the east side the mill.

The guard waved them over.

Mike cut the truck lights and pulled parallel with the fence.

Hand on the butt of the pistol hanging at his side, the guard's gaze flicked from the front of the pickup to Mike's face. He peered inside. "Good evening, gentlemen. Need help finding your way?"

"We were hoping to get a look at the mill." Mike pointed to what he could see of the structures behind the fence. Kate was somewhere in that maze.

The man folded his arms. "You expecting a midnight spook tour or what?" The white stitching on his name patch read *Harold Ivins, Deep Anchors Security Service.*

"Uh, well…" Mike shrugged. "We just got into town."

"Drive all the way from Wyoming?"

How did—? Mike gave him a questioning look but then nodded. The guy had seen the license plate.

"The mill has been closed for several years now," Harold said. "Really hurt the economy in this area. Lot of people lost their jobs, including me and my brother. However, I'm one of the lucky ones. The security agency took me on as a watchman—at a third of the income." He pressed his lips together. "Thank the good Lord the house was already paid off. I didn't have to move away like so many others did."

With a slow, sad shake of his head, he indicated the road they'd just exited. "Best way to see the mill is to get back on the highway, or McLoughlin Boulevard as we call it, and turn right. During daylight— you won't see much right now—follow the road to the overlook. Can't miss it. You can see the falls from there as well as this mill. You'll also see a power plant and an active paper mill on the far side of the river. Great view."

Clint leaned toward the man. "Speaking of spooky, do you patrol that huge place? Looks like a good setting for a horror movie."

"We have flashlights and guns. And a person gets used to the quiet, the echoes, the strange noises…the rats. Even the sound of drips."

"Ever see anything unusual?"

"You mean, besides partying, graffiti-painting, hooligan juveniles?"

Clint chuckled. "Yeah."

"It's a big place with access by foot *and* by boat." Harold rested his hand on a fence link. "If someone didn't want me to see them, there's plenty of places to hide. Fifty-some buildings in all, yet Deep Anchors only hires one watchman per shift." He shook his head again. "Guess they feel the place is so decrepit trespassers can't do much damage.

"To answer your question…" He motioned to Clint. "I hear suspicious noises now and then and see flickers of light. But by the time I get there…" He shrugged. "I don't see anything unusual, except the graffiti the gangs leave behind."

Mike nudged Clint and murmured out of the corner of his mouth, "Should I tell him?"

Clint's focus shifted from Mike to the watchman. "Seems like a decent sort."

Propping his elbow on the door panel, Mike said, "You may have heard about the woman and three kids who disappeared in Wyoming several days ago."

"I saw something on the news about an ex-con named Duncan, which is my wife's maiden name, and some orphan kids. Dark-haired woman, cute little kids. Are those the people you're talking about?"

"That woman is my wife. Despite what the media says, she's a wonderful person. Kate had a tough childhood, but that's all behind her now."

Mike had seen the pictures. He wasn't sure where the media obtained the photos. Neither he nor his mom had spoken with reporters, so he assumed the kids' pictures came from either Wyoming or Texas Family Services.

Kate's photo, which must have been provided by the Pennsylvania Department of Corrections, showed her in an orange jumpsuit. Because she had few pictures of herself from age eight on, this was the first one he'd seen of her as a young adult, other than her senior picture.

The image hadn't remained long on the television screen, but it saddened him, nonetheless. Kate was as beautiful as ever, but she looked so young, lost and alone—and frightened. The children's expressions were similar. He had to find them and take them home.

The man studied Mike as if he was trying to decide whether or not to believe him.

"What you probably didn't hear," Mike added, "is that the trail leads to the Blue Heron Paper Company. That's why we drove here from Wyoming, to look for them."

The watchman's brow furrowed. "How do I know you're not making that up?"

"Show him your driver's license," Clint said. "You have the same last name as Kate."

Mike pulled his wallet from his back pocket, extricated the license and offered it to Harold. He'd do whatever it took to speed things along. They were so close.

Harold took a flashlight from his belt and scrutinized the card. He stared at Mike and then at the license again before he pushed it between the links. "I heard the search was called off. The authorities decided it was a marital issue." He peered at Mike. "You and your missus have a spat?"

"The detectives found no evidence of wrongdoing, so the marriage thing is the excuse they came up with to end the search. And that's why we're here—to find Kate and the kids. No one else is looking for them."

"Why do you think your wife ended up at the Blue Heron?"

"We think she and the kids were kidnapped."

"Are you sure?" Harold frowned. "That doesn't—"

"We suspect they've been taken by human traffickers, probably for sex purposes."

Harold snapped to attention. "Traffickers?"

"Yeah."

"The newspaper has had a bunch of articles about that." He scowled. "Fries my gizzard to think people would steal kids and sell them to pimps or to factories or farms overseas. If that's what's going on in this mill, I'll put a stop to it, pronto."

"Better get your local authorities involved," Clint suggested. "People who buy and sell other people are rotten to the core and don't let anyone stand in their way."

Mike leaned out the window. "What would it take for you to let us in? I have cash." He'd never bribed anyone before, but maybe it would help the guard understand how desperate he was to find Kate and the kids.

"I don't take bribes." Harold raised his palm. "However, I'm sympathetic to your cause. If I were in your shoes, I'd do everything in my power to find my wife, even if we'd had a squabble. When you get hitched, you make a promise to hang in there, for better or for worse."

He started for the gate. "I'll let you in. If this becomes an issue with the boss, I'll face the consequences. It's about time for me to retire, anyway."

"Thanks, man. I really appreciate your help. But I hope you don't lose your job over this. Where should we leave the truck?"

"Over there. In front of that office." He angled his chin at a small building on their side of the fence.

Mike parked the pickup and gave the keys to Clint. Pulling the metal box from under the seat, he handed it to Clint to unlock. They assembled and loaded their guns as fast as they could and then belted their holsters over their jeans. Clint found a flashlight in the glovebox.

Mike pulled his cell phone from his shirt pocket. "Better put the phones on vibrate. We don't want to miss calls from Kate or Cal, but we also don't want ringing phones to alert the kidnappers."

When Harold opened the gate, he glanced at their guns but made no comment. Instead, he stepped into the guard shack and brought out a two-way radio and another flashlight. "I'll walk the streets that run between the buildings. You can go around the backside, down by the river, and search beneath the mill property." He held up the two-way. "We can radio each other with information."

"What do you mean by *beneath* the property?"

"Several of the buildings extend out from the hillside and are supported by concrete pillars. As a result, they have lower levels that are something like open-air basements."

"How likely are we to find my wife down there?" Mike hated to doubt the man's judgement. After all, he patrolled the complex. But they needed to get inside, not underneath, the mill. And they needed to do it fast.

Harold aimed the flashlight at the buildings. "If she's here, she could be anywhere. Like I said, it's a big place—twenty-three acres and fifty-some buildings. I know my way inside and outside those buildings. You don't. I can let you know if I spot anything suspicious up top.

"But down there..." He focused the light on downward-leading metal steps that ran alongside the nearest building. "Down there is the river access. If anyone is coming or going by boat or hiding out underneath the buildings, you'll see them."

Mike was about to take the stairs, when Harold said, "Come to think of it, you might be better off waiting here. The shore down there is no sandy beach. It's covered with boulders, machine parts, logs and who knows what else has washed up. Rough going. Stay here and I'll let you know—"

Mike raised a hand. "I'm going down. We might see something you wouldn't see up top."

Harold held out the flashlight and the two-way.

"We can use another flashlight," Mike said. "Radios make too much noise. You have a cell phone?"

"I do."

"Add our numbers and put it on vibrate. We'll add yours to our phones."

The task took way too long, but finally they parted ways, promising to report any suspicious sightings.

Mike and Clint had just begun the descent, when Harold called to them. Clint turned back but Mike kept going. He was too close to Kate to stop. He hurried down the long stairway to the river, breathing in the humid air and the stale smell of damp, aging structures. The distant roar grew in volume as he rounded a corner and saw what Harold had warned them about—rocks, and plenty of them.

The stones varied in size. Some were of football and basketball proportions but many were bigger, some much bigger. The rubble covered the ground all the way down to the river and along the shore as far as he could see. Beyond the basalt boulders, moonlight sputtered across the Willamette's current like shredded cloth in the wind.

Chapter Twenty-Nine

The sound of metal rasping against metal roused Kate. She opened her eyes and lifted her head. Ramsey's light glared in her face. She looked away.

"Get up," he ordered. "Showtime."

No, God. Kate's heart thumped. She'd prayed and prayed this moment would never come. *This can't be the end. You can't let them sell the kids! Please, no—*

"Here, let me help you up."

Surprised by Ramsey's change of tone, Kate looked over in time to see him take Tara's hand and raise her to her feet.

"Why, thank you, Jer," Tara said. "My legs are half asleep from sitting on the—" Her syrupy voice turned sharp. "What are you doing?"

"Just relieving you of your weapons, for your safety. You don't want to look like a threat to these guys. They're as skittish as alley cats."

"But I could sweet talk them. You know that."

"Yeah, I know all about you and your sweet talkin'."

Kate helped the children stand. She couldn't tell if Ramsey was making fun of Tara or flirting with her. Whatever his intent, he sounded unusually eager.

Once again, Ramsey shined the light at them. "Look alert. Don't let them see how stupid you are."

Tieno, Shannon and Lupi clung to Kate, shaking and whimpering.

He kicked the door all the way open.

Kate knelt before the three children. "No matter what happens," she whispered, kissing each of them on the forehead, "never forget that Jesus loves you, now and forever."

The children fell into her arms, weeping.

Ramsey was beside her in one step. He grabbed her hair and yanked her upright.

Pain shot up the side of her head.

"Move it." He pushed her toward the opening.

Kate staggered behind the children as he marched them to their doom. The traffickers were here, ready to take them away—to separate them forever. She'd promised the kids Jesus would go with them. But where was he now?

Mike glanced at Clint, who was climbing onto a neighboring rock. "Sorry I took off like that. Had to get moving."

Clint looked from the river to the buildings above them. "Harold wasn't joking. It's a big place." He pointed upriver. "He said he'll make his way building by building to the south end of the property and that we should do the same. He'll be at street level on the hill above us."

The few structures Mike could see were random-shaped and dark. One had an outside light but no lights glimmered in the windows.

"So that's where all the noise is coming from." Clint looked across the water. "The place is lit up like a Christmas tree."

"I'd like to think it's the factory Kate mentioned."

Below them, a black cat sniffed at a dead fish lying at the water's edge. The cat's dark coat reflected moonlight.

Mike swept his flashlight beam over the shoreline. Rocks and old machinery cluttered the slope that slanted from the office buildings above them down to the water's edge.

Clint whistled. "Looks like a space-station junkyard."

"We've got some climbing to do."

"Yeah. Wish I was wearing my hiking boots."

"Think we have enough moonlight to make it through without a flashlight?"

"Worth a try."

Mike switched off the light and started across the boulder field.

The cat vaulted into the shadows.

~:~:~

From the moonlight that seeped around the blinds in the outer room, Kate could make out the outlines of four hooded figures. Each person held a flashlight, the lights aimed at the floor. Before she could get a better look, they raised the beams and blinded her.

A young-sounding male voice barked, "Line up in front of the wall!"

Kate wished she could see what she was up against, but with the light in her eyes, all she could do was look down. She pulled the children to the wall.

"Separate."

The children clung to Kate, sobbing.

"Now." A loud snap followed by a jarring thump on the wall made them all jerk and gasp.

Kate recognized the sound of a whip and quickly pushed the children to either side of her.

"Whoa, I'm outa here." Tara stepped to the side.

The whip cracked again. "Back in line, you blonde bitch."

"But I'm not—"

"Oh, yes, you are." Ramsey thrust her toward Shannon, who tumbled against Kate.

"No, not me," Tara cried. "You're here for her and the kids, not me."

Another loud pop.

Tara screamed and grabbed her arm. "You hurt me!"

"Next one will break the skin *and* the bone."

Kate turned from Tara's terrified expression. She should have known this would be the time and place Ramsey dumped the gullible woman.

Tara's breath came in short, choking wheezes.

Ramsey growled, "Quiet."

"Spread out. Face the wall."

Kate spun and placed her hands on the shoulders of the nearest children, Shannon and Tieno. If only she could touch Lupi.

"Hands off the brats."

Kate dropped her arms to her sides. Lights crawled up and down the dusty wall. They were being inspected like cattle in a sales barn. No, it was worse than that. She clenched her fists. *We're slaves on an auction block.*

"No matter what they say or do…" She spoke to the wall. "You're worth far more than any amount of money they give Ramsey. That means you, too, Tara."

A crackle sizzled through the air. Kate felt a sharp sting on her calf and her knee buckled. She fell against the wall.

"Shut it, slut."

She flinched. She hadn't been called that word in a long time, except by Ramsey.

"Turn around."

Tara was now crying so hard she hiccupped between sobs. The children's cries were muted. Through the broken window came the roar of the waterfall's crash over the rocky ledge.

Again, flashlight beams roamed their bodies, up and down, back and forth, lingering here, pausing there. The traffickers murmured among themselves, never addressing Ramsey. She heard only snatches of conversation. "Good legs ... bigger butt ... hormones ... injections ... porn shots ... that guy in Vegas is looking for ... make babies ... ship off to ..."

Sickened, Kate could only pray. Against four armed traffickers plus Ramsey, she was powerless. But if God set things in motion and gave her strength, she'd—

"They'll do," the leader said. "Mr. Ramsey, my men will escort the merchandise down to the boat while you and I negotiate in the next room."

Ramsey swore. "First, the cash, Adolph. Then you take 'em away."

Adolph. She would remember that name.

Four bright beams fastened on Ramsey's face. The intense white light made his angry features look even more cruel than usual. His forehead vein throbbed.

"Up to this point, we've had a good understanding, Mr. Ramsey." Kate heard a new level of menace in Adolph's voice. "If you'd like to continue to do business with us, I'd advise you to operate according to our rules."

"These are my people. I call the shots."

"My men will take the goods—now. Then we can talk."

"No!" Ramsey jumped in front of the kids, a pistol in each hand.

The flashlight rays followed him.

Snarling, he pointed the guns at the men. "Get outa here."

Adolph muttered something and the lights switched off. For a brief instant, all was silent. Then Kate heard a rustle of cloth and a grunt followed by two gunshots, one right after the other.

"Get down!" She pushed the children to the floor.

Tara shrieked. "Don't shoot!"

Bright shafts of light shattered the darkness, rocketing about the room.

Kate squinted into the chaotic beams. A hooded man shoved Ramsey aside. Ramsey growled, lowered his head and charged at the group, knocking someone to the floor.

Others joined the fray, swinging and kicking. Expletives spewed like shrapnel. Tara screamed. The floor shook.

Kate rushed the children along the wall. A handgun skidded across the floor. She grabbed it and steered the kids around the corner, where they stopped, their progress blocked by the desk and the fighting. She lifted Lupi onto the desk, whispering in her ear, "Climb to the other side and jump off."

Gun poised, she glanced at the men. From what she could see in the flashes of light, Ramsey was cornered and Tara had crouched by the wall.

Lupita and Tieno clambered over the desk, Shannon right behind them. Kate was about to follow when someone grabbed her neck and hooked her in a headlock. She clawed at the man's arm. "Run, kiddos, run!"

He tightened his hold on her throat.

Her vision dimmed. Kate dropped the gun, grabbed his forearm with both hands and twisted it downward. Backing out from under his armpit, she stepped behind him, rammed his arm toward his shoulder blade, kneed the back of his knee and pushed him away. He flew onto his face, landing with a loud bellow. She took off for the door, but he snagged her ankle and she hurtled to the floor.

Before she could stand, he jerked her upright. "Cuffs! Someone give me cuffs."

Kate fought hard, but she was no match for two of them. They threw her against the wall, wrenched her arms behind her back, handcuffed her and stuffed a dirty cloth into her mouth.

Fighting her gag reflex, she searched for the children in the fleeting, shifting light and saw that gags had been tied over their mouths. Their hands were secured in front. Her heart broke for them even as she willed them to be brave.

Kate sucked in a ragged breath through her nose and looked for Ramsey. All was quiet now, except for the background rumbles, sounds of heavy breathing and Tara's muted moans. Apparently, she'd also been gagged. The office smelled like a locker room.

Three flashlight beams bounced over Tara and across each child to Kate. Back and forth, back and forth the lights swung. That accounted for three traffickers. Where was the fourth man?

She heard voices and saw a light in the next room. "Mr. Ramsey…" Adolph's rock-hard voice again. "That's just a taste of how we operate. With your cooperation, we can continue to do business for a long—"

"How you operate means nothin' to me." Ramsey sounded breathless—and as belligerent as ever.

"Hold on." A hooded form, vaguely silhouetted in the dim light, appeared in the doorway between the two rooms. "Take 'em down." She recognized Adolph's voice. "We'll follow."

Adolph's henchmen rushed Kate, Tara and the children to a set of metal doors she hadn't seen before. The screech of rusted hinges grated painfully against her eardrums. One man grabbed Shannon and another took the younger children by their thin arms. The third trafficker waved Kate and Tara ahead with his gun.

The men's lights revealed a narrow landing and wide metal stairs descending into darkness. Kate lurched downward, barely able to keep her balance. Their clanging footsteps echoed between the concrete walls. Tara fell and bounced down a handful of steps to another landing. Ignoring her frantic moans, the trafficker set her back on her feet and crammed her foot into the high-heel sandal that had tumbled after her.

"One of the men hollered, "Keep her moving." He prodded Kate in the back. "That means you, too."

She descended the next step but hesitated when she heard what sounded like a gunshot—and then another.

"Was that what I think it was?" one of the men asked.

"We'll find out soon enough." The man elbowed Kate downward again.

They exited the stairs through another set of tarnished doors into an open area with tall, wide windows. Enough moonlight filtered into the cavernous chamber that she could see it was a place they'd already traversed. Hearing loud clomps on the stairs behind them, she turned her head and saw Adolph's hooded form jogging toward them.

"What a bozo." He caught up with them. "Thought he could call the shots." He brandished a shotgun. "Too bad, really. Could a been a regular supplier. Blade, text Lizard about both stiffs—the security guard we offed on the way in and the Wyoming guy upstairs. Use the code. And tell him to collect their weapons."

Kate twisted away from the traffickers. Two men? They'd killed two men in a matter of minutes but talked like it was all in a day's work. And Ramsey dead... The thought was too much to digest. Far more crucial was figuring out how to save the kids from these coldblooded maggots.

From the big room, Kate and the others were herded down cement stairs into a subterranean chamber with a rock-strewn floor. Concrete pillars supported the edifice above. By the sound of it, the waterfall wasn't far away.

The mold was stronger beneath the building. She couldn't stop the sneeze. Blocked by the gag in her mouth, the pressure felt like it would burst her sinuses.

The group struggled between rocks and sloshed through stagnant pools that smelled like sour mud. Flashlight beams reflected the water's lime-green sheen. Kate's sandals snagged something slimy. She cringed but kept moving.

Tara slipped and landed face down in the goop, legs flailing, shoes flying. She gurgled like she was being strangled.

Adolph kicked her side. "Stand up, slut."

Like a deflated balloon, her body sunk into the pool.

"Pick her up, Blade. Roach."

Two men walked over and lifted her to a standing position, but she hung limp between them.

Adolph cursed. "Cut the drama, bitch."

Kate tried to tell them Tara couldn't breathe but her sounds were unintelligible. And she couldn't use hand motions.

Shannon stepped in front of Tara, reached up with her bound hands and pulled the soggy rag from her mouth. She dropped it in the muck and moved away.

Tara coughed, sputtered and coughed again. She took a breath, stood a little taller and took another breath—and another before she lifted her head. Filth dripped from her face and hair. Someone shined a flashlight on her face.

Awareness sparked in her eyes. "What…?" The word burbled from her throat. She spit out a mouthful of green liquid. "What…" She retched and coughed up more fluid. Then she stuck out a foot. "My shoes. Where are my shoes?"

"Forget the shoes."

Tara started to cry.

Kate shook her head. Only Tara... She'd come within seconds of dying and her only thought was for her shoes.

Adolph trained his flashlight between two of the columns that supported the massive edifice above them. "We'll take 'em through there."

"Shoes, I need my—"

"Shut up!" Adolph pivoted. "I hate whiny women. Who has an extra bandana?"

"I do." Blade patted his back pocket.

"Use it."

Grabbing a handful of Tara's hair, Blade jerked her head back and stuffed the cloth into her mouth, muffling a cry.

Adolph led them out from under the big building into the night.

Kate recognized the rocky shore that stretched between them and the river below. She tried to remember how long ago she'd rowed across from the other side. Was it hours or days?

Chapter Thirty

His back against a pillar, Mike caught his breath while he waited for Clint. Climbing over rocks and creeping through jumbled debris tangled with slippery vines was slow going. He switched on his flashlight, shining it at the huge buildings and rough shoreline that lay ahead. Eventually, they'd be stopped by the waterfall, which was louder now. And then what? He turned the light off.

For all he knew, the kidnappers had taken Kate and the kids and left the premises. He hadn't heard even a whisper from Harold and he didn't respond to phone calls or texts. Mike slapped the flashlight in his palm. What if Harold was in cahoots with the traffickers and had sent him and Clint on a wild goose chase?

He should call Cal. The lack of action was killing him.

Clint worked his way up the rocky slope to Mike. When he arrived at the pillar, he leaned against it and slid to a seated position. "You'd think chasing cows up and down gullies would keep a guy in shape."

"Slick-soled boots don't help." Mike kicked a rock. It plunked against a boulder. "We're getting nowhere fast."

Clint pulled his cell phone from his belt. "Forty-two minutes from the time we parked the truck. Getting through this rock pile is taking longer than I expected."

"Way too long."

"Did you hear that?" Clint's voice was low.

"All I hear is the waterfall."

"Over there. Voices." Clint pointed toward the base of the next building.

They strained forward.

Featureless forms stepped from the shadows into the silvery moonlight. Clumped together, individual people were difficult to distinguish. Mike couldn't tell if they were men or women.

He signaled Clint. Skirting rocks and rubble, they crept toward the next column. Mike's heart pounded like a runaway horse. Was Kate in that group?

Kate sucked in the river-scented air, a welcome relief after the fetid pools. She'd just begun to check out that section of shore when Adolph directed his light along the shore. The bright beam landed on a boat tethered below the rocks.

"Roach, was that a smart place to park the boat?" His voice had an ugly tinge to it.

"You said to get close, Adolph." Along with an accent she couldn't place, his high-pitched voice had a nasal whine.

"I said, 'Get closer, *if* you can find a good loading area.'" Adolph shoved Roach.

Roach fell backward onto the rocks but quickly pushed himself to a seated position. He stared at Adolph and rubbed his arm.

"Any moron would have done better than that. Get up," Adolph ordered. "And move it to the usual spot." He turned to Blade. "Light the way."

Adolph slid behind Kate. "I'll cover this one." He grabbed her hair and yanked her head so far back all she could see was stars. "I hear you and your little friends have experience in the industry." His mouth was close to her ear. "I'll have to check out your skills."

His breath sickened her. "If you're good enough, "he continued, "I'll make you my bottom girl and call you Delilah. You 'll be in charge of training new recruits. Most of them have no idea how to please a man." He snickered. "You can use me for show-and-tell."

Kate gagged, jerking from his grasp. Her scalp felt like her hair was being pulled out by the roots.

Adolph sneered and stepped to the side, his gaze on Roach, who was making his way between boulders down to the shore, moving in and out of the light. He splashed into the river, climbed over the side of the boat and must have started the motor because the vessel swung away from shore. No engine sounds were discernible above that of the waterfall.

"Let's go." Adolph hurried them along the building's pillars in the direction of the waterfall. The men pushed the women and dragged the children through the rocks and debris. Finally, they cleared the building and the rocks and stopped in an open area covered with nugget-size pebbles. Adolph aimed his light down the incline to where Roach was tethering the boat to a rusted pipe.

Kate eyed the factory on the other side of the river. If she could free her hands, she could jump in the river and swim across. With all the noise and steam that belched from the place, people probably worked there around the clock. She'd been attempting to break free all along, but she had no tools and she could tell the effort was making her hands swell.

Adolph sniffed Tara. "You stink."

She snarled, her tears apparently replaced by anger.

"I like 'em feisty." He chuckled and turned to Roach, who'd just joined them. "You guard skunk slut here. I'll steer the boat."

The others laughed.

Tara whirled and darted up the hill.

Adolph slammed her with his gun, knocking her against Kate, who dropped to the rocks. Her breath whooshed from her lungs and sharp pains shot from her leg to her head. She blinked, but all she could see through the star-spangled fog was a gun barrel pointed at her face. She blinked again. Beyond the gun, waterfall spray glinted beneath a full moon.

Adolph hissed, "Stand up."

Neither Tara nor Kate stirred.

"We're getting in the boat, now." He jerked Tara upright. "Understood?"

Adolph grasped Kate's arm and yanked her to her feet. Swaying like a reed in the wind, she fought to remain conscious…for the kids. *For the kids—and for Mike.* If not for them, she'd gladly give in to the darkness.

Mike slipped behind a cement barrier and peered over the top at the people they'd been following. The bright moonlight allowed him to see them almost as clearly as if it was daytime.

A moment later, Clint crouched beside him, pistol in hand.

"Looks to me like four men," Mike whispered. "Three of them have the kids. The other one is guarding Kate and another woman."

"You sure?"

"I'm sure."

Step by step, the group maneuvered down the incline toward the river. Any noise they made was smothered by waterfall din. Someone tripped and fell. Mike groaned. "Kate." He coiled, ready to spring to her rescue.

Clint grabbed his arm. "I see at least two rifles. You run out there now, they'll mow you down."

Mike gripped his pistol. Kate's hands were cuffed behind her back.

It took everything within him not to jump up and open fire.

A hooded figure pulled her into the cluster again. They continued their slow descent.

Kate tripped again.

And again, Clint stopped Mike. "Not yet," he whispered, "not yet."

Still crowded together, the knot of traffickers and prisoners shuffled down the shore to a boat that looked to Mike to be about twice the size of a rowboat.

As soon as they'd dropped the kids into the boat, two of the men crawled in and then took hold of Kate's arms. The other two steadied the boat while they hauled her and the other woman over the side.

Mike started forward.

Clint held his arm.

"But Kate…"

"Has to be a way to rescue them without anyone getting hurt."

"Like what?"

"We could trail 'em."

"How?" Mike pointed at the rocks they'd just traversed. "You know how hard it is to walk on this stuff, and we don't have a boat."

"We could hang onto that one. Looks like it has a swim platform on the back."

Mike studied boat. He'd noticed the swim platform but hadn't thought much about it. He turned to Clint, knowing they didn't have time to debate the pros and cons of the idea. "It's a longshot but worth a try." He unbuttoned his shirt. "You have a retention holster like mine, right?"

"Yeah."

"Good. Our guns won't slide out." He glanced at the sky, where a dark cloud had floated beneath the moon and was slowly eclipsing its light.

They deposited their boots, shirts, phones and wallets in a rock crevice and tightened the gun belts on their waists. After making sure the holsters were still strapped to their legs, they darted from behind the cement barrier to crawl between the boulders to the river.

Mike's breath caught when he slid into the cold water coming off the waterfall. Head low, he dogpaddled against the current that tugged at his Levis.

"Roach. Druid." The ringleader's voice carried over the water. "Push us farther out."

Two men slid over the edge of the boat and into the water.

Mike heard grunts and saw the crowded craft wobble. The boat moved deeper into the river. It looked like it was made for five or six people, not nine, if his count was right, and sat low in the water. The two men clambered back on board.

Out of the corner of his eye, he could see Clint's dark head bobbing with the waves. He paddled closer to the boat. Clint did the same.

The moonlight dimmed. Mike looked up. Above the waterfall, a dense cloud covered most of the moon. Only a thin shard of light silvered the cloud's ragged edge.

Riding the ripples, he floated close enough to thrust his fingers into a wide slit on the teak swim platform. Clint worked his way to the other side and found a handhold in another slot. With any luck, they wouldn't be seen at the back of the boat. But they'd have to remember to keep their legs away from the propeller.

The cloud obliterated the moon, shrouding the boat in darkness.

Kate was only inches away. Mike longed to lift her out of the vessel into his arms. *Soon*, he promised himself. *Soon*.

Raindrops plopped around him, haphazardly at first, creating bubbles that reflected the light on the other shore. And then, like feverish fleas, the drops began to dance on the water. The drizzle, which wasn't cold, seemed to warm the air above his shoulders.

The motor whirred and the boat made a slow U-turn.

Swallowing a mouthful of cold river water, Mike tightened his grip. The boat headed downriver, away from the falls. Head low, he clung with all his strength, praying the two of them could hang on until the traffickers arrived at their destination.

"Can't we go any faster?" someone asked.

"This thing has an electric motor," the leader responded. "Lizard's idea. He thought our other boat was too loud. This one is quiet, but the faster we go, the more battery power it sucks, and it's needed for another job besides ours tonight."

Moving at a crawl, the boat barely made a splash. The waterfall roar receded and the noise and light from the paper mill on the far side of the river intensified. A craft with lights trained on the water traveled upriver across from them at a fair rate of speed, hugging the shore beneath the active paper mill, its motor muted by the mill's rumble.

"Did you see that sign?" one of the men asked. "The one that said they're gonna turn the Blue Heron into a tourist attraction?"

"Yeah." The leader cursed. "We'll have to find another transfer station. Boils my blood. That old mill is the best place we've found so far."

They left the factory racket and glow behind. Other than an occasional duck quack, all was silent until they motored under a bridge and three cars rolled over their heads.

The boat pulled noiselessly alongside a dark sternwheeler that looked like it had seen many a day on the river. On the other side of the riverboat, a handful of sailboats were moored at a dimly lit marina. Mike was surprised to see a well-lit Clackamas County Sheriff's Department Marine Unit office in the marina. But now that he thought about it, it made sense for deputies to patrol rivers as well as dry land. Too bad no officers were in sight.

Chapter Thirty-One

Mike didn't know how far they'd traveled—one, maybe two miles, but when he didn't think his cold, numb fingers could hang on any longer, the boat rounded a short peninsula and slid into an inlet overshadowed by tall trees.

His toe banged against a rock and he let go. Hunkered in the stone-studded shallows, he stretched his cramped fingers and squinted into the gloom. Where was Clint?

Mike turned, careful to not disturb the water and draw attention. Clint was several feet away, head barely above the river's surface. They'd both made it this far, thank God.

Rain came down harder, veiling the lights on the bridge in the distance. The current drifted past him, gurgling beneath the rain patter.

The boat stopped several yards ahead. A moment later, a dim red light materialized from the trees and bounced toward them. A male voice whispered, "Throw me the line."

Mike's eyes adjusted enough to the murkiness that he could see the man wrap the boat's dock line around a tree stump before he hastened to help the others remove the victims.

"Take 'em up to the bus." The leader's voice was low. "After we dunk the skunk." He sniggered. "Hey, I made a rhyme. Dunk her, Roach."

Following several seconds of whimpers, grunts and violent splashes, someone whispered, "Done."

"Did you put her all the way under?"

"Three times."

"So the skunk slut's been baptized." The leader chortled. "She'd better smell like a rose or we'll have to tie her to the top of the bus."

One of the men snorted. "Or drag her behind."

Mike frowned. Were they doing something to Kate or to the other woman? He thought he'd seen Kate in the group that was now on the shore.

Clint whispered. "What's that about?"

Mike shook his head and watched the traffickers lead the victims into the trees. If he and Clint opened fire now, Kate and the kids could get hurt or killed. As anxious as he was to rescue his wife, they'd have to wait for an opening. He signaled Clint and was about to walk out of the water when he saw movement on the shore.

One of the men had remained behind. He unwound the line, pushed the boat into deeper water, climbed in and took off downriver. The motor's quiet whirr faded as the vessel merged with the mist.

Mike stood up and started for the trees. Sharp rocks tore at his feet.

"Boss." Clint's hoarse whisper came from the direction of the river.

Mike stopped.

"My foot's caught in the rocks. Go on ahead. I'll be right behind you."

Mike darted across the stony slope and into the water. He took a breath and lowered beneath the surface to claw at the rocks that pinned Clint's foot. Unsuccessful, he rose for air and tried again. The third time he sucked in a breath, Clint said, "Follow Kate. I'll figure a way out of this."

Mike stared at the trees and then back at Clint. "We're in this together."

"Go."

"If you don't get loose or we're separated—"

"Go." Clint waved him away.

Mike sprinted for the trees, ignoring the pain in his feet and scanning the dark woods for movement—or a flashlight. Anything. Though he saw nothing, he pushed forward. The bus couldn't be far.

Hazy light blurred by rain and striped by trees broke into the night. *Headlights.* Mike's pulse, which was already pounding, erupted. They were on the bus. He broke into a run but tripped on a tree root and smashed into dense foliage. The branches tore at his bare chest. He rolled out of the bush and hurried after the bus, which had begun to move.

By the time he reached the edge of the trees, the dark vehicle was crunching across a graveled stretch between trees. Breathing hard, Mike steadied himself against a tree trunk. He pulled his pistol from the holster strapped to his leg, shook out the water and aimed for a back tire.

He fired three shots but the bus kept going. Before he could fire again, it turned and sped out of range, weaving through the trees. He was just starting after it when Clint charged to his side, gun in hand. "I'm with you, man. We can catch it."

They darted between bushes and trees into a dimly lit open area with grass, picnic tables and a narrow asphalt lane. The big vehicle passed under a light. "Looks like a camouflaged school bus," Clint said. "A long one."

They ran after it.

The bus exited the park, turned from the lighted entrance onto a dark two-lane road, passed a group of motor homes parked by the river and picked up speed. Ignoring the pain in his bruised feet, Mike ran until he could run no farther. He holstered his gun. Breathing hard, he bent over, hands propped on his knees. He'd gotten close enough to Kate he could have touched her. But then he lost her.

Neither man spoke as they sucked in breath after breath and watched the bus's taillights disappear when it turned left.

Once he could speak again, Mike asked, "Did you see the license?"

"Yep." Clint straightened. "A California one. Memorized it."

"So did I. Now to remember it 'til we can call Cal." He looked up the road. "This should lead us back to town."

Clint ran his hand across his wet chest. "At least the rain stopped."

"I hadn't noticed." Mike looked down at his own chest, where raindrops and blood dripped and merged. He pulled a soggy bandana from his back pocket and wiped it over the scratches.

They jogged along the road, which followed the river, until they came to the corner where the traffickers had turned. A McDonald's anchored one side of the T-intersection and a Best Western the other. Up the short hill was another intersection, but the bus wasn't there.

"There'll be someone at the hotel." Mike started toward the office. "I'll call—"

"Not so fast."

Mike frowned. It wasn't like Clint to impede progress. He looked at his foreman, who stood next to him but had turned the opposite direction.

"We have company."

Mike was about to ask what Clint was talking about but swallowed his words when his foreman's face turned red and then blue and then red again. He swiveled and found himself squinting through the rotating lights at a SUV with "Clackamas County Sheriff" stenciled on the side.

A similar vehicle pulled up behind the first one, windows down. *Oh, yeah, the marine unit.* By his estimates, the office wasn't more than a quarter mile away.

A spotlight flared in his face. Mike blinked and stepped back.

The SUV's doors opened and two officers crouched behind them, guns balanced on the doorframes. The nearest deputy, a woman, ordered, "One at a time, lower your guns to the ground and raise your hands."

First Mike then Clint released their pistols and stooped to place them on the grass. When they straightened, the deputy said, "Take two steps forward."

They complied. Mike said, "We were—"

"Continue to face me while Deputy Phillips collects your weapons."

Mike stifled a groan. The bus was getting away. The deputies could stop it, if they'd just let him explain.

The other deputy came around the door. He wore Latex gloves and was aiming a revolver at them. Giving them wide birth, he walked behind the two men. Mike heard clicks and knew the officer had released the ammunition magazines from the guns. He then backed to his vehicle, holding a plastic bag filled with their weapons and ammo in one hand and his own gun in the other.

The female officer stepped from behind the car door. "Are you gentlemen from Oregon City?"

They spoke in unison. "No."

"Where are you from?"

"Wyoming," Mike said.

"Do you have an Oregon City concealed handgun license?"

"No, but I have a Wyoming concealed carry permit."

"So do I," Clint added.

Neither man mentioned the fact they didn't have their wallets with them.

"Your Wyoming permits are not valid here. Oregon City prohibits open carry of loaded firearms in public places by individuals who don't possess a State of Oregon concealed handgun license."

Clint lifted his palms. "We weren't planning—"

"You're wet. Were you in the river?"

"Yes, briefly," Mike said.

"Did you just come ashore at Clackamette Park?"

Mike pointed at the road they'd traversed. "We were in the river for a short time, and yes, we landed at a place down the road that looked like a park. I don't know the name." Why the park mattered, he didn't know. The officer needed to stop the pointless questions and listen.

"We received a complaint from an RV resident there. Said he heard shots and saw two shirtless gangsters running through the park, guns drawn."

Mike looked at his wide-eyed foreman. Gangsters? Things were going downhill fast. He turned to the deputy. "My wife was on a bus that was driving out of the park. We were trying to stop it." He pointed up the hill. "They got away. You have to—"

She looked at the other officer. "We're taking them in. Disturbing the peace, illegal firearms, discharging firearms in a public place, attempted assault, domestic dispute. The tall one is yours."

"But we—" Mike held out his hands.

Officer Phillips walked over to Mike. "Tell your story to the booking officer. He'll read you your rights." After locking Mike into the back, he got in the car and started up the road.

"We were following my wife's kidnappers," Mike said. "We have the license number—"

Raising his hand, the deputy glanced at Mike in the rearview mirror. "Later."

The drive up the hill and through the small town to the county jail didn't take long. Mike and Clint were booked by an officer who read them their rights but refused to hear their story, other than to ask why they were barefoot and shirtless. After they told him where they left their clothing and changed from wet jeans into orange jumpsuits, he locked them in an interrogation chamber. Before he left the room, he said they could tell their story to the detectives.

Mike paced the tiny room from end to end, corner to corner, avoiding the metal table and folding chairs in the center. "What's taking them so long?"

Clint, who sat at the table, said, "You look good in orange, boss."

Mike glowered at him. "The detectives better get in here soon and they better believe us about Kate and the kids."

"Yeah…" Clint drummed his fingers on the metal table. "Could be they're ignoring us. After all, we're just a couple hick Wyoming gangster-ranchers running around half-dressed, brandishing illegal weapons and disturbing the peace."

"Yeah, but for some reason, they want us to talk to detectives." Mike kicked a chair. "While that bus is driving farther and farther away."

Clint motioned him to come closer. "There's a high probability…" His voice was low. "That we're being watched through that window over there."

"In that case, I should knock the table over or pound on the window. That'd get their attention." He dropped into a chair. His feet still hurt from running barefoot over rocks. "In the movies, people are allowed to make a phone call after they're arrested. What about us?"

"We should ask."

"The only way we're going to get any action is to call Cal."

"Yeah." Clint hesitated. "But…"

"But what?"

"His number is in our cell phones."

"Then the deputies will have to call him for us."

The door opened. An officer with a clipboard and an iPad stepped in and held the door for a second officer carrying two clear plastic bags that appeared to contain clothing. The men walked to the table. The one with the clipboard looked at Mike. "Mr. Duncan?"

Mike nodded and stood.

Clint stood with him.

"Mr. Barrett?"

"Yes."

"Have a seat. I'm Deputy Salazar and this is Deputy Rankin. We'll be interviewing you this morning." He placed the tablet and clipboard on the table and pulled out a chair.

Mike clenched his fists. At least it was still morning. They'd been kept in the jail for way too long. And they'd already talked with three other deputies, deputies who had no interest in listening to them—or instigating a search for the bus. Would these two be any different?

Rankin set the bags on the table before he sat. One was labeled "Barrett" and the other "Duncan."

Mike wondered how they knew whose stuff was whose.

As if sensing his question, Rankin said, "We ID'd clothing by the cell phone owners. And the prints on the phones."

Salazar handed Rankin the tablet.

Fingerprints? Surely they hadn't taken the gangster comment seriously. They were making a federal case of a couple gunshots, when the kidnapping was the real issue. Palms on the table, Mike faced the officers. He was about to speak when Salazar set his elbows on the table, folded his hands and said, "I'm curious."

His steel-gray eyes drilled into Mike's tired brain. "Why did two Wyoming ranchers," he asked, "two *armed* Wyoming ranchers, trespass onto private property way over here on the coast?"

Mike took a breath and blew it out.

"I thought parks were open to the public," Clint said.

"I'm talking about the Blue Heron Paper Mill. That private property is closed to the public." Salazar fixed his gaze on Mike again. "You were saying?"

As succinctly as he could, Mike described the kidnapping the officers surely knew about and the call from Kate that led them to the Blue Heron. "We came here to search for my wife and the kids," he concluded. "But now—"

"But you didn't find them, did you?"

"We did find them." Mike folded his arms. "They left the mill bound-and-gagged and guarded by four armed men. We saw them get into a boat. And we saw where the boat landed. Then we saw the kidnappers drive away in a bus with my wife and the kids inside. That's when I tried to shoot the tires."

Rankin lifted his chin, doubt sharpening his gaze. "How'd you see all that?"

"We were below the mill," Clint said, "down by the river, when we heard voices. We got closer to see who it was—"

"And saw the kids and my wife," Mike said, "plus another woman. They were being forced at gunpoint into a boat."

"So you took off your shirts and swam after them." The officers looked at each other, eyebrows arched.

"No." Clint shook his head. "We hitched a ride on their boat."

"Oh, yeah?" Salazar let out an exasperated snort. "Just hopped in with the bad guys, who said, 'Welcome aboard, buddy.'"

Chapter Thirty-Two

"It was a small boat," Mike said. "Made to hold five people, six at the most. They had nine, three of them children, so it sat somewhat low in the water. We held onto the swim platform at the back."

"You were found a mile and a half downriver from the paper mill." Rankin's brow creased. "Are you trying to tell us you hung onto a moving boat for over a mile?"

Salazar wrote something on the clipboard.

"Actually, more than that. They docked the boat downriver from there."

"The officers who arrested us said it was a park," Clint added. "Clack-something-or-other."

"Clackamette Park?"

"Yeah, that's it. The boat had an electric motor. It was slow and quiet."

Determined to finish the story and call Cal, Mike jumped in again. "As soon as they stopped the boat, a guy came running from the trees to secure it. Then they herded my wife and the kids through the trees to a school bus painted in dark camo colors."

"Is the boat still there?" Rankin asked.

"No, someone took off downriver in it. Earlier, the leader said it was needed for another job."

"Did you get a license number for the bus?"

"Yes," Mike said. "I'd like to give that information to the Wyoming deputy who's been following the kidnapping."

"Tell us, and we'll tell him."

"He's in the contacts on my phone. You can dial him, put the call on speaker, and listen while we give him the license number."

Salazar frowned. "Like I said, we'll pass along that information."

"I'm entitled to a phone call, right?"

Salazar motion to Rankin. "Dig out his phone."

As soon as Rankin found the phone, the two men left the room.

"Why is it everybody has access to my phone but me?" Mike rapped his knuckles on the metal tabletop. "If Kate tried to call from the bus and I missed it..." He turned to Clint. "I hate to hold things up, but I want to be sure Cal gets that license number."

"Good move." Clint gave him a thumbs-up. "I'm counting on him to get us out of here."

"You still remember it?"

Elbow on the table, Clint nonchalantly balanced his chin on his palm, half-covered his mouth with his fingers, and repeated the number under his breath.

"Yep." Mike nodded. "That's how I remember it. But it's not doing us any good stuck in our heads." He pictured the dark bus speeding down the highway, the kidnappers with their hooded heads hanging out the windows, laughing like hyenas at their easy getaway.

The deputies returned, each man with a phone in his hand. Rankin returned Mike's cell phone to the plastic bag. Salazar set another phone on the table between the four of them. "Deputy Gardner, we have a Mike Duncan and a Clint Barrett in our interrogation room. Do you recognize those names?"

"Yes." Cal's voice came through the speaker. "Duncan is the husband of the missing Wyoming woman. Barrett is employed on Duncan's ranch."

"Mr. Duncan says he has knowledge of his wife's whereabouts and wants to pass along that information to you. Is that information of interest to your department?"

"Most definitely."

"Go ahead, Duncan."

"Hey, Cal, this is Mike."

"Hi, Mike. The sheriff just walked in. He's decided to take up where the Cheyenne police left off. I'll put the phone on speaker."

"This is Sheriff Gilmer. Where are you now?"

Mike sighed. "Clackamas County Jail in Oregon City, Oregon."

"How'd you end up there?"

"Maybe these deputies could fill you in later. Telling our story again and again only delays finding my wife and the Freedom House kids."

No response.

Mike tapped his fingers on the table. "Okay, but I'll make this quick 'cause the longer we talk, the farther down the road the kidnappers get with my wife and three children." With that, he condensed the short version he'd told the Clackamas County deputies to an elevator speech.

"You say it was a camo'd school bus?" the sheriff asked.

"Yes, dark colors, from what we could see in the dark."

"It's one of those long busses," Clint interjected. "Had California plates. We got the license number."

"Why didn't you say so earlier?"

"You wanted the story of how we landed in jail. You got it." Mike nodded at Clint, who recited the number and then repeated it.

"We'll get on it," Cal said.

"How about you vouch for us?" Clint angled closer to the phone. "And ask these guys to release us."

"That's out of our jurisdiction," the sheriff said. "But for your information, deputies, Duncan and Barrett are clean. No history of disturbing the peace or illegal firearms in these parts." He chuckled. "Or assault or trespassing."

"Thank you," Clint said. "I appreciate it."

"And thanks for your help tracing my wife and the kids," Mike said. "Please keep us informed."

"You two stay out of trouble."

Kate rubbed her earlobe, missing Mike and wondering where she'd lost the earring. She stared at the black brocade curtain two rows ahead that blocked her view of the front of the bus. Incongruous. That was the word. The classy curtain was incongruous with the outhouse stench that saturated every breath she took.

The odor emanated from the bus "toilet," a dangerously full five-gallon bucket parked by the padlocked exit door three rows behind her. As the day wore on, the bus interior had warmed, intensifying the smell.

The heavy curtain ruffled with a breeze from open windows at the front of the bus, but only slightly. In the midst of the ever-present urine aroma, she occasionally caught a whiff of sagebrush and sometimes grass. Earlier, she'd smelled pine.

Had they driven over mountains and then down to prairies or desert? She wished she knew more about Oregon. All she remembered from geography class was that it was a coastal state.

The way the bus had earlier careened around hairpin curves,

lumbered up hills and shot down the other side could suggest a coastal highway. But so far, nothing else indicated they were anywhere near the ocean. They'd left water smells at the river.

The bucket contents sloshed with the turns. How it remained upright, she didn't know. Or maybe it had toppled. She wasn't about to check.

The old bus creaked and groaned and bounced like Mike's pickup truck. The vinyl seats they sat on were slick and cracked and the padding had long ago hardened. Upper corners of the metal-framed seatbacks had been left open, which made for great handholds but hurt when the rough ride knocked her against a corner.

Kate massaged her shoulder, another injury to add to her collection of bruises. What were the authorities doing? Did they know where she and the kids were? She'd heard what sounded like gunshots when the bus first took off. And their captors had instantly gone on alert. However, nothing more had happened.

With all the modern technology, they had to be tracking them by satellite or drones or something. Any moment she'd hear sirens and officers would stop the bus. But if a rescue attempt went wrong…

Before her imagination could take her down a dark path, she reminded herself that God could work miracles in the worst of situations, which was what they needed right now—a miracle. She had to trust him rather than think about how much worse things could get.

Tara sat beside her, next to the window, sniffing and shuddering. The bus swerved through a curve and Kate slammed into Tara, who cussed a blue streak. Their guard told her to shut-up. Kate ignored them both and twisted to check her three charges, who sat together in a seat behind them and across the aisle.

Lupi was rocking, arms rigid against her chest. Shannon was staring straight ahead and pulling at her hair, a disconnected emptiness in her eyes. And Tieno, who leaned against Shannon, was asleep. Kate offered them a sympathetic smile but they didn't respond.

Earlier, Tieno had been jounced out of his seat. He'd curled in the aisle until a kidnapper on the way to use the bucket tripped over him. The man snatched him up and dropped him onto the seat. That's when Shannon traded places to sit on the outside. Kate was proud of her thoughtfulness.

Somewhere along the way, they'd stopped to take on five more children who were as somber and wary as her own wards. Just as incongruous as a fancy curtain amidst filth was a school bus populated with silent children. She'd smiled at the newcomers when they walked between the drapes into the dim light at the back of the bus. But she could tell they didn't trust her any more than they did their captors.

One of them shook uncontrollably and his nose ran. Kate wondered if he was sick or suffering from drug withdrawal. Trafficked individuals were often forced into addictions to keep them desperate for another hit and willing to do whatever was demanded of them to get it. She wished she could rock the child and sing a lullaby to him.

Mike checked his phone, ran his fingers through his hair, jiggled his knee and looked at his phone, again. Not even a minute had passed. Sitting for miles on end doing nothing was torture. They were in the mountains, without cell service. He couldn't call Cal to ask if he had any new information. He couldn't update his mom and the others at the ranch. And he couldn't finish talking with Doc Hall.

He'd caught a phone call from the vet just as they were leaving Oregon City and learned that the university wanted permission to test his cattle herd as well as the bison herd. Doc's contact had said they wouldn't charge for the necropsy or the MCF testing, for which Mike was grateful, and that the sheep flock would also be tested. But when he'd asked Doc about a timeframe for results, they'd driven into a valley and lost the connection.

At first, he'd been frustrated, but then he remembered what his dad used to say. *What will be will be.* The last few days had reminded him of an important truth. People, specifically his loved ones, were far more important than the bison, far more valuable than the ranch. The sooner he got to Kate, the better.

Mike rolled his wedding ring around his finger. He would offer to drive but he'd already done so, twice. Clint had refused both times, saying they could switch drivers when they stopped for gas.

They raced—if you could call fifty-five miles an hour racing—up and down mountains and across valleys to more mountains. Based on earlier texts from Cal, he knew the Oregon State Police and county and city authorities had been notified to be on the lookout for a camouflage-painted school bus. Although troopers throughout the state had been alerted, the assumption was that the traffickers were on their way back to California and most likely using sparsely traveled highways. For that reason, he and Clint had headed inland through the Cascade Mountains toward Bend, Oregon.

Mike turned to Clint. "You never said how your foot got stuck in the rocks back at the river. It was jammed in there tight as a sparkplug."

"I was just thinking about how that happened." Clint lifted a hand from the steering wheel. "Remember how slick those rocks were?"

Mike nodded. "Yeah, like sliding in fresh manure."

"I was crouched in the water with my feet on separate rocks. Most of my weight was on the foot that slipped, and when it did, it was like a cow going through a squeeze chute. Before I could get my balance, my whole foot was wedged between rocks."

"So, how'd you get it out?"

Clint grinned. "I prayed."

"Oh, yeah?"

"Not too long after I said that quick prayer, something jabbed my arm. Have to admit I let out a yelp." He gave Mike a sheepish side-glance. "I thought one of the traffickers had come up behind me, but it was a small tree branch, less than three inches in diameter. I shoved it into the rocks and was able to separate them just enough to pull my foot out."

Mike raised his eyebrows. "That's quite a story. Is your foot okay? I didn't notice you limping."

"Feels like it might be a little bruised, but it's fine. The bottoms of my feet are what hurt after all that running we did while barefoot."

"Same here."

They neared Bend. Mike's phone dinged. He looked at the screen. "It's Cal. Voice mail."

He put the phone on speaker. "How's it going?" Cal asked. "You getting close? We finally made it to Oregon. Right now, we're headed for Burns. Thought you'd like to know we searched Hughes's house shortly after midnight this morning. Found evidence of his connection with the kidnapping.

"We took his computer and his cell phone, a box full of kiddy porn and miscellaneous other, uh…garbage. And placed him on house arrest again. I hope they put him in prison, so I don't have to visit him twice a week and put up with his big mouth." He paused. "That's it. I'll check in later."

Clint pounded the steering wheel. "Should have strung him up on one of his own trees and left him for the vultures."

Too disgusted to respond, Mike shook his head.

Kate studied the thickset guard who sat on a stool facing her and the others, his back to the dark drapes. He looked all of seventeen and wore a bored expression beneath the bill of his ball cap. He held a shotgun in one hand. With the other, he twirled handcuffs. Kate hadn't seen him before and assumed he'd been waiting for them at the bus.

The painted windows darkened the interior. Yet, enough light penetrated the curved ceiling gap above the curtain that she could make out some of the details of their latest prison—like the handcuffs that dangled from a bicycle hook screwed into the bus wall.

Kate looked the boy in the eye. "Thank you for releasing our hands so we could use the, uh, toilet. And so I could assist the children." She'd helped Lupita and Tieno straddle the smelly bucket.

"Didn't do it to be nice." He sneered. "Just didn't want to deal with the mess if you dumped the crap."

"Still…" She forced a smile. "I appreciate what you did."

He tossed the handcuffs upward. They banged against the ceiling. The child across from Kate jumped at the sound of metal clanging against metal. The guard caught the cuffs on the downward spiral. "I'm in charge of handcuffs, so you'd better stay on my good side."

"I didn't realize your, uhm, organization designates individuals to be in charge of certain responsibilities."

Tara snorted. "What's with the fancy words, Neilson? Trying to impress the kid?" She pulled off her t-shirt. "It's hot in here."

The guard puffed his chest. "I'm the go-to guy for handcuffs." He spread the cuffs between his forefingers. "I can put these on with one hand behind my back."

Kate folded her arms and gave him a disbelieving look.

Using only one hand, he snapped both cuffs onto the corner of the seatback in front of him and then raised his hands in victory. "Ta-da."

She tried to look impressed. "That was fast."

He pulled a set of keys on a retractable keyring clipped to his belt, sorted through them, found one and unlocked the cuffs. "I've been practicing. Not much else to do when we're on the road."

"Have you been with these guys long?"

"Only since they started running brats. Before I came along a couple years ago, they used this old bus to run drugs up and down the California coast."

Kate was about to ask him about his travels, when a siren sounded behind them. Her heart rocketed to her throat. Just what she'd been praying for—law enforcement.

The guard turned and stuck his head between the curtains, facing the front. "Do you guys hear that?"

She couldn't see through his wide torso, but she could hear obscenities gush from the mouths of his henchmen.

"What's the fuzz doing out here in the middle of nowhere?" someone asked.

"Told you not to drive so fast." Kate recognized Adolph's voice.

A whiny, accented voice said, "Oregon's fifty-five limit is stupid." That had to be Roach.

"Should I pull over or make a run for it?" *Ah, so Blade is the driver.*

"This is a bus, not a sports car." Adolph again.

"Got a get me one of those."

"We can't outrun him," Blade called over the bus noise, "but you could shoot him from the back door."

"Yeah, but someone might see us."

"Hardly any traffic out here."

"Only takes one do-gooder to ruin our day."

"I say schmooze the guy." Roach again. "If things go south, we—"

"He could be contacting another trooper right now," Adolph interjected, his voice firm. "Stop the bus."

Chapter Thirty-Three

"Hang on, kiddos." Kate grabbed the seatback in front of her, hoping the children did the same. The bus jerked to the side and shuddered to a reluctant stop.

Adolph cursed. "First you slow down, you son of a—"

"My nose," Tara cried. "You broke my nose." Pushing away from the seatback she'd smashed into, she clasped her hand against her face. Blood poured between her fingers and ran down her hand.

Despite his bulk, the guard was on her in an instant, his gun pointed at her cleavage. "Cut the hysterics, lady, or you'll be dinner for the vultures and the coyotees." The word hissed between his teeth. "They get awful hungry out here with nothin' but snakes and lizards to eat."

Tara fell into the corner, clutching her nose. Red rivulets striped her forearms.

Kate picked Tara's shirt off the floor and tossed it in her lap. If she wanted, she could use it to mop the blood.

The guard pointed the shotgun at the children. His lip curled. "Brats are their favorite."

A harsh whisper came from the other side of the curtain. "Keep 'em quiet back there, Lardo. If anyone so much as breathes loud, we'll have to shoot them *and* the copper."

"I see him in the mirror." Blade's whisper could be heard all the way to the rear of the quiet bus. "He's looking at the back tires on the driver's side." A moment later, "Here he comes."

A commanding though faraway voice filtered into the hot, silent, smelly bus. "Good afternoon. You waited long enough to slow down."

"Didn't realize you were after us."

"Driving eighty in a fifty-five zone, no other vehicles in the vicinity, and you didn't consider you might be the one who needed to stop?" The man sounded incredulous as well as irritated.

"I, uh…"

"Driver's license, please."

A semi-truck whooshed from behind and shot past, jolting the bus. And then all was quiet again.

"Thank you." The trooper spoke again. "Who's in the bus with you?"

"My buddies. We have a band. See our name on the outside?"

"Bottom Girl Scouts, huh? Quite the paint job you got going."

Kate cringed. *Bottom Girl Scouts. Of all the horrid, brazen—*

"Mind if I take a look inside?"

"Uh, no. I'll open the door."

Adolph whispered, "Stash your weapons, but keep the ankle guns. You know the drill."

Kate held her breath. He was coming in. Surely that awful name had clued him in to the real purpose for the bus.

The bus floor jittered. She heard footsteps and movement on the other side of the drapes. Lardo stuck his head between the curtains. Someone hissed, "Your feet are showing." He pulled back between seats but kept his ear close to the brocade partition.

Kate tensed, ready to spring at him. She'd grab his gun while he was distracted and—

The door wheezed open.

Lardo whipped around, his bored expression replaced by a ruthless glare. He swung the shotgun barrel from Tara to Kate to the children.

This time, the patrolman sounded closer. "Hate to say it, but it stinks in here."

"Yeah, our toilet overflowed."

"What's with the curtain?"

"Our equipment is stored back there."

Eyes squinted, jaw clamped, Lardo continued to fan the gun from one side of the bus to the other.

"We're making a CD next month," Adolph said. "We can send you a demo copy."

"That's okay, boys. Just watch the speed limit." After a long pause, the man added, "This is a warning. Next time, it'll cost you. No more lead-footing it." Another extended silence, and she heard the sound of paper being torn. "You ought a hose this thing down before the smell warps your guitars or knocks you out."

"We'll do that when we get to town…sir."

Kate planted her feet, ready to spring. She had to act fast. He was about to leave.

"One more thing." The officer's voice again. "There's what…four of you?"

"Uh, yeah," Adolph said. "That's right. Four of us."

"I'd like all of you to step outside with me and take a look at the condition of your tires. I should give you a ticket, but this time I'll…" His voice was drowned by the grumbles of those following him off the bus.

Lardo chuckled and stuck his head between the curtains. "Told

Adolph this thing needs new tires."

Kate jumped to her feet, took a flying step and slammed the side of his neck.

The shotgun clattered to the floor. He collapsed to his knees, falling through the drapes. A triangle of light surged into the dismal prison just before the heavy fabric dropped, returning them to semi-darkness.

~:~:~

Mike's phone buzzed again. He held it out. "Another message from Cal." He pushed the speaker button.

"Oregon State Police just reported one of their troopers stopped a speeding camo-painted bus on Highway 20 out in the desert halfway between Bend and a wide spot in the road called Riley."

"Yee-haw, they found them!" Clint honked the horn, startling a driver in the oncoming lane, who stared up at them as the vehicles passed. "When did he leave that message?"

Mike checked the phone. "Ten minutes ago."

"We'll be way behind the eight ball by the time we get gas."

"You're telling me."

"At least we know which highway to take out of Bend."

By now, they were on the city's outskirts. They stopped long enough to top off the gas tank and ask directions to Highway 20. Mike took the wheel.

Clint accessed the Oregon map on his phone. "We're driving into flatland, which is good. We'll make better progress." He tapped the screen. "About a hundred miles from Bend to Riley."

Mike frowned. "That's a haul."

"Yeah, but Cal said the bus is halfway between the two. If you floor it, we can be there in no time."

~:~:~

Kate knelt beside the big teen. He was unconscious, but only God knew how long he'd stay that way.

"Neilson, what are you doing?" Tara's blood-smeared face emerged through the gloom. She clutched the seatback with bloody fingers and gawked at Kate.

"Getting his gun." The barrel protruded from beneath one leg. With no small effort, Kate wiggled the shotgun out from under him and laid it on a seat. Stepping over his hefty, inert form, she slipped two sets of handcuffs off the hook attached to the bus wall.

"I'll guard him for you." Tara reached for the gun.

"Sure you will." Kate shifted her weight, lifted her foot and kicked Tara in the head, knocking her against the metal seat corner. Tara slumped, half on, half off the seat.

The trooper's voice came through the bus wall. "See the tread on this one? If you as much as brake fast, it could blow. And then this tire here..."

A truck swept by, its wake shaking the bus. Kate hoped traffic noise and wind blasts would keep their captors from becoming suspicious of interior activities.

She motioned to Shannon, who helped her drag Lardo's body into the aisle behind the curtain. Moving fast, praying for time, she cuffed his wrists to seat legs on each side of the narrow aisle. Shannon tied his Nike laces together and slid the key clip off his belt while Kate tugged the bandana from his back pocket and wrapped it around his head. Pulling it through his mouth, she double-knotted it in the back.

Tara groaned and rolled to the floor between seats. Her head landed on Lardo's side.

Kate snatched another set of restraints from the wall. Straddling the bulky boy, she lifted Tara's left hand, yanked off the wedding rings and slid them onto her finger again. She'd dwell on the satisfaction of having her rings back where they belonged later. Now wasn't the time. Hooking Tara's wrists around a seat leg, she shoved as much of her bloody shirt as would fit into her open mouth.

The crunch of footsteps and the sound of men's voices came through the back door. The group walked to the highway side of the bus. The kids stared at Kate with wide, anxious eyes. She whispered, "Pray," clambered over Lardo, grabbed the shotgun and parted the curtains.

Mike slowed the truck to a stop on the shoulder. "If I were a swearing man..." They'd barely escaped the Bend city limits and gained the freedom of the open road when a siren sounded and lights flickered behind them.

Clint groaned. "I know what you mean. Your dad would have said, 'oh, fiddle,' but that doesn't have quite the kick this situation warrants."

In the side rearview mirror, Mike watched the trooper slowly exit his vehicle and saunter toward the pickup. Tugging his wallet from his back pocket, Mike rolled the half-open window all the way down.

The officer stopped just behind his door. "From Wyoming, huh?"

"Yes, sir."

"May I see your license and vehicle registration?"

Mike opened the wallet and pulled out his driver's license.

Clint retrieved the registration from the glovebox, and Mike handed it and the license to the officer.

The trooper spoke as he perused the documents. "Speed limits a little higher in Wyoming?"

"Well, yeah..."

"Have you seen the posted speed limit on this highway?"

"Yes, but my wife—"

"What *is* the limit?"

"Fifty-five. You may have heard about my wife—"

"Is she in labor or some other emergency?" The officer stretched forward to peer into the cab. "Who's that?"

"His name is Clint Barrett. My wife is with the kids who were kidnapped in Wyoming and driven to Oregon."

The patrolman straightened. He eyed Mike. "What's the name?"

"Kate Duncan. Katherine Joy Neilson Duncan."

Through the man's sunglasses, Mike saw recognition spark. "The former convict?"

"Yes." Mike offered a reluctant nod. "She spent time in prison several years ago."

"How many children with her?"

"Three. And another woman, plus four kidnappers. We saw them last night—or early this morning, that is—in Oregon City."

"You saw them?"

"We saw them taken by boat to a camouflaged school bus, where they were loaded up and driven south. A deputy told us the bus was seen on this highway. Sorry about the speeding, but I want to be there for my wife and the kids."

The officer checked Mike's license again, as if making sure he was who he said he was, and handed both the license and registration through the window. He stepped back. "The road ahead is clear. You don't have far to go. State, county and federal authorities are converging as we speak." He saluted. "Best of luck to you and your wife."

"Thanks." The officer had barely cleared the back of the pickup when Mike took off. "You take that to mean I can exceed fifty-five?"

Clint adjusted his hat. "That's how I took it."

~:~:~

Kate hurried to the front of the bus, checking seats as she went. Ball caps, cell phones, iPads, earphones and porn magazines were strewn across the bench seats. Candy bar wrappers and pop cans littered the floor.

She peeked through one of the unpainted windows near the front. The patrolman was standing beside the bus, telling the others the next town was small. It didn't have a tire shop. But the town sixty-five miles beyond the first one did.

Eyes squinted against the light pouring through the windows, she quickly surveyed the landscape. Flat desert landscape colored gray-green by sagebrush. Blue mountains in the distance. A haystack on the left. And a yardstick-straight highway stretching all the way to the horizon.

Kate grasped the door lever with both hands and wrenched it to the side. The door rasped closed.

"What was that?" someone asked.

Kate dropped into the driver's seat. Just as she'd hoped, the key was still in the ignition. She laid the shotgun across her lap, jammed the clutch to the floor and turned the key. The engine roared to life as she gripped the gearshift knob. Thank God Mike had taught her how to maneuver his truck's shift pattern. Shoving the gears into first, she checked the mirror for traffic and caught the men's startled gazes.

Adolph charged her direction.

Kate hit the gas, let out the clutch and cranked the steering wheel hard to the left.

The bus jolted onto the highway.

Shouts and curses blustered through the open windows. She glanced at the mirror again. The trooper was running toward his car, followed close behind by the traffickers. *God help the man. He doesn't stand a chance against those four.*

She shifted into second, fighting to keep the wobbly bus on the road. Pushing it to go faster and faster, farther and farther, she shifted into third and then fourth. The patrol car and the men now clustered near it grew smaller and smaller in the right-hand mirror.

"Hey, kids!" The speedometer hit fifty. "Come join me up here in the sunshine." After so much time in the dark, the bright desert light hurt her eyes, but it was a small price to pay for freedom. She'd adjust and so would the children. Warm wind laced with the tangy scent of sagebrush blowing through the driver's window was like a balm to her body as well as her soul. Fresh air and sunshine. Finally.

In the wide overhead mirror, she saw Shannon peek between the curtains. She motioned to the girl and yelled over the road noise, "Bring everyone to the front." This new freedom was for them, too. They needed to leave the kidnappers and the dark, smelly back of the bus and step into daylight.

The drapes dropped and Shannon's face disappeared.

At the sound of a siren, Kate checked the side mirror. The patrol car was shooting up the highway. She frowned. *That didn't take long.*

The state vehicle pulled directly behind the bus, lights flashing, siren blaring. Kate rammed the gas pedal to the floor. Someone other than the patrolman had to be driving the car.

One by one, the children tiptoed between the drapes.

Kate waved them forward. "Sit up here by me."

The Freedom House three filed into the seat behind her. But the newcomers hesitated. They watched her in the mirror, their small bodies rigid, their eyelids narrowed against the glare.

Kate swerved to miss a rock that had rolled off a boulder-studded cliff.

The children standing in the aisle grabbed at seatbacks.

"Sit down, please," Kate said, "so you don't get hurt."

They settled into two seats on the other side of the bus.

Now the patrol car was in the oncoming lane, driving alongside the bus. The windows were down. She could see two of the traffickers but not the trooper.

A loudspeaker blared, "Stop, now!"

Even though she recognized Adolph's voice, the sound of it bellowing through the open window startled Kate. She jerked the wheel and the bus veered toward the patrol car.

The driver backed off, hovering near the rear of the bus. "Pull over," Adolph demanded. "Now!"

A truck crested the hill ahead and the patrol car dropped behind the bus.

The rising slope was a long one. The bus slowed. Sixty-seven, sixty-three, fifty-nine...

Kate whispered, "Bus, don't fail us now."

The truck passed and the patrol car swung from behind the bus into the oncoming lane again. "Stop!" Adolph's loud voice was in her ear again. "Or we'll shoot."

Kate was fairly certain the traffickers wouldn't chance harming the children, who were worth a fortune to them, thousands per child. But they were evil men. Who knew what they'd do?

They made it to the top of the hill and started the long descent. The bus picked up speed. An endless asphalt stripe parted the desert, with no sign of life on either side of the highway other than the three cars climbing the hill toward them. The patrol vehicle withdrew behind the bus, siren still blaring.

Chapter Thirty-Four

Mike glanced at the speedometer. Eighty-six miles per hour. He hadn't driven that fast since high school. Clint's pickup shimmied and the tools in the back rattled. But the road was dry and straight. He could see for miles. Sagebrush-spiked wind currents sparred noisily between the partially open windows.

Pressing the gas pedal, he scanned the horizon. "You'd think we would have come across the school bus by now."

"If it was yellow, maybe. But from a distance, that camo paint could make it blend with the highway and the desert."

A jack rabbit popped from the barrow pit and shot across the road a fraction of a second before it would have collided with the pickup tires. Mike gripped the steering wheel and focused on the road. A wail pierced the wind rushing past his ears. He checked the mirror. Flashing lights were coming up fast behind them.

Clint turned to look between the rifles racked in his back window. "So much for permission to speed."

Mike groaned and took his foot off the gas pedal.

The wind noise lessened but the siren grew louder.

"Sheriff." Clint shook his head. "We're on everyone's radar today."

Mike let the truck roll to the shoulder. The county vehicle sped past, siren blaring. Clint read the logo on the side out loud. "Harney County Sheriff." The SUV disappeared over a rise.

Stomping the gas pedal, Mike jetted back onto the highway. If the deputies weren't after him, they had to be chasing the bus, too. They crested the hill. Near the base, a SUV was parked alongside the road. Two men stood near it.

One trooper held a cell phone to his ear and the other was removing rifles from the back of the vehicle. That could mean only one thing. The bus wasn't far ahead.

Clint dug into his pocket, pulled out a solitary key and unlocked the cable that secured the rifles. "Might need these."

Kate shifted into fifth gear, pushing the old bus to its limit. She knew outrunning a patrol car with the cumbersome vehicle was impossible. But she couldn't help but try to distance herself and the kids from the thugs who rode the bus's tail like a burr.

What next, God? She glanced at the gas gauge. Half a tank. They could drive for a while but not for forever. All she could see in the distance was sagebrush and telephone poles. No towns were within sight.

A loud bang burst like a gunshot through the clamor of sirens, motors, creaks and rumbles. The bus shuddered and the steering wheel jerked to the right. Kate clasped the big wheel with both hands, struggling to keep the off-balance vehicle on the road. Whether a tire had been shot or one had blown of its own accord, she didn't know.

"Everybody, grab hold of a seat," Kate called, "and hang on tight!" The bus lurched onto the shoulder, listing to the side. She yanked the wheel, steering back onto the asphalt.

A second blast shook the bus. The children screamed as the bus zagged to the right again and plunged off the road. Noisily churning up a dust cloud, the big vehicle thumped over grass and sagebrush and careened into a barbed-wire fence. Metal screeched against metal until the wires snapped, flying like thorny vines in an updraft.

The bus hurtled toward a stubby ridge. Kate could feel the wheels grinding into the dirt. Within moments, the cliff face loomed in the front window. She whipped the steering wheel to the left and the bus ground to a halt at the base of the bluff, parallel with it. Groaning and grating, the vehicle swayed, as if readying to leap across the desert floor, but then it settled into the soil with a long, raspy, reluctant hiss.

Kate switched her foot from the brake to the gas pedal and floored it. She'd drive on rubberless rims before she'd let the traffickers have the kids. But the engine had stalled and refused to respond to her attempts to revive it.

A wave of dust rolled through the windows. Coughing and sneezing, Kate twisted to check the children. One of the newcomers lay in the aisle. She picked him up. "You okay, sweetie?"

He nodded.

She set him on a seat and surveyed the others, who were teary-eyed and sniffling but intact. She looked out a window. The patrol car was stopped above them on the highway, lights flashing, siren blaring. And their captors were already working their way toward the bus, weapons ready.

"Shut the windows!" Kate ran to the front to slide the bolt on the door lock, an obvious aftermarket addition. She hoped it worked. Knee on the driver's seat, she slammed the window closed. They only had four other open windows but the children were weak and the old windows resistant.

Together, she and Shannon managed to shut them all, including one of the painted ones near the back that was partly open. The bus would get hot, but the cliff provided some shade and the closed windows would keep their abductors out—unless, of course, they broke the glass. She'd cross that bridge when they got to it.

~:~:~

Mike topped the long barren hill. Lights flashed near the bottom of the incline. The patrol car passed them and shot down the hill.

"There it is!" Clint jabbed his finger out the window. "There's the bus. Must have driven right through that fence. Looks like it had a flat, maybe two." Long strips of rubber were scattered along the highway.

Mike slowed the truck. The dark vehicle sat off the right side of the road at the base of a bluff. A dust cloud billowed around it and deep grooves ran through the sagebrush-dotted dirt from the highway to the bus.

"They're cornered," Clint said. "No way they're getting away this time."

The patrol car passed the parked car with the flashing lights at the bottom of the hill, did a U-turn and drew nose to nose with it. Two more SUVs and a patrol car came shooting up the highway from the opposite direction.

Mike stopped the truck behind the first car, a state police vehicle, and turned to Clint. "Better leave the rifles for now."

He stepped from the pickup, his gaze on the bus. Aftershock tremors shook the big vehicle, but other than that and the diminishing dust cloud, he saw no sign of life. What had happened to those inside when it ran off the highway? Were Kate and the kids okay? He thought he heard cries and banging but it was hard to tell with the siren wailing in his ear.

He took a step toward the bus.

"Stop right there."

He turned.

Two deputies with guns in their hands faced them, feet apart. One gun was trained on him and the other on Clint.

"Raise your hands."

Clint groaned. "Here we go again."

~:~:~

Kate grabbed the shotgun, angled the interior mirror toward the ceiling to hide their activities from outsiders looking in the door or side windows, and led the children deeper into the bus. Once they were seated between the painted windows, she laid the gun on a seat and carried the sick child several rows back to join the others. He looked miserable.

Someone pounded on the bus door. "Open up!" Others scrabbled at the bus windows. The children cringed and pressed against the other side of the bus, eyeing the men's frantic shadows.

Kate retrieved the shotgun and knelt before the children. "You-all are so brave." What next? She was out of ideas.

As if he'd heard her thoughts, Tieno folded his hands, "P-p-pray."

She squeezed his shoulder. "Tieno's right. First thing we do is pray."

He bowed his head.

The newcomers stared at him. One girl closed her eyes.

"J-J-Jesus," Tieno whispered. "H-help."

The bus jiggled and rocked.

Lupi, whose hands were folded, added, "Bad guys go away, Jesus."

Kate smiled. "Amen." *Okay, God. We're in your hands.* "Thank you, Lupi and Tieno."

"Are you going to shoot them with that gun?" asked the biggest boy.

"That might work under the right circumstances and with enough ammunition." She scanned the bus's interior, wondering where she could find shotgun shells.

Hearing an oncoming siren, Kate scooted to where she could peek out a window. A state police SUV with flashing lights was stopping behind the other vehicles. She was glad for protection but prayed they wouldn't harm the kids while trying to save them.

~:~:~

Mike was about to explain, once again, who they were, when Cal came running on the asphalt, followed by another uniformed Wyoming deputy. "I'm from the Carbon County Sheriff's Department in Wyoming. I know these men. That one is the missing woman's husband."

The other deputies looked at each other, then at the pickup's license plate, and then back to Mike and Clint. They holstered their weapons. "What do you know about the bus?" one of them asked.

"We just got here," Mike said. "Saw a big cloud of dust from the top of the hill, so I'd say it slid off the road less than five minutes ago. Far as I know, my wife is still in it."

One of the deputies said, "Thanks. We'd better go set up road blocks."

A state trooper walked up, reached in the patrol car's open window and turned off the siren. "Anyone seen the trooper who drove this car?"

Mike shook his head.

The patrolman frowned. "He went silent not too long ago." He checked inside the car again and then, still frowning, walked away.

Cal motioned to his partner. "We'd better go find out what the plan of attack is." They hurried over to where the other officers had gathered.

Mike looked at the bus and then at Clint. "They'd better figure out that plan of attack fast. We need to get Kate off that bus."

"I'm with you, boss."

A slow-moving tractor rumbled past. The driver, who wore sunglasses and a wide-brimmed cowboy hat, didn't try to hide his curiosity.

Clint gave him a nod and murmured, "I have a feeling this is the most excitement this patch of desert has seen in fifty years."

Mike pointed to a herd of cows moseying down the hill in single file, following the fence line. "Those cows are thinking the same thing."

From the direction of the bus came more pounding noises. "Let us in!" a male voice yelled.

"That's strange," Mike said, "you'd think they'd be trying to get out, not in."

He heard another loud thump, this one close at hand, and turned in time to see the patrol car's trunk lid pop open a couple inches. He and Clint exchanged a glance and then he darted to the pickup to grab a shovel from the back. Clint, who was right behind him, picked up a crowbar. When they returned to the car, a black sock wiggled in the opening and muffled cries came from inside.

Crowbar raised, Clint stood guard as Mike lifted the trunk lid, inch-by-inch. Inside, wedged amidst the trunk's contents, lay a bound-and-gagged man in a blue uniform. Knees at his chest, he'd apparently twisted far enough to pull the release lever with his toes.

"So that's what happened to the missing trooper." Clint balanced the crowbar against the car and leaned in to grasp the officer's arm. Mike took his other arm and they carefully lifted him up and out of the trunk.

While Mike steadied the man, Clint pulled out his jack knife and cut the zip tie that bound his swollen hands behind him. Mike eyed the bundle of zip ties in the trunk. Someone had used the officer's restraints against him.

The patrolman shook out his hands and then yanked at the gag. But it had been tied tight. His eyes glinted.

"Hold still," Clint said. "I'll cut it off and try not to give you a haircut."

The trooper stiffened.

Mike held the trooper's arm while Clint carefully sliced at the knot. The moment the dirty cloth fell free, the man grabbed a bottle of water from the trunk, twisted off the cap and took a swig. He spit the water out, took another swig, spit it out and then drank the entire bottle.

He tossed the empty bottle in the trunk and wiped his mouth with his shirtsleeve. "That was..." He grimaced. "Disgusting." Digging through the trunk's contents, he found his shoe and put it on. "I appreciate you helping me out, but who are you? And where are the morons who put me in there?"

"I'm Mike Duncan, husband of the woman and kids who were kidnapped in Wyoming and driven to Oregon. This is Clint Barrett, our ranch foreman." He shook hands with the trooper. "But I don't know who dumped you in the trunk."

Someone cursed loud and long. "Open the door or we'll shoot our way in."

All three men turned to stare at the bus.

"Ah, that explains everything." The patrolman began to dig through the contents of the trunk again, pushing teddy bears and water bottles aside. "They got one of my rifles but not both."

"Excuse me," Mike said. "What explains what?"

Kate crawled back to the children. They all looked as hot as she felt. And none of them, herself included, smelled all that great. Her clothes reeked, she was greasy and grimy, and her stringy hair clung to her cheek.

"Maybe we could sneak out the hole in the floor," Shannon said.

"What hole?"

"The one they put their guns in when the cop stopped us."

She gave the girl a quizzical look.

"I peeked between the fat guy's feet," Shannon said, "and saw them lift a lid."

"Show me." Crouched low, Kate followed the girl. The closer they got to the curtain, the worse the smell was. Balanced on their knees, they fingered the rubber flooring, searching for a separation.

"Here it is," Shannon whispered. Her scraggly blonde hair fell forward as she peeled back the rubber to reveal a square piece of metal secured by four clasps. She twisted one to the side.

Kate twisted another. When all four were open, she tugged at the thin strap attached to one side.

"Lardo!" One of the traffickers pounded the door again. "Lardo, open up." The bus shook.

She lifted the lid just far enough for the two of them to see below. Grass blades unfolded and popped into the opening, accompanied by the smell of burnt rubber. Kate gave Shannon a thumbs-up. Instead of covering a stash bin, like she feared, the hatch opened to the ground, which was not more than nine or ten inches below.

Chapter Thirty-Five

Sitting back, Kate wondered how many times the bus had been searched when the gang ran drugs, yet no weapons or drugs were found. She pictured the cops driving away and Adolph and his gang gleefully retrieving their stashed stuff before they moved on to their next foul deed, gloating all the way.

Blade's voice came through the opening from not very far away. "We could crawl underneath and kick in the hatch."

Shannon pulled away.

"Oh, yeah?" The sneer in Adolph's voice was unmistakable. "*If* we had a shovel, you mean. This thing is half buried in the dirt. We can't fit under there."

"My iPad and my phone..." Roach's voice. "They're on the bus."

"Forget your junk. It's the brats we need. They're our way outa here."

Cell phone. We have their phones. Kate carefully lowered the metal plate to the floor and pointed to the clasps. Shannon could secure the hatch while she called for help. She checked the nearest seat, and the next. The silent children monitored her every move.

Kate found a phone, but the screen was locked. And the screen on the second phone showed no service. About to go searching for another phone, she realized she didn't need to call for help. Help was already here, parked along the highway. She just needed to figure out how to get the kids and the cops together, with God's help, of course.

Lupi stopped rocking and slid off a seat to give her a hug.

Kate wrapped her in her arms, kissed her head, dirty hair and all, and smiled at the others, who watched with cautious but curious eyes. "My name is Kate," she whispered. "And that's Shannon."

Shannon wiggled her fingers.

"This is Lupita."

Lupi blinked.

Tieno put his hands on his waist. "I, I, I Tieno."

Kate grinned. "Yes, this is our man Tieno."

She motioned to the biggest boy from the other group. He had a barcode tattooed across the back of his neck, some pimp's despicable method for tracking his sex workers. "What's your name?"

"Gregor."

Though hesitant, the other children gave her their names when asked. Kate was certain names like Stardust, Angel Eyes and Whimsy were not their real names. She also sensed they'd long ago lost trust in adults. Her heart broke for them, and she prayed this was the beginning of a better life for each child. The sick boy whispered his name. "Skylar."

One of the girls wore a tank top. The name Ramon and a phone number were displayed in big bold letters on her forearm. She'd been "owned" by a pimp, who was apparently selling her to another pimp. Would that person "erase" the name and number and substitute his own?

Kate could only imagine how painful the tattoo experience was for the girl. Tattoo removal, she'd heard, was even more painful. Faint vestiges of ink remained on the Freedom House kids' shoulders, but rather than barcodes or phone numbers, they'd been branded with the initials of the brothel owner. Thank God they'd been treated in Dallas and were healing by the time they arrived at Freedom House.

The alternative was to have a tattoo artist transform the symbols of pain and enslavement into works of art. They'd learned of someone who provided that service free of charge for trafficking victims. Yet, she was glad the Freedom House children hadn't had to endure more tattooing.

The smallest girl pulled at her lower lip, running her tongue over a blackened area. Kate looked closer and saw a phone number tattooed inside the child's bottom lip. Her stomach turned. Such callous cruelty had to come straight from hell.

She picked up another cell phone, thinking she could at least let the authorities know who was inside the bus and who was outside. They didn't know about the extra children. That phone's battery was apparently dead. She blew out a frustrated breath.

Spotting a tablet on the seat across the aisle, she slid it close and pressed the on-off button. Maybe she could use it to contact someone on the outside. The screen came to life, but she gasped and dropped the tablet like it was a live coal. Not only did it display a pornographic picture, the scene included a child.

Kate flipped the tablet over and moved to the unpainted windows to peek at the vehicles parked alongside the highway. She sucked in a breath when she saw Clint's pickup. He and Mike were standing near it, talking with a man in a blue uniform. Tears sprang to her eyes. *Thank you, God.*

Now she knew what to do. Hurrying back to the children, she motioned for Lupi to join her. "You've been a brave little girl, Lupi. Can I ask you to do one more brave thing? It won't be easy."

Eyes wide, the little girl touched Kate's cheek. "For you?"

"For all of us."

Lupi nodded. "I brave girl."

~:~:~

Mike stared at the bus, trying to comprehend what the trooper had told them before he hurried off to join the others. Kate was the one who drove the bus off the highway. The kidnappers were outside the bus, apparently hiding behind it. She and the kids were inside. That made rescuing them easier. Or did it?

He turned to watch the lawmen talking with the trooper he and Clint had pulled from the trunk. Moments later, they separated and fanned toward the front and rear of the bus.

"Back off!" a youthful male voice ordered. "Get away from the bus. We have weapons and we have the brats. Leave us alone if you want them to see tomorrow."

The men retreated but did not lower their weapons.

Mike glanced at the cows, which had stopped moving and had clustered beside the fence. Newborn calves frolicked alongside the herd, but the cows stared from the people on the highway to the bus and back. Cattle were curious creatures and also creatures of habit. He had a feeling that not only had their quiet existence been disturbed, the bus blocked their path to the water tank beneath the windmill on the far side of the cliff.

"We can't just stand here, gawking at the bus," Clint said. "I'm getting the rifles."

Mike didn't argue. They were within sight of Kate and the kids, yet they and all the law-enforcement officers with them were powerless to help her.

Kate lifted a notebook from a nearby seat. Someone had been drawing evil-looking creatures with long claws, sharp teeth and fiery eyes. She flipped through it until she found a blank page and then pulled a pencil from the wire binding. Praying for clarity, she wrote as fast as she could, tore the paper from the notebook, folded it into quarters and folded it again.

She slid the paper into Lupi's shorts pocket. "I want you to take this to Mr. Mike."

Lupi's frightened gaze flicked to the bus door.

"No, you don't have to go out the door, sweetie. I need you to crawl through the hole in the floor and walk to the highway." She pointed in the direction of the road. "Mr. Clint and Mr. Mike are there with the policemen. They'll help you. And when they read the note in your pocket, they'll know how to help all of us. Can you do that?"

Lupi nodded, her features solemn yet determined.

Kate hugged her and led her to the opening. Shannon followed. Together, they released the clamps and then Kate quietly set the metal piece aside. She studied the opening, which was about a foot-and-a-half square. She might not be able to fit through it and squeeze beneath the bus, but Lupi could, and so could the other children.

But first, she needed to see how much could be seen from the cliff side of the bus. Pulling her hair back, she held it at the nape of her neck while she lowered her head into the hole. She looked every direction as far as she could see, which wasn't far, and then sat up. Enough sagebrush, grass and rocks filled the gap between the carriage and the dirt that she didn't think the traffickers would notice the kids' departure.

She kissed Lupi's forehead, praying no harm would come to her as she wriggled to freedom. She also prayed no trigger-happy trafficker or officer would take a shot at her when she crawled from beneath the bus.

"Neilson!" All three of them jumped at the sound of Tara's loud voice on the other side of the curtain. "Neilson, get back here and help me. I'm bruised, I'm bleeding—"

"Shut up." Adolph's words boiled through the hole.

Lupi pulled back, her face ashen.

Kate frowned. Tara had not only revived, she'd somehow removed the shirt from her mouth.

"Don't tell me what to do," Tara shrieked.

Kate whispered in Lupita's ear. "It's not far. Jesus will be with you." Tara's bellyaching would be good cover.

Lupita touched her pocket and Kate and Shannon helped her into the hole. As soon as her feet disappeared, Kate climbed onto a seat and worked a window down. It opened only a few inches but it was far enough she could put her hand through the gap.

"What in the world?" Mike gaped at the hand that had just then appeared through a gap in the painted windows. Pale against the dark camouflage, the hand moved up and down, up and down, a finger pointing earthward. Muffled shouts came from the direction of the bus but he couldn't tell what was being said.

"Look," Clint exclaimed.

Something squirmed from beneath the bus. The officers tensed, guns ready. "Hold your fire!" Mike raised his hand high. It was a child, he was sure of it.

The child stood, covered with dirt.

"Lupita," Clint breathed. He laid the rifles in the back of the pickup.

Mike and Clint ran down the incline. Someone ordered them to stop but they continued and arrived at the fence when she did. Mike stomped the bottom wire into the dirt with his boot, grabbed the wire above it with his hand and stretched it as high as it would go. Clint knelt to help the girl through the gap.

Before they could say anything, she reached into a pocket, pulled out a folded piece of paper and whispered, "From Miss Kate."

Mike released the fence wire and took the note. "Thank you, Lupita."

Clint lifted her into his arms. "Lupi girl. I'm so happy to see you again."

She hugged his neck.

Ignoring the officers who'd gathered around them, he held her close. Tears misted his eyes. "What a brave little girl you are."

Mike unfolded the paper, remembering the message Kate had left him on the kitchen window not that long ago. He hadn't appreciated that note, but this one was like a letter from heaven.

The officers crowded close.

"Hey," Mike said, "let me have some privacy." He stepped away.

Dearest Mike,

Lupi is the first of eight children to leave the bus. Please help them if they get stuck or panic. One child is not well. They're all hot, hungry and thirsty. I'll send them out one after another as fast as I can.

All my love, Kate

He looked up. "Seven more kids are on the way but one is sick. Better get an ambulance out here. The others are thirsty and—"

"There's another one." Clint ran to the fence.

Mike glanced at the bus. Kate's hand was signaling again.

He stuck her note in his pocket and hustled back to the fence to stretch the wires while Clint helped a dusty child scramble through.

Cal and the other Wyoming deputy rushed to stand guard on each side of the escape path.

"Tieno." Clint tasseled his hair.

The boy coughed and smiled up at the cowboy.

Then another child appeared beneath the bus and another, children Mike had never seen before. Clint led them one by one to the trooper they'd pulled from the car trunk. The man spread a tarp on the asphalt in the shade of Clint's pickup and gave the children water and snacks—and teddy bears.

"You should see the way the kids' faces light up when he hands them the bears," Clint told Mike. "And the way they hug 'em like they'll never let go."

But then the silent trickle of escapees stopped. Mike waited. Where was Shannon? And the sick child? What about Kate? Although she wasn't a big person, the space looked too narrow for an adult.

"Miss Kate," Shannon whispered. "I'm too big. I can't fit down there. That boy, Gregor, he barely squeezed through."

Kate brushed the girl's hair away from her eyes. "You've got to try, honey. And when you do, you can help me slide Skylar out."

Shannon slowly shook her head. "I can't—"

Tara's loud voice just the other side of the curtain made them both blink. "Get me off this big lug. He stinks and he's making me sweat."

"Shut up." Adolph's voice coming through the opening was as loud as Tara's. Shannon backed away. The sick boy's eyes opened and then closed.

"You shut *your* mouth," Tara retorted.

Kate knelt beside the feverish, trembling boy sprawled across the seat. She touched his arm and his eyes fluttered open. Pointing to the opening in the floor, she whispered, "Your turn after her, Skylar."

He didn't respond.

She heard Blade's voice and lowered her ear to the hole. "…outa here. We need to leave, now."

"We don't got nowhere to go," Roach said. "And nowhere to hide in this God-forsaken desert."

"The boss has a hideout near the California border," Adolph said. "We'll go there."

"But how?" Druid's voice this time. "This bus ain't going nowhere."

"We'll borrow a couple cop cars."

"They'll kill us first."

"Not if we have the brats with us."

"Aren't you forgetting something?" Blade asked.

"What?"

"The broad. She's trouble."

"As long as we have the brats, she'll cooperate. She's a sucker for them."

~:~:~

Mike fixed his gaze on the bus, determined not to miss another signal from Kate or overlook a child scrambling out from under it. An ominous thud made the vehicle shudder, as if the earth had moved beneath it. Another thump followed, and another.

He gripped the fence post. Kate was trying to get out. She needed his help. He lifted a barbed wire strand and was about to crawl through the fence when the sound of grinding metal and breaking glass shattered the desert stillness. The officers beside him stiffened to a new level of alertness and trained their weapons on the bus.

The noise had barely died down when a male voice shouted, "Listen up, you cretins. We just trashed the bus door. When we bring the brats out, we'll haul them to the last two patrol cars on our left. Leave the keys in the ignitions and get out of the way. If you try to stop us, we'll off a kid. There are plenty more where these came from.

"Two cars," he repeated. "With food and water. Got it?"

A truck braked to a noisy standstill at the rear of vehicles queued behind a highway barricade. The smell of diesel fuel wafted through the hot air. Cattle bawled and a hawk circling above them screeched and then screeched again.

One of the troopers lifted a bullhorn to his mouth. "Kidnapping children will put you in prison for a long time, son." His amplified voice was clear and direct. "Release the children *now*, and we'll recommend a lighter sentence for you."

The trafficker, who needed no amplification, spewed f-bombs like gnats splatting a windshield.

Mike shook his head. Negotiating was a waste of time. The traffickers were antsy. Trying to talk sense to them just made them angry. He had to get Kate and the kids out of the bus before the dangerous situation became even more volatile.

He walked across the barrow pit to where Clint was standing. "While they're chitchatting," he murmured, "I say we take advantage of those cattle over there."

Clint spoke out of the side of his mouth. "Got a plan?"

Chapter Thirty-Six

M ike leaned closer to Clint. "It's a decent-size herd. We slip into the middle and drive them around the backside of the bluff. Then we climb on top, where we can get a bead on the thugs from above." He gave Clint a side glance. "What d'ya think?"

"I'm with you, man. Time to act." Clint's jaw muscles twitched. "Handguns or rifles?"

"Handguns. If all goes well, we'll be at close range."

Clint quietly edged to his pickup parked alongside the highway and opened the passenger door. A moment later, Mike followed. All six rescued children were peering over the hood, their foreheads taut and their eyes frantic. He looked for the trooper and saw that he'd joined the other officers.

Mike knelt before the children and the teddy bears clasped against their thin chests. They studied him with somber eyes. "I know all that yelling sounds scary." He indicated the bus. "But those fools don't know how brave you are. They don't know you snuck out. You're safe here. You have all those officers and me and Clint to protect you."

"Miss Kate…?" Lupita whispered.

"Sh-Sh-Shan-non." Tieno pointed at the bus. "A-and b-b-boy."

"Mr. Clint and I are going after them right now." Mike stood. "Stay here, okay? There might be shooting, but you'll be safe if you keep your heads down."

"W-w-we p-pray." Tieno's expression was solemn.

Mike shook the little boy's hand. "Thank you, Tieno." He motioned to the others. "Remember, stay low. We'll be back soon."

Another profanity barrage burst from the bus's vicinity. "You're not listening to me!"

"*You* listen to me." The trooper's voice boomed across the sagebrush expanse. "The offer is open to all of you. But you have to act now."

Mike joined Clint, who stood behind the open door on the passenger side of the truck, assembling guns. He handed one to Mike. "It's loaded."

Mike pulled out his shirt and cinched his belt tighter. Moving closer to the truck to ensure privacy, he stuck the pistol between the small of his back and the waistband on his jeans and covered the gun with his shirttail.

Clint closed the door. They checked the officers, who were intent on the exchange with the trafficker. Mike in the lead, they sidled along the fence toward the herd. The cows jumped away from the fence line when they came close but didn't go far.

Mike was holding a barbed-wire strand for Clint when one of the patrolmen came charging up the barrow pit. "What do you two yahoos think you're doing?"

Clint slipped through and pivoted to lift the strand for Mike. He adjusted his hat. "Roundup time."

Mike crawled under the wire, turned his back on the trooper and followed his foreman into the herd.

Rifle pointed at the bus's front window, Kate knelt on one knee in front of the curtain and listened to Adolph bellow orders at the officers.

After the kicks that broke the lock and destroyed the door, she'd expected the traffickers to come storming inside. But evidently they were determined to have cars ready and waiting before they made their big move.

She motioned to Shannon and then pointed at the escape hatch, whispering, "Close it, please." She didn't want the gang to realize what had happened to the other children, and she didn't want to trip into the hole while fighting for the two left behind.

Shannon's pallid skin had paled even further, but she did as Kate asked. She placed the cover on the opening, secured it with shaking fingers and flipped the rubber mat on top before returning to her hiding place between seats.

"Neilson," Tara called, "What's going on out there?"

"Enough talk." Adolph was addressing the officers again. "We're bringing the brats out now. Back off." Kate could tell he was crouched by the door, just far enough behind the hood that no one could get a shot at him.

"You go in first, Roach," Adolph said.

"Why me?"

Adolph snarled. "Do it."

Roach stumbled up the steps.

Kate pulled the shotgun trigger. But the gun didn't fire. She pulled again. Nothing.

Roach turned and saw her staring at him. "What the—? His gaze dropped to the shotgun and he hastily backed out. "The broad's got a rifle."

Kate heard the traffickers whispering, but she couldn't catch what they were saying. She quickly checked the gun's chamber. Empty. Frustrated she'd forgotten to look for shotgun shells earlier, she stood up to check the bus again. They had to have an ammunition stash somewhere. That's when she remembered the plastic bins by the urine bucket.

She turned to Shannon, who was tugging at her hair with one hand and chewing a nail on her other hand. Keeping her voice low, Kate asked, "Would you please search for shotgun shells in the back for me?"

The girl shrunk farther into the narrow space between seats.

"You can crawl over the seats so you don't have to walk on those two."

Shannon stared at the curtain. Finally, she stood up, parted the curtains and stepped through.

Mike slipped into a cow's blind spot directly back of her hindquarters, grabbed her manure-spattered tail and twisted it. The cow let out a startled bellow and spurted forward, setting the others in motion. Half stooped over, he ran after them, hissing short, sharp whistles and waving his hands at his sides.

Clint, who also ran in a semi-crouch, clapped his hands and prodded the cattle with, "Git up, git up, git up."

Jogging to stay with the herd, Mike moved to the left and Clint angled to the right to keep the cows together. If the herd split, they'd be exposed to the traffickers. His goal was to drive the animals to the backside of the bluff, despite their natural inclination to follow their well-worn trail to the water tank beneath the windmill. That path followed the fence, which ran between the highway and the bluff.

Mike had seen changes in their environment, even something as slight as a shadow, stop cattle in their tracks. These were accustomed to the shade cast by the cliff. Had the camouflaged bus within that long, wide shadow confounded them? Or was it the officers and the commotion along the highway that deterred them?

In theory, whether the cows intended to avoid the people or the bus, they'd veer to the right and around the hill, which was exactly what he wanted. But that was only theory. Cows were unpredictable animals.

Mike glanced at the ridge. Topped with a smattering of sagebrush bushes and a couple scrubby junipers, the bluff was high enough to shade the bus. Yet, it was low enough they could easily climb it from the backside, if they could maneuver the herd that direction. But then they'd have another problem—the late afternoon sun. Cattle did not willingly head into direct sunlight.

They were nearing the bus. Still jogging, Mike bent closer to the earth, grateful the cows hadn't taken off in a full run. Despite his efforts to steer them to the right by working into their left-side flight zone, they seemed determined to follow their usual route to the water tank—until someone behind the bus yelled, "Go away, you stinkin' cows. Get the hell outa here." Other voices joined in.

At the sound of gunshots, Mike hunkered even lower. The cattle shied to the right and picked up speed. Moving as fast as he could, he angled to the center of the herd, struggling to keep up with the big animals as they skirted the bus and the hill, never slowing.

Once they were out of sight of the bus, he stopped. Hands on his thighs, he caught his breath while the stragglers charged past.

Clint, who had stopped three or four yards away, ambled over to Mike. A fresh splat of manure trailed down his pant leg to his boot. "We did it, boss. We ran with the herd."

Mike managed a weary thumbs-up.

The herd disappeared around the curve of the hill, drawn to the water tank like ants to sugar. Mike straightened, grateful the cattle had moved on. They didn't need cows tromping all over the hill while they figured out how to ambush the kidnappers.

Kate shifted to her other knee and listened. The shouting and shooting had stopped and the thunder of hooves that had moments ago vibrated the bus was fading into the distance. All she heard now was Shannon sorting through the boxes in the back and Skylar's labored breathing.

She placed her hand on the boy's chest. He needed a doctor. People who could rush him to a hospital were nearby, yet their hands were tied. She also had limited options. By one means or another, she was going to find a way out of this, for Skylar and for Shannon.

She felt a check in her spirit. *Sorry, God. I did it again. It's up to you, not me, to rescue them.* Kate sighed, weary to the bone. She wasn't sure which smelled worse, the slop bucket or her armpits. A long shower and a long sleep would be the height of luxury right now.

She turned to the curtain and whispered, "How's it going back there?"

"This is torture," Tara blustered. "I won't live much longer in this heat. You've got to help me."

Kate whispered louder, "Shannon, did you find anything?"

The girl's murmured response was barely discernable. "Maybe. These big boxes are hard to open."

Kate focused on the front of the bus again, where Adolph was badgering the negotiator, demanding the officers ready the cars for them. Any moment now, he and the others would storm the bus. *God, I trust you, but it's just me against so many.*

Phrases from Mike's song came to her. *I will give you strength and help you, hold you with—*

"I got one open," Shannon whispered. "What do I look for?"

"What're you doing, girl?" Tara demanded.

"The shells should be in a small box," Kate said. "It'll have a metallic clinking sound when you shake it. If you find them, great. If not, I'll go with Plan B. The most important thing is for you to duck behind a seat when they come in, in case they start shooting." She had no idea what

Plan B was. That was up to God.

~:~:~

Mike and Clint approached the crest of the hill, their long shadows undulating over sagebrush, rocks and grass. Mike lowered to his knees and motioned for Clint to do the same. He didn't want their shadows to give them away. Gun in hand, he crawled between sagebrush bushes and over rocks toward the rim of the bluff.

The afternoon sunshine heated the vegetation, releasing the sagebrush's sharp aroma. He slid beneath a juniper, close enough to the edge he could see the tree's shadow on the bus roof. The dark vehicle sat a good dozen feet away from the cliff wall and at least that far below him and Clint.

Mike checked the men lined up along the highway, fully aware they were watching his and Clint's every move. At least one trooper was using binoculars. They'd put Cal in the awkward position of straddling the fence between friends and colleagues. But all the officers did was negotiate. As far as he was concerned, the traffickers had the advantage because they had what the officials wanted—Kate and the others who remained on the bus.

In the far distance, he saw two helicopters topping a rise. *About time the feds showed...*

Clint elbowed him, pointing to dark forms on the ground below.

Mike scowled. The men behind the bus hadn't been shooting at the sky. They'd shot three cows. One was still moving.

Hearing voices from near the rear of the bus, he wormed toward the ridge's rim but stopped short of the edge, one hand on a warm rock the size of a milk jug. He nudged the rock to see if it would budge and when it did, he began to work it loose from the soil, millimeter by millimeter.

"I was just thinking..." The voice was male and the tone nasal. "I didn't see no kids in there."

Another male said, "They're all in the back, behind the curtain."

The one who'd been doing the negotiating, said, "Listen up." His voice came from the front of the bus. "I'm tired of talking to those SOBs. Time to ditch this piece of crap. Blade and Druid, you keep an eye on the cops. Take 'em out if they get close. Blade, you guard the back of the bus. Druid, I want you up front. Roach, you come with me to grab the merchandise."

"What about the broad with the rifle?"

"I got to thinking, the only weapon in there is Lardo's shotgun. Somehow, she got her hands on it, but it ain't got no shells. I took out the ammo in case he got trigger happy with the goods."

Mike grimaced. All Kate had for protection was an empty shotgun. He had to stop them before they got to her.

"Druid, Blade. When we come out, everyone takes two brats. Lardo will handle the broads."

"We ain't heard nothing out of him since the bus slammed through the fence."

"If he can't do his job, we waste him," the leader declared. "And we waste the whores. They're both trouble. Come on, Roach. We're going in."

Hearing footsteps in the gravel and knowing two of the men were headed into the bus, Mike shoved the rock over the brim. He heard a thump and then a cry. "My shoulder..." The man groaned. "My shoulder..."

"What the—?" the leader demanded. "What're you bitching about, Blade?"

Blade moaned. "My shoulder's broke, I can feel it."

"That big rock got him," someone said. "Fell down from up there."

"Move your arm."

"I can't. It hurts, bad. I need a doc—"

His cry was interrupted by a distinct double-click.

"No, Adolph, don't, please. I'll be—"

The sound of a gunshot erupted between the bus and the cliff. For a moment, all was quiet. Mike glanced at the officers on the road and saw two of them climb into a SUV.

Adolph growled, "Quit gawking and get busy. Roach, cover the back. Druid, get up front. I'll grab the merchandise and we're outa here."

Kneeling beside Skylar, gun in hand, Kate tried to piece together the action outside the bus. Someone had been injured and someone had been shot.

"Devil woman!" Adolph's shout came through the front door. "You must think you're hot stuff, stealing our bus. But that was a stupid thing to do 'cause now you have to deal with me. I'd kill you now, but I'll get more satisfaction from watching you *suffer* and beg for mercy."

Kate stood and aimed the shotgun at the front of the bus.

"Help me," Tara called. "Somebody help me. I'm dying."

"Shut up, slut. I'm coming in. Get the brats ready."

"Stay out!" Kate yelled. "I have a gun."

"Yeah?" Adolph snorted. "Well, guess what. I have one too. But mine has shells."

Chapter Thirty-Seven

Kate pulled the trigger and the front window exploded. The blast shook the bus.

Tara screamed.

Ears ringing, Kate ducked between seats, reloaded and propped the gun barrel on the seatback in front of her.

Adolph swore a string of oaths. "So you think you can play with the big boys?" Another blast and several front windows on the cliff side of the bus shattered. Glass shards shot across the aisle.

"I'm coming in, whore." The contempt behind his threat was unmistakable. "Drop the gun and raise your hands or we'll shoot out *all* the windows and kill *all* the brats."

Kate slipped behind a seat.

The bus shifted and through the seat's handhold, she caught a glimpse of dark hair above the short wall that divided the bus stairs from the passenger seats. A shotgun barrel slid toward her over the top edge of the metal divider.

She was about to pull the trigger again when a shadow hurtled past the cliff-side windows near her, followed by a thump and a grunt. Adolph's gun barrel wavered. Kate glanced at the side windows but saw nothing more. She redirected her attention to the front of the bus and

Adolph's gun barrel. Beyond the barrel and the busted window, a flash of denim dropped from above and a black cowboy hat bounced off the hood. *Mike.*

Another thump, but this time the groan was louder.

"What the—?" Adolph straightened and started to swing around.

Before he could fire at her husband, Kate shot him, praying Mike was out of buckshot range.

Adolph's gun fell over the divider and clattered onto the bus floor. He faltered only momentarily before he swiveled, roaring, "Bitch, give me my gun!"

Kate ran to the front, shotgun leveled at his head.

Blood dripping from his wounds, he pulled himself up the steps and bent down to retrieve his gun. She kicked him in the shoulder, sending him into the console. He bounced back, teeth bared, but she sidestepped and knocked him down the stairs with the gun barrel.

Adolph rolled out of the bus and landed on his hands and knees.

Kate bounded down the steps. She kicked him, which sent him flying onto his stomach.

The trafficker flipped over, his angry features smeared with blood and dirt, and reached for his ankle. He pulled out a pistol.

Kate leveled the shotgun at his chest. "Drop it!"

Adolph sneered and lifted the pistol. "You're dumber than I thought."

A black boot stomped his forearm and the sneer vanished.

Adolph twisted to reach for the pistol with his other hand and a brown boot clamped that arm like a vise. The trafficker howled and swore and kicked, but the boots held firm.

Standing on the bottom step, shotgun trained on Adolph's chest, Kate said, "I can't begin to say how much I'd love to fill your greedy gut with buckshot. But I'd rather testify at your trial. I'll get far more *satisfaction* watching a judge sentence you to life in prison. I've done time. I know what the *big boys* do to bottom feeders like you."

"Whore!" He raised his head to spit at her then fell back.

Two men appeared beside Mike, guns in their hands.

Kate lifted the shotgun.

Mike held out his palm. "It's okay, Kate. They're good guys. Here to help."

"Kate, it's me," one of them said. 'Cal."

She blinked and lowered the gun.

The other man spoke into a radio and more officers came running. Two of them yanked Adolph to his feet and cuffed him, while others dealt with the three fallen men.

Adolph glared at Kate. "My people don't like to be messed with. They'll take you out."

She returned the glare. "My God isn't afraid of you or your people. You ought to be falling on your knees before him, begging for mercy."

He snorted.

The moment Adolph was led away, Cal asked, "Is anyone on the bus?"

"Yes. Two children and two adults. I'd like for Clint to go in first to get Shannon. She knows him and she trusts him." Without waiting for Cal's response, she turned to Clint. "The sick boy, Skylar, is in front of the curtain. You'll need to carry him."

She stepped into the bus. "Shannon, you can come out now. Clint's here. He'll meet you by the curtain."

The girl's response was faint. "Are you sure the bad guys are gone?"

"Yes, they're all gone except the two back there with you. Clint's coming for you. He'll keep you safe."

"Clint, Clint Barrett, is that you?" Tara called. "You have to get me out of this mess. Neilson chained me to these seats. She treats me worse than a dog."

Kate sighed. The sooner the authorities removed Tara from her life, the better.

"Who's that?" Clint asked.

"Tara Hughes."

"What's she...? Oh, forget it." He headed toward the back of the bus. "Smells worse than a feedlot in here."

"Careful of the bodies. It's dark behind the curtain."

"What bodies?" Cal asked.

"You'll see." She stepped from the bus so he could climb inside. His partner followed.

Like a dam had burst inside her, strength drained from Kate's body. She fell back against the bus, smiling at her husband but too sapped to speak.

Mike moved closer. Gently taking the gun from her hand, he placed it by the tattered remains of the bus's front tire. And then he stood and pulled her into his arms, clasping her against his chest.

She buried her face in his shirt. Oh, how good he smelled, sweat and dirt included. And how wonderful it was to hold him and to feel his arms embrace her again.

His cheek against her hair, he said, "Words can never say how much I've missed you, sweetheart. I thought I'd lost you forever."

Kate lifted her head to look him in the eye. "I thought I'd never see you again, Mike. I'm so sorry—"

"No." He touched her lips. "I'm sorry. If I had gone with you, you wouldn't—"

She wrapped her arms around his neck. "I could use a kiss right now."

He grinned. "I thought you'd never ask."

Epilogue

Kate watched Lupita scamper up the sandy dune toward Gianna, who waited at the top. "With a smile like that," she told Mike, "I think we can safely say Lupi is pleased with our surprise."

He squeezed her shoulder. "Both girls seem pretty happy right now."

Kate and the three Freedom House kids had spent a night and a morning in a Bend hospital, an afternoon being interviewed by FBI agents and social workers, and then a night at a Portland hotel. This morning, Mike had rented a car and driven them all to a shopping center to purchase food and supplies for a day at the ocean.

Kate had told the kids they'd have lunch at the beach before they drove home to Wyoming. But she hadn't told them their friends would join them. The moment Laura learned of their rescue, she'd put Coach in charge of the office and Fletcher in charge of ranch activities, called the Curtis twins to assist with housekeeping duties, rented a twelve-passenger van and organized a road trip. They'd arrived less than fifteen minutes after Mike and Clint finished setting up the canopy, with Tieno's assistance.

Shannon and Tieno followed Lupi up the short hill, digging into the sand with their bare toes and waving their hands at the newcomers. Mike and Clint trailed behind. The group's arrival was as much a surprise for Clint as for the children. Tears pricked Kate's eyelids when Amy crested the top, saw Clint and ran into his arms.

Tieno and Shannon headed for Laura, who already had Lupita and Gianna wrapped in a hug. Tears running down her face, she held the children and whispered in their ears, one-by-one. Kate wiped tears from her own cheeks.

Clint lifted Amy off her feet and swung her in a circle. Kate couldn't tell what they said to each other when Clint put Amy down, but she could tell she was a bystander to another sweet moment.

Amy looked over his shoulder, spied Kate and scuttled down the hill, her skirt swirling. "Kate, oh, Kate, oh, Kate, my friend." She hugged her hard and then leaned back. Tears in her eyes, she said, "I'm so happy to see you again. I was afraid…"

"Me, too, but God stepped in." Kate lifted her eyebrows. "I'm ready for a little bit of normal. Is that how you felt in Dallas?"

"Oh, yes. Normal is good."

"Want to help me get the food ready for the party? I promised Shannon fried chicken and coleslaw, so that's what we're having, along with some other goodies." She'd found premade tiramisu in the grocery store. Mike had agreed it was the perfect dessert for the occasion.

"I'd love to help. You know how I adore parties. This will be the best celebration ever."

"You're right. Can't get any better than this."

Gianna at her side, Lupi tapped Amy's leg.

Amy opened her mouth wide. "Lupi, my love." She clutched both girls, her eyes bright with tears. Gianna flinched but didn't try to wiggle free.

Kate smiled at her friends and family making their way down the dune. Laura, Shannon and Tieno were first. Mike followed with Dymple on one arm and Aunt Mary between him and Clint. Behind them, Marita carried Frankie, and Cyrus carted Mary's walker.

Running circles around them all was Tramp. The big dog seemed to know this was a special day. He darted down the hill to Kate and let her pat his head before he hurried back to Mike.

Laura pulled Kate into a long embrace. "You are my hero forever, Katherine Joy Duncan." She wiped her wet cheeks with the back of her hand. "Thank you for all you did for the children."

"You would have done the same," Kate said. "Life must have been really crazy for you, with looking after the ranch, the kids and Aunt Mary."

"I had lots of help." She touched Kate's cheek. "You're bruised. And look at your arms."

"I feel like one of Mike's bison bulls ran over me, but at least nothing's broken."

"I'll make sure you have plenty of rest and recovery time when we return home." Laura moved aside to let Kate hug her aunt.

Mary released her grip on her walker and held Kate's cheeks with her soft palms. She looked deep into her eyes. "Safe in the Shepherd's fold, my sweet Katy." Her voice was gentle. "Safe in the Shepherd's fold."

"Yes, Aunt Mary. Safe in his fold, thanks to your prayers. That's the story of my life." They held each other for a long time, the waves breaking on the shore and sliding away, breaking and sliding away.

Kate helped Mary sit before she greeted Dymple and Marita. "Thank you, dear friends." She hugged their shoulders. "I felt your prayers."

"God answers prayer." Dymple pointed her wrinkled finger upward. "I think the whole tonsil was praying for you."

Marita winked at Kate. "Everyone was thrilled when they heard the good news. Prepare for a community-wide celebration when you return."

Cyrus, who'd never before hugged her, drew her into his sinewy arms. "Someone's been beatin' on you, girl." He held her at arm's length. "Was it that low-down snake-in-the-grass Jerry Ramsey?"

Kate nodded. "And others."

"I hear the scumbag is dead and gone. How does that feel?"

She touched the side of her head where Ramsey had hit her with the gun. "You'd think I'd be happy, but I feel more numb than anything. And grateful he'll never be able to kidnap or abuse another child."

"I'll say 'amen' to that, sister."

"You probably heard that the security guard who helped Mike and Clint search for us was also killed. That makes me sad. And Blade, one of the traffickers, was murdered by the leader. He was so young. I can't help but think that prison could have been life-changing for him, like it was for me."

"Hey, did you hear the news?" Amy asked. "*National* news?"

"If you will recall, Amy…" Kate smiled. "I've been out of circulation for a few days."

Amy gave her a smug look. "But you have been circulating, from what I heard, and the news is about you."

Kate sighed. "I wish they'd find someone else to talk about."

"Governors of five states are now applauding you. They say you're a modern-day hero. Or heroine, as the case may be."

"Five governors?" Kate hated being the media's latest hot topic.

"If you ask me," Cyrus said, "They're a day late and a dollar short. Just a couple days ago they were callin' Kate a kidnapper."

"Wyoming, Idaho, Texas, Oregon." Amy held up one finger at a time. "And even Pennsylvania."

Clint joined them, standing next to Amy. "You busted a human trafficking ring, Kate. I heard it on the radio earlier."

Amy smiled up at him.

He put his arm around her. "Seven major gangs, most of them out of California, linked forces a couple years ago to buy and sell victims from

San Diego to Portland and Seattle and back down the coast. They also loop over to Spokane and Boise and then work their way south through Reno and Vegas to California.

"Authorities suspect distribution is far greater than that. But from what they've learned so far from those they arrested the other day, they'll be able to significantly slow trafficking on the West Coast, and maybe elsewhere."

"That's great," Kate said, "but—"

Laura clapped her hands. "Let's eat. The kids are hungry."

"'Bout time," Cyrus groused. "My gut is growling."

Laura swatted his shoulder. "That's enough bellyaching, buster."

The group formed a circle, holding hands. Tramp, who'd already rolled in the wet sand, plopped in the middle. "I'm so happy we're together again," Kate said. "Thank you for coming all this way to celebrate with us. We missed you and can't wait to go home with you."

"We missed you," Laura said. "All of you."

The others nodded, their eyes moist.

"Let's pray." Mike bowed his head. "Dear God, I'm grateful for your goodness to us, more grateful than words can say." He stopped. Kate could tell he was choking back tears. She leaned her head against his shoulder.

"You saved…" He cleared his throat. "You saved Kate, Lupi, Shannon and Tieno plus five other children from a terrible future. Thank you. We ask you to heal their bodies and souls from all they endured. We're happy to have our Freedom House children together again. I pray you give the others good homes, too. Bless my sweet wife for all she did for them." He stroked her thumb with his.

Kate smiled. Her husband's understanding and support meant more to her than all the governors' accolades combined.

"We're forever awed," Mike continued, "by your amazing love and care. Thank you for this food, for our family and friends, and for this happy occasion. In your Son's name, Amen."

Blinking away tears, Kate saw Shannon raise her hand. "Can I say something."

Laura said, "Sure, sweetie, go ahead."

"That was not fun being in that creepy place and on the bus and all that. Right?" She looked at Lupita, who shook her head. Tieno said, "N-n-no w-way, b-bucko."

Amused grins spread through the group.

"But because of us, those bad people are in jail, where they can't hurt other kids. I'm glad for that."

Kate nodded. "So am I."

Shannon shrugged. "That's it. I don't have anything else to say."

"Bravo," Laura said. "I'm so proud of you, all of you." The others clapped and cheered.

Amazed by the maturity Shannon displayed, Kate could only look at her and the WP crew and smile. These sweet people were her family, bonded and blended like no other family on earth.

Cyrus raised a finger. "We gonna stand here gawking at each other or are we gonna eat?"

Tramp's ears perked. He jumped to his feet and shook his wet fur, sending sandy spray all directions. Everyone groaned and backed away.

"Tramp, stop it." Mike shooed him out from under the canopy.

Lupi watched him go. "Messy puppy."

After lunch, Kate and Mike, along with Amy and Clint, played in the water and made sand castles with the children. When she'd had enough sun, Kate grabbed a bottle of water from the cooler and joined the others who sat under the canopy's shade. Relaxing in her chair, she watched the waves crash and roll across the shore.

Seagulls screeched overhead. Sandpipers skittered on the flat, wet sand. Although she was anxious to return to the Whispering Pines, she was glad they'd decided to end their time in Oregon at a beach.

"Kate, you must be exhausted," Marita said. "I'm sure we don't know the half of what you've been through."

Kate released a long sigh. "I wish I could say what we went through was worth it. But this could be a huge setback for our Freedom House kids. And the other children…" She made a sad face in the sand with her toe. "I hate to think what they've experienced in the past and I wonder if they'll get good care in the future. Will they get the specialized support and guidance they need?"

"I called the Oregon Department of Human Service," Laura said, "and offered to take in those who don't have homes to return to. They may decide to place them elsewhere, but at least they know our facility is available." She smiled. "And then I asked to be transferred to the counselor who talked with the children after they were rescued. I wanted to get a feel for what to expect when we take them home.

"She told me your presence was a stabilizing factor for all of the kids, Kate. Escaping the bus and being cared for by people who wanted to help them not harm them, plus seeing their abusers led from the bus to the patrol cars in handcuffs did wonders for their emotional and mental health."

Kate wiped away tears, like she'd been doing all day. "Thank you, Laura. It helps to know something positive came out of that nightmare."

"Of course, they'll still need plenty of TLC after what they've been through, but I think the positive ending to the situation will give them a jump start on their healing."

"Say, Dymple…" Cyrus set his drink in the chair's cup holder. "What's this I hear about you entertaining Cheyenne detectives at your house?"

Dymple smiled an innocent smile. "I invited them over for a glass of Dymple's Delight, that's all. They stopped by on their way out of town."

"And..." Kate knew there had to be more to the story.

"Well..." Dymple brushed invisible crumbs from her lap. "I just happened to have homemade chicken pot pie and chocolate chip cookies fresh from the oven sitting on the counter—and extra plates set out."

Cyrus chuckled. "Bet they were in hog heaven."

"It's true," Laura said. "The way to a man's heart..."

"Then what?" Kate asked.

"Let's just say we had a come-to-Jamaica conversation about you and Mike, not that it changed their chief's decision."

Kate tilted her head. "Come to Jamaica?"

Dymple sighed. "Come to Jesus. I meant come to *Jesus*."

Later, as they climbed the slippery hill to the parking lot, Amy took Kate's elbow. "Do you mind if I ride with Clint? With you in the van, Laura won't need me to help with the kids and Aunt Mary."

Kate grinned. "That would be great. Good time for you two to..." She hesitated. "I'd better check with Mike. In all the excitement, we haven't talked about the rental car. He may be planning to drive it to Wyoming." She felt like she should be with the kids while they traveled, in case they had panic attacks or became skittish at rest areas. Mike would probably understand, but she should discuss travel plans with him before she made a commitment.

They crested the hill. Lupita, who was in front of Kate, released Gianna's hand and ran to Kate just as Shannon made a strange noise, whirled and bolted toward the ocean.

Tieno cried, "No!" and dropped the ball he was carrying. He raced down the dune behind Shannon.

Kate lifted Lupita so that they were face to face. "What's wrong, Lupi?"

The girl pointed to the rental van, her eyes wide.

Kate moaned. She'd felt her own gut twist when she saw the big white van, but she'd known it was coming, bringing loved ones their way. She'd been so excited to surprise the kids that she'd overlooked the potential trauma.

"Hang on, Lupi!" She flipped the little girl to her back and charged down the incline after the other two, who were flying along the shore, hand in hand. "Shannon, Tieno, wait." She tried to shout above the sound of the surf, but the frantic children appeared not to hear her.

Running as fast as she could, desperate to not lose them, Kate got close enough to yell, "Wait for us, Shannon. Wait."

Shannon pulled Tieno to a stop.

Kate set Lupita on the sand and fell to her knees before the frantic children. Their eyes were wild with fright. Wind whipped their hair about their faces, which had paled beneath sun-burnished cheeks.

She drew them close, trying to absorb their tremors into herself. "I'm so sorry I forgot to tell you Miss Laura rented a van so she could take everyone home in one vehicle."

Shannon sank onto the wet sand. "They came in *that*?"

"Yes. Did you notice it has windows on all sides? I'm sure it has air-conditioning, too."

Tieno and Lupi sat on either side of Shannon.

"Our friends all came in that van—and so did Tramp," Kate said. "You'll have a fun time riding home with them."

"Are you going to ride with us?" Shannon asked, her eyes wary.

Kate hesitated.

Mike, who'd just caught up with them, knelt beside Kate. He put his hand on her back. "We'll both ride in the van after I return the rental car. I can help with the driving."

Kate kissed his cheek. "You're a sweetheart." She turned to the children. Tramp was licking their faces. "What do you think? You ready to go home?"

Resilient children that they were, they stood, weak smiles on their troubled faces. "C-c-cowboy h-hat?" Tieno asked.

Lupi laid her cheek on Tramp's neck.

"Yes." Laura came up behind Mike. "Your cowboy hat is in your bedroom at Freedom House. It's hanging in your closet, where you left it."

Mike was helping Kate to her feet when Amy and Clint approached, barefoot and holding hands. Amy's sandals dangled from her free hand and Clint's boots were balanced on his shoulder, heels aimed behind him. "Okay with you if my buddy Tieno rides with me?" Clint asked.

Kate looked at her mother-in-law. "What do you think, Laura?"

Laura smiled. "I think that's a wonderful idea, Clint."

His grin was almost as broad as Tieno's.

"I want to ride with Miss Kate and Miss Laura," Shannon said, "and the others."

Kate was glad to see color returning to her cheeks.

"Me with Gianna and Aunt Mary." Lupi looked up at Kate. "We go home."

"Yes, let's go home."

Tieno between them, Amy and Clint ambled along the beach, squishing wet sand between their toes. Laura wrapped her arm around Shannon. Mike took Kate's hand, and Kate took Lupita's little hand. Together, they walked the beach one last time, Tramp running up and down the shore alongside them.

Home. They were going home.

Kate loved the ocean's invigorating spray, the sound of the waves and the salty taste on her lips. But she'd missed the brisk mountain air that rattled the quaking aspen leaves outside their bedroom window and ruffled the curtains. She'd missed the sound of the wind whispering through the tops of the evergreens. She'd missed sunshine, wide-open vistas and white clouds floating unfettered through the big blue Wyoming sky.

Most of all, she'd missed her family.

She smiled at Mike. Together with Jesus, they were going home. Home to Wyoming. Home to the Whispering Pines.

Acknowledgements

As you might guess, writing is a solitary endeavor; however, no author can type "The End" without the encouragement of a host of friends and family members. My husband, Steve, is an unwavering supporter as are those in our immediate family—Alissa, Jim, Toby, Jessica, Brady Maverick, Dakota and Grace. Sibling support also means a lot, whether my loved ones are related by birth or by marriage. Thank you Lanny, Roger, Becky, JoDee, Joe, Pam, Dennis, Karen and Don for praying for me and for *Winds of Change*.

Many thanks also go to the sweet ladies in my Bible study group and other wonderful friends and family members who prayed me through the process. Researching and writing about child trafficking was a challenging endeavor.

My brilliant critique partners, Lisa Hess and Valerie Gray, steered me back onto the path each time I rabbit-trailed or lost my bearings in the story. They also reviewed the final version. Others, like a photographer named Barry, provided much-needed information along the way. To see inside the Blue Heron Paper Mill, check out Barry's fabulous photos on sowewent.blogspot.com.

The Willamette Falls Legacy Project (rediscoverthefalls.com) offers a fascinating look at Willamette Falls, including the history of the area and plans for the future. To get a feel for the river and the mill, I must have viewed Frank Blangeard's YouTube video, "Kayaking Willamette River: Oregon City," a hundred times. You'll enjoy it, too!

Jennifer Borboa, Park Maintenance Supervisor in West Linn, Oregon, kindly answered my crazy questions. Diane Wolski, Rick Spencer, Brady Lyles and Jessica Johns checked out the Cheyenne, Wyoming, city park for me. When our family lived in Cheyenne, we picnicked and biked in Lion's Park and swam in Sloan's Lake; however, the children's village was created after we moved away. I was able to visit it several years ago. What an amazing place! To view the Paul Smith Children's Village online, go to botanic.org/discover/childrens-village.

Robin Durkee, Jean Thompson and Bob Thompson, experienced counselors and family therapists, graciously shared their expertise and guided my fumbling attempts to understand characteristics of severely traumatized children. Alissa Ketterling, a speech-language pathologist who works with young children, helped with Tieno's stuttering.

Lanny Carey, a long-haul trucker, talked me through the bus crash. Police officers Ray Ellis and Mike Miraglia advised me about guns. Dale Thackrah, who has trained for police work and done ride-alongs with his police-officer brother, told me wonderful stories of teddy bears and trapdoors.

Merikay Jost, a courageous woman who's fought a long and difficult battle to raise public awareness regarding human trafficking, graciously shared her library of pertinent books, articles and documents. Like a good massage therapist, Chris White, editor extra-ordinaire, found all the kinks and knots in the story and suggested excellent ways to unravel them. Kristen Ventress of Blue Azalea Designs labored long and hard to create the perfect cover for *Winds of Change*.

Last but not least, my wonderful team of beta readers sifted through *Winds of Change* for weaknesses as well as errors. Bob Thompson's input changed significant events in the story, Patricia Watkins not only helped me brainstorm fixes for a couple rough scenes, she tweaked boat and ocean descriptions and reviewed the manuscript three times (what a trooper!). Jill Carey shared her experience with Alzheimer's care, and Ginger Jordan made valuable suggestions plus shared her knowledge of horses, cattle and cowboys. Steve Lyles and Alissa Ketterling dug in deep to search line-by-line for needed corrections.

Thanks to all of you, *Winds of Change* was transformed into a better book than I could have written on my own.

Anti-trafficking Organizations

Organizations that highlight the horror of human trafficking and efforts to rescue its victims include but are not limited to: Destiny Rescue (destinyrescue.org/us); Wipe Every Tear (wipeeverytear.org); A Heart for Justice (aheartforjustice.com); Loved 146 (love146.org); Shared Hope (sharedhope.org); International Justice Mission (ijm.org); Abolition International (abolitioninternational.org); Rebecca Bender Ministries (rebeccabender.org); The Salvation Army's Initiative Against Sexual Trafficking (salvationarmyusa.org/usn/combating-human-trafficking); and the Polaris Project (polarisproject.org).

Polaris BeFree Textline: Text "BeFree" (233733)

Government websites: US Department of Health & Human Services, Office on Trafficking in Persons (acf.hhs.gov/endtrafficking)

National Human Trafficking Resource Center (https://traffickingresourcecenter.org)

National Human Trafficking Resource Center **Hotline:**
1 (888) 373-7888 (If you or someone you know is a victim of human trafficking, call now for assistance!)

About the Author

Rebecca Carey Lyles grew up in Wyoming, the setting for her award-winning Kate Neilson novels. She and her husband, Steve, currently live in Idaho, the beautiful state that borders Wyoming on the west. Together, they host a podcast called *Let Me Tell You a Story* (beckylyles.com/podcast). In addition to writing fiction and nonfiction, she serves as an editor and a mentor for aspiring authors. *Winds of Change* is the third and final book in the Kate Neilson Series, serving as a wrap-up to the adventures of the Whispering Pines characters found in *Winds of Wyoming* and *Winds of Freedom.*

Email: beckylyles@beckylyles.com

Facebook author page: Rebecca Carey Lyles

Blog: widgetwords.wordpress.com

Website: beckylyles.com

Note from the Author

Thank you for reading my stories and caring about those caught in the human-trafficking web. I hope you enjoyed *Winds of Change* and that you'll consider leaving a review or rating on Amazon, Barnes & Noble, Goodreads, or wherever you like to share your thoughts about books. If you'd like to learn about future releases, I invite you to go to my website – beckylyles.com – to register for my (rare and random) newsletter. You'll receive a free eStory as a "thank you."

Other Books by the Author

Fiction —

WINDS OF WYOMING (Book One in the Kate Neilson Series)

Fresh out of a Pennsylvania penitentiary armed with a marketing degree, Kate Neilson heads to Wyoming anticipating an anonymous new beginning as a guest-ranch employee. A typical twenty-five-year-old woman might be looking to lasso a cowboy, but her only desire is to get on with life on the outside—despite her growing interest in the ranch owner. When she discovers a violent ex-lover followed her west, she fears the past she hoped to hide will trail as close as a shadow and imprison her once again.

"Though Rebecca Carey Lyles knows how to mix suspense with the perfect amounts of warmth and humor, I found that the flaws in her characters were really what drew me in. *Winds of Wyoming* is the kind of book that gets readers hooked and asking for more."

Angela Ruth Strong, author of *Lighten Up, The Fun4Hire Series, False Security, Finding Love in Sun Valley, Idaho,* and *Finding Love in Big Sky, Montana*

WINDS OF FREEDOM (Book 2 in the Kate Neilson Series)

Winter storms blast across the West and fuel the bitter wind that ravages ranch-owner Kate Neilson Duncan's soul. In the midst of shattered dreams, she learns her best friend has not only disappeared, she's been accused of murder. Kate vows to find her and prove her innocence. When the Duncans' Wyoming ranch is threatened and Kate's mother-in-law becomes ensnared by evil, Kate and her husband, Mike, join forces with their foreman to fight for all that is dear to them. Can the three ranchers defeat the lethal powers determined to destroy Kate, their loves ones and their ranch?

"*Winds of Freedom* by Rebecca Lyles is not only an entertaining read, it is another courageous assault on the hideous crime of human trafficking. I applaud the author's willingness to tackle this topic and to help educate us in the depth of its evil. Awareness is the first step in setting the captives free—and then the challenge to each of us to get involved. Together we can make a difference! Do not miss this excellent book!"

Kathi Macias, award winning author of more than 50 books, including the *Freedom Series,"* novels written around the topic of human trafficking

PASSAGEWAYS: A Short Story Collection

Four authors who also happen to be friends. Sixteen unique short stories. From tales of spies and trains and John Wayne, to monks, magic and marriage, readers will be entertained, challenged and inspired. Valerie D. Gray, Lisa Michelle Hess, Peter Leavell and Rebecca Carey Lyles met several years ago at a newly formed writers group in a back corner of Rediscovered Books, an Idaho indie bookstore. Over time, they became critique partners who share the ups and downs of the writing life as well as act as first readers for one another's work.

Great stories, very eclectic variety, which was uber enjoyable for me! Each story was like opening a surprise gift. Sandra Doerty

While the authors, their styles and their stories are very diverse, Passageways is a uniformly excellent read. Entertaining to the very last page! Pat W.

Nonfiction —

IT'S A GOD THING! Inspiring Stories of Life-Changing Friendships"

When it seemed the best years of his life were over, Larry Baker gained a new passion for living through unexpected, life-changing friendships and adventures. He invites you to join him in the daily exhilaration of discovering the surprises and relationships God has waiting for each of us, just around the corner.

"It's a God Thing! is a very inspiring book that shows how God will use any willing heart in helping others come to the saving grace of Christ Jesus." Teresa Britton

ON A WING AND A PRAYER: Stories from Freedom Fellowship, a Prison Ministry

The night God told Donna Roth he was sending her to jail to share his love with incarcerated individuals, she said, "Lord, you have the wrong house!" She had no experience or interest in prison ministry; yet, she was obedient, and Freedom Fellowship was formed. "On a Wing and a Prayer" features stories of inmates who found freedom inside prison walls through the ministry of Freedom Fellowship.